Praise for *Newton's Cannon*,
Book One of The Age of Unreason

"*Newton's Cannon* features the classic elements of science fiction: high-tech gadgetry, world-threatening superpower conflict, a quest to save the world and a teen hero who's smarter than most of the adults. The historical setting gives this book something extra."

— *USA Today*

"Keyes' elegant alternate-history fantasy begins a series entitled *The Age of Unreason* that, on the evidence of this beginning, promises to follow honorably in the footsteps of Card's *Alvin Maker* saga . . . Keyes knows his history, knows his science, and knows how to tell a story. Eminently worthwhile reading for both fantasy and alternate-history lovers, not least because, with skill and scholarship, it uses an era and historical figures that have not been picked to the bare bones by other alternate-historians."

— *Booklist*

"Colorful, intriguing."

— *Kirkus Reviews*

By J. Gregory Keyes

A Calculus of Angels

Book Two of The Age of Unreason

J. Gregory Keyes

The Ballantine Publishing Group • New York

A Del Rey® Book
Published by The Ballantine Publishing Group

Copyright © 1999 by J. Gregory Keyes

All rights reserved under International and Pan-American Copyright Conventions. Published
in the United States by The Ballantine Publishing Group, a division of Random House, Inc.,
New York, and simultaneously in Canada by Random House of Canada Limited, Toronto.

Del Rey and colophon are registered trademarks of Random House, Inc.

http://www.randomhouse.com/delrey/

Library of Congress Cataloging-in-Publication data
Keyes, Greg, 1963–
    A calculus of angels / J. Gregory Keyes. — 1st ed.
        p.   cm. — (The age of unreason ; bk. 2)
    "A Del Rey book"—T.p. verso.
    ISBN 0-345-40607-9 (alk. paper)
    1. Franklin, Benjamin, 1706–1790—Fiction.   I. Title.   II. Series: Keyes, Greg, 1963–
Age of unreason ; bk. 2.
PS3561.E79C35   1999
813'.54—dc21   98-30776
                                                                                    CIP

Cover illustration by Terese Nielsen
Maps © Jaana Mattson

Manufactured in the United States of America

First Edition: April 1999

10 9 8 7 6 5 4 3 2 1

For my grandparents,
Earl and Helen Ridout

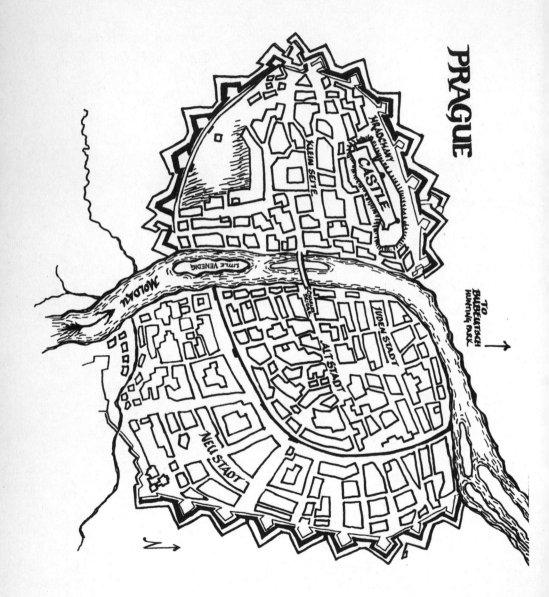

CONTENTS

PART THREE

THE DARK AER

Acknowledgments

By necessity, these acknowledgments are cumulative—everyone I noted in *Newton's Cannon* deserves another mention here. In the interest of saving space, I'm limiting this list to those I didn't mention last time.

My thanks to:

Terese Nielsen for great paintings, Jie Yang for the production work on the cover, and Jaana Mattson for the maps.

Robert Stauffer and Allison Lindon for proofreading, Erin Bekowies and Becker Strout for cold reading.

Jennifer Lattanzio and Adrian Wood for their work on *Newton's Cannon*. Shelly Shapiro—who should have been mentioned long before now—Christopher Schluep, Anh Hoang, and Tim Kochuba.

Eleanor Lang, for keeping me safe on the road.

William Ridout—my uncle—for his expert knowledge on the crafting, use, and history of black powder weapons. And for sneaking me black powder now and then when I was a kid . . .

The instructors and fencers at Salle Auriol Seattle, and especially my foil coach, Charles Sheffer. Thanks also to Marshall Hibnes and Allen Evans for their comments and opinions on eighteenth-century fencing, my cadre mates Bobby Cortez, Mel Gregory, Adam Herbst, and Zabette Macomber—and of course to our Maitre d'Arms, Leon Auriol.

The supportive enthusiastic members of Flanders Fantastic, and especially Didier Rypens. Helen Stack, for her very interesting and informative comments about her ancestor Charles Portales and his good friend, Fatio de Duillier . . .

Don McQuinn, Dave Gross, Ben Diebold, and Gavin Grow for general moral support. Add to them the whole Keyes clan, and especially Nell K. Wright and Mary K. Skelton.

PRAGUE CASTLE

1. First Courtyard
2. Second Courtyard
3. Stag Moat
4. Powder Bridge
5. Mathematical Tower
6. St. Vitus' Cathedral
7. St. George's Cathedral and Convent
8. White Tower
9. Black Tower
10. Lobkovicz Palace
11. Royal Palace (Newton's Quarters)

PROLOGUE

Confession

Peter flinched at the single drop of blood that spattered onto his coat. Even thirty feet away, one ran that risk when the knout was being used. In experienced hands, the brutal short whip could cut to the bone and raise a fountain of blood; and the man wielding this knout was a master. Peter watched impassively as the last of the strokes fell. The victim was long past screaming. Instead he croaked pitifully, face more confused than anguished, as if his mind refused to accept what had been done to his body.

Peter approached the tortured man, who was suspended, arms tied behind his back. His weight had dislocated them, so that now he looked almost comical, as if his head had been put on reversed. Peter wondered if they had gone too far—if Alexis would even be capable of speech—but finally, breath rasping, the prisoner looked up. He was weeping, tears turning sanguine where they crossed the lips he had bitten through.

"I am sorry, my Emperor." He groaned.

Peter's throat tightened. It was only with difficulty that he said, "I have heard you wished me dead."

Alexis convulsed, his face contorting almost beyond recognition, as if it, too, had been beaten. "I am a wretch," he sobbed, "and now I will die. I hope I will. I have wronged you, and do not deserve to live."

"You mean you do not have the strength to live, Alexis," Peter softly replied.

The prisoner coughed in what might have been a parody of laughter.

"All men are not like you," he managed. "If you are the measure of strength, what other man is strong?"

Peter trembled slightly. *If you only knew*, he thought. He again cleared his throat.

"It grieves me it has come to this, Alexis. It is my own failure, I know."

"What you asked was impossible," Alexis spat. Peter suddenly, almost gladly, understood that Alexis was angry, angry enough to overcome his shame and agony. "*It—was—impossible.*" The words were measured out, to ensure they were understood. To be certain that Peter comprehended that one thing, if nothing else, knew *he* was the cause, the murderer.

"You have never understood," Peter responded. "Every day I work— every single day—to make Russia what it can be, what it *should* be. Every day! Each time I relax, each *instant* I relax, to sleep, to sail, to read a book—something goes wrong. This senator becomes a grafter, that boyar raises the Strelitzi against me. I have marched with my armies. I have with my own two hands built many of the ships that guard our shores and carry our goods abroad. The very shoes I wear on my feet I earned working as an iron founder! That is what it takes to rule Russia, to bring her into a new age, to make her strong enough to survive in this new world. Not your muttering superstitions and backward-looking ways. When I came to power we were barbarians, lost in the old ways, a joke throughout the world. Now look at us! It will not all be lost when I die. No matter what, Russia will not tread backward!"

Alexis was silent for a time. "I know," he said at last. "But you must understand, I think you wrong. You strangle the old church, cut us off from the religion of our fathers. You consort with demons—"

"They are not demons," Peter said, feeling his own temper rise. "They are things of science. You would have us go back to the old ways? Would you have us give back our ice-free ports? Would you have us sit in Moscow, as the winters grow longer and colder, until the glaciers grind over our country? Would you give us back to the darkness from which we came, and worse?"

Alexis raised bruised eyes, already the dark hollows of a skull. "Yes. If it means we perish as Christians and not worshippers of things like that." He spat blood in the direction of the ifrit that floated behind

Peter. Peter barely glanced at it. It was always there, his guardian, more faithful than any man, a whirling nimbus around a single, burning eye.

"It is a thing of science," Peter repeated. "My philosophers discovered it."

"They summoned it from hell."

Peter bit back a retort, took a few breaths to calm himself. His face had begun to twitch, and he did not wish to bring on a seizure. "So you are unrepentant?"

"I suppose that I am, knowing I am to die."

"You need not die."

"I want to. There is nothing for me. You have taken everything, even my Afrosinia. . . ."

"Your little Finnish wench betrayed you, Alexis. She told all and perhaps even invented some things to save her own pitiful neck."

Alexis bowed his head, so that his hair hung to cover his face. "Tell me she will live, even if it is a lie," he whispered.

"She will live," Peter said, and turned to leave. But found that he could not, yet.

"They were using you, you know," he told Alexis, "the old boyars, the Church. Using you to strike at me."

Alexis looked up again. "I'm sorry only that I wished your death," he said. "I was afraid when I wished that. I have always been afraid, most especially of you and what you wanted. I could never have been enough for you, Father. I could never have *been* you—and that is what you need, not an heir. But I am not afraid anymore. God will take me in soon, and so I ask you to forgive me, and I will forgive you, and perhaps we shall meet again—" He choked off into a new bout of tears, and Peter's own eyes grew moist.

"I forgive you, Alexis, my son. I'm sorry I failed you."

And then he turned and walked away, unable to bear any more, his ifrit following like a faithful dog. He went back to his palace in Saint Petersburg and sat staring at the order for his son's execution, pen gripped in a trembling hand. He sat for many hours, and he still had not signed it when they came to tell him that Alexis had died.

He went to his balcony and looked out across his sea at the ships coming into his port, and he wept.

1722
The Council Meeting

"Halt there 'n' bide, stranger," a hoarse voice shouted over the groan of the wind and hiss of sleet. Red Shoes squinted toward the light and made out four figures, obscured by night and frozen rain, silhouetted before the dim lanthorn. At least two were armed with muskets, so he stopped as commanded, knowing they could see him far better than he them. He hoped that they would quickly get to whatever business they had with him, for the wet cold had long since worked its way into his bones, and his feet were as numb as stones. The city lights were visible ahead, where warmth and food awaited for the first time in many days.

"State your business," the same voice demanded. A tingle of alarm crept up his spine as he made out a faint creak and click—the hammer being drawn back on a flintlock.

Red Shoes cleared his throat. "I have come for the council meeting," he said.

"Council meeting? You mean the town council?"

"The council meeting," Red Shoes repeated.

"God, John," another voice sputtered. " 's an Ind'yun."

"Hold still," the first voice—John's—snarled. "I can see that. Are you armed, fellow?"

"Yes." He did not elaborate. The musket slung on his back was easy enough to see, but there was no reason to tell these men that he had no powder or shot. His pistol was hidden beneath his calf-length coat, every brass button of which was fastened against the murderous cold. His war ax was there, too, equally inaccessible. He had not expected to have to fight his way into Philadelphia.

"John, you know there's more out there," a third man said. "If there's one, there's more. And that's a French coat he's wearing. Damn you, I didn't bargain for this."

"You a Delaware? Mohawk?" John demanded. "Are you alone?"

Red Shoes could tell that they were craning their necks, looking for his imaginary red army. He had heard rumors that the unseasonable cold had provoked warfare between some of the northern tribes and white towns like Philadelphia—but surely no one would mistake *him* for a Six Nations man or a Delaware. He was Choctaw, and *looked* Choctaw.

"I'm alone," Red Shoes assured them. "I have a paper."

"A paper?"

"An invitation. To the council meeting."

"The council meeting," John repeated again.

Something was wrong here, something more than their worry about Indian attack. These men did not know what he was talking about, though if they were Philadelphia warriors, they certainly should. The trip had been long and hard, but not so hard that he had lost track of the days. The meeting was tonight, and he would not be the only one attending from outside the town. Gate guards should know that.

But of course the lanthorn behind them might not mark the gate as he'd originally thought. Stupid of him.

"Let me see your paper," John crisply ordered.

Red Shoes reached into the deerskin haversack slung at his waist, but even as he did so, the shadow named John suddenly lunged toward him.

His only option was to fall. His muscles were too fatigued and numb to react any other way. He twisted to catch himself, and struck his elbow against the ground as his right hand fumbled into his coat, knowing he could never withdraw his pistol in time. He did the only thing that remained: With his outblown breath, he released the shadowchild from its prison in his lungs. In less than an eye flicker it leapt to protect him, shrieking its displeasure as the descending sword cut into it, and then it was gone, a dying ghost bound for the Nightland. And so it felt as if a club struck him rather than a sharp-edged blade, slamming his face into the flinty earth rather than decapitating him. What was worse—far worse—was the pain of losing his shadowchild.

As he lifted his head to gaze at his death, thunder boomed, and the world lit in a yellow flash. As through a curtain of diamonds he saw John, mouth wide, a gaunt man in a black coat and tricorn, sword in hand. The three men behind him showed only eyes and mouths like round dark holes before the night closed again. Another explosion, another flash of light, and John was on his knees, while a second man twirled, and then it was black again, with a groaning louder than the wind.

The shock in his arm had quickened to pain, as if his bones were aflame. Grimly he flopped across the cold ground, still fumbling for his gun.

"Aye, flee, you fools," a voice shouted from behind him, a cannon of a voice firing words like red-hot iron.

Red Shoes assumed that his remaining attackers had fled. *He* would have, if he could.

Footsteps crunched toward him as at last he managed to free the pistol from its place in his inner pocket. A boot settled on the center of his back and pressed down.

"Hold on there," the new arrival said. "Let's not get off to a wrong start. I've just saved your life and expect a bit of gratitude. Now get up slowly, or I'll be forced to open y'like I did those two."

Red Shoes let the pistol slide back into its place and painfully pushed himself to his feet. Not only did the man have the advantage of him, but as his ears adjusted after the gunfire, he realized that the newcomer was not alone. This was confirmed an instant later as a warm yellow light was born nearby, expanding to envelop him. This came from a small lanthorn borne by a boy of perhaps sixteen years, perhaps younger. The light bearer hardly held his attention, however, for as Red Shoes stood he found himself face to chest with the wearer of the boot.

He was huge, a bear, clad in a dark red coat faced blue, a black waistcoat, and a tricorn trimmed in silver. His face was mostly beard that was twisted into many braids bound with black ribbons.

"I'll be damned," the bear said. "You *are* an Indian. What tribe do you belong with?"

"Choctaw," Red Shoes answered distractedly. He was busy counting the other men in the party—ten, including the whiskered giant.

"Choctaw? Son, but you are far and far from home."

"Yes. Thank you for helping me." He noticed that John had stopped moving and a second man lay equally still. Of the other two there was no trace.

"Would have had to shoot 'em anyway, I imagine. Common highway thieves. Might have let them have *you*, though, save I heard you say something about the meeting. You goin'?"

"Yes, that's so."

The man seemed to grimace, but it might have been a smile. "How old are you, boy? How many summers have you seen?"

"This is my eighteenth."

The man laughed harshly. "Doesn't much seem like summer, does it? A hell of an August, wouldn't you say?"

Red Shoes didn't see any point in agreeing. The world had turned upside down, and weather made no more sense than anything else. Besides, he still wondered what the man wanted. He might end up dead yet in this strange country so far from everything familiar. He hoped not; it would be stupid to have made it this far only to die at the very doorway of his destination.

When he didn't answer, the man chuckled again and shook his head. "Indians," he grunted. "Well, come on, boy. You best travel the rest of the way with us. We're going the same place anyway, me and you."

"You're going to the council meeting, too?"

"Yes, of course. Why else be out in this?" He waved at the surrounding night. "On account of my reputation, I thought it best not to bring my ships up in their harbor. But let me introduce myself. The name is Edward Teach."

"Teach," Red Shoes repeated. "The king of Charles Town."

"Oh, then you've heard of me? All away and over in Choctaw country?"

Red Shoes nodded. "We've heard of you."

The streets of Philadelphia were empty, but Red Shoes' eyes longingly turned to the warm yellow gaze of the windows surrounding him. He had meant to inquire his way to the town house where the meeting was to be, but Teach seemed to know where he was going, and Red Shoes followed silently.

Philadelphia was like the other three white towns he had been in: Biloxi, New Paris, and Charles Town. Like them, it was square. The buildings were square, the windows were square, the streets were square. It appeared to be a sort of obsession with white people, this squareness. It seemed to Red Shoes that it was almost a ritual, might even be the thing—or one of the things—that they derived their vast power from. In particular, there seemed to be some link between this squareness and the magic called science, but just when he thought he understood what it was, it eluded him.

Maybe here in Philadelphia he would come to understand.

He blinked—had he been asleep on his feet? They were mounting the steps of a large building. Teach's fist made explosions on the heavy wooden door.

The portal swung open, and heat flooded out like a summer wind, so delicious to his exposed skin that he nearly moaned in ecstasy. Privation strengthened one, to a certain point—but beyond that, it only weakened you. He was very weak right now, and pleasure was far more unnerving than pain.

He entered with Teach and his party, and terrible silence came in with them.

"Merciful God," someone muttered. "It's Blackbeard."

A number of men sitting at a large table came slowly to their feet. To Red Shoes, they were diverse only in the way they dressed. Three were clad in austere black with only a bit of white lace at their throats to brighten them. Others wore brighter clothing—notably the four red-coated soldiers who cast dithering glances at muskets leaning against the wall. Five more at the table were arrayed quite splendidly, at least by European standards, complete with the strange mounds of false hair that so many of them affected. It was one of these—a corpulent fellow with ruddy cheeks—who stabbed a finger toward Teach.

"What gall you manifest by presenting yourself in this place, pirate. I will have your head posted in the harbor."

Teach grinned broadly and placed his hands on his hips. "That is no fashion in which to address a fellow governor, Mister Felton," he proclaimed, his voice booming in the hall.

The other man—Governor Felton, Red Shoes presumed—reddened further. "You are beyond all insolence, Edward Teach. Do you think there is one man in this room—or alive on the face of this Earth—

who believes that because you have moved your campaign of terror from the high seas to the statehouse of Carolina you have any legal status except that of a loathsome and hunted criminal? Do not mock us. If you have come here with sword and pistol to bend us to your will, then have done with it or stand to do your worst. If not, get thee hence. This council is of the gravest possible nature and touches upon the fate of us all. We cannot countenance theatrics."

"Then perhaps you should cease performing them," Teach grunted. Red Shoes thought he detected a hint of strain in the pirate's voice, as if the effort to remain amiable were paining his throat. "Who have you invited to this council? The other governors, I see, every man jack of them as helpless as a kitten. Can they provide you with what you need? You know that they cannot. I see a small coven of ministers—the good Cotton Mather, I presume, and his progeny? But I am sure that they have brayed—ah, pardon, me—*prayed* long and loud for what I have come to give you. Now, I admit that the Crown has not yet given me a paper allowing that I govern my colony—"

"Never shall it!" sputtered the scarlet-faced Felton.

Teach paused. When he spoke again his voice carried a palpable danger. "That may be, and when any of you *gentlemen* think to deprive me of what I have won and the order I have brought from chaos in the South, then I welcome your efforts. But until such time as His Majesty across the ocean sees fit to back the paper currency of your opinions with a more solid standard, I will keep my place and claim my due. Is there any of you who has ought than bones in his head and understands I have come to do you a favor?"

"And what might that favor be?" The dark-clad man Teach had addressed as "Cotton Mather" asked quietly. His pendulous face and bulging eyes should have made him seem ridiculous, and yet Red Shoes sensed authority in him, strength. And perhaps—something more, something that teased at the edge of his vision in a familiar way. When he blinked, however, the something vanished.

He was tired.

"I know well the purpose of this council," Teach explained to the preacher. "For two years, no word has come from England, no ship, no aetherschreiber communication. Likewise none from Holland, from Spain, from France. Nor have any ships you sent come back. Nor do you have spare ships left to send, not when you must watch for the prowling French corsairs north— 'Tis true?"

The roomful of men had no answer. They gazed sullenly back at Edward Teach. He surveyed them all with satisfaction. "Nor can you build more than a handful, not with this witchy cold and the Indians gone wild amongst the trees you might use for masts."

"We have ships!" another of the splendidly dressed men claimed, at last returning his lips to the pipe that had smoldered unsmoked since the pirates had made their entrance.

"Oh, indeed, one small sloop and a frigate that has seen far better days. But 'tis all apparent now that whatever has befallen Albion is an eater of ships and men, an unknown thing, and 'twill require men-o'-war to go and return, to discover the truth of our long isolation."

"And why should you care about that, Blackbeard?" Felton asked, picking an imaginary hair from his velvet coat. "As you say, you have benefited by our isolated state. Why would you want our enterprise to succeed?"

Teach trembled perceptibly as he answered, the muscles of his great shoulders bunching beneath his coat. "I will say this once, Lord Governor, and I will ne'er repeat myself save to write it in your blood. Whatever else Edward Teach might be, he is an *Englishman*. There is evil blood between myself and his German majesty, King George, and there was wrong done me which I have returned fivefold. But I love my country, and I fear what may have befallen her."

"Beside all that," Mather quietly added, "if you were to aid us in restoring our link with the sovereign, what benefits might not befall you? A pardon, perhaps?"

Teach shrugged. "I can't say that would displease me, but it is nevertheless a risk to my neck, is it not? And if I risk that, then you gentlemen should be willing to risk my aid. I offer you not one ship, but four ships o' the line with forty cannon on each, the men to crew them, and my personal service as admiral."

"A pirate in command of His Majesty's ships? Preposterous!" Felton exclaimed. But his eyes were those of a small dog backing away from a larger one.

"Well, good sirs," remarked a fellow in a blue coat, "the choice now comes to a devil or a Frenchman. Which more frightens you?"

All eyes turned toward the speaker. He had a strong face, careworn about the eyes, and a round chin that stuck out a bit. He was perhaps in his fortieth summer. By his silver gorget and plumed hat, Red Shoes took him to be the selfsame Frenchman he spoke of.

"Monsieur Bienville," Felton said in a heavily taxed tone, "surely you can understand our position. The last we heard from England or Europe, our countries were at war, and now the raids on our coast from your brethren in the north occur almost daily."

Red Shoes shook his head to clear it. Bienville? He looked more closely, and the recognition came. He had seen this man perhaps five times as a boy, come to the village of Chickasaway to parley with his uncle and the other leaders. He and his companions had been the first of the white people Red Shoes had ever seen.

The Frenchman cleared his throat. "I name you governor, Sir Felton, because your king has made you one. Will you do me the same courtesy, please?"

Felton blushed and nodded briskly. "My apologies, *Governor* Bienville."

"Thank you, sir. As to the matter you justly raise, I cannot speak for the men of New France and Acadia, Governor, save to say that if winters are hard here, they are most assuredly harder in those latitudes; and men made desperate by cold and hunger will do awful things. I have had little communication with them, and I believe that the government has fallen into the hands of ruffians—something the English colonies surely understand." At this last he boldly rested his gaze upon Blackbeard, who shrugged.

"And yet, as governor of Louisiana, have I not ceased all aggressions in Florida and the West, and concluded an armistice? Gentlemen, we all of us must discover what has become of the world. Are we truly alone? If so, we must know of it. We must prepare ourselves, and we must ally. For I tell you that without our mother countries, we are all of us at the mercy of a thousand evils. None of us can imagine what happened across that great ocean sea. Some say they saw lights in the heavens, a red glow like sunset. Your eastern harbors were flooded, and many ships at sea were never seen again. Even our miraculous aetherschreibers have been of no use. And yet we have some rumors—of fire falling from the heavens, of forty days of darkness. I know for a fact that Paris was in flames almost two years ago. Have the devils been let loose on Earth? What man knows the truth? If there is one, let him speak it. Here is the truth that I know: Each of us alone has sent ships, and each of us alone has failed. My harbors were untouched by flooding, but I had fewer ships to begin with. The great naval actions of the Flanders War were elsewhere, as you all know, and thus were the ships of France and Spain. Now I offer you what I have left, asking only that I act as co-commander of the expedition. I give you my word as a gentleman that our armistice will hold, no matter what the case, until our ships are safe back here. Even the Sun King himself could not cause me to break this vow. I will fight against my own French brothers, if need be. My word of honor, sirs, something this pirate cannot give you."

An uncomfortable silence followed the Frenchman's words, and then one of the men with Teach stepped forward. Like the soldiers, he wore a red British coat. He was perhaps forty, his faced tanned and hard.

"It is understandable that you do not accept the word of Edward Teach, but perhaps you will accept mine."

"And who, sir, are you?" the governor inquired.

"I am Captain Thomas Nairne. I believe Mr. Teach is sincere, and I will stay at his left hand to insure the interests of the Crown."

"That is surely not sufficient, sir," Felton complained. "Any man can don a red coat and call himself a captain, and any captain can turn pirate, for that matter."

"Nevertheless," Nairne persisted, "I urge you to consider my opinion. Like you, I do not consider the position Mr. Teach has taken in South Carolina to be a lawful one, but someone had to establish order there. He is not an unpopular ruler, though you may not credit it."

"I will not strike a devil's bargain," Felton insisted.

Bienville shrugged. "Then perhaps Mr. Teach and I can come to an agreement on our own."

"Is that a threat?" Felton snapped.

"It is not. It is an option. I would see the shores of France again, sir, and know what has become of my king."

"Right well said, sir," Teach added. "What use have we of these popinjay do-nothings when *we* have the ships?"

Mather crooked a finger at Teach. "He needs us," the black-clad minister asserted, his voice as confident as an iron tower. "Or he would not have come. He wants the sanction of the Crown insofar as you governors can give it."

"Out of the question," Felton said, but a man in a cinnamon coat plucked at his sleeve.

"Not so quickly, sir," he said softly. "There is much here to consider." His rather lean face was puckered into a frown beneath a curling white wig. "Who is this Indian? Is he with you, Mr. Teach?"

"No, indeed. He represents the Choctaw."

"Is this true?" the man asked. "We did invite representatives from your people, but we have had ill luck with Indians of late."

Red Shoes cleared his throat. "I am Red Shoes of the Sixtowns people of the Choctaw nation. I have a paper summoning me to this meeting."

"I wrote that paper," Cotton Mather said. "I invited your chief."

"I am his nephew. My uncle and the rest of our party were slain by the Shawano while traveling here."

"Yet you came on alone."

"I did."

"You speak well for an Indian."

"I have been taught English. I have learned to read and write and do figures. I know something of history."

"And what do you offer us? More ships?"

"No, of course not. I only offer myself, and later my words to my people."

"Why should we value those?"

"My people are split in the matter of the white people. Many think it is time for us to be rid of you."

Though his words were quiet, they had the effect of a thunderbolt. Good.

"Of all the insolent . . ." Felton began.

"Are you such a one, boy?" Mather asked.

"No. The British and the French have many things we desire, and we have many friends among them. I see no virtue in a war that might end as badly for my people as for yours. You invited my uncle, the chief, to this meeting. That was good, because it shows us that you care—or worry—about what we think. It also admits your desperation. Some of you know the trouble that waits among the Choctaw and our allies. You would have us at least remain quiet until you learn what has caused these strange changes in the world. We would know that, too. My word: Until I am dead or return, my people will not wage an unprovoked war."

"How do your people know that you are alive?"

Red Shoes smiled. "Through a certain science, they know. When I die, they will know that, too."

"And if you should die?"

"That will depend on many things, and I cannot speak of a situation that might exist when I am dead. I am the eyes and ears of my people. They know what I know."

"Fantasy!" Felton asserted. But he believed. They all did. This time the pause stretched long, and there was some whispering at the table before the governor looked up, bleak eyed. "We will discuss this matter," he said weakly. "Rooms have been arranged for you gentlemen at a nearby inn."

"Don't think too long," Teach growled, and then, as if to offset the threat, he bowed clumsily.

Back on the street, the man named Thomas Nairne approached him. "*Chim achukma,*" he said.

"*Achukma,*" Red Shoes answered. Continuing in Choctaw, "*You speak my language.*"

"*Indeed. What do you think of what you heard today?*"

"*I think they will accept Governor Bienville's offer, and the Blackbeard's, too. I think we will all sail across the Pale Water.*"

Nairne switched back to English. "A fair assessment, I think. How is it that you speak English so well? I have always known the Choctaw to be solidly in the French camp."

"We are in the *Choctaw* camp. Years ago, my uncle saw we should send someone to learn English ways. I was sent to Charles Town for five years."

Nairne nodded. "I'm sorry to hear the rest died. I knew your uncle,

I believe—I was an agent among your people some years ago—and I mourn his passing."

"He died well." Red Shoes felt a constriction in his throat and swallowed.

"Tell me," Nairne asked lightly, perhaps to keep the names of the dead from being spoken, "do you really want to sail across the sea?"

Red Shoes nodded wearily but grinned. "As I said, I know something of history. I know of Columbus, and how he discovered this New World. It amuses me to think of discovering the old one."

Nairne chuckled, and they went to the inn together.

Part One

Evening Wolves

The Evening Wolves will be much abroad, when we are near the Evening of the World.
—Cotton Mather,
   Wonders of the Invisible World, 1693

1.

Der Lehrling

Distracted as he was, the sudden pounding at the door captured all of Benjamin Franklin's attention. Sticking his head above the bedsheets, he stared for an instant at the source of the noise, completely at a loss.

"Katarina!" A man's voice shouted, *profundo*, followed by ever more violent thuds.

The appropriate reaction occurred to Ben, and he swiftly disentangled himself from milky limbs with as much enthusiasm as he had earlier entangled in them.

"It's my father!" Katarina whispered.

"Oh, only your father," Ben hissed back, reaching frantically for his breeches. "Ask him to come back later, then, will you?" He tumbled out of the bed and began struggling into the breeches, wondering where the rest of his clothing and his haversack had gone to.

"Katarina!" her father roared again. "Open the door. I know you have a man in there!"

"I don't think he will listen to me," Katarina replied.

Diving for his shirt, Ben yet allowed himself an admiring glance at tousled honey hair, half obscuring a softly rounded face still rosy from exertion. "Well, should I introduce myself?" Ben asked, yanking his shirt over his head and starting toward where his waistcoat lay crumpled in the corner. He made a mental note to learn to undress more neatly, even when passion ruled.

"I wouldn't. He has a pistol."

"A pistol?"

"Well, he has a commission in the army."

"What? You didn't think this worth mentioning?"

"I wasn't thinking much about my father just now. Besides, I thought he would be gone all day."

"Quite understandable. This window opens?"

"Yes." She sat up in the bed, allowing the sheets to drop away from her upper body, and despite himself, Ben grinned. The floor-length mirror behind Katarina grinned back at him from a face still rounded by the last traces of boyhood and haloed by thoroughly mussed chestnut locks. "Sorry to leave in such a rush," he apologized, pleased at how smooth his German had become.

"Don't forget you promised to show me the palace."

"I shan't, never fear. Expect my letter."

He bent to kiss her and heard a key suddenly grating in the lock.

The kiss turned into a quick nip on the lips. "Remember me," he said, grabbing his haversack and rushing to the window, flinging it recklessly open.

"Don't think ill of me!" she called from behind him. "I don't do this all the time. But I know more than I showed you. . . ."

Ben was no longer listening, concentrating as he was on gripping the windowsill, looking down at his feet superimposed over cobblestones two stories below. He did not hesitate, for at seventeen his body was long and strong, near six feet, and he was confident of his athletic ability—at least, more confident than he was of his capacity to withstand a pistol shot.

The pavement shocked up through the bones of his legs into his belly, forcing out a pronounced *oof*, but he straightened quickly, looking about to see if he had been noticed. Happily, the street was deserted—but he had gone fewer than fifty yards when the door banged open behind him. He was running already, not up the street or down it, but straight toward the Moldau River.

"Goddamn lech!" a man's voice roared, accompanied by a bright barking sound. Something whizzing struck sparks on the pavement two yards to Ben's right.

"Beelzebub!" he grunted, and then leapt again, this time vaulting over the wall that kept high waters from swallowing Kleinseit. He paused for just an instant to slip the metallic key dangling from his waistcoat into the tiny pocket near his belt—and disappeared.

Or at least to the casual observer, he reminded himself. Among other things, the aegis built into his waistcoat bent light around it, a trick that fooled some mechanisms of the eye but not others. From the corner of his eye, the vengeful father might catch a glimpse of Ben, and staring straight on he would perceive an eye-hurting blur. Of course, the aegis also emitted a repulsive gravity that turned such objects as musket balls, but Ben's experiments had shown that as a shield the device sometimes failed. Rather than further test it, he scrambled down the stone and sand embankment to the river. There he drew out the contents of the haversack—a pair of odd-looking shoes, stiff and solid like a Dutchman's but comically larger and more boat shaped. Behind him, the hollering continued—albeit with a somewhat confused quality—as he donned them.

Katarina had been *so* sure her father would be gone until nightfall. Or had she? Might it be some plan of hers to trap him into marriage? After all, these days he was a fine catch, and she not without ambition.

As quickly as he dared, he placed first one foot and then the other onto the surface of the river and awkwardly glided away, around the shielding bulk of little Venedig Island. The shouts faded behind him, and once he was certain he was far enough away to risk it, he drew out the key. Wearing the aegis restricted its wearer's vision as well, faded the world to rainbow at the edges, as if one stared through prism eyes. Much like being caught in a girl's bedroom by her father, it was a less-than-comfortable sensation.

He finally found his stride, sliding his feet from side to side as if skating. It was rougher than skating, however, harder to keep his balance, but at last he was sure enough of himself to take his eyes off his feet. Just in time, too, for looking up he noticed a boat with an instant still to avoid it. He had a glimpse of a wide-eyed boatsman, heard his terrified *Gott!* before he was beyond, bouncing perilously over bow waves, and then weaving in front of the small craft.

People were staring and shouting from the shore as well as if they had never seen a man skating upon the Moldau before. But perhaps they had not, he thought smugly. Not when it wasn't frozen.

Grinning, he pushed on, still marveling at the way his shoes pressed against the flowing water without touching it, like two magnets with like poles shoved together. He turned back upstream, laughing at the peculiar resistance, Katarina and her father already forgotten, sliding two steps forward but nevertheless moving back with the vaster sweep of the current. Turning again, he lost his balance and teetered precariously on one foot, arms windmilling, but he did not fall. He knew all about falling from practice the day before: The shoes stayed out of the water, making it hard to get his head up; the only solution was to take them off, a clumsy business.

After an instant or two, he relaxed, marveling instead at his surroundings. It was a beautiful day—or as beautiful as days got now. Fingers of sunlight groped down through billowy clouds, tearing blue portals to a more cheerful sky. In the past two years blue sky had been so rare a sight that, if it could be minted, it would replace gold and silver as the currency of nations. Sweet, honeyed light traced languidly across the eldritch rooftops of Prague, quickening copper and gilded steeples, dancing across the gray waters of the Moldau as easily as he did. For a moment, he seemed beyond himself, a part of that singular gift from the heavens, and it came to him like a wind at his back that if he could walk upon water by the labor of his own mind, his own hands, he could do anything. He could bring sunlight back to the world. He *would*.

It was, he thought with a trace of an old anguish, the least he could do for having taken it away.

The inconstant sun was hiding again when he reached the Charles Bridge, and neither the span nor the baroque iron saints that stood watch upon it cast a shadow as he slid to the river's edge and the quay below them. A small crowd had gathered to watch him with a sullen and superstitious curiosity he had come to know well. Even though they whispered, he still heard one of them hiss "der Lehrling," the Apprentice. That was what they called him, these people of Bohemia. They did not say whose apprentice he was, for everyone knew the unspoken part of the phrase: the Sorcerer's Apprentice—Sir Isaac Newton's apprentice.

The lone person actually waiting for him was not frightened, however, but stood, arms akimbo, an irritated expression on his handsome face.

"Oh, 'tis a fine thing!" the auburn-haired man shouted, Ben pushing back his gold-ribboned tricorn. "Walkin' on water whilst I wait on you! The other fellow as performed that feat had more consideration f'r his friends!"

"Yes, and look how they treated him for his troubles," Ben rejoined. "Anyway, by the toll of the clock—or its lack, I should say—I'm not yet late for our appointment."

"Any moment that separates me from a beer is a moment too long."

"Well, Robin, let's remedy that, then." The solid stone felt strange beneath Ben's feet, as if he had been on shipboard for some time. He considered taking his new shoes off—they were clumsy and thick, for he was no cobbler—but going about in stocking feet would quickly ruin his stockings. So he left them on, noting with satisfaction that not a single drop of water adhered to them.

Robert was looking at them, too, shaking his head as they started up the stairs. "I don't know as I should show out an' you've been doin'," he said, more softly than his greeting. "These affrighted Catholics might pitch you up and make a torch from you an' them."

"Let 'em try," Ben replied, trying to smooth a wrinkle on his waistcoat with the palm of his hand. "They'll learn a hard lesson in science from me and a harder one in politics from their emperor. Anyhow, suspicious as these folks are, they know who keeps the Turk from the gate and food in their bellies. Don't worry about me."

"Never that!" Robert assured him. "I worry about *me*. How would I explain to Sir Isaac that I, your s'pposed bodyguard, let his little homunculus end up at the bottom of the Moldau?"

"If I'm at the bottom of the Moldau, it'll be to hunt mermaids," Ben replied.

They reached the top of the stairs, and Robert started to turn left and cross the bridge.

"Let's not go that way," Ben suggested.

"Ain't we goin' back to Kleinseit, to Saint Thomas'?"

"I thought to go to the Vulture," Ben said.

"Ain't you meetin' his sirness in three hours?"

"A few hours is plenty," Ben replied. "It'll—eh—give a certain fatherly sort time to calm and quit roaming the streets of Kleinseit."

"Indeed? The father of a certain golden-haired lass?"

"Ockham's razor," Ben supplied. "The least complicated answer—"

"Is the best," Robert finished. "I saw ya throwin' sparks at each other in the square t'other day."

"She has considerable spark," Ben acknowledged.

Robert shrugged. "Well, then, to the Vulture and a pint for your adventures."

"And to celebrate my new invention," Ben added. "Then we're back across the bridge."

"A pint," Robert agreed, turned right onto Charles Way, and began to walk into the Old Town.

Ben loved the Old Town. Across the river in Kleinseit and Hradčany there were castles and palaces, pomp and splendor. In Old Town there was life. The streets—even Charles Way, a central thoroughfare—were narrow, darkened by several stories of buildings on each side. And such buildings! Medieval edifices like the tower of the bridge behind them, brooding and black. The strong heaven-seeking arches and spires of gothic cathedrals and state buildings, scrolled and ornamented baroque houses from the last century. It was like something from a fairy tale—from all fairy tales—and it was nothing at all like Boston, where he had been born and where nothing was even a hundred years old. Prague was a city with its foundations sunk nearer the creation, the memories of a thousand generations in its walls and streets. Even London had never struck him in this way, for the core of London had been gutted by fire and rebuilt according to scientific plan, a vast structure designed by a single architect, Sir Christopher Wren. It had been modern, not a hodgepodge from every human age.

But, of course, London was dust. It was worse than dust, and with very few exceptions, everyone who had ever lived there was dead. Like the blotted sun, that too was his fault.

London was gone, but Prague he would save.

They went on, past the Italian Chapel, past the Golden Serpent and its fountain of red wine, out into the Old Town square. Just as they arrived, the clock began to toll, and Ben quickened his steps.

"Now what's your hurry?" Robert asked.

Ben didn't answer, instead skirting to the opposite side of the Old Town Hall, so he could see the clock.

It was a magnificent creation. Dancing its minuet of brass and time, it displayed not only the hour and minute, but the movements of the spheres. As it tolled, Jesus and his apostles shuffled behind small windows, bowing to the watching square before receding into the mechanical labyrinth where they dwelt.

"I should think such frippery would not impress you, Benjamin Franklin," Robert said. "You've made much greater magic than this."

"I suppose," Ben replied, "but perhaps that's what impresses me. This clock was here for hundreds of years before true science came to be. It's just a clever machine. But *so* clever, Robin, and with so much attention to beauty. It is entirely practical and entirely a thing of art at the same moment—and that moment stretched to centuries."

"I'm sure he was very clever with his hands, the man who built this," Robert temporized, "but p'rhaps not so quick-witted in other ways. As I hear it, he was blinded so he couldn't repeat his feat. A truly intelligent man would know t' be wary of the whims o' kings 'n' lords."

"Is it my imagination, or are you still mothering me?" Ben asked softly. "Do you know something I don't, Robin?"

Robert chuckled. "I know *plenty* you don't, boyo, and don't you f'rget it. But nothin' specific worrisome—just an itch I have today."

"Maybe it's time you settled down and became a father. That'll scratch that itch right well."

"Hah. Some cures are worse than any affliction."

A gilded cockerel suddenly stuck its head from the clock face and flapped its wings. "Let's on," Ben said. "The performance is at an end, and the Vulture is a stone's throw that way."

The Vulture was indeed only a few doors away, but the beggars in the square had noticed them now and swarmed about, hands thrusting out, eyes and mouths pleading. Ben set his gaze straight ahead and brushed through them—the children, the nursing mothers, the old men. In his first months in the city, Ben had been wont to give them what he could, but by degrees his heart had hardened; for the simple fact was that there were too many of them, and for each he satisfied with a coin, twenty were left to stare grudgingly after him.

Prague was bursting its walls with refugees of all sorts, from peasants driven from the land to the emperor himself, fleeing the fall of Vienna. The most and poorest of them dwelt in New Town, sleeping in whatever tents or shanties they could piece together; but many made their way here, to the heart of things, during the day, despite the periodic rounds of soldiers who cleared them out.

Ben also knew that none of them were starving, due to the manna machines he had helped Newton design. Manna might be unpleasant, but it was food and free for the asking.

A man at the door of the Vulture looked them over in case *they* might be beggars, but he let them pass without comment. Even at this time of day the tavern was nearly full, though it was no small place. Soldiers in uniforms rough and fine, gentlemen in stylish frock coats, workmen in stained shirts stood or sat at the long wooden tables, both in the darkened rooms and outside in the beer garden. Ben and Robert chose a table in the corner mostly because there was still room on its benches. Almost as they sat down, a serving girl with a thin face and lank brown hair brought them each a beer.

"Thank you, my dear," Ben said, flashing her a smile.

Robert lifted his wooden tankard. "To your new invention, the Jesus shoes!" he pronounced.

"Hush, you butter-head!" Ben said, nearly choking on his drink. "Now who's being incautious around the Romish?"

Robert grinned and took a gulp of his beer. " 'An eagle abroad but an owl at home,' " he quoted. "So what *do* you call those things?" He gestured vaguely beneath the table.

"Aquapeds," Ben replied.

"Of course. Nothing is scientifical unless you name it in the Latin," Robert remarked, a bit mockingly.

Ben didn't bite at the bait, but instead tasted his beer—it was black, bitter, and solid going down. "God save the king," he toasted automatically, and then wished he hadn't.

"The king!" Robert agreed, and they tipped their tankards hard.

When they settled them back down, however, Robert looked at him thoughtfully. "Do you think there *is* a king, anymore? Do you think he might have escaped?"

Ben resisted frowning. He would rather discuss more pleasant things, but he had started it with his thoughtless toast. He shrugged, hoping Robert might think his blunder a sardonic jest. "It depends upon how convincing Heath and Voltaire were. I wouldn't bet a single crown upon it."

"Well," Robert said, "well . . . let's just drink to England, for even without London there must be Englishmen, and as there are Englishmen, there is England."

"Hear, hear," Ben agreed, but his heart wasn't really in it. It always felt as if his chest were stuffed with thistles when the subject of London came up.

"So what will you do with these magic shoes of yours?" Robert asked, probably to change the subject.

"I will present several pair of them to the emperor and his daughters for their amusement. Perhaps he will not have my eyes put out."

Robert shrugged his shoulders and gestured with one hand, like a dandy indicating a painting. "If they did, ya would have only the challenge of inventing a new pair t' see with." He glanced again at the table, as if looking through it to Ben's feet. "Is Sir Isaac pleased?"

"Pleased? With the shoes? No, he thinks my continued experiments with affinity a useless divertissement. I must work on such things in my spare time."

"That provokes you," Robert observed.

"Dogs and damsels, yes, it provokes me!" Ben agreed, following his words with a substantial quaff of his beer. "He's at work on some New System of his—biblical stuff with angels and such—while I'm left to keep the emperor happy." He considered for a moment. "Not a bad job all in all—it keeps us in high style—but it's not practical. Who knows when another comet may be called upon our heads?"

"Wouldn't the airy shield around the city stop it?"

Ben shook his head. "No, that's just an aegis built large. We should have written a real countermeasure two years ago. The thing you have to know about Newton is that he does not care about the useful, only about philosophizing. His research is directed not by what might produce something good, but by impulses of—of I know not what. He seeks to understand God's universe, to know its depths. Not for me or you or Prague or even England, but for himself. Because he thus believes to curry God's favor."

He finished his beer and called for another.

"And what make you of all of this, then?" Robert asked.

Ben was silent for a moment, and then he smiled and lifted his mug. "I make I'm being too serious about it all. Let's just drink and be merry."

Robert shook his head. "This is not the same lad I met just come from Boston."

"Nor is it the same world we live in," Ben rejoined. "Our wonderful new age has come, and so let us enjoy it."

The two men emerged from the Vulture an hour and a half later, several pints heavier, their moods and feet much lighter.

"We'd best walk this off," Robert suggested, "else the emperor might notice that the apprentice has some sway in his stance."

"He will be so pleased by his new toy that he will not care if I vomit on his rug," Ben scoffed. "Especially when he discovers that I'm having one of his boats fitted to operate thus. Can you imagine what speeds a seagoing craft might travel with no resisting friction from the water?"

"With no ports he'd have little account to test such a craft. Best you build a rowboat, unless you can make such as the fairy tales tell of, that sails both land and sea."

"That has more difficulties involved," Ben said. "Water is simpler than soil." He cocked his head. "But I shall think on it."

"What of the aerial ship by which we arrived here? Could you not combine the two?"

Ben shrugged. "Perhaps, if Sir Isaac would ever give up the secret of its operation. At first I thought it built on the principle of some repulsive affinity, but Newton claims that it is not."

"You know," Robert began hesitantly, "I always fancied that there was some sort of—well, *creature* in the globe that bore our boat aloft."

Ben nodded. "I believe that there was, a sort of creature that he names malakus. But he will say nothing else on 't."

"Could it be some sort of demon?"

"No. Yes—I don't know," Ben said. "Nor at the moment do I much care."

"Aye," Robert grunted. "But there's the stories about him 'n' demons, you know."

"Told by whom?"

"Servants. Them that cleans his laboratories. They whisper things about."

"I'm sure a spark of electricity seems a demon to them."

" 'Tis more than that. What of the weird lights that accompanied that fellow Bracewell? The one as killed your brother and did his damnedest to kill you? I saw those, and you did, too. What would you call them?"

"An enigma, that's what. A scientific man does not make hasty conclusions based in superstition."

"Ah. Very well. But the emperor is no scientific man. What if these rumors of weird lights and strange sounds come back to him?"

"*Pfuh.* The emperor is like a child. Did I publish to him that rain was the splashing of angels in a heavenly tub, he would agree to it."

They continued on for a moment, and then Robert chuckled. "For a colonial lad," he said, "you have little enough awe of emperors."

Ben shrugged. "Why should I? An accident of birth makes him no better than me. The age of monarchs is ending, my friend. Who are the great men of this day? Isaaac Newton, a yeoman's son; Leibniz, the son of a professor; John Locke, an attorney's boy."

"Yes, and Jesus was the son of a carpenter, but a king still had him killed. You may not live in awe of them, but you best not turn your back, Ben, or give your tongue pr'miscus liberty."

"Returned to that lesson, have we?" Ben said, but playfully. He didn't mind Robert looking out for him, and the older man had saved his life more than once. Besides, he was certainly right. The court of the Holy Roman emperor was not the safest place in the world at the moment. With Vienna fallen, Hungary in revolt, Prague laid siege to twice in the last year, and a huge influx of refugees, the emperor and his ministers were often short-tempered. Still, if anyone at court had a secure position, it was Newton and thus himself. Without them, Prague would join Vienna beneath the red banner and white crescent of the Ottoman empire or fall prey to a Moscovado army. The Emperor Karl VI, if not a brilliant man, at least knew that. No, the Habsburgs needed their miracle workers.

At Robert's suggestion, the two of them had taken a roundabout way back to the bridge, crossing the Old Town square again and wandering vaguely north. Their ultimate destination was the banks of the Moldau, which bent eastward around the city. There they could walk a circuit along the embankment back to the bridge. In the meantime, they were in no real hurry; almost two hours remained before Ben's appointment with Newton, and unexpected sights hid around each corner of the great city, even in the meanest and most out-of-the-way street.

The unexpected this time was not some architectural gem or tucked-away shop, however.

"Someone follows us," Robert hissed.

"You are certain?"

"Five men, all from the Vulture," he said.

"What can they want, I wonder?"

"I don't know. Perhaps it is an angry father and his friends."

Ben strained his ears and heard what Robert heard: footsteps and voices muttering in a language unintelligible to him and yet familiar in cadence, in tone. . . .

"Russian," Ben hissed. "They speak Russian."

"Then probably not simple cutthroats."

"Five, eh? Robert, let's give 'em a surprise."

"Ben, don't place too much faith in your wild inventions. Five is still a lot of men. If they've guns—"

"I want to know what they're after. We'll just run around that corner and turn on our aegises, then clobber 'em."

"Ben . . ."

"Come!" he shouted, and broke into a trot, glancing back as he did so. There they were, five men in nondescript clothing. One of them shouted, and they, too, began to run.

"Ah, shit!" Robert groaned.

And from the corner in front of them stepped a sixth man, pistol cocked and raised.

2

Brigands

Outside, smoke clung to the earth like a bitter fog, mingling fumes of gunpowder, flaming thatch, and charred flesh.

"Yes, keep you quiet, little one," Adrienne whispered, holding her son more tightly to her bosom.

"It is a strange child who does not cry at gunfire," the man nearest her hissed. Le Loup was the only name she knew him by, a graying fellow with tangled hair, face as cratered as the moon by pockmarks.

"He came into the world to the sound of muskets," Adrienne told him. "He cries when he does *not* hear them." She peered wearily out the narrow door of the cottage, caught a flash of cobalt through the haze, as if a bluebird were winging through the bleak morning. From quite near, a gun roared.

"It is good," Le Loup said. "I have been known to smother children when they raised the alarm for my enemies."

Adrienne met his gaze. She needed no words to make Le Loup uncomfortably return his attention outside.

Adrienne kissed her toddler on the forehead, wondering what thing it was in a child that could demand life of its mother. As a girl, she had not much considered motherhood, and it had never pleased her to be around children of less than seven or so years of age, and not often then. Her own son was really no different from any she had met save that he belonged to her. He was greedy: He gnawed at her breast, even when she had no milk to give, when her own ribs were visible through her starving flesh. He was stupid: stupider than any cow, goat, or dog, which by the age of one and a half would be capable of foraging for its own food and have the sense to remove itself from its own excrement. Not so her darling child. It seemed impossible that he might one day read, speak in sentences, dress himself.

And yet this creature, this child, was the only reason she still lived. It was as if everything in her that yet wanted to survive had congealed itself into him so that she could see it, be reminded by it, demand that she continue the motions of life, though her soul felt dead.

She kissed her son again. "Sleep, Nico," she said, and lay the fatigued child on a bit of straw.

Almost as tenderly, she lifted up the carbine next to her and primed the pan. Stretching out on the stinking dirt floor of the cabin, she propped the short weapon on a hearthstone, sighted the door, and waited. Outside, the nameless little village continued to smolder.

"Hsst! Awake!" Crecy's voice came in her ear. Adrienne blinked and realized that she had nodded off—for one moment or many she did not know, since the scene outside had scarcely changed. Adrienne glanced up at Crecy. The redhead's chiseled features were lovely in the faint light, but there was no other outward sign that Crecy was female. Her rangy frame and narrow chest were easily disguised by her stained waistcoat and heavy gray justaucorps. Perhaps Le Loup and his bandits suspected her true sex, but if they did, they assented to the fiction, for they had all had ample demonstration of her speed, strength, and skill.

"They've passed. We must go before they return."

"They left no sentries?"

"Tonio has already disposed of him."

Adrienne eased up, searching for her things. She looped the dirty sling that Nicolas rode in about her shoulder and lifted him into it. He was awake, watching her with gray eyes clear of human thought— and yet communicating something, a hint of some weird secret, an enigma only mute pupae such as he were privy to. Something like a feather stirred in her chest, quite near where she had once kept her love for another Nicolas. It was a place she could prod as one might prod a sore, but it was no longer painful; what she felt there was only a cold cavity. The gangrene that nearly destroyed her was gone, but the scar of it still clung.

Le Loup was already outside, encircled by some ten or so of his band. Adrienne and Crecy emerged from the house, and, with as little sound as possible, they all began to move off.

Half an hour later, the village was a plume of smoke in the sky, then a memory. Le Loup and his brigands had hoped to raid it, but it had already been abandoned by all save corpses when they arrived. While they were searching the ruins for food, clothing, and other valuables, the bluecoats had come, more than they could ever hope to deal with, and so they had hidden and waited. Bandits did that often, as Adrienne had discovered in the past several months.

Now they wound through muddy, overgrown pasture, weeds and thistles waving higher than their waists. The sky was an iron skin upon the heavens, as it had been since the comet had come at a madman's call and ruined the world. But at least the rains had slackened.

"We cannot stay with these men much longer," Crecy confided, as the line stretched out and they were able to achieve relative privacy near the middle of the column.

"We need them, I think," Adrienne said.

"Oh, indeed, but they will soon decide that they do not need us. Or me, at any rate."

"Le Loup is jealous," Adrienne admitted. "He knows you are the better leader, and his men know it, too. But that can be managed."

Crecy was silent for a score or so steps. "He hasn't touched you, has he?"

"Touched me, yes. More, no. But I fear—"

"Fear nothing. I will kill him, if it comes to that."

Adrienne shook her head. "We need him."

"Not that badly."

Adrienne frowned. "You still treat me as if I am some delicate flower. You would do it, if it meant the survival of your son, your friend."

"And you still treat me as if you think me a whore," Crecy shot back, "and a stupid one. If you lie with Le Loup, he will have made his conquest. He will then pass you along to his men. Do you want that? Is that a sacrifice worthy of you?"

"If it keeps us alive."

"Listen to yourself. Listen. Is this how you were brought up by the sisters at Saint Cyr?"

Adrienne snorted. "They brought me up for nothing, nothing at all. What use have they made me to the world or myself? The only thing they prepared me for was to take vows, and if I had done that I would be raped or dead or both now, for the convents are the first place men like Le Loup go; and in these days all men are like him. Yes, all that I learned in Saint Cyr, my skill in mathematics and science, literature, the ways of grace—all useless. What has my fortune always turned upon? In Paris, at Versailles, now? The organ between my thighs. That is the way it is. How dare you confront me so, Crecy? You have always known this about the world, and I do not mean by that that you are a whore. Only that you were never a fool."

"I never thought you a fool," Crecy softly replied.

Adrienne did not meet Crecy's gaze. She had come to understand when the other woman was exercising her caustic sarcasm and when she was sincere by the set of her strange, pale eyes. Just now, Adrienne did not want to risk seeing sincerity there.

"Listen," Crecy said, still softly. "Do not lie with him. It will gain us nothing and lose us much. Le Loup thinks you are my woman. He will not take you by force."

"No, but he may kill you in your sleep. What then?"

Crecy shrugged. "It is simple. I shall not sleep."

"Crecy, I—"

She broke off because one of the bandits ahead—a thick, stupid Picard named Roland—folded to the ground. She blinked once before she heard the faint report.

"Flame!" someone shouted. The tall grass hissed as if full of snakes, followed by more distant gunfire, like hands clapping. Adrienne turned and saw a neat row of little blue clouds in the field behind them.

Two more bandits fell and another ran screaming, gripping an arm that flopped like the broken neck of a chicken.

Crecy's musket was already up, and now it spat fire. She knelt as the smoke enveloped them, reloading with enviably smooth motions.

"Crawl that way thirty feet and then run," the redhead hissed.

"Not without you."

"I'm coming. One more shot." She grinned nastily. "I think our decision is made, by the way. Monsieur Le Loup has grown a third eye."

"You saw?"

"I put it there."

"God will damn you, Crecy—"

"Run. For Nicolas."

For a heart-stopping instant, Crecy thought her friend meant the *other* Nicolas, the man she had loved, who now rotted somewhere near Versailles. But of course she meant the child.

And so she ran, the tough shafts of the weeds tearing and scratching at what little was left of her dress. As she ran, finally, little Nico began to wail.

Behind her, Crecy shouted orders. The remaining bandits had clumped behind her and were retreating with a certain amount of order; half kneeling to fire while the others ran and reloaded, and then reversing places. Most were old soldiers, and so had the training in their bones, but Crecy could reach into that marrow in a way that Le Loup never could.

She realized that she was glad Crecy had shot the foul little man. To hell with him.

Adrienne topped the rise of a hill, and her heart sank. Three men on horses—wearing the familiar blue coats—were fast flanking them from that direction. She shouted toward Crecy, to warn her. Whether from the gunfire or her own barking voice, the other woman did not appear to hear but continued retreating toward the riders. In a moment, she and the bandits would crest the hill and be visible.

Adrienne sank down. As the retreat continued, it began to lose its illusion of order. She had not counted survivors before, but they were fewer. Cursing, Adrienne unslung the carbine from her back and reprimed the pan, noticing as she did so how precious little powder remained.

Crouching in the brush, she took aim at the nearest rider. Her weapon was shorter than a normal musket, designed for firing from horseback, and it was thus less accurate. The mounted man had a pistol, however, which was less dependable still—unless it happened to be some sort of scientific weapon, in which case she was doomed. She let him come closer, not certain whether he had yet seen her, determined to use any advantage she had. The other two horsemen still rode at right angles to her, completing their flanking motion.

Something familiar about the man's uniform nagged at her. It was blue—most of the robber gangs had formed from army regiments, so that held no surprise for her—but the facing was silver, like that of a Hundred Swiss, the old personal guard of the king of France. Nicolas had been a Hundred Swiss.

She let him come closer, closer. Still he hadn't seen her, or had lost her if he had.

And then Nico screamed, a long wail that only the deaf or the dead could not hear. As the horseman located them, she fired. The recoil rocked her back, and as she recovered she saw her foe still sat his horse, his pistol leveled. It spat flame, but not at her—over her—a wild shot.

Or so she thought. The horse pivoted broadside, rearing, and the man fired a second pistol, also over her head; and this time Adrienne turned to follow the deadly ball.

Crecy had just come over the hill, but even as Adrienne watched, crimson erupted from the center of her waistcoat and she twisted around, the sword at her side leaping out like a silver eel. The horseman drew his own broadsword.

He got a surprise. Crecy darted under his scything attack as if he were a child and then sprang up, her weapon a steel fan. Blood fountained from suddenly uncaptained shoulders.

Then a second invisible fist struck Crecy and she pitched over and did not move.

3

Winter Talk

Red Shoes raised his face to the familiar, welcome scent of hickory smoke that the wind whipped by him as he and Bienville rode past the house at the edge of the woods, a lean, gray building, a wolf sort of building, ready to grow thin in the bleak winter but not destined to starve. Some Europeans, he had gathered, came from frozen countries, and they brought with them the art of living in ice. Gazing up at the slate sky, at the hills in their white coats of water-cut-to-pieces, he wondered if they had not somehow managed to bring their weather with them.

"*I appreciate your company,*" Bienville said in Mobilian, the trade language. It was like a child's version of Choctaw with a funny accent and a few strange words. Red Shoes had never much cared for it.

"It's good to get out upon the land," he replied in French. "It's good to hunt again."

Bienville chuckled. "So you *do* speak French. Your English was so good, I began to wonder if you were really a Choctaw at all."

Now Red Shoes smiled. "I am Choctaw, Governor. We have met, in fact—or at least been in the same house before."

"We have? You've the advantage over me, young man."

"At the time, my uncle was the *Tishu Minko*, the speaker for the chief. You stayed one night in our *chukka*, in Chicasaway. It was only a few months after you took the heads of the Natchez chiefs. We thought much of you, then, for the Natchez had been trouble to us for many years."

"I remember that," Bienville said. "I remember a boy, too, a boy with a strange look in his eye who never spoke."

"Me," Red Shoes acknowledged.

"You've learned to speak."

"So I have."

The trees were denser, but it was young growth, the churned ground between them bearing the frozen record of men, horses, swine, and cattle. How far would they have to go to find game? It didn't really matter. He had spent a month in the town of Philadelphia, waiting for the ships to be provisioned and the winter to pass. He had busied himself studying maps, reading books, improving his English. But English towns were claustrophobic, and he still had months yet to spend there. Merely being outside was worth the bitter cold—and the simple fact was that Bienville had not asked him hunting for the purpose of hunting, either, but to talk.

"And in many languages," Bienville concluded.

Red Shoes sighed. "Governor Bienville, you wish to ask me of my relations to the English."

"That is true," Bienville answered. "You have exposed me. The Choctaw have been French allies for many years, now. And yet, always I have suspected that some lean toward their Chickasaw cousins and the English."

Red Shoes shrugged. "The old men tell me we turned to the French in the first place to get guns to protect ourselves from the Carolina slavers and their Chickasaw allies. The French have been our friends, and they still are."

"Then—"

"But the French have also been the friends of the Natchez, and yet you yourself, Governor, have led troops against them."

"Choctaw troops in part, I seem to remember."

"Exactly, Governor Bienville. Do you think that we are like children, that we see only what you want? The French are our friends because it suits them to be, because it is to their advantage. The Choctaw, likewise, ally with the French because you help us against our enemies. That is honest. But when you set grass fires, you must watch for a shift in the wind."

"Then you cultivate no secret alliance with the English?"

Red Shoes grinned broadly. "I? No. But if the day comes that we must, I will be there to do so."

"I see. What if the day should come that the French cannot provide you with trade goods as cheaply as the English?"

"Governor, we have seen no goods from France or England in several years now. We should like new muskets, powder, shot—wherever it may come from. We will negotiate with whoever has it, I think."

"You are an honest man," Bienville said.

"I have heard you are, as well," Red Shoes answered. "You are still respected among my folk, and I do you the honor that my uncle would have."

"In that case, my friend, I fear I must ask you a favor."

"I must hear the favor, of course."

"Of course." Bienville chewed his lip for a moment, and then drew his musket from its place at his saddle and laid it across his lap. "It may come too late, for I have seen you much with Nairne, who was an English spy during the last war."

"He visited my folk, if that's what you mean."

Bienville nodded absently. "Everything that I've said in the meetings is true. I do have ships, and my oaths concerning the voyage are good. But I have not told them the condition of Louisiana."

"Ah."

"Red Shoes, have you told them that we are dying? That there are scarcely a thousand Frenchmen and -women left in the colony?"

"I have not mentioned it."

"I beg you, do not speak of it. They must believe me strong. They must believe I allow them to crew my ships because of my goodwill, not because I cannot do it. Otherwise . . ."

"You think they will turn on you?"

"I do. Or they will turn the expedition to their own ends. I have agreed that we will visit England first, but I *must* be able to insist on a visit to France, you understand? I must renew trade, or else all my people will die—and your own be without goods, as you say."

"And if I make you this gift?"

"I know your people are fond of trading gifts," Bienville said. "I will give you this in return."

He reached into his holster and pulled out something that looked much like a pistol, save that its shaft was coal-black iron, solid and drawn to a point. He handed it to Red Shoes.

He took the weapon, feeling the ornately carved ivory of the grip. "A *kraftpistole*," he breathed.

"It is yours," Bienville said.

Red Shoes raised the deadly weapon and pointed it at the ruggedly laced trunk of an elm. "How many charges remain?"

"Twelve."

Red Shoes held the weapon for a moment longer, and then reluctantly proffered it back to Bienville.

"I had no plans to tell the English how poorly the French fare," he replied. "It is better for the Choctaw if the English think we have strong allies, not sickly, dying ones. So you need not present me with a gift."

Bienville's hard face softened somewhat, and he nodded. "Then I give it to you in hope that it may begin the two of us on a path to friendship."

"Well," Red Shoes said, admiring the *kraftpistole* once more, "on those terms, I will accept it. May we walk a white path together."

"Thank you," the Frenchman said. "And now, I think if I am not mistaken, those are the droppings of a deer."

Red Shoes looked down, saw the spoor. "Indeed," he replied. "And so shall we hunt now, or is our business not done?"

"Hunt, I think," Bienville replied, and together, they continued into the forest.

Red Shoes found it difficult to concentrate on eating, with Mather watching him. There was something about the man—quite apart from his words and appearance—that he found troubling. Part of this was the rude use he made of his eyes, but that was a common trait of most white people. It was as if they spoke with glances, the many words they uttered no more than a noise to accompany a battle of wills. Choctaw engaged in such combat, too, but not when discussing the flavor of food or the color of the sky—only when insult was intended or a lie was suspected, or before a fight to the death. For the white people, each exchange of pleasantries seemed a contest that must produce a winner and a loser.

But Red Shoes had grown accustomed to that peculiarity, and this was not what disturbed him about Mather.

"I've asked you here to speak on certain matters," the preacher said after a time.

"I guessed as much."

"It concerns this 'science' you speak of, by which your people might know your fate. Did you speak truly, or was that a tactic to protect your person? If it was the latter, I assure you no such pretense is needed."

"It was the truth."

"Might I inquire how this 'science' operates?"

"You might," Red Shoes answered, "but I cannot answer."

The wrinkles about Mather's eyes tightened. "I wonder if you can tell me if it involves the invisible world."

Red Shoes did meet Mather's gaze then. "You must explain what you mean by that."

"The invisible world. The miles of dark air, the evil angels which dwell therein, the angels of light, so distant from us."

Red Shoes could feel the man's eyes, measuring him. "Go on," he said.

"My father and I have long ministered to your people—"

"You have been among the Choctaw?"

"I mean among the Indians native to Massachusetts."

"Ah. Then you do not mean *my* people."

Mather frowned. "I shall not quibble with you, sir. Hereabouts, many of the natives have been brought to see the clear light, to acknowledge Jesus Christ as their savior, and to forswear their ancient, evil ways. Many of them admit to me that their *powawes* make use of the invisible world against their enemies. To be plain, they have summoned unclean spirits, evil angels, to do their bidding."

Red Shoes pursed his lips. "You speak of *Hattak Hohlkunna*. Of—" he struggled for an English word. "—witches."

Mather raised an eyebrow. "Yes. Every folk has them. Even in my own country, in Massachusetts, a conspiracy of devils threatened the domain of our Lord. So I do not say that I single your folk out. But you do admit that such evil persons exist."

"Of course."

"And what is your opinion of such persons?"

"We kill them when they are discovered."

"Why?"

"Because they are our enemies. They are accursed, living only to cause harm. Why should we tolerate such as they?"

"Why indeed?" Mather pressed. "And yet, you admit to not being a Christian."

"I am not a Christian, it is true."

"Then I fail to understand your position."

Red Shoes now stared openly at the man. "They bring disease, cause misfortune, murder people, lead us down black trails. We do not care for this. What do you not understand?"

Mather returned his stare. The conversation was clearly not going as the white man had expected.

"And yet you yourself claim to have some commerce with this invisible world."

"Do I? I did not say so."

"You imply it."

"Perhaps. Tell me, Reverend, do not you? Is not your god a part of that world? Is he not a holy ghost?"

Now the preacher's eyes lit, and a certain satisfaction came to his face. "Indeed. I have seen proof of witches—I have performed scientific experiments that confirm their existence and their nature—and I find comfort in discovering this evil, for it proves to me also that good exists. But what I must make you understand is that as a heathen, you cannot possibly know the difference between a good spirit and a bad. If good angels claim to serve you, then they are liars. They are devils in disguise, for good spirits will not minister to your sort."

"My sort?"

"Have you never wondered how your people came to be here, in this America, so far from the rest of humanity?"

"I know how we came to be here."

"You have legends, I am certain. But how can your history be reliable, when it was taught you by the devil?"

"I no longer follow you," Red Shoes admitted, trying to keep anger from sharpening his tone.

"Scholars have long pondered your existence on these shores—"

"And we are much gratified by that interest," Red Shoes assured him.

The preacher glared briefly before going on. "It seems clear that Lucifer showed you the way to these lands that he might have whole continents of damned men and women. Those same *powawes* I have converted admit as much, and admit as well that their dark lord is angered by the presence of Jesus in these colonies. Do you deny that your people have used their familiar spirits to sicken my people, to try and drive them away?"

"Yes, I deny it. Though I suppose some witches might have directed their ire toward you."

"And yet you yourself speak of being 'rid' of us."

"Yes. With the war club and bow, not by communion with the accursed beings."

"But I remind you, you seem to admit to having familiars yourself."

"Not as witches do."

The preacher banged his fist upon the table. "If you are served by spirits at all, I tell you that they are devils, though you may not know it."

"And these witches who infested your Massachusetts. Were they Christians? Why could they not tell the good spirit from the bad?"

"An excellent question. Some sought the Black One on purpose, for their hearts were evil. Others were fooled, but that only strengthens my contention, you see? Even those who strive to keep the covenant can be fooled. How much more so your own people?"

"I assure you, sir, that I well know the difference between an accursed being and the powers that serve me."

"Will you allow me to examine you? To prove this is so? Will you listen to my words about Jesus, and take the first steps toward the covenant of grace?"

Red Shoes grinned. "You may speak as you wish, and I will listen. I promise nothing, however."

"I cannot allow you to accompany us on this quest if I consider that you might be a warlock. This is to be a Christian undertaking, and it is already compromised by the Popish French, who are closer to the devil in some ways than any heathen. Indeed, it has been shown that Indian sorcerers and French ones conspire against us from the wilderness."

"I know nothing of that," Red Shoes said.

"I cannot trust it. Will you accept conversion?"

"I will not, nor will your word keep me from this expedition, I believe. Governor Bienville or Teach will take me on their ships."

"I will argue against it."

"And you will fail. I do not say this to anger you. I know your concerns, and I would not keep company with someone I thought a witch. Nevertheless, you must."

Mather simmered over that quietly for a few moments. "I have more influence than you might think."

"Do you? Since I have been in Philadelphia these past months, I have heard some talk of you, and of those witches in Massachusetts. Many now believe that you were party to the murder of many innocents."

Mather hesitated. "Much of that is slander," he whispered, for the first time seeming unsure of himself. "But it may be true that some died innocent. I was not a judge, and at the time I spoke against much of the evidence presented—most especially the spectral evidence— but in vain. Yet it is clear from all indications that the devil came into Salem. Few doubt that."

"I think that many doubt it, to be blunt."

"They will not doubt a man of God speaking of a savage."

"They will doubt you about *this* savage, in *these* times. They fear my people, and they fear our alliance with the French."

Mather bowed his head down to the table, and began muttering in that way that Red Shoes understood to be praying. He waited quietly, picking at what remained of his food.

Finally Mather looked up, and Red Shoes met his gaze, in the white man's way. "Will you at least let me assure myself? Perform the simplest examinations? Can you read?"

"Yes, some."

"Will you read the commandments, aloud?"

"Yes."

"And the Lord's Prayer?"

"Yes."

Mather nodded grimly, somehow triumphantly, and a sudden dart of unease pricked Red Shoes, making him wonder suddenly just how wise he had been.

4

Peter Frisk

Ben reached for his aegis key, but in the same instant Robert crashed into him, knocking him from his feet. Ben cursed as his elbow crunched against the hard stone, but Robert was a blur of continued motion, the gleam of his rapier arcing up to meet the newcomer who had just emerged from the alley.

"Hold, fellow," the man shouted. "Mark that my muzzle confronts your pursuers, not you."

Indeed, the pistol was pointed over Ben and to the right of Robert.

"Draw your swords, both, and we shall deal with these," he went on.

Robert, always quickest in such situations, had already turned to face their pursuers, albeit with one wary eye on their new comrade. Ben scrambled to his feet, clumsily drawing his own blade, still swearing at Robert's misguided attempt to protect him. The steel felt ungainly in his hand. Robert had shown him a few passes, but Ben had not managed to work up much enthusiasm for swordplay. No matter; his other hand now clutched the aegis key, poised to activate his magical cloak.

He waited because the five men following had halted, some twenty paces away, indecisive in the face of the pistol. They were a dour, dark bunch, mostly quite large men. All bore swords, and several seemed to have sidearms, though only one held his drawn: a man with piercing blue eyes, smaller than the others.

"You'll find no easy prey here, carrion crows," their seeming ally shouted at the men. Though Ben was still new to the German language, it seemed that the fellow had an odd accent. He wore some

sort of military uniform, but not one that Ben could identify as be-
longing to the empire.

"We've no business with you," the small man yelled back. "Only
with these two."

"Then you have business indeed with me as well," the man
shouted.

Ben straightened. "What call have you to accost us?" he shouted at
the five. "I recognize not a man jack among you, and so don't think I
have wronged you. If we have given you offense, then lay it at our feet
so we can know what we are charged with. Otherwise be off with you."
He gritted his teeth at the pain in his arm, hoping his sword was held
in a way that conveyed at least some competence.

"You mistake us, sir," the blue-eyed man said, edging a bit closer.
"Our intention was never to assault you but to speak with you on a
certain matter."

One of the other men grunted a word in what Ben was now absolutely certain was Russian. The small man snapped back in the
same language.

"You know who I am, I gather?" Ben called.

"Indeed, sir. You are Benjamin Franklin, apprentice to Sir Isaac
Newton."

"Then you may know as well that I am under the emperor's
protection."

"Of course. But as I said, this show of steel and pistol is unwar-
ranted. I only wished to state a proposition."

"State it, then."

"I had hoped for a more—private—venue."

"I am quite sure you did," Ben replied. "But if you will not speak,
than I cannot help you."

"I would prefer—"

"Come and see me at the castle," Ben interrupted. "I extend you an
invitation. At the moment we are in something of a hurry."

The small man regarded him for a moment, and then bowed. "Very
well. I apologize. I saw you in the tavern and thought to take advantage of my good fortune, but I see I have overstepped the bounds of
politeness. I will present my offer another time."

"And I will be happy to hear it, I am certain," Ben replied.

The man bowed again, and with an air of reluctance, the five turned and went back the way they had come. Ben noted that neither Robert nor their benefactor allowed their weapons to waver until the Muscovites were well out of sight.

"Now, then," the newcomer said, finally returning his weapon to its proper place at his belt. Robert's rapier lingered in the air for a second or two longer, and then hissed back into its scabbard.

"I would not believe them, if I were you," the man advised. "I heard them in the tavern. Their plan was to take you hostage."

Ben looked the fellow over. He was a year or two one side of forty, with sea-gray eyes peering over a regally arched nose, lips tight with a sort of grim humor. A battered tricorn jutted over a high, balding forehead. He exuded the sort of competence that Robert did, but more so, giving the impression that he could have easily dealt with all five men.

"You've done us a damn good turn," Ben said, sticking out his hand. "I'm Benjamin Franklin, and greatly grateful to you."

"Yes, so I heard them call you," the man replied. "My name is Peter Frisk."

"Pleased to meet you, Peter Frisk," Ben replied, as they shook hands.

"And me," Robert added, taking Frisk's hand next. "And might I suggest that we move along? Rats'll scurry away, but they always come back f'r the cheese."

"Indeed," Frisk replied. "I'd be happy to escort you wherever you might be going."

"No need fer that," Robert answered. "We're just headed back t' the Charles Bridge."

"Well, I've a mind to see that side of the river myself. Would you allow me to accompany you?"

"Please," Ben said. "I want to hear more of this kidnapping plot."

Robert shrugged acceptance, and the three of them began winding their way back toward the river.

"I take it," Ben said after a moment, "that you speak some Russian?"

"Some," Frisk said, a tinge of surprise in his voice. "What makes you ask?"

"Those fellows were Moscovados, I think. If you heard them speaking amongst themselves. . ."

"Ah. I see. Yes, you are quite right. They are Russian—in speech at least."

"And did you gather why they wished to abduct me?"

"Not really, only that they did intend to do so. They seemed to think you a person of some importance."

"You don't know who I am?"

Frisk smiled. "Take no offense, sir, but no, I do not. I heard them tell that you were the apprentice of some man named Newton— whose name I believe I have heard remarked—but that is my balance of knowledge concerning you. I am recently come, you see, to Prague. I have scarce been here for two days."

"I understand you never having heard of me," Ben allowed, "but how odd that the name of Newton is not prominent in your mind."

"Mr. Franklin, I have been on campaign for so many years I have had little time for news of any sort."

"With what army?" Robert asked.

"I marched with Charles XII of Sweden in the year seventeen hundred. I have not seen my home or family since that time."

Robert whistled. "The Muscovy campaign! I should say you *have* been busy for a time. I commend you on your survival."

"I thought Charles defeated," Ben remarked.

"We were broken at Pruth, but not destroyed. Charles rests with the Turk, watching for his chance."

"And you?"

"I have decided that enough of my life has been wasted in a war that will never end, and I have no great love of the Turk. And so I have come here in hopes of earning my way back to Sweden."

"I fear that you will not find the north as you left it," Ben replied softly. "You may have been better off with the Turk."

Frisk shrugged. "I hear the stories. That may or may not be, but I shall find out for myself."

They had now reached the Moldau and the dark, massy bridge that spanned it. The castle looked down from their right, banners whipping in the wind.

Ben smiled at Frisk, trying to hide his suspicion. He had been taken in before, and by fairer spies than Frisk—Vasilisa Karevna, for instance, from whose lips he had first tasted Russian. Who was to say that this Swede had not authored the entire confrontation, to present himself as an ally? Certainly the Muscovites had given up easily enough.

"Well, Mr. Frisk," Ben said, "again, we are in your debt. If there is some way I can compensate you . . ."

"I must admit," Frisk said, "that my decision to aid you was not without some self-interest. As I said, I gathered from your would-be attackers that you were men of no small importance. . . ."

Robert chuckled. "We are not so important as we think we are," he joked, glancing meaningfully at Ben. Robert didn't trust the fellow either. Still, if he was honest, they did owe the man a debt. If he wasn't, it might be better to have him near, where his movements could be watched, rather than plotting unseen in the deeper labyrinth of Prague.

"I meant what I said," Ben asserted. "If there is anything I can do, publish it to me."

"Only to mention my name to someone," Frisk said. "I am looking for employment, for a time. I had the commission of captain in the Swedish army, and I was hoping to find some small position with the emperor's forces."

Ben considered the man for a moment. "That is the least I can do," he said at last. "Where is your lodging?"

Frisk smiled wryly. "In New Town. But I shan't be there long, as my gold credit is done this afternoon."

"Very well, Captain Frisk. Meet us across the river here, in the tavern of Saint Thomas this time tomorrow, and I'll give you what news I can. At the very least I might find lodging for you."

Frisk stuck out his hand, but at the same instant there came a hollow boom, and the Swede grunted and spun drunkenly. Ben had a brief impression of red—spattered on the nearby building, a fine spray like powder on his extended coat sleeve.

"Shit!" Robert snarled, and vanished. Frisk crumpled to one knee.

A second explosion followed, and Ben understood at last that the Muscovites had not gone far after all, only just so far as to choose another moment to attack. He fumbled for his aegis key, found it, and vanished as well.

Robert was a faint suggestion of drawn steel, already ghosting toward the enemy. All five men had produced pistols, though two now quickly traded their smoking ones for swords. Angrily, Ben drew out his own smallsword and edged toward the men, wishing he had brought along some more potent weapon.

He at least had the satisfaction of seeing the dumbfounded confusion at his and Robert's disappearance, and that in turn gave him confidence. Who did these men think they were attacking, anyway?

The nearest man, a monstrously large fellow with dirty blond hair and a face like a pig, trained his pistol on the obscured Robert and fired. An instant later he yelped, clutched at the back of his knee, and collapsed to the pavement. Taking a deep breath, Ben chose his own target—a second large fellow—and advanced, wondering what it would feel like to pierce flesh. He would do what Robert had done, simply wound the man, he decided. He was not a killer.

As he hesitantly planned his attack, an unseen sledgehammer struck him in the chest, and the air leaked darkness and constellations into his eyes. He sat down hard on the cold stone and heard, distantly, the metallic laughter of his sword bouncing away. Blinking, his vision cleared enough for him to make out the small, blue-eyed man jogging toward him, looking determined, shoving a pistol in his belt with one hand and drawing a broadsword with the other. Ben groped stupidly for his errant blade, which lay perhaps two yards away, but his limbs felt like lead; and with sudden chagrin he realized that the world no longer had a rainbow frame. His aegis was no longer functioning.

He scrambled back, trying to gain his feet, as another of their attackers spied him and started forward.

Near his ear, Frisk howled, leapt up, and hurled himself like a thunderbolt at the blue-eyed man. The fellow scarcely got his blade up before steel dissected the hand that held his weapon, and he clutched at the stump, eyes wide with disbelief.

Frisk did not even pause but swept past him, launching the edge of his saber at the burly fellow approaching behind. The Muscovite cried out and swiped wildly with his sword; Frisk beat the blade away as if it were a toy wielded by a child and pressed on. The fellow fell back, grunting, cut viciously at the Swede's head; but Frisk wasn't there, was instead skipping to the side, bolt upright, sword flicking like a snake's tongue despite his shirt and waistcoat being drenched in his own blood.

And then the larger man was down, wrapped around his own belly and its deep new navel.

In the ten or twelve seconds this took, Ben struggled to his feet. All but one of their foes had fallen, and the fifth vanished around the corner as Ben watched.

Robert reappeared, rushing toward him.

"Ben? Are you injured?" he shouted.

That hadn't even occurred to him yet, though his chest throbbed as if a horse had stepped on it. He looked down, fearing to see a hole gaping in his breast, but there was nothing save a dark scorch on his waistcoat, and the aegis key dangling loose, apparently jogged out of his pocket by the concussion.

"It would appear not," he gasped. "But Frisk . . ."

Frisk was kneeling by the now-one-handed man, wrapping his gasping foe's wrist with a cloth. "Here is one to make some explanations," he said grimly.

"You need a surgeon," Ben grunted. "Your shoulder—"

"Is not as bad as it looks," Frisk asserted, turning back to them. "But if you have a surgeon handy—"

"Get him to the castle," Robert said. "I'll watch these. Send back the guard."

Ben nodded. "Come along, then, Captain Frisk. You'll get your recommendation sooner than you thought."

"I am in your debt, sir," Frisk replied.

Ben stared at him, unbelieving, and then laughed.

Newton's eyes flicked around the room nervously, refusing to actually settle on Ben, a sure sign that the great philosopher was agitated. "Were you injured, dear boy?" he asked.

"No, sir. Bruised is all."

"Good. I am relieved to hear it. I would be— I would be unhappy if anything happened to you."

"I'm sorry to have worried you."

"Worried? What cause had I to worry?" Newton's voice was suddenly a bit sharper, his eyes focusing on Ben.

"Sir?"

"What cause had I to worry? What baffles me is how a gang of assassins roamed so freely here in Hradčany, where the emperor's guard patrols in such numbers." His brow creased in a frown. "You *were* in Hradčany, weren't you?"

"Ah—no, sir."

"In Kleinseit, then? You were perhaps in Kleinseit, acquiring the books I asked you to borrow from the library at the Wallenstein Palace?"

"Umm—no, not in Kleinseit."

Newton nodded grimly. His face was a young one, thin lipped, dimple chinned—he could have been twenty, if his eyes did not give it the lie. They seemed subtly polished—almost eroded—by some eighty years of vision, jewels handled by a million fingers, and yet still luminescent with passion. "Well, look here," he grated, his earlier concern suddenly fled, "this is passing—*passing* odd, Mr. Franklin, for though you seem to have been set upon by ruffians, this does not seem to have happened in Hradčany or Kleinseit. Now in that part I am not surprised, for in these two sections of town the guard is most efficient and well staffed, and thieves and murderers keep well away. Now if you had been attacked in Old Town or New Town or Judenstadt, *that* would be no surprise, lawless as they are. And yet I am entirely certain that you were not in any of those places, because I have told you time and again to avoid them. So it is most surpassing strange that you could have encountered these men you speak of."

Ben nodded throughout the tirade, and when it was done, he met Newton's ancient eyes square on. "I was in Old Town," he admitted distinctly.

"Yes, of course you were, you imbecile. And *that* is what I am sick unto death of. I think, indeed, that it is high time that I found a new apprentice."

Ben managed a weak grin. "I'm glad that you were concerned about me, sir."

Newton stared at him incredulously for a moment, and then rested his forehead on his fist. "Benjamin, what am I to do with you? How can I keep you from the hands of the devil?"

"Sir—" Ben considered for a moment, then plunged on. "Sir, I was never so proud as the day you made me your apprentice. Proud I still am. But of late, you do not include me. I hardly feel your apprentice anymore."

"This excuses your behavior? Is that what I shall tell the emperor when he hears of your exploits?"

"It is no excuse, I agree. I do not offer it as such."

"It seems to me that you do," Newton said, his voice suddenly weary. "I have perhaps neglected your education, somewhat. But I do what is for the best, and you are good at educating yourself."

"But, sir, to be barred even from your new laboratory—"

"My current endeavors are of too delicate a nature to disclose. This is as much for your sake as anyone's, I promise you. Meantime, you still have the old laboratory to putter about in."

"But it is my wish to help you."

"You help me in what you do."

"Making toys for the emperor? Scientifical baubles for the archduchess? Forgive me, sir, but I had hoped for more. I thought you promised me more."

"Perhaps I did, but we must suit our actions to the times. Had I all leisure, I would devote myself to your education. But the world is at the edge of a fearful precipice, and I cannot fail it to serve you."

"I don't understand," Ben said, feeling a little angry. "If the importance of your present work is so great, would it not serve us all better for me to aid you?"

Newton's eyes lit with an answering fire of their own. "I have said I cannot discover these things to you now, Benjamin. In time I will. That should be enough for you."

Ben nodded in sudden understanding. "You don't trust me."

Newton tapped his finger on the armrest, looking at the floor. "I have already been betrayed by one I trusted deeply," he said, softly, "the only one I ever gave my trust to. You are bright, and have a good heart somewhere in you, but you are also reckless. I cannot risk your becoming another Fatio de Duillier."

Ben kept his tongue still, a dam against a flood of angry words. *Perhaps it is this very sort of mistreatment that made de Duillier betray you*, he thought. But he could not say that; it would only make matters worse. Instead, he took another tack.

"I have been working at affinity," he said. "I've found a method to repel against water."

"And made something amusing for the emperor?"

"Yes, I think so. But in working with repulsions, I hope to eventually solve the problem of the comet."

Newton smiled indulgently. "My new system has that in hand, never fear. Now, clean yourself up. We are to see the emperor in an hour, and your present appearance would, I daresay, displease him."

After undressing and dabbing at himself with a cloth, Ben felt more human but no less frustrated. Newton's casual dismissal of his work stung, and the admission that he did not trust Ben was even worse. After two years of being Newton's apprentice, it was almost as if they had come full circle to the day they first met.

Except that it was worse now, because in those days he had thought Newton a god, and now he had begun to have his doubts. What he could glean of this "new system" seemed very dubious to him, as Newton drew chiefly on strange, superstitious texts. It hardly seemed science at all to Ben. If only he could get a glimpse of what his master was working on, find some assurance that the elixir that made Newton young again had not also driven him into a subtle insanity. Newton had a history of periodic madness, and the last time he had been mad, a comet had destroyed London.

Ben was certain he knew where the new laboratory was: a floor below the old one, in the Mathematical Tower. He was certain, too, that the key that would open its mysterious lock was somewhere in Newton's private chambers. If only he could enter them, get the key, find Newton's notes on this "new system."

Pondering this, he selected a shirt of white linen and struggled into it. It felt good against his bare skin, better than the rough linsey-woolsey of his childhood, and he reminded himself that he owed such luxuries to Newton.

As he turned to select a suit, someone rapped at the door.

"Who knocks?" he called.

"The maid, sir."

"Indeed?" Ben replied, perking up a bit. "Enter, then."

The door squeaked open and a young woman of perhaps fifteen entered. Her eyes widened at his near-undressed state.

"Your pardon, sir," she said, "but I can return at another time." She had a sharp, almost birdlike face, not unpleasant but not exactly beautiful either. She composed herself quickly, and he reasoned that she was not the giggly sort of chambermaid but one of the more serious kind. One he might consider as a challenge at some other time, if he did not have so much to worry about—and if she were a bit prettier. She looked familiar, too.

"Where is Ludmilla?" he asked her.

"She has taken ill, sir. I'll be your maid until she recovers."

"Nothing serious, I hope."

"No, sir."

And then, like a breeze returning as a tempest, he remembered his earlier conversation with Robert about the servants and the things they said. And he remembered also where he had seen this one before: she was the customary maid for Newton's apartments.

"Good," he exclaimed. "And now you can do me a most wonderful favor."

"Oh, can I?" she said, a hint of sarcasm in her voice.

Ben tried to appear taken aback. "Well, yes," he replied.

"There are some sorts of favor I am not required to do," the maid said, stepping in and closing the door.

"I am quite certain I have no idea what you are talking about," Ben said.

She flashed him a crooked little smile that made her suddenly more compelling. "They talk of you, sir."

"Who? Who talks of me?"

"Ludmilla. The other girls."

"Oh. Well, I can tell you that slander is a high art in this castle, and so I hope you haven't taken much of what you've heard to heart."

"I take little to my heart, sir, or any other part of me. I wonder if you might consider dressing?"

Ben grinned. "Well, that was the help I was after. I wondered if you could help me select a suit to attend court in."

She curtsied, though Ben thought he detected something faintly mocking in her carriage. "If you wish, sir."

"And please call me Ben. All of my friends do."

"I understand that, sir," she said, strolling over to the wardrobe. "I should think you would want some black and red. Red hose, of course . . ."

"I had thought to wear white hose," Ben murmured, studying her back, wondering what sort of shape was beneath those petticoats, if it was fairer than her face. God often rewarded in some areas what he had penalized in others.

She seemed a bit on the slim side.

Unaware of this attention, she shook her head. "No, white won't do, as you must know. The emperor will call you a Frenchman and have you thrown from the hall. No, it must be in the Spanish style, so your hose must be red or black."

"Red, in that case. You see how desperately I needed you?"

She ignored that, continuing to paw through his wardrobe. "And for your coat . . ." She pushed through a few and then pulled out a rather full-skirted coat of watered black silk. Starting to hand it to him, she frowned and reached back in. "No," she said, "I should like to see you in these, first." And she handed him a pair of black knee breeches with scarlet bows.

Ben accepted them, stepping a bit closer to do so. "I have not met you before," he said. "I wonder if you would tell me your name."

She raised her eyes to meet his, and they were nearly black. "I am a servant, sir, and so what need have I of a name? Call me what you will."

"There's no need to be unpleasant," Ben remarked.

"Was I unpleasant? I hoped to be accommodating." Her smile was bright and probably false as she returned to selecting clothes for him.

A sort of funny feeling rumbled in Ben's stomach, a slight vertigo, an uncertainty. He thought furiously for something else to say, but his throat remained empty of words until she had laid out the last of his suit. He pulled the breeches on, suddenly feeling foolish. "Thank you," he finally managed.

"You are welcome, sir."

"Please call me Ben."

At that she only smiled enigmatically, returning to her work, leaving him feeling as stupid as a child.

5.

"**G**oddamn," Blackbeard muttered, tugging at his braided beard, and then more forcefully, "God*damn*. Where's the *Thames*?" The pirate shook his fists at the coastline. Red Shoes stared at the brackish mudflat, verdigris with sickly and crouching scrub, trying to understand what the problem was. It bothered him that there were no trees anywhere—it was alien to his eye—but he had gathered in his time among Europeans that trees were scarce in Europe.

"The longitude and the latitude are correct," Thomas Nairne insisted. "Of that I have no doubt."

"No? Then where'n hell is the river?"

Red Shoes turned to study Nairne and caught him staring sourly at Blackbeard's back. Beyond Nairne the Pale Water stretched endless as time, dwarfing the remainder of the ships in their flotilla. They were eight, all told, and to Red Shoes they had once made an impressive sight, each larger than anything made by his own people. Swallowed by sea and sky for two months they had diminished in his eyes, and now, come to this strange, dead shore, they seemed smaller than ever, bubbles in the eddy of a swift stream.

They had sailed toward Sun-Emerging, a direction where his people had always believed the sources of life were. And yet this place more resembled legends of the Darkening Land, where the sun dies. Even with his ghost vision he saw nothing save a few birds. It worried him, this place.

And the Europeans were confused, too. This wasn't what they had expected either.

"But them's the cliffs, han't it?" one stout, knot-nosed sailor—everyone called him Tug—muttered.

"Aye," Blackbeard assented. "But not one damn house, not one single church steeple, not a tower, nor nothing, an' we've been on this coast for days. An' this *looks* something like the mouth of the Thames—but where is the river?"

"Could it have been stopped?" Red Shoes asked quietly. "The river—could it have been dammed up?"

Blackbeard shot him a withering glance, and to Red Shoes' surprise, he saw the rage there mixed liberally with what must be fear. In his experience, if Blackbeard was afraid, then the rest of them ought to be terrified.

"You don't know what a mad thing that is to say, Choctaw."

"Stupid In'yun," Tug added.

"Nevertheless," Nairne quietly put in, "it is a possibility."

"Why? What army could do this? Raze all the buildings on the coast, yes, but steal the Goddamned *Thames*?"

"The latitude and longitude are *correct*," Nairne insisted, voice determined. "This is—or was—the mouth of the Thames. London lies yonder." He pointed west and north.

"Well then"—Blackbeard scowled—"you're the overlander. You go find it. And while you're at it, find me a port, before the men mutiny over lack of food and rum."

"We need to talk with Bienville and Mather, first."

"By my leave," Blackbeard grunted, still staring at the shore. "Invite Bienville over."

Bienville shook his head and took another puff from his pipe. "I am loath to send my men there," he said. "Better that we sail on until we find some sign of life."

Blackbeard, red eyed, downed another cup of Portuguese wine, his eighth. "You mean sail on to France?"

"Yes, that is precisely what I mean. If this is truly the mouth of the Thames, then the world has gone more mad than ever we thought. It is safer for us to stay in numbers until we have some idea what has befallen here. If the coast of England is silent, perhaps in France we will find answers."

"More answers generally are gotten from the murderer than the murdered, though perhaps not truthful answers."

Bienville reddened and blinked angrily. "Sir, I suggest you restrain yourself from drawing conclusions. If this expedition is to stay of a piece—"

"If you want it of a piece, then give me command of your men."

"That was not the agreement, as well you know, Mr. Teach," Cotton Mather interrupted, clasping his hands together on the table they all sat around. He had been sickly for most of the voyage, and his voice still shook a bit, but his words were firm enough. "This armada is governed by council, something that you should also keep in mind, Monsieur Bienville."

"I have not forgotten it, sir. I was only making a suggestion."

Mather nodded. "You are a gentleman, Monsieur, and I do not doubt your word. Nor do I doubt your commitment to this flotilla. We will sail to France, on that we are all agreed. It is just a matter of when. For now, as we are here, I believe a closer look at England—by a small number of men—prudent."

Bienville nodded thoughtfully and glanced at Red Shoes. "And you, sir? You are a part of this council as well."

Red Shoes blinked. That had been said, of course, but this was the first time he had been consulted on anything since the voyage began.

"I think it a bad idea to set foot here," he said at last.

"Why is that?" Mather asked mildly, perhaps with a trace of annoyance.

"It is not right, this place. I see that you are all afraid, and I know these are not just my feelings."

He did not mention the other thing: that he had sent a shadowchild to reconnoiter, that it had died somehow, that the loss haunted him deep. It would only anger Mather.

"I find little sense in that," Mather said, a trifle coolly, "but thank you for your opinion. Gentlemen?"

Bienville sighed. "Choose your men, and I will furnish a matching number."

"Agreed," Blackbeard said. "And who shall command the trek across land?"

"I will," Mather said quietly.

"You?"

"Yes, me. I am the only man of science among you, the only member of the Royal Society. We have here a puzzle, gentlemen, and it is, I believe, a scientific one. I shall go, and the governor's men with me."

"Well, the whole council represented on foot then," Blackbeard noted. "And so who will you send for your people, Choctaw, into this land that is 'not right'?"

There was, of course, only one answer to that.

The earth beneath the grass was as black as charcoal. In fact, it *was* charcoal, as Mather noticed almost immediately.

"Evidence of conflagration," he murmured.

"You mean 'twas burnt," Tug said, looking about worriedly at the featureless landscape.

"Burnt, yes. But by what?"

"Fire, I'd expect," Tug answered nervously.

"Yes, one would expect that. Captain Nairne, which way?"

"London should lie in that direction," Nairne replied, pointing.

"We are to be as quick as we can," a third man reminded them, one Lieutenant du Rue, a rather frail-looking Frenchman in a plain blue coat. His hand stayed nearly constantly on the wire-wound hilt of his colichemarde as his eyes picked suspiciously at the landscape.

They were ten in all. Nairne, Tug, and a compact black man named Fernando made up Blackbeard's portion; du Rue and two stocky Normans, Saint-Pierre and Renard, the French. Mather was accompanied by two soldiers from Philadelphia: a hulking but amiable fellow named Charles and a tough man with straw-colored hair who went by the name of Wallace. And then, of course, there was himself.

"So you've discovered England," Nairne whispered to him. "What do you think?"

Red Shoes grinned slightly. "I meant to claim it for the Sixtowns, but I wonder now what would be the point."

"We shall find the point, I hope," Nairne said and took the lead.

They kept to the higher ground, skirting the noisome fens on the west, and for a few hours found or saw nothing remarkable. But then Mather, who walked somewhat stooped, as if reading the ground, grunted.

"Look here," he said, and held up a brick.

Soon enough they found many more bricks and building stones, most shattered and blackened. After a time they found something more.

"Foundations," Nairne observed. Red Shoes had guessed that as well, for here he noticed the land touched by white man's squareness again, though now reduced to walls a few inches high. Some had lost their regularity, cut into pieces by something that had incised a furrow in the earth that went on for as far as they could see. In other places the ground was dished out, as if poked by a giant's finger.

"Could have been Tilbury. Or Sheerness."

"God's balls, I don't like this," Tug said, gaping. "No sair, not a Goddamn bit!"

"Hush your blasphemy," Mather snapped, eyes suddenly blazing.

"Sorry, Reverend. But this is the sort o' thing'll upset a man."

"It is nothing next to God's wrath," Mather reminded him.

"Indeed," du Rue said. "But suppose this *was* God's wrath?"

Mather shrugged. "Everything is a part of God's plan, and so this—whatever it is—surely is. If He is willing, we will understand something of it."

"I feared for London before," Nairne said grimly. "How much more so now."

"All things are judged in their time," Mather replied enigmatically.

The land became more blasted as they went, the vegetation ever more spotty, until they crossed a lifeless plain of soft white stone that Mather called chalk. To Red Shoes it was bone, the skeleton of a dead land, picked clean by buzzards.

The sun's funeral went unnoticed as gray, drizzling sky became black. They huddled beneath canvas tarps on that plain, glum and almost without conversation. Near midnight the rain finally stopped, and he stepped into the damp air, carefully placed a measure of Ancient Tobacco in his pipe, and filled his lungs with living smoke. Eyes closed, he chanted lightly beneath his breath, opening his ghost eyes and ears, searching. At first nothing came, but then a distant chittering. He stayed at the edge of it, not wanting *them* to notice him. Over the years he had become good at listening without being heard, a mouse, and had thus learned a great deal about spirits. If he would learn more, he would have to risk more.

He would not do that tonight. His shadowchild was dead and he did not yet have the strength to create another. If they found him, he would be defenseless, and he had seen what happened to those who were caught, their minds turned inside out by the *Na Lusa Falaya*. He had discovered what he wanted to know: as dead as this place was of people and animals, it was very much alive with spirits. He could not know their intentions, but his heart warned him not to expect anything good from them.

"Why don' you hush up so's we can sleep?" a voice growled from nearby. It was Tug, a brutish shadow a few paces distant.

"I apologize if I bothered you," Red Shoes said.

"Your sort, always singin' to the damn devil, han't you? What're you doin' here, In'yun? Why come this whole damn way? Hopin' to roger a white woman, maybe? Think you'll have more luck here than wi' them nuns down Looweeanna way?"

"I came because I had to," Red Shoes explained.

"Uh-huh. Well, I'll tell ya this. You hain't gettin' in back a' old Tug. You stay clear o' me, hear? These fancy types like Nairne and Mather might give pretense as they believe you dependable, but Tug knows savages. One minute all nice and the next slittin' yer throat an' thrummin' yer corpse. So keep where I can see you."

"I'll try to," Red Shoes said coldly.

Red Shoes had been into the Cherokee country before and seen mountains, but the one they encountered the next morning was like nothing he had ever imagined. It looked more like a wall than a mountain, an almost perfectly regular line against the sky, cutting nearly the whole horizon. As they approached it, the stone beneath their feet turned up gradually to meet the slightly serrated line, and then ever more sharply. The stone itself was blistered, in places glassy.

"What do you make of this, Reverend Mather?" Thomas Nairne asked quietly.

The older man shook his head almost imperceptibly. Sweat stood out on his brow, and Red Shoes wondered if it was from exertion or fear.

"At least we can see what happened to the river," du Rue offered. "This wall—or mountain, or whatever it may be—has stopped its progress, or at least redirected it."

"What could do such a thin'? God help us." Tug shivered. He looked shyly at Mather. "Reverend," he said, "I do repent of my earlier blasphemy. Would you—I mean to say, could we pray?"

"Were you raised Puritan?"

"No, sair. But as you're the only man of God hereabouts . . ."

The rest of them waited while the two of them and the governor's men prayed. Saint-Pierre, apart from the rest, prayed as well, fingering his rosary while his companion Renard merely rolled his eyes heavenward. Nairne folded his arms impatiently and joined Red Shoes in contemplating the strange horizon.

It was hard work reaching the summit, and in some places would have been impossible. They had the good fortune to locate a sort of crack in the side of the mountain that gave them egress. Nairne tried to convince Mather to let the younger men go on and bring report, but the Puritan would have none of that, and so their progress was limited to his speed. It was thus nearly an hour from sundown when they finally reached the summit.

But it was no summit; it was a rim. Only an arm's span wide, the mountain sloped down even more steeply than on its other side. The narrow edge curved away and slightly inward from them, misting in the distance. Below lay a valley that Red Shoes guessed to be the shape of a gigantic bowl.

For long moments, no one said anything, until Nairne managed to whisper in a brittle voice. "Gentlemen, there lies London." Tears streamed down his face.

A muffled choking sound betokened Tug weeping, too.

"*Pardieu,*" du Rue muttered. "*Angleterre c'est passé.*"

Tug's sobs suddenly turned snarl. "Fu't y', Frenchman!" he shrieked, and while the rest stood stupefied, flung himself at the officer. Du Rue half turned to meet the enraged sailor, hand barely to his sword when Tug struck him. The two grappled for an instant and then plunged inward over the rim, striking hard, bouncing and sliding thirty yards. All around Red Shoes swords and pistols snaked out as the remaining two Frenchmen faced off against the English pirates and colonists. The tableaux locked that way for a few moments.

"Put those up," Nairne shouted. "*All* of you." His voice carried a firm snap of command.

"For God's sake, yes," Mather added.

Red Shoes peered down. Tug and du Rue lay perhaps twenty feet apart, both moving feebly.

"Tug!" Nairne shouted down. "Stop that damn nonsense." He turned back to the others, found them still eyeing one another over their weapons. "You, too. The truce still holds."

"If you please, sir," Renard said, "my companion and I are outnumbered, and the aggression was on your own side. I respectfully suggest that English steel be covered first."

Nairne stared at them, and then drew forth his *kraftpistole*, an ugly, dangerous-looking weapon.

"All of you put up your toys by the count of three, or someone— English or French, I care not—dies."

"Perhaps they should keep them out," Red Shoes said.

"What?"

He pointed. Along the rim, from both directions, dark figures hurried toward them, hooting like distant owls. Out across the valley floor, red lights rose like fireflies.

"I want two guns on each side," Nairne commanded.

"What about Tug?" Fernando asked, nodding toward where the sailor and du Rue were weakly struggling up the slick side of the hill.

"The best we can do for them is to hold this position," Nairne observed. "Fernando, you'll hack anyone who gets close to the musketeers."

"Aye."

"I wonder who or what they are," Renard remarked, sighting down the barrel of his musket.

Red Shoes regarded the approaching figures, wondering the same thing. They seemed naked, or nearly so. Some of them had a bluish or blackish cast to their skin. All bore weapons—swords, axes, clubs. Except for their white hair, they might have been Chickasaw or Natchez, or any other of the traditional enemies of the Choctaw.

"Their intentions seem clear," Nairne said. "Shoot as soon as you can hit one."

"That would be about now," Renard said, squeezing the trigger. The shot boomed hollowly in the vast bowl.

The lead figure on that side pitched squealing into the valley.

"But wha' abou' them?" Fernando asked, gesturing at the glowing balls of flame rising all around.

"*Nishkin Achafa*," Red Shoes said. "A kind of spirit. You can't harm them with your weapons."

"Can they harm us?"

"Not easily."

"Ignore them, then," Nairne ordered.

"But there are other things that can," Red Shoes went on. "Things you *can't* see."

The Englishman darted him a glance. "Can you?"

"Sometimes."

Mather's head snapped around, eyes shining with a cold light, and opened his mouth as if to speak; but about then, there was no more time for conversation. The second wild man fell as Charles' musket barked, and then a third as Saint-Pierre fired. By that time, Renard had reloaded and loosed another round.

Skirling like madmen, they came on, reminding Red Shoes now of *Hacho*, the berserk warriors of his own people. Death did not worry them, these men. That was bad.

He cast his ghost sight about, searching for the more dangerous sorts of spirits, but he saw only the one-eyes, watching them. A few were picking at his guard, trying to reach his mind, but he kept them out, drawing the *kraftpistole* Bienville had given him. This seemed to be a battle of arms rather than sorcery—which, considering his weakened state, was a good thing.

Charles and Wallace were both still reloading when the next berserker came within striking distance. But Nairne fired his *kraftpistole* over Wallace's shoulder, and three of their attackers fell, engulfed in flame. Taking his cue, Red Shoes took up a position behind the Frenchmen.

Still their attackers didn't flinch, and some began scrambling around the lip, forcing the defenders to divide their fire. Fernando hacked at them with his cutlass, but it was like striking at the incoming tide. Red Shoes fired his *kraftpistole* for the third time, aiming at a brute twice the size of a normal man, hair spiked up with some sort of paste. The man caught fire well enough, but he did not stop, slamming into Saint-Pierre and Renard, both of whom lost their footing and fell over the side. With no time to reprime his weapon, Red Shoes whipped out his ax and buried it in the skull of the next man who bounded toward him. Unfortunately, the ax stayed in the head as it went by; and in the next heartbeat a blurred figure lifted him free of the earth and crushed him back against the hard slope. Skittering down together, rocks tearing at their flesh, Red Shoes managed to get hold of an ear—but there was suddenly a second man grappling him and then a third. Shortly he couldn't move at all, and they bound him. As the roar of blood in his ears receded and awareness of his surroundings returned, he noticed that the sounds of battle seemed to have ceased, and now only the weird hooting remained, echoing triumphantly in the hollow which had once been London. He closed his eyes, wondering what sort of tortures the wild men of England might have prepared for him.

Night came, but their captors lit no torches. The one-eyes remained the only light, and they illumined only themselves. Red Shoes could hear more spirit-whispering now, but even bound and beaten he still had the strength to resist them. The one-eyes were essentially weak, the weakest of all spirits. Dealing with them had been his first lesson as an *isht ahollo*, a lesson he had learned almost at the cost of his sanity. He was not likely to forget it. He did not sleep, and the sun awoke a gritty gray sky for his still-open eyes.

From the rim, the valley had looked like a bowl; here it seemed a flat plain, ringed about with a palisade, a fort built by giants and now abandoned.

And yet not abandoned, for after a few more hours they came to a camp—if such a tattered collection of tents could be called that. The fabric seemed rich enough—silks and brocades, linen, furs—all draped on poorly built frames of saplings. Red Shoes wondered how far away the saplings had come from, for since leaving the coast they had seen no trees.

The largest tent was long and narrow relative to its length, as he had heard Iroquois houses were. His captors carried him toward it.

During the night, the naked warriors had calmed and become quiet, but now they began hollering again, and answering calls went up from the tents. They brushed through the flap.

Red Shoes was dumped unceremoniously onto the ground—or rather onto the rugs that served as a floor. They were so filthy that Red Shoes wondered why they bothered; after all, a dirt floor could be swept.

The others were dropped near him. His heart sank as he saw that they were all there; he had hoped that someone had escaped to bring back rescue. At least all seemed alive, with the possible exceptions of Fernando and Mather, who he hoped were merely unconscious.

"Cut their bonds," an oddly muffled voice commanded, "all but those on their hands."

Red Shoes looked up to see who was speaking. It was a white man of middle height, his skin pricked blue with tattoos. He wore a sort of kilt made from what appeared to be silk, and a cloak of similar material. Most notable was the bone-white mask that covered his face, a blank oval with no eye holes, fringed with raven feathers. Behind him stood a number of men similarly clad and masked.

Their bonds were cut, and they were dragged roughly to their feet. Mather's eyes opened, and he looked confused. Fernando they could not rouse.

"Well. Who have we here?" The man's voice was muffled by his mask. Red Shoes noticed two one-eyes hovering behind him.

"O God, the God of hosts, shield me in thy hand—" Mather began.

"Shut that one up," the masked man snapped.

"Deliver me from mine—" Mather coughed off suddenly as an open hand cracked across his face.

"Leave him be!" Charles snarled, starting forward despite the three men with weapons pointed at him. "That there is a reverend!"

"Yes, I recognize his costume," the masked man remarked silkily, confirming Red Shoes' suspicion that the fellow was seeing through the one-eyes—a foolish thing to do. "But I shall not tolerate his pitiful whining. Not here, in this sacred place. Not today, on this sacred day."

Mather looked up, blood streaming from his mouth. "Sacred to whom? Satan?"

The masked man laughed, a sick, grating sound. "Where are you from that you are such fools?" he asked.

"What happened in this place?" Nairne asked.

The man turned his eyeless face to Nairne. "What *happened*? Can you really not know?"

"We're just come from America. How could we know?"

A general gasp went up, but the masked man silenced them with a wave of his hands. "Very good. Very good. I knew you would come. And I knew you would tell these lies. So here we came, and here we waited, and here you are."

Nairne ignored that. "What happened to London?" he asked again.

"The apocalypse, you imbecile. The end of the world. Your God and your devil fought until both were dead."

"Blasphemy. Utter madness," Mather spat. "God is eternal."

"Oh so? Did you see it, Reverend? Did you see the flaming sword of God? Did you see his blood falling from the heavens? I did. It was the last thing I ever saw with fleshly eyes. Now I can see more. Now I know the Truth."

The Europeans merely stared at the man, apparently stricken.

"You say this place is sacred," Red Shoes heard himself say. "Sacred to what god, if yours is dead?"

"Sacred to the old gods. To the ones here before that upstart Hebrew god, Jehovah. Sacred to *me*, Qwenus. Sacred to the Anointed, who saw the battle, who testify to it."

"*Pardieu*," du Rue said. "Madmen. Blind madmen."

"What do you want with us?" Nairne asked quietly. "We only came to learn what happened here."

"Now you know," Qwenus said matter-of-factly.

"I'm not certain I do," Nairne replied.

"Then you are a heretic. Fortunately, heretics are just as palatable to the old gods as believers are, their screams sweeter to them than honey."

"Palatable?" Tug grunted.

But the audience seemed to be over. The masked fellow waved his hand, and they were hauled roughly to their feet.

"Come on," one of the warriors holding him said, the first intelligible noise Red Shoes had heard from any of them other than Qwenus.

"Palatable?" Tug repeated, as he was dragged from the tent.

"Apparently," Nairne said.

"No, sair, I mean what in hell does 'palatable' mean?"

"It means, I think, that they intend to eat us."

6

The Duke of Lorraine

The battle was over in a few instants, with all but a few of Le Loup's brigands stiffening in the field. Adrienne sat next to Crecy, Nicolas clutching her arm, watching the bluecoats go about their business. A young man watched them nervously from ten paces.

Crecy was still alive, blood bubbling from her nostrils, mouth sucking air in brief hiccups. She had two wounds—one just above the heart and a second through her ribs. Adrienne had seen enough injuries in the last two years to understand that they were fatal in most men.

Crecy, however, was not like other people.

Adrienne was dressing the wounds as best she could when a second soldier approached. His face might have once been pleasant, before his nose had been broken and healed into a sort of parrot's beak, before the warmth had drained from his deep brown eyes. Like the man Crecy had decapitated, he wore the colors of the Hundred Swiss. She glanced angrily up at him, but found him studying her with a quizzical expression. He looked first at her, then at Crecy, then back at her, and she saw the puzzle solved behind his eyes.

"Sweet Mary," he swore. "Mademoiselle de Mornay de Montchevreuil." He doffed his hat.

It had been so long since Adrienne had heard her family name, she nearly didn't recognize it. A name from another lifetime.

"You have the advantage of me, sir."

"My apologies, Mademoiselle. My name is Hercule d'Argenson.

I—" He knelt next to Crecy. "—I regret that we meet under such circumstances. How is she?"

Adrienne raised her eyebrows. "You know her."

He nodded. "She was a member of the Hundred Swiss, once. Posing as a man, of course, but a few of us knew. I was a friend of Nicolas d'Artagnan, Mademoiselle. We all envied him, that he was your guard."

"He was ill served by it, as Crecy has been. I do not think she will live."

"We will do what we can, I assure you. My doctor is nearby." D'Argenson smiled faintly. "I know that you may doubt it, but your company has improved. We are not cutthroats, like these fellows." He gestured at one of Le Loup's men who lay dead not far away.

"I am relieved to hear that."

"I thought you might be." He regarded her for a moment. "I will tell you of it in a more comfortable place. Here, we are in danger. Indeed, you are fortunate that we found you. Soon, this may well be a true battlefield."

Adrienne shrugged. "I do not even know where I am," she replied.

"Presently, it is a part of Lorraine," he said. "But in a few days, time, I fear it shall be Muscovite soil."

They reached the main road from Nancy near nightfall and found it flooded with a stream of men, women, children, beasts, and creaking wagons.

"Where do they think they are going," Adrienne wondered, "that will be better than whence they came?"

"They would rather take their chances in the countryside. Evil tales are told of the Muscovites," d'Argenson replied. "Some say they are sustained by the blood of their victims, that they have made pacts with the prince of hell."

Adrienne absently stroked the mane of the horse d'Argenson had given her to ride.

"They will find nothing in the countryside," she told him.

"How well I know, Demoiselle."

They moved upstream through the stream of refugees for a few hours but parted from it before reaching the town, following instead a smaller track which quickly gained in elevation, until the horizon stretched out behind them as a blue smoke. Above, a few blurred stars shone down, and Adrienne remembered a night, long ago, when she had lain with Nicolas d'Artagnan and beheld a sky of jewels, and known that she was in love. She had been twenty-one, then. Now she was twenty-four, and could only just barely recall the feeling, and could visualize the splendor of a clear night not at all. She absently stroked the head of her child, the namesake of that lost love, wondering if he would ever see the stars that clearly.

The road tunneled through a dark wood, but after a time, the light of many campfires appeared. Sentries questioned them and they entered a city of camp sites. They passed near some men who were singing a bawdy but not unpleasant song. Her nose twitched at the scent of meat, a rare thing these days.

They rode between stone gateposts grown over with ivy, across ill-tended gardens to a manse in the style of two centuries before. There liveried servants hurried out to meet them, and Crecy was borne off by a pair of soldiers to where d'Argenson assured her a doctor waited.

D'Argenson dismounted and then offered to help her down, but she had already taken her son beneath one arm and thrown a leg over the saddle. She grinned ruefully at his extended hand.

"I have not been in the company of gentlemen in a long time," she apologized.

"That is the loss of gentlemen everywhere."

"You are gallant. I know what my appearance must be." Her hair was a rat's nest, her stolen dress in tatters.

"A diamond is always a diamond."

Suddenly embarrassed, she looked away from eyes not as cold as she had thought on first glance, and waved at the manse. "Are you the master of this place?" she asked.

"Not I," d'Argenson answered. "I suppose I am something of the prime minister. No, yonder comes the master."

Adrienne blinked. In the light of a single fitful alchemical lanthorn, she saw approaching a fair-haired boy, perhaps some thirteen years old, outfitted in riding clothes.

D'Argenson stepped up and bowed. "Sir, may I present to you Mademoiselle de Mornay de Montchevreuil."

The boy smiled broadly and bowed, then approached to take her hand. "It is an honor," he said softly, "to meet the betrothed of the late king of France." He kissed her hand lightly. "I am Francis Stephen, duke of Lorraine, and if there is aught I can do for you, please name it."

"I . . ." She suddenly felt very tired. "A bath?"

"The servants shall see to it," the boy replied.

Reclining in the bullhide tub, it came to her that there could be no civilization without hot water. For two years she had lived like some wild beast—living in filth, washing only in cold, dirty pools. It had made her brain like an animal's, uncaring, thinking only of survival.

One taste of hot, soapy water on her skin changed all, changing her nature from beast to human. She reminded herself how illusory it was, how a week on the road would prove to her again that the society and works of man were silly ephemera, and yet, for the moment, it did not matter.

And the room was warm, too. There was a toilette with perfumes and powders, and laid out on the bed were three dresses such as she had not even seen since fleeing Versailles. She chose a dark green manteau, the least ostentatious but the most comfortable of the three.

As she was dressing, a girl of perhaps twelve came in, a pretty thing save for a few pockmarks on her face.

"Perhaps I could comb Mademoiselle's hair?" she asked.

It took a painful hour to get the tangles out, but with each stroke of the brush, Adrienne came more alive, felt her skin going from stone to flesh. She would regret that, when she needed stone again, but in her last days at Versailles she had learned that the world would harm you whether you were prepared or not. Pleasure was a rare fruit that should be tasted when it came one's way.

"Where is my son?" she asked the girl, suddenly, as it came to her that he was not in the room.

"He is with a nurse," the girl replied.

"A nurse." She had never been apart from little Nico, save for an hour here or there, and then Crecy had been his guardian. And yet, for the space of half an hour, she had not even missed him.

But of course, her child was a part of that cold, dirty life in the fields. He did not fit here. But with some luck, he would. As she woke from the dream of cold roads to one of hot baths, she would bring him with her, the way she had brought herself a new hand from the land of dream and ghosts.

She studied the hand absently as the girl combed her hair. It *looked* like a hand, until you peered closely and saw that it had no pores, no trace of hair. Until you realized, over the months, that its nails never grew, that briars never scratched it. But it could feel, and grasp and sometimes—sometimes it seemed capable of doing other things, as well, vague and frightening things.

Her hand had been burned off by an angel, and somehow had been replaced. How? She had thought about this before, but she had never really puzzled at it. She hadn't cared. Now she cared, and the remains of a formula danced in her brain, the fragments of a great proof that, in a dream, she had once known entire.

The girl answered a knock on the door, and a moment later returned to Adrienne.

"The duke requests your presence, milady," she said.

"First I will see my friend," Adrienne replied. "Do you know where she has been taken?"

"Yes, milady, but—"

"Then please take me there."

The girl bowed.

"And have my son brought to me, please."

The physician attending Crecy was a slim young man with little in the way of a chin.

"She must rest," he insisted, when she entered.

"Will she live?" Adrienne murmured, nestling a sleeping Nico against one shoulder.

"She should not, but she may," he replied. "Her constitution is very strong."

"She is my dear friend, sir. I will be very much in your debt if she lives."

He shook his head. "Not in my debt, but in God's. I have done little here, for there was little to do save remove the balls and sew shut the holes."

"Nevertheless," she replied. "May I look at her?"

"If you like."

Crecy was always pale, but now she was as translucent as finest porcelain. Her hair fanned on the pillow like a halo of flame. Her chest rose and fell only slightly.

"Be well, Veronique," she whispered, bending to place a kiss on her friend's cheek.

Two slivers of blue ice suddenly appeared, as Crecy's lids opened. A hissing cough escaped her lips, flecking them with blood. Holding Nico in one arm, Adrienne knelt at Crecy's side and took her hand, but it did not grasp back.

"We have found you," Crecy rasped, in a voice like a knife on whetstone. "We have found you."

And then she closed her eyes again.

Adrienne felt her strange hand tremble, then almost hum. She suddenly realized that she had gripped Crecy's fingers with it. She let go of her friend, a terrible icy chill working up her arm and into her spine. Suppressing a cry, she backed from the room.

Nicolas woke as she fled to her room, staring at her. Before reluctantly returning him to the kind-faced nurse, she sang him a lullaby, trying to escape Crecy's strange words. They were no doubt simple delirium, and yet there had been something utterly un-Crecylike in her eyes and tone.

Un-Crecylike, or perhaps Crecy *par excellence*: the cold-eyed stare she usually hid, the remorseless tones she commonly draped in the silk of emotion and care—an actress not acting.

Adrienne loved Crecy, but even now she did not trust her. Even now she feared her.

"Mademoiselle, the duke . . ."

The girl had followed along, fidgeting restlessly.

"Thank you, my dear. I would be honored to see the duke now."

Neither the duke Francis Stephen of Lorraine nor Hercule d'Argenson seemed much put out by her late arrival. They sat at the table, wine and soup untouched, awaiting her, conversing in low tones. When she was shown in, both rose.

The chamber was quaint, almost antique, though it was brightened by an alchemical lanthorn in the form of the moon depending from the high ceiling. A tapestry of men pursuing a stag draped one wall, the Lorraine crest another. A haunch of venison lay steaming on a platter, and Adrienne understood suddenly how very hungry she was.

"Mademoiselle, please join us," said the young duke.

Adrienne sat, her frame vibrating with appetite, but she waited until the duke began to sip his soup before touching hers. A lifetime of etiquette had been swept away in the dark months after the fall of the comet, but now she understood just how entrenched her training had been.

Once she actually tasted the soup, however, her will broke, and she gobbled at the meal like a starving dog, never pausing to touch the utensils near her plate.

The duke smiled brightly. "I take it you are unused to good meals, Demoiselle?"

Adrienne nodded, speaking between mouthfuls. "It is true, Your Grace. I have not eaten meat in—" She counted. "—more than a month. And then it was not nearly so good as this."

"Mutton?"

"Dog."

"Oh, dear!" Francis of Lorraine laughed again. "We shall try to keep you better fed than that." He glanced at d'Argenson. "Though I fear we shall have to put you back on the road quite soon."

Adrienne looked up.

"He means with us, not to your own devices," d'Argenson clarified. "We must abandon Lorraine, I fear. We have not the men to hold it against the Muscovite force."

"This is all strange to me. I have lived . . ." How much did they know about her? Did they know that she and Crecy had tried—and failed—to murder the king? Probably not, or she would not have this reception. Or if d'Argenson had been a friend of Nicolas d'Artagnan, perhaps they did know but did not care. "I have lost touch with things, I fear."

"So have we all, my dear," d'Argenson said. "After your abduction, as you know, the great flame fell from the sky, and the world went mad. Much of the coast was drowned, Versailles and Paris burned and then soaked in the hundred-night rain. The king, you understand, died."

Adrienne nodded. That much she knew.

"What became of you and your friend?" the duke asked.

Adrienne frowned, and decided to lie. "Our kidnappers took us to the Midi; but as you say, flame and flood washed out roads and bridges. Torcy and d'Artagnan were killed, and the rest fought amongst themselves. They then met with ruffians rougher than they."

"Those men we found you with?"

"No. Crecy and I escaped, you see, and fled to stay with an acquaintance of hers." Half truths. The truth was that there had been no kidnapping. They had all fled Versailles together after trying to kill the king. "We stayed with this friend—Madame Alaran—for some months, but as you know the weather only worsened. Her servants turned on her, in the end, and we barely escaped with our lives. We wandered, but the whole country had fallen into barbarism, like the days of the Goths, and everywhere there were bands of evil men. We finally were captured by Le Loup—the captain of the brigands you saved us from. We had no choice, so Crecy lent them her sword arm. As evil as they were, they were our only protection."

"I am sorry that we killed them, then," d'Argenson said.

"No, do not be. They were not good men. Soon they would have raped and killed us both, I am certain. No, Monsieur, you have saved our lives."

"It was a privilege, as I said before. And so you know nothing of the state of France?"

"Rumors only, and undependable ones at that."

D'Argenson took a long draft of his wine. "There are three kings of France now, or perhaps a hundred, depending on your reckoning. Many of the noble houses have simply declared themselves sovereign, or formed pacts of mutual protection, effectively carving France to bits. Worse, the duke of Orleans has declared himself king, though he really rules little more than Paris. Philip of Spain, of course, claims all France, and has of late sent troops inward to secure the southern portion—"

"Ah! We met many fleeing that army."

"Just so. The third king is the duke of Main, whose whereabouts are presently unknown, though some say he has gone to New France."

"Who controls the army?"

"No one—everyone."

Adrienne nodded. "Many of the gangs on the roads and towns were once of the army, but surely some remain loyal."

"Yes. Some to Orleans, some to Main, others to their old commanders, who do with them as they see fit. Orleans has had to split his forces—half to defend against the Muscovites coming from Flanders, half to defend against Philip in the south, though Philip claims, of course, that he is only coming to aid France against the Muscovite foe."

"The Netherlands?"

"Holland drowned; the dikes were broken and the sea came in. Tsar Peter sent thousands of men and ships to their aid. Much rebuilding has been done, but now the Muscovite grip on the Netherlands is strong, and he marches on Lorraine and Paris—a long front, but he has the men and weapons to sustain it. Terrible weapons, even more fearsome than those we saw used in the Flanders War."

"And so now we must flee my duchy," the duke broke in. "But I will return for it, one day. Those bears will not dance in Nancy and Metz forever!"

The young duke sounded more excited than chagrined at the prospect of losing his duchy, she noticed.

"Where, then, shall you go?" she asked.

The boy's eyes shone. "It shall be a grand adventure, I promise you, Mademoiselle. My army and I shall march to the east—through Muscovite and Turk—and we shall offer ourselves to the Holy Roman emperor in Prague. And, God willing, with our aid, we shall free Vienna besides!"

Adrienne asked, "You have a large army, then?"

"Almost two thousand souls!" Francis of Lorraine said, raising his glass. "To the empire and the glory of God!"

"The empire!" d'Argenson echoed.

Adrienne wondered if she had just fallen from one fire into another.

7

At Court

Karl VI, the Holy Roman emperor, was the first monarch Ben had ever seen, and now as at that first meeting, he found himself far from impressed. Eyes drooping, jowls pendulous, ringleted wig falling like gigantic, floppy ears, Karl more resembled a mournful hound than the heir to a lineage said to date back to Aeneas. Today he seemed more melancholy than usual.

It was an informal audience, and while Ben preferred those to formal ones, he still found them anything but relaxed. The room—one of the smaller galleries in the palace—was nevertheless crammed with gaudily dressed halberdiers, the Gentlemen of the Golden Key, the Gentlemen of the Black Key—all of whom Ben thought of as merely "the old men"—assorted courtiers, advisers, and servants. And, of course Sir Isaac, Sir Isaac's valet, and Sir Isaac's apprentice. Newton himself wore a vermilion coat embroidered in gold, while Ben wore the comparatively somber black coat and waistcoat chosen for him by the maid.

A string quartet played something dreadful in a nearby alcove as they waited, hats tucked under their arms, for the "informal" audience to get under way. At last, the chamberlain beckoned them forward. Newton went first, performing the Spanish genuflection, bowing deeply thrice and then dropping to one knee. When it was Ben's turn, he did the same, sweeping his hat gracefully before him.

He was rewarded by a gasp from the entire court, and for an instant he was well pleased with himself, believing that his performance had been somehow superlative—until he suddenly understood his mistake. At the end of his bow, he had—quite inadvertently—replaced his hat on his head. That made exactly two people in the room wearing hats: himself and the emperor.

He hastened to remove the offending headgear, and though Karl deigned not to notice the breach of etiquette, the "old men" stared angrily at him for the remainder of the audience.

The emperor nodded at Newton and cleared his throat. "How fare things scientific, Sir Isaac? Have you discovered anything of gravity?"

Ben chuckled aloud, but he was the only one in the room who did so. No one ever dared to laugh at the emperor's jokes, probably because the emperor himself never even twitched a smile. "A very clever pun, Your Majesty," he said, bowing once more. The emperor inclined his head toward Ben, but then returned his attention to Sir Isaac. A few belated and forced titters drifted about the room, accompanied by additional venomous gazes directed at Ben.

"Indeed, Sire," said Newton, "I have been making great strides of late in the development of a new system, one which, by comparison, shall make even my *Principia* appear rather pale."

"That is good to hear. The empire has need of such 'new systems,' I am certain." He raised a brow. "I hope in this new system you make certain matters clear."

Ben knew what he meant. Everyone was aware Newton had discovered some means of recovering his youth, and the emperor—and a good number of others—took a rather extreme interest in that, though the interest went mostly unspoken or couched, as now, obliquely.

Newton understood him, however. "Yes, Sire. It is a matter of regularizing an accident, of making it mathematically predictable. It is the difference, you might say, between taking—accidentally—enough of a virulent poison to cure an illness but not kill and being able to reliably *prescribe* that dosage. His Majesty will understand that I hesitate to experiment upon him in such matters."

"I should say I do," the emperor replied. "But I speak of more important things than this 'medicine.' "

"Yes, Sir Isaac," another man put in. "How will this new system aid us in our struggle to reclaim the empire from its enemies?" This speaker was nothing like the emperor. Though an older man, he hardly looked it. If the emperor was a weary bloodhound at the age of thirty-eight, Eugène of Savoy at fifty-nine was a wolf. Though childlike in size and proportion, what there *was* of his slight body seemed made of wire, piano string tuned so tight as to be near the breaking point. Still, just as Karl VI did not, at first sight, strike one as being an emperor, the prince of Savoy did not *look* like the greatest general of his age—not, that is, until you noticed the metallic glitter of eyes, windows into a head full of dancing knives.

"I durst not say," Sir Isaac replied, keeping his gaze upon the emperor's knees. "Unless His Majesty should ask me himself, and even then I would beg for a private audience."

"Quite right," the emperor said. "That is as it should be, given recent events. Considering all you have done for the empire, it pleases us to trust you. And yet, I could wish for some results soon, Sir Isaac, something of practicality. You must know how heavily it burdens me that Spain, our rightful possession, languishes under Bourbon rule. Harder still that glorious Vienna, queen of all cities, cracks beneath the weight of fat Turks. But as you well know, Prague herself is now threatened. Why, we have heard even today that a Russian mob threatened our sorcerer's apprentice." He gestured with thumb and forefinger at Ben, who bowed, wondering how long one's knees could last at court.

"I apologize for that incident, Majesty," Newton replied. "I have instructed Mr. Franklin to remain, henceforth, on this side of the Moldau."

"The matter is weightier than that," the emperor said. "We have had cooperation from the prisoner taken this morning, the leader of this gang, and he has admitted to being an imperial Muscovite agent. His charge was to steal one or both of you away from us. Gentlemen, we do not care for this at all. Prague—all Prague—must be more secure, and we must have weapons that will make the Russians think twice of trying to shuck this oyster for its pearl."

"I assure you, Sire, that you will have such weapons soon enough."

"Very well. Is there anything else that either of you have to say, then?"

Ben stepped up and bowed once more. "Yes, Sire. I have a present for you."

The emperor did not smile, but his eyebrows rose, a sign of his pleasure. "How thoughtful," he said, and gestured for the chamberlain to take the box Ben indicated, the one that Newton's valet had carried in a few feet behind them. The old fellow took the package and drew out the shoes, which Ben had hastily painted black.

"Well, how *unusual*," the emperor said, and this time the laughter around the court was a bit freer.

"If it please Your Majesty, like the men who accosted me, they are more than they seem."

"I guessed as much. Well, there are no wings upon them, so I suppose they are not the fleet shoes of Mercury."

"No, Sire, more those of Poseidon. With them, you may skate upon the liquid surface of water."

"What a delightful thought. I should like to see this." He paused for an instant. "I should like to see this now."

The move to the first courtyard and its fountain pool took a full hour, though the distance traversed was less than a hundred yards, because moving the party meant that everyone present had to sort themselves into the proper order, from emperor to servant and all of the somewhat-disputable degrees between. Ben had never seen a more profound waste of human effort and ingenuity, and he reflected privately that it was no wonder that the empire had withered to a single city if this ossified ceremony was indicative of how affairs of war and diplomacy were also conducted.

They at last reached the courtyard, and he bounced lightly up onto the edge of the fountain pool, donned his inventions, and began to shuffle about upon the marble-confined puddle. Only silence greeted his performance until the emperor gave an enthusiastic exclamation and a single clap, and then the applause pattered around Ben like rain. This cheered him up, and that the courtiers could not even decide whether something amused them eased his anger into jovial disdain.

He twirled about and bowed, still standing on the water, and then stepped down from the fountain, bowed, presented the shoes to the emperor.

"I shall furnish more for your daughters, if you wish, Your Majesty," he said, "and I have taken the liberty of engaging a boatwright to modify one of your pleasure craft in like way."

"A boat that touches not the water?" Prince Eugène mused. "I think I might see some advantage in that."

"Yes, yes!" the emperor exclaimed. "Sir Isaac, again you have amused the court and shown us something useful. We are very pleased, and it would please us *mightily* if you would attend Mass with us tomorrow."

Ben felt a bit of guilty delight; though Newton always got the ultimate credit for *Ben's* inventions, it was Newton who had to pay the price by attending state functions—and worst of all, church. In all the world, Newton despised nothing so much as the Catholic Church, and in Bohemia, there was no other church, unless one counted the Jewish temples. Newton felt it a mortal sin to attend—as he put it— the "lying, pagan rituals" of Catholicism.

But Newton knew his limits, too, and the boundaries of the emperor's favor. "If it please Your Majesty," he conceded, bowing.

Yes, let him have the credit—and let *him* be the one lying prostrate in the cathedral whilst Ben found diversions with less devout playmates.

The audience began breaking up. It was nearing the dinner hour, and as soon as it was polite, Ben took his leave. As he crossed the courtyard, however, he found himself suddenly confronted by a bizarre procession.

Some ten or so dwarfs in miniature courtly garb were marching into the yard. First came halberdiers, followed by bearers supporting a small sedan chair, behind which trailed pygmy versions of courtiers, "gentlemen," "ladies," and most interestingly, one small man all in red, wearing a peaked astrological hat and little round spectacles.

As the weird cortege drew up abreast of him, the window of the sedan chair lowered a few inches. Inside, Ben could see a little girl, perhaps five or six, with strikingly blond hair and unreasonably serious eyes.

"Hello, Mr. Franklin," the girl called. "Could you come here for a moment?"

Ben bowed thrice and went down on one knee before he approached the chair. "Good afternoon, Duchess," he said.

"*Arch*duchess," she corrected him, with a bit of childish petulance. She was dressed exactly as a great lady—in a blue and silver gown trimmed with gold and large, dangling sleeves: an empress with a court made to scale.

"Beg pardon, Your Highness, Your *Arch*duchessness. How can I be of service?"

The archduchess Maria Theresa smiled slyly. "You see that I have my own philosopher?" she asked, pointing back at the little man in red.

"Indeed," Ben replied. "He seems a smart fellow."

"Yes, I suppose," she said, complaint in her tone. "But the scientifical inventions he makes aren't nearly so jolly as yours."

Ben glanced back at the dwarf, who was doing his best to look cheerful but was being only moderately successful.

"Well, we scientifical philosophers all have our feasts and famines," he replied.

"Yes, I guess so. But I would like to have *you* with my court, Mr. Franklin."

"Well, Archduchess, that is highly flattering, but I'm afraid I already have a position."

"Well, *leave* it then." She pouted. "My father has too many scientificals. I want one of my own."

"Well, but as you said—"

"No, a *real* one," she insisted, "like you."

"I think perhaps I am too tall to be in your court," Ben replied.

"You could be my giant. Father has a giant. Besides, I shall not always be small. One day I shall be grown-up."

"But for now, I'm afraid I have to do what your father, the emperor, says," Ben explained. "Now if you could but convince him . . ." He had a sudden, horrible thought. What if she *did* manage to convince her father to put him in her service, forcing him to parade about in this play court of dwarfs all day?

He cleared his throat and then lowered his voice secretively. "A thought, Archduchess. What if I were to be your *secret* court philosopher? Wouldn't that be more fun, more mysterious?"

"No," she considered, "I don't think so."

"Oh, yes, but it would. We could meet in secret, and I could show you inventions that no one else has seen, and only you and I and your guards would know about them."

"Even my father would not know about them?"

"Not even he," Ben lied.

"Well. *Maybe* that sounds like fun."

"Well, if you decide, send me a *secret* note by only your most trusted servant. Don't forget that the Turk has spies all about us, watching everything we do."

"I don't like that."

"Well, that is why we must be careful. In fact, let us have a secret password, so that no Turk can disguise himself as me and intercept your communiqués."

The archduchess clapped her tiny hands. "What shall our password be?" she asked.

"Well, as you are the archduchess, that is for *you* to say."

"Very well. Then I say it is . . . um . . . I don't know. I command *you* to choose one."

"Very well, then. It shall be . . . *Rehaset Ramai*."

"Rehaset Ramai? Why, that *sounds* Turkish."

"Very good, Majesty. That will fool them all the more. In Turkish it means—um—'all is well.' But it really is your name."

"My name? That's silly."

"No, no. 'Tis an anagram, you see? 'Rehaset' is Theresa, 'Ramai' is 'Maria.' So when I hear the note is from Rehaset Ramai, I shall know it is from you, but if a Turk hears, he will think, 'All is well.' "

"I do see. This is fun."

Ben bowed again. "I shall await your next communication, Archduchess Ramai."

She nodded, and, looking pleased, put up her window. The dwarf court began marching once again.

Noticing that Newton was still engaged in conversation, Ben finished his stroll across the courtyard and out onto the Powder Bridge. From there, he stared down at the green depths of the Stag Moat, wondering what he should do next. Not go back to Katarina's, that was certain. In fact, he now had an excuse not to go back there for a good long while, if ever. Besides, what he was hungry for at the moment was food, not female diversion, so best he find Robert—or perhaps this Captain Frisk, if he was able—and make his way to a tavern to dine. And then, perhaps, return his attention to that maid, whatever her name was. Cold and imperious she might be, and no great beauty, but she had something in her gown he much desired.

Her *keys*.

Something was moving down in the moat. The Stag Moat was not one of water; it was a narrow canyon planted with lemon trees, figs, and other exotic plants. Usually, the emperor and his nobles kept game for their frequent hunts there—wild boar and stag, of course.

The long shadow Ben saw gliding through the trees was not a stag or a boar, however, but the lithe black panther. Even from here, it looked dangerous, as if the mere touch of its sleek fur could kill or the light reflecting from it give one a fever.

It looked up at him, exactly as if it knew he was there, and for an instant its eyes flamed red. Ben gasped and jerked back from the edge of the bridge, heart twisting. He had seen eyes like that before, on a man named Bracewell, a man who had killed his brother and tried to kill him. But it wasn't the cat's eyes that shocked him so—for he had seen dogs and housecats with red night eyes—but rather the third, rather faint orb, floating above the panther, blinking open for only an instant and then closing lids of air to vanish.

One of the things that Newton named the malakim. Such creatures had accompanied his brother's killer as well.

Drawing a strengthening breath, he looked back down.

Cat and unnatural eye were nowhere to be seen.

"Something disturbing in the moat?" a voice asked from almost in his ear. Ben jumped a second time: he had not heard the prince of Savoy approaching, pantherlike in his own way.

"Perhaps, Your Highness, perhaps a trick of the light," Ben replied, affecting the briefer, less complicated bow that was due nobles other than the emperor.

The prince nodded knowingly. "In Prague, one is never certain what one sees from the corner of the eye. It is a haunted sort of place, one I do not find comfortable."

"Neither do I," Ben replied, gazing back down into the moat.

"No? I would think that a scientific man would find the ghosts of Prague quite fascinating."

"Ghosts? Do you speak metaphorically, sir?"

Eugène shrugged his narrow, hunched shoulders. "I suppose. The marks of the past, I suppose I mean. Poor Mad Rudolf stained this city so deeply with alchemy and the necromantic, there are more than a few echoes still. The soothsayers, right here in the castle, on Golden Lane, the arcane books in the libraries—why, even your own presence in the court could be said to arise from that lingering ghost of Rudolf."

"How is that?"

"They take such things very seriously here—astrology, alchemy."

"Science is taken seriously in all civilized countries, sir. That is the pursuit of my master and myself. These other things you speak of— the astrology and alchemy of a hundred years past—these were not science."

"What difference do you see?"

"Your pardon, sir, but the difference between superstitious non-sense and empirical experimentation."

The prince laughed briefly and seemed to examine the sky. "Which is which?" he wondered.

Ben stared at the man. "What do you mean?"

"You just walked upon water. You and Sir Isaac arrived here in a flying boat. Sir Isaac himself, a man of some eighty years, wears the face of a man just twenty—these are things I heard about long ago, in fairy tales. Are these things scientific? They do not seem so to me. A few years ago, philosophers said that the world was like a great clock, a machine that God set in motion and is now merely watching, knowing how it will run. That seemed scientific to me. But Newton has returned us to mysterious attractive forces, the weird harmonies of the spheres, the unseen and the unknowable. To a simple man like myself, Mr. Franklin, the new science seems like the old sorcery."

"But these forces are not mysterious," Ben countered. "Or they need not be. That is the crux of our work, what makes us different from those alchemists of the past. We discover the laws by which God operates the universe, create mathematical systems that can explain them. That is what allows us the invention of the things the old ones merely dreamt of, told tales of."

"Or perhaps remembered? From an earlier day? That is what your master seems to think."

Ben nodded. "I know. I disagree with him there. I think him too humble in that respect."

"Sir Isaac? Humble?"

"In that he believes that he is not the first to discover the wonders of gravity and other sympathies, to create the calculus, and so forth. Yes, he believes that the ancients had them all, and more, and we but merely rediscover what has been long obscured."

"But you think not? The apprentice has his own head in this matter?"

"Yes, sir, I do. If these things had been once discovered, on what possible account would they have been lost?" *I am arguing with a prince*, Ben thought. Just the sort of thing that Robert would warn him against. But Eugène seemed to take the argument as just that, not something to find offense in. In fact, he was nodding again, as if he accepted Ben's verdict. But then he turned back, a taunting smile on his lips.

"Perhaps . . . let's see. You claim that you have systematized the laws by which God operates the universe."

"Some of them, yes. Much remains to be done."

"And yet, without a fullness of knowledge—without the complete knowledge that God has—you have taken it upon yourself to meddle with those laws, to operate with them, to build devices which never were and do things that were never done."

"I . . . that is true, insofar as it goes, Sir, but—"

"No, no, hear me out. Let us say you were, for instance, God. Might you not perceive that this fiddling about with the divine laws had consequences of which the meddlers were unaware? That, in fact, it upset the rightful order of things? Were you God, might you not take steps to set things to rights? Perhaps the ancients *did* have the knowledge of Newton. Perhaps they created many strange and scientifical things. And perhaps God simply *stopped* them."

Ben's scalp tingled. "Do you fear he will stop us?" he asked, trying to sound suitably skeptical.

"Look about you, Mr. Franklin. The world has descended into madness. Fire rains from the heavens, and winter sits enthroned in August. Perhaps he has already begun."

Ben fidgeted. He and Newton had not explained what had really happened two years before: that the meteor had been intentionally summoned, not by God, but by men.

The prince laughed at Ben's expression, perhaps mistaking it for an intense effort to address his argument. "Who can know how God works? Certainly not I. I am no theologian."

"Do you wish for Sir Isaac and me to cease our experiments?"

"I? Heavens no. You are our only hope. I merely voiced some vague misgivings I have. I have misgivings about guns, too—occasionally they explode in one's fist. But if I see an enemy, I will sight down my barrel and fire. No, I dearly value Sir Isaac's work for us, especially now." He faced Ben fully, all trace of levity gone. "The Muscovite who led the attempt to kidnap you was not a strong man under torture. Few are, really. It rarely takes more than a few hours to learn all there is to know. First they are silent, then they threaten, then beg, and finally tell. When this man made his threats, he said we would all die, every one of us, that the emperor would be humbled, that Prague would fall. 'Death from the sky,' he said."

Ben stared back down at the moat, stiff, his pulse beating like some cannibal's drum in his temples.

"Does this mean aught to you?" the prince asked.

For an instant, Ben's tongue lay frozen in his mouth. There were more comets in the sky than grains of sand on a beach. But if he said, he would have to explain: and if he explained, he would have to admit that there was nothing he could do. But there *had* to be something he could do. There had to. He had to think, alone.

"It means nothing to me," Ben lied. "But with more information— Did this Muscovite say anything else? When this death would come or how?"

"He did not."

"Then he must be made to."

"If you have some science by which to speak with corpses, you may ask him yourself," the prince replied. "He was indeed a weak man, weaker than we thought."

Ben blinked, remembering the fellow's blue eyes, the intensity of his voice. *But he would have killed me,* he remembered. "The others, then? Weren't two others captured?"

"We are still discussing matters with them, but I think they know nothing—just big hands to hold swords and carry apprentices." He paused, and his eyes narrowed a bit. "You are certain that it means nothing to you?"

"It could mean so many things," Ben said, a little weakly. "But I swear to you I shall discover it for you. It will have my every thought. Have you told Sir Isaac?"

Prince Eugène shook his head. "I leave it to you. But let me have some word from him soon."

"I shall, sir," Ben replied. But in his mind, he was watching the fall of heaven, God smiting London with the fires from which hell had been built, the blackening of the sun.

"Oh, God," he murmured, just at the edge of breath, as he watched the prince move back into the castle, "if you wanted us to stop, why didn't you just tell us so?"

8

Shadowchild

They were cast into a pit some ten feet deep and as many square, dug into the loose soil of the valley and buttressed by black stones. Saplings lashed with wire formed the roof. He supposed that if they could reach it, they might tear their way through it, even without tools. But even Tug—the tallest of them—could not reach it. Someone standing on the big man's shoulders might, were it not for their guardian, now armed with Saint-Pierre's musket.

So they lay in the pit, tired, stinking, and wounded, trying out ideas for escape in hoarse whispers, discarding each in turn.

"Very strange," Red Shoes told Nairne, "that I should travel so far to die as I might have died among the Chickasaw or Shawano."

Nairne chuckled dryly. "Your people talk of some rather miraculous escapes."

Red Shoes nodded. "So they do," he said.

"If you have any ideas, let me know."

"I will." But he lied. If he told Nairne, the one-eyes might find out, and the one-eyes would tell the blind men.

Night came again, and most fell fitfully asleep. When all was quiet, Red Shoes closed his eyes and imagined a rhythm. He imagined a song, and he gave himself up to the ghost vision, to which his lids were meaningless.

Most of the *Nishkin Achafa* had gone or were attending the blind men, not paying attention to him as he dropped deeper into the soul behind the flesh of the world.

It was an unknown place, a terrifying one, one that human eyes could not see. Instead, they made figures of reality—the way that the white man's writing was a figure of actual speech, and speech itself only an echo of thought. And so he descended into a square that was not a square, surrounded by houses that were not houses, looking into a fire that was not a fire, regarded by a little man who was not in any way a man. He was *Kwanakasha*, a powerful spirit.

"What have you come for this time?" Kwanakasha grumbled. He was naked, so brown he was almost black, and no taller than Red Shoes' waist.

"I've come to make another child."

"Why? When I could do anything you want with so much less trouble? I can draw down the lightning, command the winds, see the future, perceive the far distances. I can find what is lost, summon game or a woman—" He grinned. "—rend open cages."

"Yes, I am certain you can do all that. That is why you are chief of the world," Red Shoes sarcastically replied.

"Ungrateful wretch! I chose you, came to you when you were just a child, spoke into your ear. . . ."

"Yes, you did. And if my elders had not noticed me listening to you, I would have grown up to be your tool, a sorcerer, an accursed being."

"More powerful by far than you are now."

"No, I would be dead, for my people would have wisely killed me. My people long ago learned the danger in the 'aid' you offer us. And I tire of this conversation, which you insist on each time I summon you."

"You may have me in your grip, but my speech is still my own."

"And as crooked as ever. Now, be still."

Kwanakasha watched sullenly as Red Shoes produced a knife made from the stuff of ghost. Tapping his chest, he passed the knife to the little man.

The dwarf pursed his lips in anger, leaned over, and stabbed the knife into Red Shoes' chest.

There was agony, but not the agony of the flesh he was likely to endure soon enough. This was a mother dying, a homeland lost—a taste of death.

"Leave me now," he told Kwanakasha.

Without another word, the creature did so.

Tears sparkling down his face like diamonds, Red Shoes fought against the black gloom, reached into the incision, and withdrew the substance of his shadow. It was both spongy and malleable, and he began to knead it into a new shape. Quietly, the cut in his chest closed up as his soul—abhorring the vacuum—stretched itself thin to make up the loss. Soon he would be whole, but with altogether less essence.

After some thought, he made his child a falcon. He searched above him for the ghost world trace of the grill above them. The wood itself was too complicated to scent and understand, but the metal wire had a simple taste. He awakened the falcon to the scent of iron, trying to ignore the dislocation he always felt when he made a new child, as if he were two places at once. The child tasted the iron, knew it, and slept.

Black clouds boiled overhead, and Red Shoes knew that he had tired himself too much. If he fell asleep in the ghost world, he would be at the mercy of whatever spirit happened along. He began withdrawing, hoping he could do so quickly enough to avoid being caught.

Kwanakasha reappeared, and, as the square darkened and blurred, he began to resemble a dark, winged creature with many eyes. "The great ones are awakening," Kwanakasha purred with mixed glee and disdain. "A new time comes. You will see, my friend, how different things can be, and you will wish you had accepted me on my terms."

"Go to sleep," Red Shoes commanded, and the eyes of the thing dimmed.

His own lids flickered open long enough for him to see Nairne, awake, staring at him, to hear Tug's loud snores before closing again, sealing him in sleep.

He awoke to frantic whispering a few hours later, feeling no more rested and perhaps a bit feverish. His falcon was still dormant, traumatized by its birth, and might well be of no use until he was dead, depending entirely upon what the intentions of the wild men were and when they decided to do something about them.

The whispering was from a shadowy form, kneeling above their prison. "I'm not sure, Reverend. How can I be sure?"

"Search your heart, your faith, and you will know that God still lives," Mather answered.

"I once was a Puritan," the shadow confided. "And yet I have been convinced—if there is indeed a God, how can he so treat the world?"

"Son, the world is a place of sin. God hates our sin, but He allows it to us. He also allows us to escape it."

"I want to believe, Reverend. But after all I have seen and felt—and I have *seen* the old gods, Reverend."

"You have seen devils and specters," Mather replied. "You have seen through the eyes of godlessness and fear."

"Fear? Reverend, I have seen more than fear. I have seen towns and forests wiped clean off the Earth from here to forty leagues. In all that distance, not one person lived. Were they all sinners? Could they have all been sinners? Beyond that, I have seen the dead heaped in the streets. I have seen the living, their skin blistered from them, eyes blasted, eardrums shattered. For the love of our Lord, Reverend, could they have all been sinners? I prefer that God be dead than to think him capable of such cruelty."

"What you prefer is of no matter," Mather replied. "God is, God was, God will be. And, no, all of those dead were not damned, but neither are all those in a ship that sinks, a town drowned by hurricane. But there are those among the dead who are elect—who live on—and those who are not and do not. Son, you have been drawn into worship of the devil, because you have lost hope. But does the devil give you hope? Do these so-called 'old gods' give you hope?"

The shadow was silent for a time. "No, sir. But we live better than some. And it makes the despair—" He paused, searching for words. "There's different kinds of despair. There's a kind that makes you mean, and it's better, you see? Better than just watching your family die, better than thinking everything is done, that the Lord has come and gone and didn't think you worthy."

"It isn't all done, friend. You can still be worthy, still hope for the covenant of grace. When this life is over, hope you for nothing better?"

"How can I hope?" The man was weeping. "Reverend, how can I hope?"

"You can hope because God is real, and His love is real, and His justice is real. And thus if you stay in the ways of sin, depriving yourself of the covenant of grace, you may despair of the same things. Regain your faith!"

The man above was openly sobbing now. "You have faith, though you will die tomorrow under torture?"

"Torture?"

"The old gods are said to like torture, to eat it."

"Very well, son. I will not like the torture, but I will not despair, no more than did Jesus on the cross."

"But didn't he despair, Reverend?"

"For an instant. Perhaps I will, too, for an instant. But let that instant stretch too long and it becomes eternity. And if you think your life is wretched now—"

"It must be good," the man wailed, "to die knowing you have God's grace."

"None can know for certain that they are elect," Mather replied quietly, "but that is the essence of faith."

The guard was silent, then, and though Mather tried to get his attention a few more times, he did not respond. Finally, the old man fell silent.

"Torture," Nairne replied quietly. "Are you brave enough for that, Red Shoes?"

"We are brought up to torture, to expect it—but still I hoped to avoid it."

Nairne smiled. "I've lived with the Choctaw, you know, and the Chickasaw, and the Muskogee. I've seen how the children attack hornet's nests so they can endure their stings, to learn stoic ways."

Red Shoes smiled at the memory of childhood. "Many are not so brave when the first hornet stings."

"Many find the same when the hot iron touches them the first time," Nairne muttered. "They find that it is to a hornet's sting as a hornet's sting is to nothing at all."

"I have heard this said as well. Have you ever known the iron, Thomas Nairne?"

He nodded. "Yes. And I have known the pitch pine."

Red Shoes stared at him. "And you yet live?"

Nairne chuckled mirthlessly. "They pushed splinters of lighter knot everywhere in my body, so that I was more porcupine than man, but they never lit them. The next day they let me go. I still don't know why."

"That's the way war is."

Nairne shook his head. "With your people. For you, war is a way to glory, sometimes a matter of survival. Torture is to punish the enemy, but also gives him a chance to die well. Whatever it is to these men, it isn't that."

"How can you know?"

"These people are not like you. Some call your people savage, and perhaps in some ways you are. But you have laws, love, marriage, children, games to go along with war."

"And these do not?"

Nairne shook his head. "Whatever these people pretend they are— Picts or Druids or God knows what—they are not that. Two years ago they were yeoman, tradesmen—their leader has the accent of gentility, and I'll wager him noble born, no matter how he disguises it. No, these are men who have nothing at all. They've thrown all away and only pretend to have something to replace it with. They are, in short, merely mad, not savage. To be savage is to have redeeming qualities."

"I take that as a compliment," Red Shoes told him. "But that makes our lot all the worse, doesn't it?"

As if to comment on their whispered conversation, the shadow leaned close to the grate again.

"Reverend?" The voice sounded calmer somehow.

"Yes?"

"Reverend, I accept what you say. You must be right. God must still live. Thank you, Reverend, for you have made me a Puritan again."

"It brings me joy to hear you say that, son," Mather replied. "You will not regret. When we walk together in the golden city, all this will seem a distant dream."

"I long for that day, Reverend. My decision is made."

"That mean yer goin' t' help us out o' here?" Tug hissed, hopefully.

The shadow paused for a moment. "I can't," he said at last. "Evil as they are, I can't go against them. But I will preach to them, you can be sure, and I will martyr myself. I will ask to die with you!"

"Son, have you thought that perhaps God still has work for you to do? For *us* to do?" Mather asked, voice a little strained.

"It can't be," the shadow whispered. "He can't. I don't have the strength, Reverend. The one thing I can still do is die a Christian. Didn't you say that He would forgive me? Didn't you say that He would allow me into the kingdom of heaven if I let Him back into my heart?"

"Son, that is only the first step, not the last. Sometimes dying is not the bravest nor the truest thing."

"Aye, come along, feller." Tug grunted. "I've had me a talk with God, and He has plenty and more plans f'r *me*."

The young man was weeping again. "No," he said. "I've made up my mind. It's all I have the strength for."

He fell silent again, and after a moment, Nairne nudged Red Shoes. "See?" he whispered. "All any of them want is a way to die. They've just gotten it twisted up."

"Let us hope," Red Shoes replied, "that we can *untwist* it."

At the first gray of morning, the grate was lifted, some twenty of the wild Englishmen crowded around it. Red Shoes' heart fell. His shadow-child was not yet strong enough to free them, and even if it could, it hardly mattered at the moment, with so many armed men to prevent their escape.

The man in the white mask stood above. "Who will be the first to honor the old gods?" he asked.

No one in the pit spoke up.

"Very well," the man said after a moment, "if none of you understand the honor you are being given, I will let the old gods choose."

"No!" Mather exclaimed. "No, let it be me."

"Ah! The reverend! Then you understand now."

"I understand that you can sacrifice me to the devil, but he will not have my soul. In sacrificing my flesh, you sacrifice your own eternity and assure mine."

The masked man shrugged and signed to his men, who made to reach down for Mather.

"No!" someone shouted from above. "No! Let me be the first!"

The masked man and others turned at the shout.

"You are one of us," the man said.

"No! No, I am a Puritan. I have fallen from grace, but God has shown me the way back."

"Your dead god has only shown you doom," Qwenus said. "But very well. Let us see how well your god keeps you."

Red Shoes had never seen the young man's face, but shortly he heard his screams.

Unlike his companions, whose faces reflected a dwindling of hope, Red Shoes began to feel a glimmer of possibility, for as the torture began, his shadowchild came awake. Torpid, weak, but awake.

He set it to working on the wire. If the young man took long enough to die, they would at least have a chance.

The young man did not last very long, however. He did not die repentant, as he wished, but instead died begging for his life, swearing his allegiance to the old gods. After a brief pause, in which the wild men chanted some sort of song in a language Red Shoes did not understand, the grate lifted again.

"Now," the masked man said. "Reverend?"

Nairne stood straight up in the pit. "Cowards," he shouted. "Cowards! Give me a sword, and I'll show you and your 'old gods' what fear is. I'll show you slaughter!"

"Aye!" Tug yelled. "Cowards every one of you. Not a one—not the whole damn lot o' yer—could stand against old Tug."

General pandemonium broke out then, as the anger and fear in the pit spoke. Meanwhile, Red Shoes' spirit gnawed at the wire bonds of the grate. But when it came apart, this was not what they needed. All eyes had to be focused *away* from them, and soon, or his whole effort would be useless.

Which meant that someone had to be tortured.

And so Red Shoes gave a war cry.

The war cry was something that Choctaw children spent considerable time learning. A man's war cry said everything about him that was important; whether he was brave, determined, reckless—or weak, frightened, unsure.

Today Red Shoes was sure and reckless, because otherwise he would not live. The cry cut through the surrounding tumult. Following his shout, there was silence, and he screamed again, glaring defiantly up at the leader, pointing at him.

"What have we here?" Qwenus asked.

"You have a man who doesn't fear you. You have a man who laughs at you. You have a man who will piss on your corpse before the day is out! You have a man who sees you trying to play that you are Indians and would show you how absurd your playacting is!"

Nairne gripped his arm. "Do you have any idea what you are doing?" he hissed.

"A red Indian?" the masked man said. "We have a red Indian among us?"

"Your one-eyes didn't tell you that, woman?" Red Shoes shouted. "Did they tell you how I will treat your mother when I've done with you?"

The man laughed, but Red Shoes smiled savagely, for he heard the anger in the laugh. He had won the right to be tortured.

The sane part of him did not think this a good thing. But he could not let the sane part of him have any say now. To live, he had to let the *Hacho* out, the madman, the shedding snake.

He continued shouting at them as they hauled him out of the pit. He spat on the man in the mask, and the anger felt better and better.

When he saw how the young man had died—tied to a frame and burned in the genitals and face by a hot gun barrel—he laughed again.

"You have a mighty high capacity for amusement," Qwenus observed.

"I'm just laughing at your stupidity. You think to torture me in *that* way? You think I fear *that*?"

"I think you do," the masked man replied, a hint of uncertainty in his voice. Most of the other wild men were staring at Red Shoes as if he were some kind of strange, rabid animal.

"My people have been torturing since the beginning of time," Red Shoes went on. "There has never been a white man who did not beg for his life in the first seconds of torture, calling for his mother—and that with our little children doing the deed. Do you know how many white men I have watched shit themselves before the brand even touched them?"

"We will see how brave you are," the man assured him.

"I will *show* you how brave I am." Red Shoes spat. "I will *show* you how to torture a man! Unless you fear me, a helpless captive surrounded by armed men, you geldings!"

It didn't work. The masked man nodded for him to be tied spread-eagle to the frame. While they did so, Red Shoes continued his tirade, escalated it when the cherry-red gun barrel approached him, held in a large pair of tongs. Behind him, he was dimly aware that his shadow-child had nearly finished its work.

The barrel touched him on the left nipple. In his maddened state he did not register pain, but rather a dull shock that ran up to his scalp. He laughed again, laughed harder at the expressions on the faces around him.

"You see?" he shrieked. "You see? Let me up from here, and I will show you how to torture."

The man with the barrel paused, uncertain. He looked to the leader. The rest of the men watched him uneasily.

"Very well," the masked man said finally. "Let us see what he has to show us. Let him amuse the old gods."

They cut him loose, and he tried not to look at the ugly pucker where the iron had touched him. He whooped some more and began a song, his head light and tingling. The man with the hot iron still stood there, unsure what to do.

"Well? Show us, Indian."

That was when Red Shoes took the rifle barrel in his bare hands. He spun and swung it at Qwenus, imagining that his hands had simply become wood, that the smell was meat burning on a distant fire. He struck the "god" at the juncture of shoulder and neck. The barrel resisted coming away, fused as it was to the man's flesh, but he managed it and swung again, catching another of the blind men who stood in ranks behind their leader. He swung it three more times before his body realized what he had done to it and brought down the night.

He awoke to pain, and a gentle up-and-down motion.

"What?" he muttered. He was cradled in someone's arms.

"Aye! He wakes!" called the person carrying him. Through blurred vision, he made out Tug's face.

Other faces crowded around him. He recognized Fernando and du Rue, closest.

"I've never seen nothin' like that," Tug whispered, "what you did."

"How are you?" Nairne asked.

"Not well," Red Shoes replied.

"The wire on our cage just fell away," Tug continued, enthusiastically. "*Then* we showed 'em. I boosted Fernando out, an' he threw down the rope. None of 'em even noticed, they 'uz too busy watchin' you. Hell, most of 'em didn't even stay for the fight."

"Where are we?"

"Be still," Nairne said. "And the rest of you leave him alone, you hear? He needs rest." He turned back to Red Shoes. "We're almost to the ships. Will you live?"

Red Shoes nodded. It was difficult to move. Now that the madness was gone, he couldn't imagine how he had picked up a hot gun barrel.

He had no intention of looking at his hands. He knew that given time he could heal them, though he guessed it would be months before he could grasp anything with real strength. But at least he was alive.

"Did anyone die?" he asked Fernando, after Nairne and the others fell away a bit.

"Aye. Some seven or eight English."

"Any of them ours?"

"No. Saint-Pierre was shot, but only through the shoulder. He should live."

"Good. Do we have any rum left?"

"No. The crazy Englishmen drank it all."

"I hope Blackbeard gives me some, then. I shall need it very soon."

"If he refuses," Fernando promised, "I will strangle him."

Part Two

SECRET KNOTS

The World is bound by Secret Knots
—Athanasius Kircher,
   The Magnetic Kingdom of Nature

*A Devil is a Spiritual and Rational
Substance . . .*
—Cotton Mather,
   Wonders of the Invisible World, 1693

1.

His skin was a coat of ice, thickening toward his bones. The night was cathedral windows stained only with the pale hues of the moon, mosaics of umbra and uncertain light filtering through the bare branches of the trees. Curiously, those branches knit together tightly enough that he could not make out the actual source of the wan illumination. Ben did not know where he was or how he had gotten there.

Wandering aimlessly at first, now he began to make out vague geometrical shadows amongst the twisted tree trunks. Buildings, he realized with a start, or the remains of them.

He approached the yawning portal of one of the structures, its lintel framed in dead briars, the flagstones, crumbling, barely evident beneath his feet. Inside, it was lighter, the luminescence of alchemical lanthorns coppering the walls. It was like discovering some lost Babylon—one of those cities in the desert that travelers to Arabic lands reported, visible one day, lost again the next, buried here not by sand but by root and branch.

Wandering into a room, he saw his mistake, for amongst the cobwebs and tendrils dangling from the roof, dozens of metallic orbs spun lazily, suspended in air. In the center was one that radiated a dim light—that one was the sun, of course. He named the rest beneath his breath: Mercury, Venus, Earth, Mars—all the planets there, and amongst them, like airborne marbles, the moons and comets.

No antediluvian ruin, this. This was the orrery room at Crane Court in London, where he had become a Newtonian, where once this model of the solar system had been a tool for refining natural law. He gazed about with mingled horror and sadness.

Perhaps in response to that thought, something in the depths of the building stirred and scratched, something whispered his name, and he recalled that more than architecture had died at Crane Court.

He fled outside, recognizing other ruins—the coffeehouse where he had met his first lover, the Tower of London, the dome of Saint Paul's. The Grecian Coffeehouse, where he had met Vasilisa, Maclaurin, Heath, Voltaire.

So it *was* a dream, for it was impossible that any stone of these buildings remained standing. But the terror was no less real, and he ran, beating at branches that grabbed him like bony fingers, murmuring indictments, as if every tree in this endless wood were one person whose death was his responsibility.

He ran, and he was running from Bracewell, he was running from the comet, every flight in his life twisted together, every cowardly motion he had ever made confounded. The faster he ran the denser the trees became.

At last another familiar house appeared, windows bright and inviting. It was his brother's shop, back in Boston. He had run at last back whence he came. His fear gripped him like gravity.

Gritting his teeth, he worked the latch of the door.

There was James, grinning crookedly at him, the rusty stain still on his shirt. James, his brother, dead, beckoning him in.

Of course it was a dream.

"I never meant for it to happen, James," he whispered, sure he was meant to say something. "I never knew he would kill you." But ghosts knew, knew intentions didn't matter so much as results. James' eyes mocked him, and through his brother's features, Ben suddenly saw their father, as in an imperfect looking glass. He shrank back even before James licked his cracked lips and began to speak.

"Among the many reigning Vices of the Town which may at any Time come under my Consideration and Reprehension, there is none which I am more inclin'd to expose than that of *Pride*." James spoke the words glacially, sightless eyes fixed on Ben. His voice was familiar but strange—lacking breadth and character, human quality. And his words struck a sickening discord in Ben. They were familiar, too.

"It is acknowledg'd," James continued, "to be a Vice the most hateful to God and Man. Even those who nourish it in themselves, hate to see it in others."

James, please, Ben tried to say, but his tongue clove to the back of his throat, threatening to choke him. James spoke Ben's own words— from one of the letters Ben had written as "Silence Dogood" for *The New England Courant,* James' paper.

His brother blinked angrily and stood, finger stabbing outward like a pastor's admonishing the congregation, voice rising. "The proud man aspires after Nothing less than an unlimited Superiority over his Fellow-Creatures. He has made himself a King in *Soliloquy;* fancies himself conquering the World; and the Inhabitants thereof consulting on proper Methods to acknowledge his Merit!"

His mocking tone boiled into fury, and Ben stood paralyzed as his brother suddenly lunged forward and slapped him, backhand, on the temple. He staggered against the wall, gagging as the sudden stench of rotting flesh filled his lungs. James stared at him, unchanged, save that the light had gone from his eyes, and with it all anger and passion. Slowly, his brother turned, went back to the press, and began to work. Ben stood there, shivering, for a time, and then he left, weeping dream tears.

Outside, it was now brighter. The trees had opened a space, so that it was as if he stood in a wide amphitheater, the night sky at last naked for him to behold.

The heavens were bright, but not from moon or star. Instead was a brilliance, the apparent size of a fist, smudging a streak of ash all across the sky.

Shivering, he awoke to terrible cold and a jabbing in his ribs.

"Waken, sweetheart," someone roughly cajoled.

Ben squinted his eyes open. He lay on cold stone. Robert towered over him, face pale in the light of a small lanthorn, hard toe of his shoe nudging again into Ben's ribs.

"What in God's name do you want, Robin?" Ben snapped.

"Now there's 'n ungrateful man," Robert observed. "We save him from icy death an' he only complains."

"What?" Ben sat up, rubbing his eyes. Where was he?

It came back to him when he made out the gleam of brass and the chill, fuzzy blobs of stars above.

"Oh." He grunted. "I must have fallen asleep."

"What is this place?" a third voice asked. Ben glanced over to where Peter Frisk curiously examined a telescope.

"Good morning, Captain Frisk," Ben managed, stretching his cold-cramped muscles. "This is the astronomical observatory of the Mathematical Tower."

"I thought I'd begin here before starting with the boudoirs of the young ladies in Kleinseit," Robert explained. "An' a good thing. A girl might've kept you warm enough to live until found, unlike that thing." He gestured at the telescope.

"Aye, and likely you would've become too distracted to carry on searching." He rattled his head a bit. "I couldn't have been asleep more than a few minutes," he continued. "And I would've wakened in a few more."

Robert shrugged. "As y' wish. So the air is thin enough t' see through this night?"

"No. Damned and thrice damned, no." He flung an angry gaze at the stars. Which one was Prague's doom?

"Y'r agitatin' y'rself, Ben," Robert observed.

Ben rubbed his arms. "I'm not just up here from idle curiosity, Robin," he muttered. " 'Tis happening again."

Robert's eyes widened, and his face went sober. "No."

"Yes. The prisoner said so."

"But how?"

Ben snorted. "That's easily done. Stirling and Vasilisa survived. Probably the Frenchmen, too, whoever they were. Fools."

"I don't suppose you two would enlighten me as to what you are talking about?" Frisk put in.

"No offense, Mr. Frisk, but what brings you up here with Robert?"

"Oh. Well—"

"The emperor," Robert interrupted, "decided that you needed another protector, and was well impressed with Captain Frisk."

Ben eyed him, noting his bandaged shoulder. Of course he was grateful to Frisk, but didn't the emperor have any damn sense at all?

Despite having helped them against the Muscovites, Frisk might easily be a spy. He knew that there were few guards or soldiers to spare, but this stretched the boundaries of wit.

Or maybe one of the "old men" had done this to him, hoping that Frisk *was* a murderer of some sort.

"Well, Captain Frisk, it appears that your desire for employ has been fulfilled. What of your injury?"

"It was only a cut upon the flesh, no bones shattered, thanks be to God. And I am quite happy to be your guardian, sir."

"I hope you shall remain happy when I delay explaining to you what Robert and I spoke of, for it will take some time to present to you." He glanced around conspicuously. "Aside from that, doors and walls are fool's paper."

For an instant, Ben thought he saw a blaze of sheer indignation on the Swede's features, but Frisk only nodded and said, "I am at your service, not you at mine."

"Have you told Sir Isaac?" Robert asked.

"No. No, I came right up here . . ." He closed his eyes, seeing again the apparitions of his dream. "I had to *do* something, you see? Talking's no good." He sighed. "But no luck. This is a simple optical telescope. What I have need of is an affinascope, like the one we had at Crane Court."

"Build one."

"I don't know how, and Sir Isaac left the plans in London. I've begged him for the secret, but he won't be bothered with it. It isn't what *interests* him now."

"But sure, wi' this new information—"

"Yes, well, we can hope, but he that lives on hope dies fasting. I will talk to him when he wakes, of course. How far the sunrise?"

"An hour. But Newton has already risen. He sent us out to find you."

"Oh. For what purpose?"

"He wants you to fetch something for him," Robert answered, handing him a scrap of paper.

"What's this?"

"The description of the thing, I suppose. He gave me the address."

"Wonderful." Ben hesitated. "What humor was he in?"

"What do you expect? He thinks you out carousing."

Ben nodded. "And damned if I shouldn't have been. I did no good here."

The ghost of James had hit the mark dead center. He was all about his pride and vanity. The truth was, Prague was better off without his supposed help.

"Let us get this thing," he grunted, "after which I'll buy you both a breakfast pint. Where gang we to, Robin?"

"Judenstadt."

" 's'z it," Robert said.

It was just a house, neither particularly large or small. Ben paused, realizing that he did not yet know exactly what it was he was after. He dug in his pocket and uncrumpled the note Robert had given him.

The Sepher Ha-Razim it said. *A book of cabalistic formulae.* Below, scribbled in an untidy hand, was the name of the same book in Hebrew characters.

Ben rolled his eyes. Another one of *those* books. Prague was one vast storehouse of occult books—he spent half his time lugging tomes from one part of town to another. Early on, most of these had been histories and chronologies of ancient kingdoms, but in the past several months, Newton had shifted his interest to cabalistic texts—most especially the rambling, obtuse *Zohar*. In consequence, Ben was having to learn Hebrew, though his lack of enthusiasm made progress slow.

Stepping up to the door, he rapped smartly on it.

Minutes passed. He knocked again. He was just coming to the unpleasant conclusion that the tenant was either not home or soundly asleep—something Newton would not be pleased at all to hear—when the door squeaked ajar.

Methuselah himself peered out at them. His eyes were almost buried in crinkled hollows, below which sharp cheekbones threatened to cut through the translucent parchment of skin stretched over them. A beard clung like some albino, alpine moss to the fissures of his lower face, depending stringily to his little round belly. Wispy hair protruded likewise from beneath a small black cap, and a blue vein stood out like a ridge on his forehead. Ben was unable to tell if the man's frown was one of puzzlement or irritation—or if in fact it was a frown at all, and not the natural creases of his face.

"It is early," said Methuselah, his voice quavering. "I was finishing my prayers."

"I beg your pardon, mister—" Ben stopped, realizing that he did not know the fellow's name. Hiding his embarrassment, he started again. "My name is Benjamin Franklin, a pupil of Sir Isaac Newton's. My master sent me—"

"I know who you are."

Ben stopped in surprise. "My master sent word ahead?"

"No. There are tales of you, Herr Zauberlehrling. You are the boy who wears the Garment of Adam."

Ben blinked. "I don't understand you, sir."

Methuselah sighed heavily. "What have you come for?"

Ben brightened. "Then you *have* had word."

The beard wagged back and forth. "No again. Young Christian boys do not venture into Judenstadt to pester old men unless they have been sent for something."

"I see. Well, it is here . . ." He handed the paper to the old man, but the fellow made no move to take it.

"I haven't my glasses on. Read it to me."

"Um—*The Sepher Ha-Razim*. A book."

Methuselah regarded him for a long moment, an enigmatic little smile on his face. The speechless gaze stretched so long that Ben wondered if he was going to answer. Uncomfortable with the silence, he asked, "I am embarrassed to say that I don't know whom I am addressing, sir."

"I never for an instant thought you did," the man replied. "I am Rabbi Isaac ben Yeshua." He pursed his lips. "I have no manners. Come in."

"Now, sir, about the book."

"Indeed. I have such a book, young sir, but I wonder what your master Newton would want with it."

"What do you mean?"

"Well, I have read his work—or some of it, you see. I am an alchemist of sorts myself. This book is a silly thing, doubtless of no use to him."

Ben shrugged. "I have long since ceased trying to guess what will interest my master. But I know that he has great regard and respect for the work of the Jewish sages. He believes that knowledge was most perfect among the ancient prophets."

The rabbi looked a bit surprised. "This is so?"

"I assure you."

Rabbi ben Yeshua nodded thoughtfully. "I still wonder if it would be wise for him to have this book. It is not a book for just anyone, I fear, but only for those who have long meditated upon the Talmud and perhaps the Zohar."

"I know him to have read both of those."

"I did not say read," the rabbi emphasized. "I said *meditate*."

Ben sighed. "Sir, had I my way, I would take your opinion. However, my master wants the book."

"He may go wanting. I am not certain I can easily lay hands upon it."

"Sir, I plead with you to discover it. My master's request carries the weight of the emperor."

"Request. I see. Request." He frowned at the floor and then shrugged. "Very well. Wait for me here."

He was gone a long while, which gave Ben ample time to congratulate himself on his acumen.

After a few more moments still, he began to worry—perhaps the rabbi had slipped out by some secret way—but then the old man returned, grunting with the weight of a massive tome beneath one arm. He handed it over to Ben only reluctantly.

"That is the book, yes?" Rabbi ben Yeshua asked.

Ben turned to the title page. It was, of course, in Hebrew. There on the far right was the first letter, *samekh*, which was like "s," and that next one was *pe*, and then *resh*. No vowels, of course, but the word was probably *Sepher*. He could look at the paper again, but if he did that—or spent any longer trying to puzzle it from memory—he would only be admitting his ignorance to the old man.

No point in seeming ignorant. Ben smiled, passing the cumbersome volume to Robert, and held out his hand to the rabbi. "I thank you, sir, and my master thanks you."

"You will return it?"

"Of course, sir." He turned to go, and then turned back curiously. "What did you mean, that I had been seen in the 'Garment of Adam'?"

The rabbi lifted a bony finger. "When Adam was cast out from the garden, God gave him special garments that rendered him invisible and untouchable."

"Oh. You mean the aegis."

"Call it what you will. It is a stolen thing, not meant for you."

"Stolen? I made it with my own hands."

"You made it with knowledge, and knowledge can most assuredly be stolen." His gaze seemed to rest on the book in Robert's arms as he said this.

"Surely knowledge is meant to be discovered," Ben countered. "Surely God is pleased that we come to understand his world, the better to appreciate it."

The rabbi grinned. "Do you know who last mishandled the Garment of Adam?"

"No, sir."

"From Adam they passed through the generations, finally coming to Nimrod. Nimrod used the garment to make himself worshipped as a god, to raise up a tower against heaven. He was punished for it. Good day."

"A nice bite y' gave 'im," Robert commented, as they settled down at a table in the Three Little Bears.

Ben thumped the book. "Whatever else Sir Isaac may say of me, he shall never say I failed in an errand."

"It is a mystical book?" Frisk asked curiously.

"I suppose. I don't know what *Sepher Ha-Razim* means exactly. *Sepher* means 'book,' I think." He opened the volume and flipped through it, hoping to find an illustration or two to give him some clue to the tome's nature. He saw a number of what seemed to be lists and possibly incantations, but no illustrations.

"Your pardon, Herr Franklin—"

"Please," Ben said, "I own no title, nor desire none. It's just plain 'Ben.' "

"Ben here has a theory that the age of kings and lords is nearly over," Robert explained.

Frisk's eyes widened. "And how is that? If people are not to be governed by their kings, then by whom?"

"Why, by themselves, I should say."

"You think that common folk are suited to govern themselves? I'm a soldier, and I say a soldier is worthless without a general."

"A good example. How many of these court popinjays do you think knows as much of war as you?"

"Prince Eugène is a great soldier."

"Name another."

"Well, you have the advantage of me, Mr. Franklin. I am not yet well acquainted with this court."

"Yes but—" Ben sighed. "There were able men in the days of the Bible, you agree? And yet you don't find them going by 'the right honorable Moses, esquire, marquis of the desert', do you? Or 'Adam, the duke of Eden.' They just went by name, for their *deeds* were their fame. If men were titled only by their merit, Prince Eugène would still be a great man. It's not his sort I begrudge, but those human slugs who have no talent or use, yet I must *bow* to them."

Frisk was frowning deeply. "But there are kings in the Bible, called as such. King David. King Solomon—"

"Whose position and fame rested equally on the backs of birth and accomplishment. Ah, our beer."

He lifted the mug up. "To such as us, gentlemen, who are the future of the world."

Frisk hesitated an instant, shrugged, and raised the glass in toast. He did not, however, drink. "In any event," he said, "our debate has interrupted my question. If you cannot read the Mosaic script, how certain are you that you got the right book?"

"Well, I can read a bit. And I have this . . ." He fumbled out the slip of paper with the name of the book scrawled in Newton's sloppy Hebrew.

"You see," Ben began, and then stopped abruptly. He had read the first word correctly enough—*Sepher*. But with a deep sinking in his chest he knew that last word was not *Razim*.

He had been given the wrong book.

2

The Monochord

For Adrienne, the next two days were uneventful, though there was a considerable bustle all around her as servants and soldiers prepared for the long march east. They got news that the Muscovite camps were still more than twenty miles away and stationary. Less dependable sources spoke of pitched battles near Paris, and d'Argenson speculated that the Russians were delaying their siege of Nancy to reinforce the more important thrust toward the French capital.

"Why not aid the French defense?" Adrienne asked d'Argenson, as they picked their way amongst the vine-fettered statues of a neglected garden.

D'Argenson grinned a bit ruefully and brushed back his thin brown hair. "Paris will fall, if not to armies, from within. You can only fight so many wars and build so many grand chateaux on the bellies of the poor before they go mad, like starved dogs. The king, begging your pardon, never really understood that."

He rubbed his chin. "We cannot even hold Lorraine, with only twice a thousand men. With that number and some good fortune, we *might* reach Prague. Myself, I would rather march down to Tuscany, for I hear that even a man with a small army can make much of himself there. But the duke—well, he dreams of the Holy Roman Empire. He fancies himself an emperor one day, I think."

"He has some claim?"

"No. But Emperor Karl has two young daughters, and he has had them named his heirs, since he has no sons."

"I see. And his men will follow him, this young duke?"

D'Argenson pulled at the facings of his burgundy coat and nodded thoughtfully. "Those with weak loyalties are long gone. Those remaining believe that the old days will return, and throw their lot with one who might be emperor."

"I take it you disagree with such sentiments."

D'Argenson leaned against the marble column of a small pavilion and folded his arms. "Know you something of history? How in the dark days after the fall of Rome, barbarians ruled? How from them came a few strong men, like Carolus Magnus, who founded empires and brought order?"

"Yes, of course."

D'Argenson smiled. "The kings of today make fine lineages for themselves, don't they? Pretending that their ancestors were once Roman senators or Trojans or what have you. And yet the discerning student of history can see that even the great Charlemagne was really just the strongest and ablest of the barbarians, of as mean a birth as anyone. That is, I believe, our sort of epoch. Rome is falling. History is killing old, diluted lines to make way for younger, cleaner blood."

Adrienne eyed him doubtfully. "Do you fancy your blood clean, Hercule d'Argenson?"

"Me? Bah! What need have I of an empire, of enemies on every front, of sons squabbling over my gains and shredding them in the process? As I said, Mademoiselle, I have read altogether too much history."

"What then?"

"Oh—enough to eat, and good food rather than slop. Entertainments that divert and surprise me. Able companions to make my days and nights memorable." His eyes sparkled devilishly at her, and she found that there was a certain charm to his broken nose, if not beauty.

"Even those things require a modicum of affluence," Adrienne remarked.

"Indeed. I never said I wanted *nothing*, Mademoiselle, nor to live contemptibly like a monk. No, I am content to watch for those who might be king, to wait my chance, to serve them, and then ask my reward. Nothing extravagant—a small duchy, an estate in the country."

"So you think the duke might be emperor after all."

"He will at least take me nearer those who might be. And I have little better to do." He shrugged. "Francis has the makings of a good king, I think, and it will be some few years before all credit of noble blood is bankrupted." He smirked again. "As to my pleasures and companions, I take them where and when I may. I will not forfeit the living of my life until it is secure."

"I am sure you will not, Monsieur," Adrienne answered, reflecting that once such a bold remark would have brought a blush. No longer; the virgin hue was long gone from her cheeks. "I was wondering . . ."

"Yes?" He arched his brows.

"Wondering if there is any good I might do in these preparations."

"But of course! You could ease the suffering of one who labors mightily in that cause."

She smiled primly. "I had rather thought to be of some use in packing necessities."

D'Argenson heaved an extravagant sigh. "It seems I will have no surcease from my sorrows."

"I am sure consolation awaits you within these walls," Adrienne said dryly, "for there are maids and cooks aplenty. If I can be of some other use . . ."

"As a matter of fact, you can be," d'Argenson said, more seriously. "The duke has a library of some size. He wishes certain volumes selected to travel with us. I am aware that you were schooled at Saint Cyr—"

"I would be glad to do that," Adrienne assured him. "Could you show me the way?"

"Now?"

"If you please."

"Other things would please me better"—he leered playfully—"but it shall be, as in all things, as you wish."

"You are a gentleman, sir."

"And see how you repay my kindness with an indictment! Ah, well, such is life and such are women."

They retraced their steps through the ruined garden to the manse, and both were silent.

"And your son?" he ventured. "How is he taking to life out of the rain?"

"Well enough. It is all confusing for him, I think."

"I have not heard him speak," d'Argenson said. "He is a quiet little fellow."

"He has not yet spoken," Adrienne replied.

"Not yet? My girl was babbling at his age."

"You've a child?"

He raised his hands helplessly. "I pray I do. God willing I will see her again someday. Another reason I would prefer Tuscany, for her mother is a Florentine. She should be thirteen, this year."

"And she spoke at just over a year?"

"It is the usual time, I think. But children differ."

Adrienne nodded, a bit disturbed. She had assumed it only natural that Nicolas had not formed words. He seemed too young for it. But what did *she* know about raising children? Only what she had learned by experimenting thus far. She resolved to have a long conversation with the nurse. Or perhaps it would be best for Nico if she . . .

No. Nico was her child, no one else's. She had learned calculus and optics. She would learn this, too.

The library occupied a large and windowless room on the second story, but it was cheerfully illuminated by an alchemical lanthorn which—considering the rarity of such devices these days—told her this was a library that saw some use. It was an extensive one, too, and she noted that many of the volumes were well worn. This was no nobleman's "show" library of immaculate and unread volumes. Someone had treasured this room.

"How many books and what sort?" she asked.

"The duke has esoteric tastes. Begin with the scientific and occult volumes. We should not carry more than half again a hundred, I should think, so be selective. Do you know enough of such matters to be selective?"

"Yes," Adrienne replied, tasting a secret irony, "I believe that I do."

"Well, then, I shall leave you to it. I will send a servant later to package them."

Adrienne nodded distractedly as she perused the spines, savoring a quickening that she had not known in years. They were here, her old loves.

There was the *Horologium Oscillatorium* and *Cosmotheoros* of Christiaan Huygens; the *Arithemetica Infinitorum, La Geometrie, De Analysi*—books she had secretly devoured as a little girl at Saint Cyr. And there, too, were the texts from her older years, chief among them works of Isaac Newton, including the *Principia Mathematica*, its binding still new and unmarred. In less than half an hour, she took down thirty books of science, opened them to their title pages, remembered. Remembered an earlier woman with her name and face.

That younger Adrienne had devoted her whole life to the love of unmasking the subtle harmonies of God and Nature. Her ambition had been to continue such studies for the length of her life, and yet even as a girl she understood the absurd constraints inhering to the female sex that must be overcome to do so. Other women, in the past, had risen beyond their circumscribed roles of wife and mother—some boldly, like Ninon de Lenclos—others in secret.

Of those two ways, she had timidly chosen the second, or perhaps, looking back, it had been chosen *for* her. Chosen that day when one of her teachers at Saint Cyr found her puzzling at an algebra problem and had slipped her—with index finger pressed tight to her lips—a book on the subject. Nourishing her with secret knowledge, that teacher in time brought her to the attention of the Korai.

How long the Korai had existed, none could say, though they claimed since antiquity. A secret cabal, all female, they abetted one another in the quest for knowledge. They were her friends, her secret mothers and sisters, her peers and judges. They discussed things scientific, published books and treatises under the names of men, and thought themselves clever. With them, Adrienne had been happy.

And then, one day, they vanished. Her old friend, the teacher, would not speak to her, the letters in cipher ceased arriving; her own letters—first quizzical and then pleading—returned unanswered. At the age of seventeen, she was alone in a way that she had never been.

In that state she was taken to court at wondrous and terrible Versailles.

While the girls at Saint Cyr were discouraged from studying mathematics and science, they were well educated in other things, and the greatest prize that a Black—a girl in the senior class—could hope for was to be selected by the queen, Madame de Maintenon, to be her secretary. In the midst of her despondency, Adrienne was dully surprised to find herself selected.

Without the Korai, Maintenon became her friend, her confidante, nearly her mother. But Maintenon was a devout, even puritanical woman. For her, science was a distraction from salvation; the only purpose for educating a woman was to make her a better Christian, wife, and mother. Adrienne could not tell Maintenon of the Korai or speak to her of her interests. Instead, she lived as Maintenon did, defending herself from the debauchery of the court with virtue and faith. But in her heart she could not give up her first love, science. When the queen died, she was again alone, confused, wishing for one thing but now hampered by the cumbersome morality of Madame de Maintenon.

Gazing at the pages of mathematical symbols, she cursed that younger Adrienne, who could have been everything she wanted. She could have become the mistress of some wealthy, married man who would support her and not care how she spent her private time. She could have spurned convention and simply done as she pleased, the way the great Ninon did. Instead, she had merely dug herself a grave and dragged half the world into it with her. It was her timidity that had brought a comet to bruise the Earth, which had murdered Nicolas, Torcy, the king. . . .

She tightened her lips. Enough of that.

Cohabiting with the scientific books were a number of more dubious titles. For instance, *De Occulta Philosophia* and *Natural Magick*—prescientific compendiums of nonsense that she would hardly place beside the *Principia*—nevertheless seemed to her to have seen much use, and d'Argenson had been specific in his mention of the occult. Better was Robert Fludd's *History of the Macrocosm and Microcosm*, which contained some good—though somewhat naïve—work on the harmonic affinity. She shuffled through its pages, musing at the quaint diagrams. One she remembered fondly, for she had first seen it at the age of ten, and by it she had begun to understand the harmonic relationships of the universe.

It depicted a sort of cosmic violin, a monochord, its scrolled head high above heaven, single string descending through the realms of angels, planets, elements, and finally to Earth. Two octaves were marked along its length, demonstrating that the ratios between the spheres were the same as those between the notes of the musical scale. It was simplistic, but for a young girl already acquainted with music it had been a revelation, an analogical doorway to the science of affinity.

Now, however, something bothered her about the picture. She looked it over again, reading each Latin inscription, searching for the cause of her disquiet.

And then, suddenly, she saw it. At the head of the "violin" was a tuning key, by which the cosmic wire might be tightened or loosened. Grasping the key was a hand reaching out from a cloud. The hand of God, of course, the master tuner of the cosmic instrument. But it was not God that it reminded her of.

Instead she stared at her own hand, remembering the sensation when she had touched Crecy, a sensation that had been somehow familiar. Now she realized it had been like grasping a vibrating wire, as if it were *her* hand on the cosmic monochord.

Still gazing at the drawing, she no longer saw it. Instead she saw an equation, the one from her dream, which had somehow made her hand from nothingness.

They were harmonic equations.

Her skin creeping as with fever, she stumbled about the room. Searching a small desk she found ink and quill, but no paper, though she emptied its drawers onto the floor. She pushed books this way and that, searching for some hidden scrap of vellum, *anything* to write upon, and in her desperation noticed a book—*Femmes Illustres*, a romance by Scudéry. Smiling grimly, she opened it, tore out pages which had space on them, and began to write. When she ran out of room, she found another useless book—*Polexandre*—and cannibalized it, too. And all the while her heart beat faster, like notes rising on a scale; and it was passion, like the time she and Nicolas had loved, like a wonderful symphony, and at times she wept, remembering how it felt to *see*, to discover, to understand.

The servant came in and Adrienne nearly shouted her away. The nurse came later, asking if she wanted to see her son, but she dismissed her, too. The window darkened with night, and at last a knock came on the door she had finally closed against intruders.

Rubbing her eyes, she answered it. It was d'Argenson.

"You are beginning to frighten the servants," he said, peering around her.

"My apologies. I became quite absorbed, I fear."

"Ah. I had not thought that choosing a few books would present such complications, but then I know little of science. If it is too onerous a task . . ."

"No, it was nothing of that nature," Adrienne replied. "I merely had a thought on one of the books and wished to write it down while it was still clear."

"A scientifical thought?" he asked, seeming surprised but not shocked.

"Indeed." She paused only for the barest instant, and then she did what she should have done in a different age. "It is an interest of mine, science."

"Really?" d'Argenson replied. "I've never been able to comprehend much of it myself. I stand in awe of you if you understand but a hundredth of what these books contain." He tilted his head. "In any case, I hope my interruption has done no permanent damage to the cause of science, but I had good reason. The demoiselle Crecy has asked for you."

"Veronique? Awake?"

"Even so, I am delighted to say."

"Well," Adrienne said. "I thank you very much for the news." He hadn't even blinked at her announcement. It did not upset him, her interest, even when laid plainly at his feet. On impulse, she leaned up and kissed the blunted point of his nose, and was rewarded by his furious blush.

"My lady!" he choked, after a heartbeat or so. "To what does my nose owe this honor?"

She turned to gather her papers and cap the ink. "Perhaps I will tell you, someday. For now, just know I thank you."

"You are much welcome, and my nose thanks you. Almost, you rendered it straight again. If you ever feel the desire to perform a similar service in other anatomical—"

"Hush," Adrienne said. "Do not make me regret myself."

He smiled, somehow boyishly despite his very unchildlike face. "Never would I that," he replied, bowed, and gracefully retreated from the room.

A moment later she followed, winding through the dark passages of the house until she found Crecy's sickroom. As promised, the redhead was awake, head propped on a pillow.

"Hello," she said, sounding stronger than she looked.

"I'm glad to see you improved, Veronique. I was worried about you."

"Were you?" Crecy said.

"I am happy to see you wakeful. You know our situation?"

"Roughly. D'Argenson explained much to me. A good man, a friend of Nicolas."

"Veronique . . ."

"Yes?"

Adrienne knelt at her side and found her hand. It was warm and gripped hers feebly when she took it with her left hand, not her strange right one.

"Veronique, I love you. You and I, we have survived much together. I do not know your heart—I don't think I will ever know it—but I tell you plainly that I love you."

"Thank you. It is good to hear that, stepping back from the grave." Her lips almost seemed to tremble.

"I love you," Adrienne went on, "and yet I know you have lied to me about some things and obscured others. The time has come for an end to that, Veronique."

"I understand."

Adrienne blinked. "That easily."

"That easily. I have set myself as your protector and yet I have failed you. I may die, I am told, when we begin to move east, for my wounds may mislike the treatment of cart wheels. Once I thought to protect you by withholding, but now . . ." She closed her eyes. "Now I must trust *you*."

"Trust me? Trust me how?"

"To be strong. To go forward." She coughed. "I hardly know where to begin."

"Then let me suggest a place," Adrienne replied. "Tell me how it is that I have the hand of an angel attached to my wrist."

3.

Thief

Ben grunted and swore as his hand slipped on the ornate cornice, desperately shutting his eyes as the world stirred itself into a kaleidoscopic vortex. Wearing the aegis at its highest calibration was worse than being blind. Even with his lids squeezed closed, prismatic annuli painted themselves in the hollows of his skull.

By feel he renewed his hold on the ledge, hoping no one had heard his feet thrash against the wall. It was not likely that anyone would see him—with the aegis at this pitch he would appear as only a faint ripple in the air—but if he made too much noise they might guess he was there.

The drawback being that, as the world was blind to him, he was nearly blind to the world.

Finally hauling himself onto the ledge, he drew deep, deliberate breaths and forced his eyes open again. Prague reappeared, a silhouette etched black upon an iridescent background. It was as if he himself were a prism, splitting light with his nose.

Once again, he wondered just what the hell he was doing breaking into a man's house. Oh, he had convinced himself he had good reasons. Sir Isaac would be angry if he failed to bring the book. More important, if Newton was not mad, *The Sepher Ha-Razim* could be crucial to saving Prague.

But, sitting on the ledge, fingers on the frame of the open window, he understood that that explained only why he had come back for the book, not why he had given Robert and Frisk the slip, waited until he saw ben Yeshua leave, and then essayed this crazy ascent.

No, the truth was, it would have been humiliating to have to face the rabbi again, to admit that he had been tricked, to beg for the right book.

Pride again. Pride that hadn't let him check the book against the paper, pride now. Well, by God, he had learned his lesson this time. Josiah Franklin had not raised a complete fool!

But since he had already made the climb, he reasoned, he might as well peek in the window.

Below, the street was alive with conversation, laughter, vendors hawking in languages familiar and strange. Bread was baking somewhere, infusing the air with yeasty perfume, and his stomach testily reminded him that he had eaten no supper nor breakfast save a few sips of beer—and now it must be near noon.

Sighing, he studied the room like a drunk, trying to sort sense into things that ought to be familiar but weren't. That large thing might be a bed, he supposed, and that other a desk. Nothing seemed to be moving. Nothing seemed to be in front of the window. To be sure, he felt with his hands until they encountered the floor.

He wondered how long the rabbi would be gone. After all, it wouldn't hurt to take a brief look around. The fellow had said he would loan them the book— If he happened to run across the *Sepher*, taking it would not be theft, but merely the collection of a promise.

Satisfied at this reasoning, he eased in over the sill as quietly as he could, listening, straining, holding his breath, though the only sounds seemed to be from the street. Warily, he removed the aegis key from his waistcoat pocket, blinking at the sudden burst of white as the rainbow folded in on itself.

It was, as he had suspected, a bedroom, ascetically furnished. A door leading beyond stood an inch or so open.

Gingerly, wincing at each creak in the boards beneath him, he padded to the door and peered through. Outside were a staircase and two more doors. Relaxing slightly at the continued lack of noise, he eased out of the bedroom and chose the left-hand door, remembering that ben Yeshua had come upstairs when he went to fetch the counterfeit *Sepher*.

The second door revealed a library, and Ben's heart whirled in ellipse—first the aphelion of finding it so quickly, to a low perihelion when he realized that there must be nearly a thousand volumes in it, most in Hebrew. Cursing under his breath, he quietly shut the door and made his way to the voluminous shelves, skirting a table of alchemical apparatus—beakers, mortar and pestle, what seemed to be a barometer—wondering pessimistically how long it would take to get through the books. Sighing, he began on the left-hand side of the room, scanning for the books beginning with the Hebrew "s." He found one, compared the title against Newton's scrawled Hebrew, and moved on.

A clock ticking against the wall marked his time for an hour, and no *Sepher Ha-Razim*. He had moved through only a fraction of the library, and a growing suspicion told him that it was no use, anyway. What would he, Benjamin Franklin, do if strangers came demanding a thing he did not wish to give up? He would hide it, of course, and when the strangers came back for it, he would claim to never have owned it. With an imperial order they might search his shelves anyway—and not find it, leaving them no choice but to believe his lie.

Why hadn't the old man lied about owning it in the first place? But he probably presumed that it was his right to refuse loaning out his own property. Ben sympathized—a man's things ought to be his own—but his greater concerns overwrote that. Besides, the fellow should have dealt honestly with him.

He turned away from the shelves, thinking now of hiding places. Did the rabbi have some clever strongbox about, some secret cabinet? He checked in the desk, beneath the rug, found nothing. He moved from room to room, confident now that no one was home, peeking into cupboards, boxes, on top of things, to no avail.

Retracing his steps through the house—wondering again how long the fellow would be gone—something in the kitchen caught his attention. Dirt—gritty, black soil—was scattered here and there on the polished wood floor. It was the first trace of grime of any kind he had seen in the otherwise immaculate dwelling.

On closer inspection it revealed itself as a faint trail, leading into the pantry. He had already searched the small storeroom, but now he did so with a new eye, and so noticed a small brass hook at the back of it. He twisted it between thumb and index finger, and with a click and a sigh, the back of the larder swung away from him into darkness.

The pitchy blackness seemed to frighten the candle flame, so did it quiver. He mused that it had been long since he had touched a candle—though he had once made the wretched things as his father's 'prentice. For a while they had been all but obsolete, but magical lanthorns were becoming less common these days. Most of them had been crafted in England and Holland, and both of those countries had other than strictly mercantile concerns at the moment. In any event, the candle did not show him much, only walls of sweating stone. His nose told him more, as the air smelled not only of grit, but of sulfur and ammoniac, the acrid scents of alchemy.

The stairs ended at a dirt floor, and there the candle flame ceased its anxious wavering and stood bolder and brighter. He saw that he stood in a sort of cyst, a more or less domed structure some thirty feet in breadth, squatting claustrophobically low upon him. What had this place been?

What it was *now* was clear enough. On a large stone table, curling Italian glass, porcelain beakers, a lamp of antique and Arabian figure winked his candlelight back at him. Moving carefully, he lit the lamp.

In the brighter light, he noted two things immediately, chills crawling up his spine. The first was that the table was no table, but the stone lid of a sarcophagus. The other was that a handbreadth from the lamp lay a single slim book, no thicker than the width of his thumbnail. On its cover in faded gold leaf he read *Sepher Ha-Razim*.

"There you are, my sweet," he breathed, lifting it with both hands, marveling at the trouble he had gone through for such a tiny book. Isaac ben Yeshua must have had a good laugh, he thought, at Ben lugging off the cumbersome decoy.

And now, away from here, he thought. Out of this tomb, this house, this strange quarter of the city.

As a precaution, he activated the aegis on its lower setting, and that was when he saw something troubling.

In the first glimpse, from the rim of his vision, he thought it some peculiar reflection of himself, some shadow-image limned in diffracted light. That was until it lurched toward him.

The motion caught into him as if a spider suddenly sat on his lip. It was so absurd and horrible at the same time that he simply froze in incomprehension as it approached, a soundless apparition without face or sex. Only when it spread fingers like a fine film of oil upon dark water toward him did he react, and then too late, as the spectral digits brushed through his chest to his heart. A sheet of white flame wreathed suddenly around him, accompanied by a somehow inappropriate crackle, and for just an instant he felt tongs close on his heart and a terrible pain, as if a horse had stepped on his breastbone. A hideous scream filled the low chamber, so unnatural and high that it was only afterward that he recognized it as his own, and then the lightning and its puny thunder redoubled, this time flinging him against the wall and sending the phantasm hurtling another way, blue fire dancing upon it.

The next thing he knew, he was at the head of the stairs, his lungs laboring and sharp pains in his shins as if he had climbed the treads by the sole use of those bones. The book, he noticed dimly, was still clutched in one hand. Groaning in terror, he slammed shut the false cupboard and made for the front door, any intention he might ever have had of exiting stealthily dismissed. It was like his dream of the night before—running, just an animal running to save its life. Except that his dream had seemed more real than this.

When he burst into the street a dozen heads turned his way, but he did not wait to see their puzzled looks, their fear, their anger. The sunlight, the normal look of the street sickened him almost physically, for it all seemed a lie, a bright, cheerful painting on a rotten canvas. Science, the paint. The thing that followed him, the canvas. Painted his life, his beating heart—death was the reality, and it was coming behind him. He could feel it.

At the corner he turned and looked back, and was sure he saw it emerge from the house, a colorful blur.

His legs turned to stone before he reached the Charles Bridge, but they worked on regardless. The bright edge of his panic had blunted a bit, though he sickened whenever he noticed the thumping of his heart, now regular if accelerated, for he could only remember how it felt when it could not draw blood, gasped for blood as a blow to the belly made one gasp for breath.

He had nearly died. He still might.

But countless glances over his shoulder as he huffed across the bridge revealed no demon following him.

It had reached through the aegis—not without consequence to itself, it seemed—but it had breached it. If it found him again . . .

He set his mouth grimly and clutched the stolen book more tightly under his arm. Newton *would* talk to him now.

"You say it *touched* you?" Sir Isaac asked, his eyes full of something that—in another man—might be mistaken for love.

"It touched my heart," Ben said, "my actual heart."

"And did you— Did it seem composed of a fiery substance or some subtle vapor?" He paced the length of his sitting room, hands clasped behind his back.

Ben blinked. "It seemed composed of nothing at all," he whispered. "It seemed an angel of death."

"Yes, but what predominate nature did it evince? What element embodied?"

"I had scant time to perform experimentation upon it," Ben answered. "Sir, it might have followed me here."

"And you believe it was guarding the book?" He held aloft *The Sepher Ha-Razim*.

"Or haunting the tomb, or—I don't know. I first saw it when I wore the aegis. Otherwise it was not visible. For all I know, it was aggravated by the sympathies of the device."

"No," Newton said. "It was guarding the book."

"Are you—" Ben took a breath to keep from sputtering. "Are you saying that you knew this thing would appear when I took the book?"

"I did not send you to *steal* the book, Benjamin, but to borrow it. You know that theft deserves its punishments."

"He would not loan it. Should I return it to him?"

Newton hesitated an instant, his dark eyes flickering to the book and back.

"Soon," he replied.

"Soon. Then you as good as stole it yourself, sir, and you should not upbraid me for a crime you share in."

"I would not that you stole it," Newton insisted. "I never hinted that you should. And yet the damage is done—and I have need of this book. But in the future I will not have you sin for me, do you understand? Do what I ask, but keep the commandments." He fingered the gold lettering. "I did not know I sent you into danger, Benjamin. You must not think that. And though you may have applied perhaps too much enthusiasm to your task, I appreciate your efforts."

"Well—thank you. But, Sir Isaac, I have more to tell you. After our audience yestereve, the prince of Savoy approached me."

"Death from the sky?" Newton paraphrased.

"Yes. He sent you word?"

"When you vanished, yes."

"I was in the observatory."

Newton nodded understanding. "A pointless gesture. How would you have known it if you saw it?"

"Then you think as I do? That the Muscovites have summoned another comet?"

"It seems reasonable. They have had the time, and likely the knowledge."

"How will we stop them?"

Newton paced a few steps, clutching the book in front of him, brows drawn tight. "In some few days I will tell you. Until then, keep a cool head."

"What if we have not so much time?"

"We do."

"How can you know that, sir?"

"I know. In fact, I assure you that we have, at the very least, a month and perhaps many more weeks than that."

"Sir, if you could but tell me how you know this, it would much set my mind at ease."

"The ease of your mind, Benjamin, is not my paramount concern. Your place is to trust my word, for now. When my new system is finished, I promise to disclose all to you. In the meantime, be calm. You and I shall have ample warning before any cosmic object strikes

Prague. Until we must, I am loath to leave this place, for it is perfect for my present purposes—"

"Leave?" Ben interrupted. "What do you mean, leave? I thought your system would protect Prague."

"Well, that it may, if I have time to perfect it to that degree, and if we have time to implement. If not, we shall have to go elsewhere."

"No. No, I do not agree to that, sir. Already London is destroyed, and look what the vapors and atmosphere of the comet have wrought upon the Earth in general. We cannot stand passive and allow another such bombardment!"

Newton regarded him levelly. "My methods are as yet unready. They are not perfected. Until such time as they are, they are of no use."

"Then let me help you! Let me edit your notes or experiment, or—"

"You have just been of immense help to me, and I have said it. How much compliment do you crave?"

"I crave no compliment!" He was aware that his voice was rising. "I want only to save Prague!"

Newton drew a deep breath, favored Ben with a steely glance, and then strode purposefully toward his study.

"I am finished with you for the day. The emperor's boatwright has a few questions for you. I suggest you go answer them. Good day, Mr. Franklin."

Ben's protest was stifled by the slamming of the door.

Halfway to his own rooms he realized that he was crying. It felt as if something were quaking inside him that would soon shake him apart, an awful thing that had no name. He hated it, resented it, for it was weakness, childishness. He quickened his step, determined that no one would see him in such a state.

Once in his room he hastily shut the door and staggered to his bed, nearly blinded by tears, where finally he sobbed aloud; once begun his eyes seemed as loath to stop as the clouds above Noah's ark. But in time stop they did, leaving behind a sort of watery warmth in his chest. Laconically, he wiped his eyes and nose and set about wondering what to do next, and it was then, lifting his gaze, that he realized the little maid was in the room, sitting quietly on a stool in the corner.

"You!" he said. "Why didn't you make yourself known?"

"I didn't want to disturb you."

"No, you would rather watch the great apprentice bawling like a child, so that you might spread the report. Well, go about it! What does it matter anyway?"

"Why would I do such a contemptible thing?" she asked.

Ben wiped his eyes again. "Do not pretend you have any love for me," he muttered. "You made your feelings clear."

"Did I? Of course I admit I have no love for you, for I do not know you—"

"Oh, but you seemed to know me well," Ben snapped. " 'I have heard about you,' you said. 'They speak of you,' you said."

"Well, then, tell me I was wrong," she demanded, digging her fists into her hips. "Tell me that you were not after me to lie with you, and then thank you for the privilege of being your whore for a night. Tell me— I'll take your word."

"Do not flatter yourself," Ben returned. "I have beauties in Kleinseit enough to accommodate me, and you, if you pardon me, do not measure well against any of them."

She colored just a bit at that. "Yet still you do not deny. So you thought me ugly, and no great conquest, and perhaps all the easier for that. Deny it."

Ben opened his mouth, but in her set expression—or perhaps beyond it—he saw himself, parading about in nothing more than a shirt, whispering sly insinuations. This woman saw him, not as he wanted to be seen—not as most of his conquests saw him—but as he was. It was intolerable.

"I do not deny," he finally said. "I would have seduced you. But that isn't . . ."

"Isn't what?"

Ben reached to massage his brow. "I need something from you, something I thought to seduce from you."

"What have I that you may not obtain without me, save my virtue?"

"Your keys. The key to Sir Isaac's private rooms."

She stared at him. "What? You are his 'prentice. What possible cause have you to spy on him?"

"He withholds something of grave importance to me."

"I see. Well, if there is nothing else . . ." She turned to go.

"No, please—wait," Ben pleaded. "I am sorry I mistook you the other day. I was indecorous, and I apologize. But I really do need your help."

"Sir, you ask me to risk my life, and in all honesty you have not moved me to do that. If you wish to explain why this should interest me . . ."

Ben shook his head. "You do not have the sound of a chambermaid. Whence come you? What is your *name*?"

She sighed. "Good day."

"No—wait again. I would tell you, but I cannot."

"Ah. Thus he will not trust you, and you will not trust me, and so all secrets stay in their boxes. Perhaps 'tis best, given the example of Pandora."

Ben closed his eyes. "Stay, then. Stay." He sighed and sat back upon the bed. "A doom is coming to Prague. My master claims that he may have some knowledge to arrest it, but he will not tell me of it, and I cannot judge without seeing his notes."

"Doom?" She faltered slightly. "But what good can you do if your master cannot?"

"Come here. Come close."

She hesitated, but came to him.

"Closer. Lean down." He rolled his eyes at her skeptical expression. "I will not bite you. Come near."

She did, lowering her face until their gazes met from a bare foot apart. Her eyes had green in them.

"What you must know," Ben whispered in a voice that was wispiest air, "is that my master may choose to leave Prague to its fate and give no warning to the populace. I will not do that. If I know there is no hope, I will raise alarm. If you love this city, that is your interest in me."

She continued to stare into his eyes, and then leaned near his ear, so that her warm breath tickled it. "I have not the key," she said. "But I can get it."

"I urge you," Ben said, "do so!"

"Conditions twain," she replied.

"Name them."

"That I go with you, so as to see you remain honest."

"Done. And the second?"

"I should like to gaze through the telescope."

Ben drew back from her until he could again see her face. Her lips were pursed, slightly wide, and for an instant he had the most powerful urge to kiss them. His brain won the argument with other parts, however, for he knew he would lose all that he had just gained if he did. He nodded, wordlessly.

She nodded in return and then stood. "Tomorrow night I shall come—let us say at midnight—and you shall take me to the telescope. Then we shall speak of keys." She curtsied, turned on her heel, and made for the door. At the handle she paused and looked back over her shoulder.

"Lenka," she said, softly. "My name is Lenka."

4

Crecy's Story

Crecy coughed and tried to smile. "The hand of an angel," she repeated.

"For want of a better word."

"So you know that." Crecy sighed. "Very well. Is there anyone near? Near enough to hear?"

Adrienne went to the door, checked the empty hall, and, closing the heavy oak behind her, returned.

"We are alone," she assured Crecy.

She tried to sit up, winced, and settled for propping her head higher on the pillow. "You were never initiated into the inner mysteries of the Korai," she stated.

"Inner mysteries? I have never even heard of such."

"Yes. After I foresaw your marriage to the king, we decided to wait until after the wedding to initiate you."

"I see. Then I was never really one of the Korai."

"Of course you were—but you were kept from the greater mysteries. The mysteries I speak of have to do with the founding of our sisterhood. It is a long story, but I can shorten it."

"Be as long-winded as you wish. This is the most you have spoken of the Korai in two years."

Crecy made as if to speak, and her face crinkled in pain. She cleared her throat and went on. "The Korai teach that in order to create the world, God had to withdraw from it—create a place where he was not—so that finite things like matter could exist. Once created, he could not enter the world without destroying it, so he created servants to do his will. These were races of air and fire—ofanim, cherubim, seraphim—the angels, in short. Through them he created all the physical world—animals and plants, man and woman. The woman was called Lilith."

"Ah," Adrienne murmured.

Crecy closed her eyes. "I know you are skeptical, but hear me through. Lilith was too much for Adam. Her craving for the pleasure of flesh was stronger than his, and she was not pliant. She did not lie passive, but straddled from above and took her joy at her pleasure. Moreover, Adam was not her only lover. She seduced some of the angels, learning from them the secret laws of the universe. For this—for being a woman of free will, for being Adam's superior, for rising above him in bed—she was imprisoned. Adam was given a new, sweet, docile wife—Eve.

"But Lilith had many children, and though some were—like their fathers—creatures of an elemental sort, others hid amongst the descendants of Adam and Eve, growing bolder in time, marrying amongst them, passing on the germ of Lilith from one generation to the next. Athena was the daughter of Lilith, remembered after her lifetime as a goddess. You and I are descended from her."

"Metaphorically, perhaps," Adrienne said. "I must say, this story is told differently than I have heard it. Is not Lilith the mother of demons? Are you and I demons, then?"

"Those lies started with Adam and Eve—of course they cast darts at Lilith. But think, Adrienne. Lilith was part of God's plan. How could she have been a mistake? Why would he imprison her?"

"And the Korai have some answer to this?"

Crecy nodded. "Indeed. They say that the god who exiled Lilith and created Eve was not God, but an impostor. One of the angels, Lucifer, took this universe—this place without God—and made it his own kingdom."

"And thus the world is ruled by the devil, and not by God at all. Yes, a pretty philosophy, one that explains the problem of evil very neatly," Adrienne said. "I refuse to believe that the intelligent women of the Korai believe such facile nonsense."

"I cannot say what they actually *believe*. But this is what I was taught. Of course, it may be all lies, a story to exaggerate our own importance. But at the heart of it may be some truth, Adrienne. The angels—do you know the Hebrew name for them, malakim? Do you know the meaning of the word?"

Adrienne sighed. "My interests are in natural philosophy."

"It means 'shadow side of God.' The Hebrews knew whom they dealt with, even if our Church has forgotten. They are *real*, Adrienne. You have seen them, been wounded by them, been given a hand by them."

Adrienne nodded, frowning.

"What do you believe, Adrienne? Do you believe in God?"

Adrienne looked at the redhead, shocked. "Of course. Do you understand how precariously the universe is built, Crecy? How exacting its specifications? Without gravity and the other affinities, there would be no order, only chaos. Where there is law, Veronique, there must be a lawmaker."

"I am no philosopher, but I agree. And you philosophers—you discover these laws of which God has writ the world, and you find how we might use them?"

"Yes."

"Then why must I convince you of the reality of angels?"

"I have never doubted their existence, Crecy, for the Bible speaks of them. But the Bible often cloaks the real in obscure symbol. I once speculated that angels represented the elements, gravity, the harmonics of sound, and trajectory. But you are right—that is lost to me now. That creature that guarded the king—angel, devil, fey, or djinn—it was something, something intelligent, malicious. But I must know what they *are*, Veronique. I must have more than hieroglyphic mysteries. Are they living things, or do they merely resemble life? Do they have souls? Are they composed of matter?"

Crecy nodded. "I knew you would ask these scientific questions, but I have little to tell you. Only that God must have made them."

"If so, they must conform to His laws. They must be understandable in mathematical terms. If they are mysterious, it is only because we have not asked the right questions, not pursued the proper experiments."

"And how will you experiment on them, my dear? How will you dissect angels in your laboratory?" Another cough rasped from her throat. "No, no, let that pass. I need to tell you something else, before I weary too much."

"I will not tax you," Adrienne vowed, suddenly a bit anxious. "If you pledge me you will live, we can continue later. You have already given me much to think about."

"I haven't answered your first question, about your hand."

"Later."

"Yes, later. But I will say one more thing, now. There are many sorts of malakim. There are those such as you saw near Gustavus, clouds with fire glimmering within. There are those such as guarded the king and burned your hand. There are many who cannot make themselves seen in the world of our senses, or only barely so, but they are there nevertheless. But in a different sense, there are two sorts of them: those who wish to destroy mankind and those who do not."

"Angels and devils."

"No. It is not so simple. In a sense they are all devils—or all angels—it does not matter what you call them. What matters is that they think first of themselves, of their own wishes, of the politics of their realm. They are cut off from God. I do not even think they acknowledge him, have forgotten him. They forget us—mankind—too, for eons at a time, consider us no more than you consider dust in the air. But in certain ages, philosophers arise, and the dust, so to speak, thickens to choking. Men and women begin to learn the laws of God—the real ones, the ones by which the universe operates. This angers the malakim, Adrienne, and worse, it frightens them. And so they work against such people. They kill them, oftimes."

"If this is so, how did Huygens and Leibniz and Newton and—and myself, for that matter—live to publish what we learn? Why weren't we killed?"

"That comes to two reasons. The first is that it is not easy for them to murder us, to touch us outside their realm."

"And yet you were just telling me tales of fornication with such spirits, of a human woman bearing their children. The Bible speaks of Jacob wrestling with an angel, of cities being blasted by them to ash."

Crecy's grip on her hand tightened almost painfully. "Imagine for a moment that you are God. You have withdrawn yourself from the world in order to create it. You built it of law, of numbers and words, of mathematical affinities. And then the very servants you send into the world to carry out your will barricade themselves within and begin to do as they wish. What do you do?"

"Destroy the world and begin again."

"Let us assume that you are the loving God of whom Jesus spoke and cannot bear to undo your creation."

"Make other servants to deal with the first."

"Ah. But how to prevent *them* from developing *their* own wills in this place you cannot reach?"

Adrienne lifted her hands in defeat. "Very well, Crecy, *you* are God. What is *your* solution?"

"I am outside the world, a world whose boundaries are made by my very will. You just said that the universe is precariously built. What if I were to change the law, just a tiny bit, a harmony here, a numeral there—not so much that things fall apart or crash together into a great lump, but just enough to deprive my renegade servants of some of their power, make them as ghosts in the world they have stolen. And what if these adjustments to the law allowed my favored creation— Man—to one day rise against his wrongful masters and cast them out of the universe?"

Adrienne remembered the engraving again: God's hand reaching from the cloud, grasping the cosmic tuning key. Could He twist it, and thus make the universe different?

She shook her head. "But they *can* kill us."

"It is difficult. It is easier if they use human agents."

"You said there was a second reason."

Crecy leaned her head back. "They have tired of killing you one at a time. The blood of Lilith is everywhere, and will not stay quiet. Age after age, you keep coming back, inquiring after the law. Some malakim think to kill you all, children of Eve and Lilith alike."

"How?"

"By making you kill yourselves, of course. London, my dear, was only the start."

That made a horrible sort of sense, and for an instant Crecy's bizarre explanation seemed perfect, a balanced equation. But then something began to nag at Adrienne, though she could not place what. The wrong integer, somewhere, the wrong operation. At the root, of course, was her distrust of Crecy, but there was something more.

"How do you know all this, Crecy? Did you learn all this from the Korai?"

Crecy chuckled, a sort of bubbling deep in her chest, and her voice faded to a whisper, her eyelids fluttering. "No, my dear. I know these things because I am one of them. One of the malakim."

Adrienne awoke, sprawled across open books, wondering where she was, trying to recall what had awakened her. Raising her head she found herself peering at the engraving she had fallen asleep regarding: a seraph, four of its six wings hugged around itself and two spread wide. The wings were covered in eyes, and eyes winked from the palms of its hand, from each finger. She recalled that she had been dreaming, and in her dream her hand had blinked at her.

Someone rather near coughed for her attention.

It was Francis of Lorraine, staring at her with an amused and perhaps slightly worried expression.

"I am sorry, Demoiselle. Hercule should never have set you such a demanding task."

"Oh, no, Your Grace," Adrienne managed, rubbing the sleep from her eyes. "The task is no trouble. I hope you approve of the volumes I chose."

"I wish I could take them all," Francis complained. "But you picked the best, almost as if you read my mind. But why do you sleep there, when a good bed awaits you?"

"I was reading," Adrienne said. "You must understand, it has been a very long while since I have had books."

"But such books!" Francis said. "These are among my favorites."

"Mine as well," she said, smiling as brightly as she could.

"Really? How delightful." He looked shy for a moment, and exactly his fourteen years. "I wonder, Demoiselle, if you would consent to ride with me at times on the journey. I would very much welcome the opportunity to discuss these matters with someone who understands them."

Adrienne cocked her head. "I would enjoy that very much, sir. Though I must also watch my son and friend."

"Yes, of course," the boy said hastily, blushing. "I only meant when it was convenient, and to your liking."

"I am certain it will be to my liking often," Adrienne replied, rising and curtsying, fully aware of the view that Francis had of her low-cut bodice. It could not hurt either her or Crecy if the young duke had a boyish infatuation with her. She presented him her hand, which he stared at blankly for an instant before nearly stumbling over to kiss it.

"Good night, Your Grace," Adrienne said.

"Yes, Mademoiselle, good night. But I should to your bed if I were you—it may be the last time you are able to sleep in one for some time."

"We leave soon, then?"

"By the noon, tomorrow, I'm afraid."

"Oh. But my friend Crecy . . ."

"She will ride in a carriage, and the doctor shall attend her. I'm afraid it is the best we can do."

Adrienne curtsied again. "That is all we can ask," she answered.

It was a long morning for Adrienne, for she and Crecy had no chance to talk, and her mind stung with questions as if full of hornets. The preparations of the last several days collapsed into seeming chaos, and no place or room was still—or safe for conversation—for long.

As Francis had promised, however, midday found them under way, beneath a miraculous sky, a vault of turquoise only lightly veined with clouds, and a golden sun. Despite everything, she felt a surge of happiness so strong that she almost wept. Others felt it, too, and the expedition was in an almost carnival spirit, the duke and his guard in bright coats and plumed hats, the horses shining, the infantry singing bravely. It was like a day from the past, before the world was all mud and gray. She wore a beautiful riding habit, practical of cut and warm against the lingering morning chill, yet fretted with gold braid on face and cuffs.

Even her horse danced beneath her, and on impulse she cantered back to Crecy's carriage and shouted in through the window. Crecy waved wanly. The doctor was still within, and so there was no chance of them talking. Still almost giddy, Adrienne worked on back through the ranks, smiling brightly at the soldiers who bowed to her, until she came to the wagon where little Nicolas rode with the nurse. Adrienne leaned near and took her son up in her arms, laughing at the excited puzzlement in his eyes, as she raised him toward the heavens.

"Look, Nico!" she cried. "That is the sun!"

Nicolas was silent, but when she brought him back down, she saw that his eyes were shut, and he seemed almost on the verge of tears.

"I know, my darling, my Nico. It is very bright, too bright for your little mole eyes. But it will come back, the sun, and your eyes will learn to love it. The world is getting better! I promise you, little one!" She rode together with her boy, and he liked the bouncing motion of the horse, grasping the coarse hair of its mane and cooing.

It could not last all day, or course. Evening darkened before the sun was low, olive clouds squatting like giant toads on the horizon. There seemed no actual danger of rain, but she returned Nicolas to the greater safety of the wagon, and rode out ahead. Her mood began to change with the weather, the strange thoughts and revelations of the past days now demanding their due, and when she looked at the heavens again it was to wonder what monsters might hide there.

They halted not much later to camp. They were still in no hurry; the way looked clear to the border and it seemed unlikely that the Muscovites would try to prevent them from leaving Lorraine essentially defenseless.

She joined Crecy in the carriage once she saw the physician leave, finding the redhead awake but flushed.

"Do you have a fever?" Adrienne asked, touching her friend's forehead but finding it cool.

"Where is Nicolas, Adrienne?"

Adrienne frowned slightly. "The nurse has him in another carriage."

"Have you abandoned your son?"

"No. He rode with me most of the day."

"I wish you would bring him so that I can see him."

"Crecy! Is this affection?"

"Perhaps."

"I shall bring him to see you later, for I think he sleeps now. I do not mean to hurry you," she said, "but we may not be alone for long. I must know what you meant yesterday."

"It is a strange story."

Adrienne shrugged.

"I was born human enough, I suppose," she began. "The Korai say that the blood of Lilith flows more strongly in some, and perhaps that is how they choose us."

"Choose?"

"Understand that I was seven years old before I knew that aught was amiss, Adrienne. Seven years before I understood that other children could not hear the voices I heard, see the things I saw."

"You were Joan of Arc, then?"

"Joan of Arc was one of us, of course." Crecy sighed.

"One of the Korai?"

"No, not one of the Korai. One of the— Well, we have no name. Call us fey, for the sake of convenience."

"Fey. Like the forest sprites of peasants."

"It is only a name. But they take human children and then leave one of themselves . . . here." She reached up slowly to tap her temple.

"When I think of my childhood, I think of the voice. My earliest memories are of songs, strange little tunes which I hummed sometimes, and my mother—my human mother—asked me where I had heard them. I told her I just heard them, and she laughed. But my mother was more distant to me than the voice. The voice was my real mother, Adrienne. It made my body grow stronger, swifter than other children. In short, my dear, it shaped me. By the time I was twelve I knew what I was to do."

"And what was that?"

"I have told you. I was to work toward the destruction of humanity, to play my part in the great plan. I have assassinated, Adrienne, and I have slept with men to gain secrets. And in the end they put me to being your friend, to fill you and Korai with false prophecies—"

"*False?*" The word burned her throat like vitriol.

"I never foresaw you marrying the king, Adrienne. It was a lie I was forced to tell you."

"A lie?" She hissed. "God curse you, Crecy. I ruined my life for that lie! And Nicolas died, Torcy died, everyone died—" She choked off, realizing that she had known it all along. "Do you know—" She had to stop again. She felt stripped naked and tied before the world to amuse it. Almost, she wanted to die, it was so awful.

"Adrienne," Crecy whispered, "you must let me finish."

"Goddamn you," Adrienne whimpered, not knowing what else to say.

"Surely God has never loved me," Crecy said steadily. "Yes, I betrayed you. But when I did that, I betrayed a woman I did not know, did not love."

"You said that you had *seen* us as friends, that you felt a love we had not yet had. That was a lie, too?"

"Not entirely. But I did not see that until the day we first met, when I first touched you in the canal."

"That was before the lie about the king."

"Days before. I was confused, Adrienne. I thought I knew what my purpose in life was. I held to duty instead of my heart. That was my sin."

"Pretty words, very pretty. And now I am to trust you?"

Crecy closed her eyes, and to her utter astonishment, Adrienne saw a tear squeeze from one of them. "I know. I can't even ask your forgiveness. Why do you think I haven't told you? But I betrayed them, Adrienne. I helped you attack the king, though it went against the command of the voices. You remember Gustavus, who tried to stop us?"

"Of course."

"A fey, like me. I fought him for you. I tore the voices out of my head for you, Adrienne, my mother and my sister, and everything I had ever known—" Her breath caught short. "You cannot hate me now. Please do not hate me. You and Nico are all that remain to me."

"Are you so certain, Crecy?"

The redhead opened watery eyes. "What do you mean?"

"As you lay injured, you spoke to me, but I do not think it was you. I think it was your 'voice.'"

"What did I say?"

"You said, 'We have found you.'"

"I don't remember that."

"I'm sure you do not." She was in control of herself again, her ridiculous bout of crying being gradually replaced by a sort of cold, hollow anger.

Crecy bowed her head. "Voices have found me again. But not the same voices."

"No? Perhaps these are the ones who spoke to Mademoiselle d'Arc."

Crecy ignored the gibe. "I think they must tune us like the chime of an aetherschreiber—the way that the elixir of life tuned the king, made him receptive to ministrations of the malakus that guarded him. I think without the potion, it takes many years; so they must begin with us as infants—perhaps even with our mothers. But somehow I shut them out, cut them from my brain— These two years, I have never heard my voice. But when I was fevered, and when I dreamed, seraphim came to me. I told you that there were two sorts of malakim. This was the second sort."

"The ones who wish us well?"

"Yes. They are those Lilith befriended, those loyal to the true God, if we are to believe the Korai mystery. Whatever the reason, they oppose the death of our race. And, Adrienne, they have been searching for us. They are willing to offer their help."

Adrienne regarded Crecy, and for an instant felt a profound pity for the woman. If everything she said was true . . .

"Will you accept it?" she asked, softly.

"It is not for me to accept. It is *you* they wish to serve, Adrienne. You."

5.

The Mathematical Tower

When Ben awoke he was so pleased to be alive that he spent a moment giving thanks to whatever powers might be listening. It seemed a sensible precaution; though he seriously doubted that the creator of the universe was paying attention to Ben Franklin of Boston, there might well be some provincial god who was doing so — especially considering what he had learned lately.

The night had been hard, as each stirring of air suggested the *thing* slipping up on him; even the flexions of his own heart became a suspicious, fragile commodity. Added to the fear was the anticipation of at last managing to gaze upon whatever secrets obsessed Newton. The sum of that computation came to sleepless hours.

But his body was wiser than he and would not bear two nights without real sleep. Near midnight it sent some physic thief tiptoeing to his brain to steal his consciousness.

Humming, he rose, changed clothes, and left his rooms at about ten to look for Robert. Emerging into the hall, he noticed a clump of servants absorbed in some serious discourse near Newton's rooms. One of them—a plump maid named Gertruda—was crying. Curious, he strode toward them.

"What's the matter?" he asked, as he drew near. He knew two of the four—Gertruda and an elderly valet named Milos. The other two—a raven-tressed beauty of perhaps twenty and a plain woman with gray-shot hair perhaps twice that—he had seen but did not know by name.

"Your pardon, Herr Franklin," Milos said, bowing.

"No need to ask for pardon," Ben said. "I was only wondering what Gertruda was crying about."

"It is Stefan, sir, the sweeper."

"What of him? Is he ill?"

"No, sir, he is dead. They found him here."

"Dead? Of what cause?"

"God took him, sir." Gertruda snuffled. "There was never a mark on him. It was as if he just—died."

An extremely unpleasant notion struck Ben. "I remember Stefan," he said. "He was not an old man. . . ." He looked more closely at the door to Newton's apartments. The entire wall seemed to waver faintly, as if seen through water.

"He was only twenty-five," the beauty said with peculiar vehemence. Ben turned a speculative eye on her—which he had done before, with other interests in mind.

"Anna," Milos said softly. "Hush."

Ben cocked his head. "No, please, speak. Better—" He looked around, and lowered his voice. "Better, come into my rooms for a moment that we might all speak privately."

They exchanged nervous glances, but Milos nodded almost imperceptibly, and they all followed.

Once the door was shut, Ben paced over to sit on his bed.

"Please, sit down." He indicated some stools. "Now, Mrs.—Anna, what do you suspect?"

"Nothing, sir. I should not have spoken."

"But you think Stefan died of unnatural causes."

Anna hesitated and looked at the others for support; but they gave her none, their eyes fastened on the carpet, the ceiling—anywhere but her.

"Anna, this is important. You say that Stefan died near my master's door. Is my master well?"

"He is well," Milos said. "The guard inquired after him, of course."

"What did he say when he learned of Stefan?"

"He *nodded*," Anna said, a little heat in her voice. "He nodded, like he knew something, and then—" She stopped, because Milos *was* looking at her now, sternly.

"We have to be going, sir," the older man said, "else we will be wondered at."

That was that, Ben knew from experience. The servants had their own ways and were as stubborn in them as the nobles they served. But he knew that that *thing* had come for *The Sepher Ha-Razim*. Newton had erected a barrier against it, and it had slain poor Stefan.

"Wait," Ben said. "Just a moment." He rose up. "Did Stefan leave relations?"

Gertruda nodded. "A wife and two boys."

Ben, feeling sicker, reached into his leather wallet. "This is nothing," Ben said. "It is not a husband for her, nor a father for her children, but it is all I have." He reached a handful of coins toward Gertruda. "I know that you will see to them."

Gertruda stared at the gold. "Yes, sir," she mumbled.

"And all of you, take care," Ben warned. "Avoid this hall when you can."

"We already do, sir," Milos answered somewhat gruffly.

He tried for two hours to see Newton, to no avail, and finally sought out Robert. He found him where he thought he might, in Saint Thomas', a dark and ancient Kleinseit tavern that served good meals and better beer.

"I could wish y' wouldn't make as free with yer life," his friend told him over a plate of roast beef and boiled dumplings, "but I'll admit y' put the bite on the old man—and Frisk an' me as well."

"I don't know who has bitten whom," Ben replied dubiously. "Have you heard about the death of Stefan?"

"The sweeper? Aye, 'tis all the talk of the servants."

"They seem to suspect something dark."

"They always do, where Newton is concerned."

"This time I think they have cause," Ben said, and then outlined his adventures in stealing *The Sepher*.

Robert took it all in, frowning more deeply each moment. "What was it?" he asked. "Another one of those things as accompanied that Bracewell fellow? Some witchy familiar?"

"A different sort," Ben replied, shaking his head. "I think Newton knows, but he will not say."

"How many sorts of these things can there be?"

Ben pressed his forehead with his fist. "Only God knows," he muttered. "There are a thousand species of life on the links below us in the chain of being. It may be that there are at least as many above, between us and God."

"Like the angels? Don't Newton call 'em angels?"

"Yes."

"That seems strange. If they're nearer t' God, I'd think 'em more perfect—we'd have naught to fear of 'em."

Ben smiled grimly. "Oh? You mean as an insect underfoot has nothing to fear from you?"

"Ah." Robert took a thoughtful bite of his beef. "And so Stefan 'uz the insect."

Ben nodded. "That's my guess. The thing scents after the book, but Sir Isaac has erected a barrier. It beats at the obstacle, enraged, and when a servant comes around . . ."

"Yet you stood near his door an' went unaccosted."

"True. I have no explanation."

"How's this? Maybe our master struck a bargain with the devil. Maybe he *gave* 'im Stefan as sacrifice."

"Oh, come, Robin—"

Robert pushed back his plate, and Ben saw his friend was really angry. "How is it that y' are so credulous an' so skeptical all in the same breath?" he snapped. "Y' concede the existence of the things, y' guess that one murdered Stefan, an' swear that Sir Isaac is makin' up a system about 'em the like of you know not what. And so tell me, if they be angels or devils or the whatnots from the dark caves of the moon, then why may they not drink Christian blood or come at a dark Sabbath? If the devils exist, why is it that what we hear of them is wrong?"

Ben regarded Robert for a long moment, ordering his words, and then leaned forward. "Robin, the sun, moon, and stars were known to Aristotle, and he could not have been more wrong about them. It isn't *what* you know, but how you come to know it—whether you can trust the *method*. Now, I will not trust Aristotle about the sun going 'round the earth, and I will not trust some medieval necromancer on the nature of aethereal beings. I will know what I know because I observe, because I experiment, because I observe again, because I keep my conclusions in the bounds of what I have seen, can demonstrate, can do again. Do you see? And so you say that the sun revolves around the earth, and I say how do you know that, and you say, 'because I read it in Aristotle.' And do you know what that makes you?"

Robert's sour expression twisted just slightly so as to form a sardonic smile. "The graduate of a university?"

"Just so," Ben replied, pleased to feel the tension ease between them. "Just so. And so you say that you heard that the Jews sacrifice Christians to demons or that the angels bleed honey. I'll agree with you that there are angels—or some things we might name as such—"

"Aye, good, stop up y'r maw. Y'r point has found me. But just answer me this. This method—is it Newton's?"

"He is the author of it. He is the master of it."

"In his madness, could he have forgotten it himself?"

Ben stared at his plate for eight or so heartbeats before replying. "God help us if he has." He sighed, reaching for his nearly untouched food. "But soon, by heaven and earth, I shall discover it."

Ben shivered beneath the weight of the cathedral rising night against night above him, its thousand knobbed spires like the spines of some poisonous insect, beautiful and terrible at once. It seemed to Ben a place built from fear of God rather than love of Him, as if its dark quills and snarling gargoyles could keep the Almighty at bay, prick His toes if He trod upon the castle.

"The air is clear," a woman's voice said, from nearby. Ben turned to regard Lenka, some ten paces away.

"I didn't hear you approach," he said.

"I didn't. I've been waiting here."

"It may not be safe, wandering the castle alone."

"I heard about Stefan," she said. "I heard that you sent his widow money. It won't work. They still won't talk to you."

He suppressed an angry retort, and instead said, "Will you?"

She pointed a finger at the moon.

"Very well." He sighed in resignation. "Come along."

They crossed the courtyard, passing a statue of Saint George battling a dragon of decidedly unheroic size. Beside the mass of the cathedral, the tower rose, slender by comparison, a fairy-tale spire decapitated by science, its ancient conical roof replaced just that year with a polyhedron of tough alchemical glass.

"Take my arm," he whispered.

"Why?"

"If you want to get into the tower, take my arm."

"Very well." She slipped her small-boned arm around his, and he was abruptly reminded of another woman holding him so—Vasilisa Karevna. Was that what disturbed him about Lenka?

A guard nervously greeted them as they drew near. "Who goes?" he grunted, hand on his sword.

"Benjamin Franklin, apprentice to Sir Isaac Newton. I've business in the observatory."

"Oh, yes, I know you now, sir. And the lady—"

"My assistant," Ben replied, winking broadly.

"I see," the man replied knowingly. "Please be free."

Ben gave him a little bow, and they passed on.

"Was that so necessary?" Lenka asked, as Ben opened the door and produced a small lanthorn to guide them. "It's difficult to keep a good reputation in the castle."

"Especially accompanying me, eh? Well, there's a cost for everything, as you've shown me."

"Some costs I will not pay," she answered, stiffening.

"Yes, yes. You have laid down your coin already, never fear," he said, and was rewarded by her arm relaxing.

"Are there more guards?" she asked a moment later.

"No."

"Good." And she disentangled her arm. Feeling a trifle insulted, he continued up the narrow, winding stair. Except for their footfalls, there was no sound, and it was easy to imagine that even those did not belong to them, but to the ghosts of John Dee, Tycho Brahe, Johannes Kepler, or the mad Emperor Rudolf himself. Legend had each of those men haunting the tower, and even his brave speech to Robert about scientific method could not rob him of all worry at such tales. Might not the soul, surely an aetheric entity, survive its corpse?

He paused briefly at the door he believed hid Newton's new laboratory, glaring at the recently added Pythagorean lock. Knowing it wouldn't work, he tried his key anyway.

"What's in there?" Lenka asked.

Ben grinned sardonically. "The wheel of Ezekiel, I expect. Come on. It's farther up we go."

The upper story—the observatory—was as he had left it, save that tonight the sky had thrown off all but the gauziest of her veils, her thousand suns and planets naked to their sight. The telescope gazed up at them already, crystal eyes tireless.

"Well, then, here we are."

"Yes." Lenka sighed, seeming a little breathless.

"What would you see?"

"I would see the moon."

"Very well." He walked over to the instrument and began to adjust it a bit impatiently. Why was this girl wasting his time, when so much danger threatened?

Squinting through the ocular, he turned the wheels until the creamy half-moon filled the view.

"There," he said, stepping back.

At the telescope, she paused. "How do I do it?"

"Close one eye and look through the eyepiece with the other."

She nodded and bent to the ocular, and stood there like a statue for a long, long moment, while Ben tapped his foot restlessly. Finally, when he was just going to ask her how long one could *look* at the moon, she raised up, and he felt an odd, warm shock at the base of his skull as he noticed streams of silver glistening down her cheeks.

"Thank you," she whispered unsteadily. "We can go."

He could not move nor answer, for her tears and the moonlight caught in the fine hollows of her face mesmerized him.

"We can go," she repeated, reaching to wipe her eyes.

"Please," he said. "Leave them."

Her hand paused and then dropped to her side. "Why? So you can say that you saw the servant girl weeping?"

"Now why would I do such a contemptible thing?" he replied, and the corners of her mouth lifted a bit. "Why?" he pressed softly. "Why do you weep?"

She seemed astonished by the question. "Why do you *not*?"

Frowning at her, Ben bent back to the scope, found the ocular damp with her tears. The night sky had shifted a bit, but he brought the satellite back into view with ease.

"It is the moon," he said, still gazing.

"Don't you see them?" she asked. "There, where the dark lies? The mountains, casting their shadows? Mountains so lofty that they must blot the Earth from the sky if you stand next to them? If you *could* stand next to them?"

Her words were soft, cadenced, almost a sort of song, and then, all of a sudden, he *did* see them. Oh, he had seen them before, known what they were—could even name some of them. But now, suddenly, the privilege of it struck him, the magnificence.

"I have gazed on the mountains of the moon," Lenka said. "In my whole life, I never thought to do that. And yet always I have dreamed . . ." Now, as her tears had held him, so did the moon. Until he heard her feet softly start down the stairs.

"Wait," he said. "Wait, please, come back."

He looked up to find her watching him expectantly.

"Let me show you something else. If luck is with us, and the air is clear, we might see the rings of Saturn."

"I'll not waste more of your time," she said. "I've seen what I came to see. I'll meet you in the morning, at ten, when I know Sir Isaac will be away with the emperor."

"No, but you haven't seen enough," he insisted. "The rings are not to be missed."

She gazed at him like some strange night bird, a pale inhabitant of the moon herself, and he thought she would refuse and knew that would sadden him. But, at last, a minute smile crooked on her face. "Very well," she agreed.

An hour later, as the sky began to cloud too much to see anything, they started back down the stairs. "Thank you," Ben said to her.

Five steps passed, and then she answered, "You are welcome." As if she knew what she had given back to him.

"There was more, wasn't there?" he asked. "What attaches you so to the moon? Why, of all the sights in heaven, did you care first and foremost to see—"

"Hush," she interrupted. "We approach the guard."

And when they reached the courtyard, she slipped off like a wraith, leaving him more confused than ever.

6.

Deep

Red Shoes wondered at the dark spangles of the ocean surface, trying to peer deeper, to see what might be below that translucent curtain. Once, he knew, the whole world had been endless deeps, before Hashtali, whose eye is the sun, covered the dark waters with a roof of earth. On land, that lower world was accessible only through narrow doorways—deep pools, caves, the densest forests. Only the bravest, most powerful *isht ahollo* dared such places, for the creatures of that lightless deep hated the upstarts of the land, nurtured poisonous revenge in their hearts. Anyone might encounter this poison—in the bite of a cottonmouth, in the fever from the swamps. But to go beneath was to enter the heart of chaos.

Out here, the deep was unbuffered by land, the ship a dark cave of many chambers. The sailors reacted to this by stupefying themselves with rum, gambling constantly, picking senseless fights, planning what they would do at landfall. Red Shoes drank some of the rum—his hands hurt constantly, and besides, there was plenty of rum and very little fresh water—but neither that nor any other diversion could dull his unease. The best that he could do was stay where he could see the sky, deny the darkness all about him, and dream of his home. He was in a place where no Choctaw—even an *isht ahollo* like himself—ought to be.

Something white moved beneath the waves, and he leaned forward to the rail for a closer look. As his hands touched the wood, he realized his mistake—too late. Pain lashed up his arms, turned him into jelly, and the rail seemed to dissolve as he tumbled through the thick air.

The underworld swallowed him gleefully. He tried to strike back toward the surface, but he had never learned to swim; and besides, strong arms grabbed him, pulled him downward. He held his breath as long as he could, fighting, but he lost, and water filled his lungs.

It wasn't so bad, the water in his lungs, once he realized he wasn't dying. As the sea grew darker, he caught glimpses of the creatures who had captured him. Pale men, whiter than any European; mouths gaping gar's teeth; wide, round eyes glowing with malice. He knew them from childhood tales. The *oka nahollo*, the pale people of the water, who stole children to eat—or to transform into one of their own. As it was pointless fighting them, he relaxed, let them take him where they were going.

It was a town of mud, stone, and rotted wood; and it smelled like sea, garbage, putrefying meat. They took him into a moldering house, where a single *oka nahollo* sat upon a dais before a black, heatless flame. He wore a diadem of eels—as a Choctaw chief might wear swan's feathers— and fixed Red Shoes with a round stare and shark's grin.

"*Chim achukma?*" he croaked, in a watery sort of voice.

"*Okpulo,*" Red Shoes responded. "*A chishno?*"

"Well enough," the chief continued in Choctaw, "considering that you people walk above my head and cast down your shit upon me, bury your dead so that they putrefy and sink into my domain."

"This is not my doing," Red Shoes said reasonably. "It was made thus by Hashtali long ago. Why have you abducted me on account of your grudge against him?"

The chief shuddered and turned a rather remarkable blue color before going on. "Because you are his creations," he said.

"And you are not?"

"We own this world. No one made us." The chief considered him a moment, and then leaned forward. "He made *you* from us. Did you know that? He stole you as children, dressed you in clay, taught you to hate us."

"I fear you," Red Shoes admitted, "but I don't hate you." He cocked his head. "Is that why you steal our children? Revenge?"

"Yes. And because, being made of mud, you can do things we cannot—walk on the land as we cannot. You can help us, and you can be rewarded."

"Ah. Rewarded with a place down here?"

"Bah. When we have again torn asunder the roof Hashtali has placed above us—"

"That which imprisons you."

The *oka nahollo* glared at him for a moment. "It hinders us, yes. But often we are content here—until you mud spawn pollute the water we breathe. At those times, we act against the offenders."

"Such as myself, I assume?"

"Your soul came from us. Inside that mud shell, you have a powerful soul. At your birth, we offered you a useful place amongst us, and instead you chose to torture yourself, eat up your own shadow merely to annoy us. But there are far worse in the world than you: people who would destroy both your people and mine."

"You mean the white people."

"You call them *nahollos*, after us. Do you wonder why?"

"No. The first Choctaw who saw them thought of you, for they were pale as sea foam and came in floating houses. It was a natural mistake."

"Was it?" The fishlike man grinned crookedly.

"Say what you have to say."

The chief stopped smiling. "What I want to say is this, my cousin, my nephew. When your kind emerged from the cave at Nanih Waiyah, when you dried and cracked out of your crawfish skins and became people made of mud—you did not lose your kinship with us. We are your elders, and you owe us respect and obedience. You were offered a chance to behave right once. Now I offer it again. If you refuse—" His eyes flashed black, then green, then pale as shell. "—refuse, and you are meat. Do you understand?"

Red Shoes met his gaze. "Eat me now, if you can." He slapped his hands together, drew on his shadow, and split the sea chief's skin. The dwarf, Kwanakasha, crawled from the slowly collapsing membrane, snarling before he, too, ruptured to reveal a black, winged thing with many eyes, an awful butterfly emerging from a fleshy chrysalis.

"You have been warned," it said.

Red Shoes tore open the water and awoke in his own cramped quarters, to the rocking motion of the ship. His hands hurt terribly, and he realized that in his dream he must have been flexing them.

For a moment he thought he would be ill, but he breathed the stale air deeply until the sea in his belly subsided. After a moment he went above to where the waters were at least below him and not all around. Perhaps he would ask to sleep on the deck from now on, save when it rained.

In the welcome wind above, he contemplated his dream and what it might mean. It had been an attack. Knowing him weakened by his ordeal in England, Kwanakasha had made its move to free itself from him. But he suspected more than that. Kwanakasha had earlier spoken of the "great ones." Red Shoes had a suspicion that he had just met one of them, through the mediation of his own little captive. If that were true, he was indeed in danger, for though legend spoke of such creatures, details on them were scanty, and the ways of defeating them—or even defending against them—were not known to him. He would have to be light on his feet, sharp of eye. He was hunted by a predator for which he had no name and knew no face.

A hoarse, spontaneous cheer went up from all eight ships when they sighted trees for the first time since leaving America. The Picard and Norman shores had looked much like England, bare of anything save grass. But when they reached what Bienville guessed was Brittany, they saw trees lying flat on the ground—as if blown over by an unbelievably high wind.

"I still would prefer that we had sent a party in toward Paris," Bienville told the council over dinner that evening, "yet I understand your reluctance. But should we see an inhabited village, I must request that we go ashore."

"And so we shall," Blackbeard replied. "We've need of supplies, if nothing else. But I'll be damned if I send another of my men where I can't see 'im from behind a cannon." He grinned ruefully. "They wouldn't go, anyway."

"Yes. But if we get news that Paris and Versailles still stand, you understand I will insist on going there."

Blackbeard nodded. "Aye. No need to 'labor the point."

The next day they did see a village, or what was left of one—more cause for jubilation.

"So it's not th' whole world 'uz dead. Not th' whole world!" Tug said.

"What did happen, I wonder?" Nairne said, watching the ruined village go by. "It's as if the breath of God blew across here, hard enough to flood harbors even in America."

"My people tell a story about wind," Red Shoes said. "They say that he is much like a man, and lives in a house, here, in the east, in the sky. He had many children and he sent them abroad to bring him news, but none ever returned. Finally he went looking for them. He looked a long time, and at last discovered that a man made of iron had captured them all and drowned them in a river. Wind killed the Iron Man with a puff of tobacco smoke."

"Strong tobacco. Did he find his children?"

"The Iron Man had a wife. Wind tortured her until she told where they were. When she told him, he threw her in a fire. Each time she crawled out, he kicked her back in."

"Nice fellow, Wind."

Red Shoes smiled. "When he got his children out of the water, they blamed him for their fate, but did not thank him for their rescue."

"Did he burn them, too?"

"No, he let them go, made them the winds we know today. Then he went to sleep in the water. He said the next time he woke up, he was going to blow away everything in the world."

"Ah. And you wonder if Wind woke up here?"

"No," Red Shoes said, shaking his head. "I don't think this was Wind at all. But maybe if we find a village with someone alive in it, we can ask."

They saw people the next day, but by the time the first of the long-boats put ashore, the village was deserted. Cooking pots, left to ruin over flame, were proof of the haste with which the evacuation had taken place. Forays into the surrounding countryside turned up no one.

Discouraged, the flotilla spent two days off the coast, watching. Though they occasionally caught a glimpse of someone stealing in or out of the village, they were never able to make any contact.

"This bodes ill," Blackbeard said, when the council met again. "These people have been taught to fear ships."

"Pirates might teach such fear," Mather suggested.

"They might," Blackbeard said, grinning, "though I doubt it. What is a pirate without ports? Without tavern keepers and wenches and fresh food? Usually the coast towns like pirates well enough, for it's on the seas we do our work and in the towns we spend our money."

"If not pirates, what then?"

Blackbeard shrugged. "Maybe a new sort of pirate. Maybe pirates more akin to those madmen we ran across in England. Reavers, sailing up the coast like Vikings."

"That *is* bad. What if we should meet these reavers?"

Blackbeard grinned more broadly. "Then we will teach them the difference between a village full of fisherfolk and a well-armed flotilla."

"I think," Cotton Mather said, "that it is time to think about the second part of our commission."

Bienville frowned. "We have not yet finished the first charge of it."

"In part we have. We know that, for all practical purposes, and for whatever reason, there is no such place as England anymore."

Bienville nodded. "Yes, but France—"

"To all accounts, France is at the very least in grave disarray. All the channel ports, great and small, are gone. If there is a Versailles, it is cut off from the sea. The fear along this coast shows that the people here enjoy scant protection from the king—if there is still a king. Most of us agree that an overland expedition, with no better intelligence than we have, is out of the question."

"Not out of the question, sir—" Bienville began, but Blackbeard cut him off.

"Out of the question."

"May I continue?" Mather asked politely.

"As you wish."

"The farther south we sail, the more agreeable things become. When last we heard, Monsieur Bienville, Spain was under Bourbon rule. We are now in the Bay of Biscay. It is my sense that we should not tarry here but sail on to Spain. Intelligence of what has become of the mother nations was an important part of our charge, but let us be frank. It is more important to both our colonies that we discover trading partners, whether they be French, Spanish, or Portuguese. These ships we have here are more than half the present sailing strength of North America. If we lose these ships in risky endeavors, we harm our peoples—for all we know, the only remaining fragments of England or France. Sir, if we find a busy port, a vital port, we shall learn what we wish to know. If we do not, all our efforts are in vain."

Bienville stared at the map unfurled before them and took out his pipe. "Your point is taken, sir. Our first priority is to find civilization from here on."

"Are we all agreed on this, then?" Mather asked.

"Aye," Blackbeard said.

"It seems sensible," Red Shoes added.

As the council began to break up, Red Shoes noticed Mather—not for the first time—favoring him with a hard glance.

"Reverend?" he asked, when the others were gone. "You have a question to ask of me?"

"I have been meaning to speak to you for some time," Mather acknowledged, lifting his chin slightly, almost in a gesture of defense— as if Red Shoes had caught him doing something wrong. For just an instant, the Choctaw felt disoriented, as if he were once again speaking to the *oka nahollo*, once again being challenged by the Lower World.

Remembering that the spirit had suggested some connection between itself and the Europeans, he idly wondered how misplaced the feeling was.

"What shall we speak of?" Red Shoes asked.

"The Invisible World, and your relations thereof."

Red Shoes blinked. "A subject we have already discussed, I believe. Did I not pass all your tests?"

"I am a man of science, and now freely admit that my tests were of no use. I *saw* your familiar spirit."

"You were able to see that? See my shadowchild?"

"I saw the demon you dispatched to make the wire burn, yes," Mather replied, eyes sparkling oddly. "I have warned you, my friend. You will damn yourself."

Red Shoes sighed. "What you saw was not a spirit as your perceive them, Reverend, but a child of my shadow."

"What nonsense is this?"

How odd it was, Red Shoes thought, that this man could claim to know of this "invisible world" and yet not know so simple a thing as the distinction between a shadowchild and a spirit.

"Each man, each woman, is made of three things," Red Shoes began, "in life, at least: the flesh, the *shilombish*, and the *shilup*."

Mather pursed his lips as if to comment, but after an instant, waved him on. "Explain those words, please."

"The *shilup* is the soul, the essence, the breathing part of a man. When we die, it goes beyond the sunset."

"And the other?"

"The *shilombish*. That is the shadow, the reflection, the image each of us carries. The *shilombish* remains to haunt the living sometimes. *Isht ahollo* send them out to see distant places or divide them to create helpers."

"Amazing," Mather said. "Do you speak of the plastic spirit? You do, I think."

"Plastic spirit?"

"The essence of pattern God has placed in all creation, that life uses to live, that angels, devils, and some men may bend to their wills. Did you read of this?"

"My people have understood the shadow for a very long time. It is our defense against witches—and those spirits which create witches."

"I know you believe what you say," Mather told him, "but you have been deceived by the devils into this practice of yours, indentured yourself to the dark forces without even knowing it. I am grateful that you saved our lives. It was that act—selfless, no matter how diabolical the aid you summoned—that convinces me you can be saved, brought into the covenant of grace, despite Satan."

"What would you have me to do?"

"Confess, and seek the covenant of forgiveness and grace. I can help you find it."

Red Shoes smiled grimly. "And what if you need me again to save your life?"

"I would rather see your own soul saved than my life." There was something about the way that Mather said this that took Red Shoes momentarily aback, as if the preacher had said something else, something altogether more threatening. But his expression remained mild, caring even.

"Believe me, Reverend, I would be only too happy to forgo my practices—they give me no pleasure. But if I were to dispense with my guardians—if I did not shape my *shilombish* to defend me—then I would be damned indeed, for the devils you speak of would drag my true soul to the Nightland and send it wandering about, naked and miserable."

"Even a pact with the devil can be broken, forgiven. Whatever he has made you think, he does not own you. You can be pried from his clutches."

Suddenly Red Shoes was very annoyed. Was his English so bad, that every single thing he said could be so completely misunderstood by this man?

"Thank you once again for your concern, Reverend," he said, just to end it. "I will think on all you have said."

"Please do. I am fully prepared to guide you and help you in your struggle against the devil. I have spoken to you honestly and openly before preferring any other action against you. What happens next is up to you."

He left, and Red Shoes remained in the cabin, staring at the air as if he could see the preacher's implied threat, hanging there, itself a sort of entity.

7

Wine, a Cup, and Two Drops of Wax

With her eyes closed she could still see, though it was not natural vision. Gone the uneasy sky of lacerated clouds, the knee-high grass of the hilltop, the melancholy silhouettes of gravestones. In their place—wonder.

In two weeks she had learned much, but answers still stood in impoverished ratio to questions. She opened her eyes again—her real ones—so that she could scribble in her book, something impossible to do while gazing at the living texture of its matter.

> What the living eye sees is a surface, an analogy. It does not see matter, but the light reflected by matter, its speed and angle determining color and brightness. It is elementary to say that matter is compounded of the four atoms, but it is another thing to see, with angel eyes, what compasses the atoms themselves.
>
> My hand is sensible to the aetheric harmonies of nature. When I gaze upon a stone I see not the light reflected from the stone, nor yet the atoms composing the stone, but rather the aethereal ferments within which the atoms are enmeshed. This is perhaps why each thing has something of the appearance of sand on a drumhead struck or the blurring tines of a tuning fork. There and not there, a remarkable thing. A more curious aspect of my vision is that what I perceive has the look of a drawing or diagram. The world becomes an etching, as if God drew His creation in pen and ink. I must conclude, that even with this hand—this manus oculatus—I cannot perceive things as they actually are, but must have them discovered to me in figures I already know.
>
> For instance, at night I see the stars, though clouds may bar the

way to my mortal orbs. They are not brighter or dimmer but more or less massy, nimbused by arcs and waves which intersect in unthought-of patterns, but which nevertheless have the look of the illuminations in Huygen's Treatise on Light. Beholding Jupiter, I perceive the knots by which its moons are bound, and the fist of the sun, on an arm unimaginably long, grasping the king of planets himself.

I can also see the malakim, or at least the ones that attend Crecy and myself. They are strange to look upon, like Jove both a part of and separate from the harmonies around them, systems, so to speak, unto themselves, and more disorderly than nature, more manifold. As yet I can see no pattern in them, no start for a calculus of angels. This much is clear: they are not things of atoms but of aether, ferments without content, or with very little content. Those that become visible to human vision—like the flaming eyes which attended Gustavus— do so, I think, by drawing substance into their emptiness, as a man might draw smoke into his lungs.

They have offered their aid, and they have shown me how to see through my hand—they speak to me through it. What they show me is wonderful beyond measure, but I must be wary, for, despite everything, I still fear damnation. I cannot believe in the godless universe of the Korai.

She sat for some time on the hilltop, absently running her natural hand over her strange one, wondering where her heart was. Her discoveries brought her joy that she had not known since childhood, and yet it was not an unmixed pleasure. Something seemed amiss, though it was hard to characterize what. Perhaps it was like being given something one did not deserve.

But, no, that wasn't it either.

And then, in the next instant, she had it. It was like being asked to guess a wonderful secret—one that you know upon hearing you *could* guess, given a few moments—and then having the simpleton who posed it impatiently blurt the answer. It was a sort of robbery, a diminishment—an insult. Now that she understood her feelings, she saw how silly they were. One could learn much of the heavens with the eye, but if a telescope made the task easier, it would be foolish not to use one.

She rose, dusting grass blades from her petticoats. Nearby, the gravestones regarded her silently, and beyond them the bell tower of the country church down the hill. As she hesitated, unsure which direction to walk, a lively whistling interrupted her solitude. She turned to see Hercule d'Argenson strolling up the hill behind her.

"Ah," he called, his voice half stolen by the whipping wind. "How fair and rare the flowers on this hillside."

"I see no flowers," Adrienne said, lifting wide her arms to indicate the bloomless vista.

"No, soft, it has just now bloomed, raised its petals at the wind," he called back. He was close enough now that she could hear the whisk of grass against his riding boots. His forest-green coat hung open, the same-colored waistcoat buttoned only half up, lending him a country air.

"Sir, by the tenor of your flattery I would guess you to have been a courtier at Versailles, but I don't recall having ever seen you there. I wonder where else they train such adroit hyperbolizers."

"I have no idea what you mean. How have I been ingenious?"

"To see a flower in this," she answered, indicating herself, "takes more than a little genius."

He clucked and waggled a finger at her as he crossed the last few yards to stand at a comfortable nearness. "Now who plays the courtier?"

"How mean you?"

He stepped back, hand theatrically to chest. " 'You are a blossom,' he says to her, and answers she, 'Not so!' And he repeats himself. 'I am so unlike to a flower,' says she, 'that it needs you must explain yourself.' 'Why in the rose blush of your cheeks, Demoiselle,' answers he, 'in the supple swell of your bosom, so like to the lotus blossom'—and the like. In denying my praise you only curry more of it."

She laughed. "You have the better of me, sir. I only thought I said you were exaggerating, when in fact you reveal to me my own true nature. I thank you humbly."

He laughed. "May I take your arm, Mademoiselle?"

"Only so you promise not to take it too far, Monsieur *Renard*."

He chuckled again, slipping his arm through hers. "No fox, I, Demoiselle, but only a loyal and stubborn hound. Were you bound anywhere in particular?"

"No. The village is empty?"

He nodded, and some of the good humor went from his voice.

"Yes. They are, perhaps, hiding nearby, for the houses show signs of recent habitation."

"The duke's men? Will they—?"

D'Argenson shrugged. "As of now they are well disciplined. They will not loot, at least not very much. But I fear before the march is over—Well, we have mountains to cross, and when food is short and fear is everywhere, even virtuous men become less so."

"How true," she murmured. "And women the same."

He tightened his grip on her just slightly. "I can imagine no deed which you could have committed that you do not redeem by your simple existence."

"You have a limited imagination, then."

"Mademoiselle," he said, uncharacteristically softly, "I have no surfeit of imagination; but better, I have intelligence. And I repeat myself. I cannot imagine—nor have I heard of—anything you might have done for which you should bear shame."

"That, sir, is because you are a rogue, without moral sense or scruples."

"Oh, yes, true. But what of it?"

"Nothing of it. Your kindness comes from knavery, but since it still has the seeming of kindness—well, I will simply thank you." And was surprised that, even as she smiled—a real smile, not her old accustomed fraud—her eyes moistened.

"You will dine with the duke this evening?" he asked.

Adrienne nodded, finding herself momentarily without speech. They could now see the camp in the valley below, tents laid out in rows more neat than any real town, the wagons massed together, horses unhitched.

"I, unfortunately," d'Argenson went on, "must scout ahead with the cavalry, for we know nothing of the roads. Treat the duke carefully, my dear. He is still just a boy, whose heart is not as well defended as yours or mine."

"I am mindful of that," she answered, patting his hand.

When she reached her tent, she found Crecy leaning uncertainly against the frame, slender as a reed in a gown of green silk. She met Adrienne's chagrined frown with a narrow grin of triumph.

"Veronique, have you no sense? Has the doctor given you leave to walk about?"

"The doctor would rather keep me on my back, I think, and circumscribed by sleep for his benefit, but I will not oblige him," Crecy answered. "My strength is returning."

"If you overtax, it will desert you again."

"Don't fear for me. My own health is of great concern to me." She narrowed her eyes slightly. "What of you and—and our friends?"

"I have been exploring," she said. "It is marvelous, what they give. So much so that I keep wondering what the price shall be."

"I would be as cautious, I suppose, were I you. Like me, you must stand before you can walk, and ease into your new estate by degrees. But I sense no deception on their part. They have sworn themselves to you."

"So it seems," Adrienne allowed.

"I think they have proved their good intentions."

"Oh? And how, pray tell me?"

"As I said, it is difficult for them to kill our kind, but not impossible. If they were of the *maléfique* faction, you and I would be dead already."

"And yet the *malfaiteurs* did not kill me when they could have— before you and I were friends."

"They had uses for you then. When you upset their plans, they changed their tune, did they not? Gustavus most certainly meant to kill you."

"That makes sense." Adrienne nodded. "I would like to believe *my* malakim good creatures, doing God's will. If they can be trusted, there is little limit to what I might learn. Still, I wonder what *they* gain in this."

"Haven't you guessed? They are as blind to the world of matter as we are to the world of aether. Through you, they see our world. Thus, you can help them to defeat their evil brethren. If the *malfaiteurs* find us now, they will not find us unguarded." She grinned and touched Adrienne's arm lightly. "You will be reassured in time," she said. "As it is, you smile more than I've ever know you to—real smiles, not that frosty thing that you kept out at Versailles."

"There is much to smile about," Adrienne admitted. "We are fed, clothed, reasonably safe. My son is well and now has a chance at a good life, and my good friend Veronique seems on the verge of recovery! Will you have the strength to join us for dinner?"

"Yourself and the duke? No, I think not. Already I tire, and you are right—I should not overtax myself."

"Good. Then you do have some sense, though I am sure that the duke would enjoy your company."

"I am more than certain you can entertain his lordship sufficiently alone. He has an eye for you."

Adrienne nodded. "I know."

"Be careful. He is our benefactor, but he is also both a boy and noble—two sorts of creature notoriously prone to jealousy, rage, and idle whim packaged in one male form."

"As usual, your advice in the matter is expert," Adrienne said, laying her hand on the other's arm. "Though Monsieur d'Argenson has lectured me on this already."

Crecy pursed her lips in approval. "A sensible man, d'Argenson. A likable man, and I have heard good things of him. Perhaps when I am capable of greater exertion—"

Adrienne thumped her friend's forehead lightly. "She-goat! Best you curb your cravings for a time, else you will return to the doctor's ministrations."

Crecy smiled wanly. "Ah, just a thought. Now if you could help me to my bed—my lonely bed . . ."

Adrienne had perhaps too much wine that night and the duke certainly did, but while sloppy drunk, he was yet charmingly naïve, so it was no trouble to kindly dispose of what might have been tentative advances. Returning to her tent, slightly unsteady on her feet, she found Crecy in deep sleep, and lighting a solitary candle did not wake her. She drew out the formula she had been working on—the one to do with her hand—and tried to read through it, but was frustrated. Each time she read it, it made less sense. Back in Lorraine, she had been certain that she could fill in the missing parts, understand exactly how her hand had been made and what its ultimate properties were. Now, drunkenly staring at the pages, at the symbols so well known to her and yet so mysterious, she wondered if it was not a sort of false start. If the malakim had *given* her the hand, then her dream of having some-how created it was simple delirium. In that case there were deep-rooted errors in her assumptions which—after all—had not come from reason but from fever. What she needed before plunging back into some deductive, intuitional cloud castle of mathematics were more empirical observations of just the sort she had made today. The method of Newton, after all, made it clear that observation and ex-perimentation were far and away preferable to mere hypothesizing. What foundation did she have to hypothesize from? Not much of one.

She stepped out into the cool night air and took a moment to enjoy the gentle buffeting of the wind. Then, raising her hand, she opened its many-eyed fingers, willing it to see. The harmonies of the world opened before her, and she searched in them for angels. She saw one, near enough. She had seen two of their kind before ever she had lost her real palm and fingers. One had been a fiery eye ringed by a mist; the other a winged, black creature. Both had been visible to her hu-man eyes. The one she regarded now had never evinced a material form. Through her *manus oculatus* it appeared as a spiculum, two cones or horns with bases together, blurred toward their ends.

"Of what nature are you, O Djinn?" she asked, lightly. The ques-tion hummed through the *manus oculatus*, and her fingertips birthed ripples, just as if she had wiggled them in still water. Whatever else her hand did, it functioned something like philosopher's mercury, transposing the gross motions of matter into fluxions of the aether.

The answer came back similarly, a resonance that became, some-where between fingertips and brain, a voice—her *own* voice. That made a sort of sense—the creature would have no physical vocaliza-tion of its own, possessing neither lungs nor tongue—and so as the varied business of the universe transposed themselves for her as lines and numbers, so too did the voice of its aethereal creatures become fa-miliar, as well. This hypothesis made her own voice answering her no less eerie, however.

"I translate," it said. "I make harmony."

"What do you mean?"

"Between like and unlike I make resolution."

"Ah. Mediation, you mean."

"If that is your word for it."

"What is your name?"

"My name is Odjinn," it replied.

For some reason, rather than being amusing, that sent a little shiver up her spine. "That is what I called you," she pointed out. "I called you Djinn, for a fanciful creature. But what is your *name*?"

"My name is Djinn," it answered promptly.

Names, then, like the visions, like the sound of its voice, came from her. How did this differ from delusional madness? "If I call you that name, you will come?"

"Yes."

"And why are you here, Djinn?"

"To serve you, lady."

"And how can you serve me?"

"You command, and I shall serve."

Adrienne bit her lip and thought for a moment. So far she had merely used the creatures as oculars to view the aetheric world. But could she do more? Could they also be her mortar and pestle, her crucible? It mediated; that was a key concept in science. Water, for instance, could not dissolve copper—the two were too dissimilar harmonically to be sociable—but if the copper were melted together with sulfur first, a solution with water could thence be formed. The sulfur mediated the change, produced a middle ground between the ferments of water and copper. Her hand mediated between the tones of sound and the harmonies of the aether, and so forth. Mediation created, in essence, sociabilities or attractions between things where naturally none existed. However, most natural mediators had limited roles, any one substance able to mediate between only two or perhaps three or four others. Philosopher's mercury was a powerful mediator, for it was changeable in nature, able to transmit any harmony or set of affinities it was supplied with; and so it was through mercury that many scientifical devices worked, whether it be the work of transmutation or turning a liquid into its natural vaporous form. Was this creature a sort of living mercury? Was that its nature?

She recalled a passage from one of Newton's books, in which he feigned to explain muscular motion—saying that the animate spirit present in living things was, in its essence, mediation between the aether and the gross expansion and contraction of muscles. Could that be what these malakim were? The same sorts of spirits that animated living things, but without bodies or with bodies of fainter stuff?

Frowning, she returned to her tent, took up a candle, and from the floor a half-empty glass of wine. She dripped a little wax into the cup, where it congealed and floated, two little islands.

"Here," she said. "Can you mediate between these substances?"

"If you see the substance for me, I will try," Djinn answered.

"Very well." She closed her eyes and concentrated through the *manus oculatus* on the cup, on the wine, on the drops of wax. They appeared as distinct entities, bounded from one another as if by capsules or walls, and yet connected by a thousand wavelet harmonies as well—gravity, magnetism, and many more she had not yet named.

Long moments passed, and she began to grow impatient.

"It is a many-sided task," Djinn admitted.

"Ah." She should have started with something simpler: water and copper, lead and tin, or some other simple, unsociable compounds.

There came a hiss and a vapor, as the bones of her hand flared sun bright through her flesh.

"I could not mediate all," Djinn told her. "Some of the substance was lost."

"Yes," Adrienne replied, absently. "I saw the vapor. But sweet God . . ." She stared at the gray, gelatinous puddle that had once been wine, a cup, and two drops of wax.

8.

A Hunting

Ben groaned at the hollow boom that seemed to rattle his eardrums from within. He opened his eyes to find his face pressed hard against the mattress.

The concussion repeated itself, and this time he realized it was someone hammering on the door. Cursing, he rose—rather drunkenly, though there was no taste of beer in his mouth—and uncapped the small lanthorn near his bed.

His bleary eyes and the clock told him it was six.

Four hours of sleep. He rubbed his eyes and found that even with such little rest, he felt good. The evening with Lenka and the telescope had been a deep breath, clearing his head, reassuring him, leaving him with a powerful sense of optimism and purpose. Today, for good or ill, he would learn what Newton was hiding from him, and know what to do.

But who in the world was banging at the door?

It might be Lenka—perhaps Newton had gone early. Or maybe she had some other reason to see him. . . .

Grinning at that latter prospect, he quickly pulled on a linen shirt, white satin waistcoat, and rather poofy black Spanish breeches. It would not do for him to appear in the slightest undressed before her, not this time. Smoothing back his hair, he trotted to the door and swung it open.

Two royal footmen replied to his welcoming grin with polite nods. "Good morning, Herr Franklin," said the one in front, a fellow Ben recognized but whose name he did not recall. "The emperor requests your presence at the hunt."

"When?"

"The company leaves by the stroke of seven, sir."

"Leaves? Leaves to where?"

"To Bubeutsch, the hunting park, sir."

"I . . ." He cursed inwardly. It was too late to feign illness, not the way he had come up to the door, all grinning and stupid. "I must first have my master's permission."

"Not that it would matter," the fellow said, "for the permission of your master is nothing next to the emperor's wish—but Sir Isaac is going as well."

"Oh." He thought furiously. Would Lenka wonder where he was, come ten o'clock? If he missed their appointment she might claim it canceled her debt, and that wouldn't do. Damn the emperor, anyway. "In that case, I'll join you at seven." He could at least find her and explain.

"We have orders to accompany you, sir. The tailor sent along your hunting clothes." The second man stepped up, offering a pile of woolen garments.

Ben stared at the suit, but he could think of nothing more to say. "I suppose I'll dress, then," he muttered.

He miserably watched the water cascade from the brim of his hat. The dawn had begun to gray the sky a bit as they approached Bubeutsch, but the day it revealed was not promising. A mat of pewter cloud lay low to the ground, and rain came and went. It was coming now. He reached up to unlace the hat, converting the tricorn to a more functional rain hat, and a small flood splashed onto his horse's mane.

"This is a fine, fine day," Robert muttered from a few yards away.

"It's a damn silly day to go hunting," Ben snapped. "What does this—" He stopped himself. Nobody was in earshot save Robert and Frisk, but he still had his doubts about Frisk, and using the words he had intended in describing the emperor could prove a very foolish thing if they got back to him. Instead, he changed the subject.

"Do you have the smallest notion of how to hunt?"

Robert's white grin appeared through the double cataracts of their hats. "Well, sure, I'm expert in these highborn hunts—I've hunted with the French king, the tsar of Muscovy, an' the pasha of Persia— but 'tis said the customs of these German folks an't the same as them courts."

"Meaning you don't know either."

"Meanin' exactly that. What in hell would I know of royal hunts? How about you, Captain Frisk? What've you to speak on the matter?"

Frisk shrugged. "I have not hunted in many a day. As a boy I hunted with musket, but the kill was so easy as to seem pointless to me—a sport for weak, fat old men."

"What did you hunt with, then?" Ben asked.

"In the end, a pitchfork," Frisk answered.

"A pitchfork? How does one kill a deer with a pitchfork?"

"Ah, one does not," Frisk answered. "The pitchfork is best for hunting bear."

"I *see*," Ben replied. "And so, in brief, none of us knows a thing about hunting."

Frisk turned to frown at him. "Are you calling me a liar, sir?"

Ben opened his mouth to retort, but he suddenly saw that Frisk was not joking, and he remembered how little he knew about this man— and what a dangerous man he had shown himself to be. "No, sir," he said. "I only assumed you were having me on, but now I see that you aren't."

Frisk's severity was cracked suddenly by a smile. "You've no reason to credit my tales. What would you know of hunting?"

"Well, what shall we expect? Not pitchforks, I should think."

"It differs from court to court. The French ride on horses with spear and sword. I believe they follow the Swedish custom here, taking the quarry on foot. I believe that they will use muskets. Beaters and hounds will chase the beast in toward the hunting party. Always let the king have the first shot, and if your shot should later fell it, you best claim it was the king's shot which was fatal, though he miss by a league."

"Hah. Small danger that I shall shoot anything." Ben grunted. "I wonder what 'it' may be."

" 'Tis in the wagon up ahead," Frisk said. "I saw it in passing. I believe it is an East Indian panther."

Ben remembered the sinuous form in the Stag Moat—and its accompanying malakus—and suppressed a shudder. "How right you are, Robert," he said. "What a *fine* day this is turning into."

The sky paused in its weeping an hour or so later. By that time they had reached the hunting park, a verdant forest with trees spaced wide and manicured, a sort of imperial simulacrum of the wild. The wagon Frisk had mentioned stood with doors wide, and perhaps three score men with pikes and expressions ranging from bored to worried stood in a van on the small meadow where the emperor and his guests gathered. Aside from the huntsmen and guards, the party was small; the emperor, Prince Eugène, Newton, their footmen, and himself, Robert, and Frisk.

Ben gingerly took the musket he was presented. It was heavier than he had imagined, and the scent of wet steel, oil, and burnt powder tickled his nostrils.

"You know how to fire it, sir?" the huntsman asked.

"Yes," Ben replied, fairly certain that he did.

"Shall I prime the pan for you?"

"Ah—please." He watched carefully as the powder was measured, then took the musket and horn for himself.

Out in the forest, a faint barbaric music began, as of metal pans being beaten. He felt as if it were a noose of sound tightening on his neck.

The emperor walked up, and to Ben's vast surprise, clapped a hand on his shoulder. "Come along, Mr. Franklin," he said, actually smiling a bit. "I've a mind to see the hunting prowess of a man bred in the wilderness of America."

"Yes, Your Majesty," Ben replied.

"This way," the emperor said, indicating the forest. They started along, his three footmen, Robert, and Frisk following at a discreet distance. The dank smell of the woods enveloped them, cleaner and wilder than any city.

"I've often wished I might hunt in the New World," the emperor went on. "I hear so much of the wild beasts and untamed forests. Is it true that it is possible to walk across streams on the backs of the fish?"

"Well, Your Majesty, such is not the case in my native Boston, though I have heard such reports of the lands in the interior. I have never been there myself."

"Oh," the emperor replied, sounding somewhat disappointed. "Well, perhaps—after we reclaim our precious Spain—I shall visit our possessions there."

Ben nodded, not sure what to say, and he wondered, not for the first time, how the colonies fared. He had made every effort to discover what he could of them, but communications were poor even in Europe, and he had found no word of Boston or any other colony. Most surprising, there had not even been communication by aetherschreiber, the miraculous invention that communicated letters instantaneously over any distance. He had hunted the unseen air for messages of any sort, and in so doing made a disturbing discovery. His adjustable variation aside, other aetherschreibers could only communicate in pairs, the glass-and-regulus chimes that lay at the heart of them having been made a single piece and then cut apart. But no pair of aetherschreibers constructed before the fall of the comet still functioned—only those made since. He had proposed a hypothesis to Newton explaining this—that the impact of the comet had created waves in the aether that had slightly changed certain ferments in proportion to the distance from London. A pair of schreibers—one in Holland and the other in New York, for instance—would have been affected differentially, enough to spoil their congruence and thus their usefulness. Like so many of Ben's theories, Newton had dismissed this as pointless speculation.

"I am not a fool, you know," the emperor abruptly said.

"Your Majesty?"

"I know that I must seem a fool when I speak of Spain. Have you been to Spain, Mr. Franklin?"

"No, Majesty, I have never had that pleasure."

"It *is* a pleasure, make no mistake," the emperor assured him. "The happiest times of my life were spent there. The sunlight is like—like a sort of honey, sweet and warm. It is almost as if you could capture it in a jar." He sighed. "I understand, you see, that Spain is forever lost to the empire—or at least for many, many years to come. I make the appearance that it is still ours because I must, because the seeming of confidence is one of the few powers that an emperor—and an emperor alone—wields. Do you know what I mean? Law must be wrestled through the Diet. War is conducted by generals and soldiers, and they find their salvation or their doom short of my word, whatever may be said. But an emperor is the soul of the empire, its hope and its dream. The difference between a good emperor and a bad one is his ability to make these things manifest to his people. And so Spain is lost to us, but I can never credit that, do you see?"

"I believe so, Sire."

"I am perhaps not as good an emperor as I could be," he admitted, "but I do what I can. And so I have lost Spain and Vienna and Hungary—indeed, I have lost all but this city and the dream." He turned to Ben, his face rather tight, eyes showing a rare sort of fire. "Whatever sacrifice is required, I will not lose Prague, Mr. Franklin. I am most determined about that, do you understand?"

"Yes, Majesty."

"Good. Prince Eugène believes that Sir Isaac is hiding something from us, something concerning the ravings of a certain Muscovite prisoner. Is this the case or isn't it?"

Ben hesitated for a bare instant, and then shook his head. "Sire, I cannot speak for my master."

"No?" The emperor's voice had a rather queer ring to it. His gaze now darted about the forest, strangely hawklike in that sad, doggy face. "It approaches, and who shall say which of us will fall, man or beast?"

"Beast, I should hope, Majesty," Ben replied.

"One hopes. But I tell you truthfully, men die on these hunts."

A sort of frozen horror evolved from the base of Ben's spine. He saw Sir Isaac, not far away, conversing with Prince Eugène. Robert and Frisk were thirty paces back, compassed by royal guards and huntsmen. He suddenly felt very alone, very vulnerable, despite the crowd. Idly, he reached to fondle his aegis key, and with a falling sensation understood that he wasn't wearing it.

"Of course, I have been most careful," the emperor went on. "Sir Isaac is valuable to us, even when he is uncooperative; and so he will be well protected, better even than myself."

Ben understood *that*. Newton was in no danger, but *he* was. If Newton would not cooperate now, perhaps he would when the emperor proved his point by killing Ben.

"I hope Your Majesty exaggerates the danger," Ben said. His pulse had moved into his head, the wet air suddenly seeming inadequate to sustain him.

"I do not," the emperor said, softly. "So look to yourself, Mr. Franklin. I am fond of you, and so is my daughter—as, I believe, are a number of young ladies both in the castle and out."

"I endeavor to guard myself," Ben answered, mouth dry.

"And so you should." They walked a few more paces, and with each step Ben seemed to hear the clatter of skeletons behind him, grinning their bony grins, of James waiting patiently in the dark cottage, of the million souls in London, hands reaching up to pull him into a hell.

"You were in the observatory all night, two nights ago—just after Prince Eugène told you that Prague's doom had been forecast as coming from the heavens. Were you doing a horoscope?"

"No, sir. I was worried by the Muscovite's claim, and I was searching for its basis."

"And what basis do you think that might be?" The beating was very near now. "Quickly," the emperor commanded, "before it is upon us."

"I don't know, Majesty. I was looking." He felt suddenly calm, as if his head had detached from his shoulders, mocked at gravity, and stared down from above at an amusing scene. When would it happen? Where would it come from? He looked around, gripping his musket, feeling the noose tighten.

"Something came from the sky and destroyed London." The emperor's voice came from far away. "What was it?"

"I don't know, Majesty," Ben lied.

"You were there. You lived. What was it?"

"I don't know." He was trembling, he knew, which was silly, but his body seemed possessed of fears of its own.

"Quickly!" the emperor snapped, and then, suddenly, threw his gun up and fired.

The shadow of a huge cat appeared, hurtling toward them, above its head a flaming eye. In a blurred instant, Ben felt a familiar touch. Two years before, he had met the villain Bracewell on the Boston

Common, seen the sorcerer's strange familiar for the first time: a glowing red sphere in a misty cloud. Somehow, it had touched his brain lightly—it had seemed to Ben accidentally—but the moment had changed his life. He had seen the solution to tuning an aetherschreiber, and that in turn had led to everything since. Everything.

Now that sickening, alien taint invaded him again, and he suddenly saw Ben Franklin, a colorless image in hunting outfit, musket gripped in one hand, gaping. The emperor stood next to him, smoke pouring from his gun barrel. Less than a yard behind the gray, astonished image of himself, a man aimed the black maw of a pistol at the back of his head.

He let his legs go and dropped toward the muddy ground. A fusillade of shots exploded, but he was already hurling his heavy gun away, legs churning him back upright and then pumping like steam pistons through the woods. He did not look back, but simply ran, and when he came to a steep bank and hurled himself down it, something like a hornet whined by. He was briefly tangled in a vine, tore free, and continued.

More running. He wasn't afraid anymore—just angry, determined. He wished now that he had kept the musket, to make at least one of these lackeys pay for serving such a treacherous king.

But of course, the damned musket had probably not even been loaded.

He curved his course, trying to remember where he had last heard the beaters, not wanting to run into them, searching for the Moldau, which must be near. He was a strong swimmer, stronger than almost anyone else he knew. If he could cross the river unscathed, his opportunities for survival would increase somewhat. But how to find the river?

He studied the treeline as he ran, trying to make out where it seemed thinner. Spying what might be a gap, he jogged toward it, as the rain began again. That brought him a sort of joy; it would be harder to find him in the rain.

His exultation diminished when the earth began sucking at his feet, and he realized that he had run into a swamp. A few more steps would have him trapped, floundering in viscous water choked with dead grasses and rotted trees. Cursing the quagmire, he searched for what pursuit there might be. The gnashing of his breath, the thunder of his pulse, and the wet susurrus of rain made it impossible for him to hear.

For an instant he saw nothing, and then two dark figures resolved themselves. He hissed in frustration and crouched down. If one would come close enough, he might deprive him of his weapon. A slim hope.

"Ben!" A voice came to him, thin through the pouring rain. "Ben, f'r God's sake!"

He blinked water from his eyes. It was Robert and probably Frisk. The question was, did he trust them?

He looked at the swamp again, saw how hopeless it would be. And now he heard more men, shouting, and dogs.

"Here, Robin," he hollered.

The two paused and then crashed through the undergrowth toward him.

"Are you hit?" Robert asked, coming closer. "Wounded?"

"No."

Frisk waved his hand impatiently. "This way, or they shall find us."

"You know this land?"

"No. But I know land, and I know retreat."

"Retreat. Now, that sounds better than 'running like a shitting hare.'"

Frisk grinned. "Doesn't it? Come!"

They started off together at a trot.

"Where is the rest of the pursuit?" Ben asked a few moments later, suspicion freshening.

"The panther proved much for them, I think. It was attacking the king, when last I saw, and being unaccommodating in its expiration."

"But you two came right after me."

"You're my friend," Robert snapped. "The emperor an't." He paused. "Beside that, Frisk saw 'em try an' kill you. Shot the man dead," he added, "just as he fired on you. How did y' know t' dodge? That was fair impressive."

"I . . . I don't know. The emperor as much as told me what they were planning."

"Well, there he made a mistake, I think."

They crested a bank, and there lay the Moldau, its surface beveled and misted by rain.

"You can both swim?" Frisk asked.

"Certain," Ben replied, and Robert shrugged.

"Once out a hundred feet, they'll have nothing to train guns on, so I suggest we haste."

Ben was already stripping. He threw shoes, cloak, coat, and waistcoat into the dark waters, and then, as he heard the shouts approaching nearer, himself.

9

Crucible

Crecy groaned as the carriage shuddered to a halt, and then, with a hideous grinding, lurched into motion again.

"Enough of this." Adrienne gasped, renewing her hold on Nicolas, who had nearly escaped her embrace in the upset. "The carriage is no longer a quieter means of transportation than horseback, and certainly no better for your wounds."

"I agree," Crecy muttered, massaging her young scars. "A horse between my legs would better suit my health."

Adrienne passed up the obvious gibe, and instead called for the driver to stop. They climbed out into the pungent mud, where Adrienne saw the cause of their discomfort: The road—really a track some two yards wide—was rutted nearly two feet deep in places.

Crecy slogged off to the side and held Nicolas while Adrienne set about finding them horses. Her own mare was nearby, but Crecy needed a steed. There was no hurry; the little army was limited by the speed of its wagons, and on this road—if a road it could be called—that was no faster than the pace of a one-legged man. The heavy wains and carriages that bore supplies and artillery were better suited for these conditions than the pretty nobleman's carriage they had just abandoned, but even these labored mightily, horses frothed in sweat and mud, axles and wheels shattering with increasing regularity.

Walking back, she caught someone waving at her from one of the wagons—a flaxen-headed girl of some sixteen years named Nicole. She waved back. Nicole was new; the expedition had grown by perhaps a hundred in the month since it had set out, most of that inflation female.

"Whore," a nearby man muttered. For a frozen instant, Adrienne thought he was addressing her, and a violent, even murderous thing twisted her to face him. But the man was staring angrily at Nicole. Beneath his mud-spattered coat he wore the habit of a priest.

"Father, what cause have you to speak so of her?"

The priest—she had never learned his name—turned apologetic gray eyes to her. "I am sorry, Mademoiselle. I should not have spoken so in your presence."

"Nevertheless, you did."

He sighed, doffing his hat. "So I did. I am concerned, that is all. The farther we travel the more of these—young women—we acquire. The duke makes no effort to turn them away, even on my advice."

"And why should he?" Adrienne wondered aloud.

"On a moral level, they encourage sin. On a pragmatic one, our supplies of food run low."

"And yet we allowed you to join us."

"Indeed, lady, but I am a man of God."

"We already had a chaplain from Lorraine."

The priest frowned. "Two priests and near three hundred whor— camp followers. Which of us eats more?"

"That is not the question," Adrienne softly riposted. "The proper question is, who better earns their keep?"

His mouth gaped for an instant, then closed angrily before he spoke again. "Demoiselle, that is a statement offensive to God, as you well know."

"I know that it is a statement offensive to you, which I meant it to be," Adrienne said, smiling sweetly. "As to God, I do not pretend to know what He thinks." He seemed about to interrupt her, but she held up one hand. "No, Father, no more debate. I have things to be about." She nearly slipped in the mud turning from him, and laughed aloud at the ruin of her dramatic exit.

It was a heady thing, berating a priest, not something she could have done in her younger days. She smiled, realizing that as she had spoken, she had imagined herself as saying what Crecy might say.

Not exactly, for Crecy would have offered to demonstrate the power of even simple fornication to build morale. She would have hated the priest, whereas Adrienne understood him; in some ways, she had once *been* him.

"There is no spirit in this nag," Crecy complained, a half hour later.

"You have no need of a spirited mount," Adrienne replied distractedly, watching her son's changeable face. Nicolas seemed intrigued by the *schlock! schlock!* that the hooves of their mounts made as they sucked in and out of the mud. It was as if he sensed the connection between their motion and the sound.

"Perhaps not, but I'm always happier on a horse I know can really race, if I need to."

"We will do better for you soon," Adrienne promised.

"How are you faring with your calculus of angels?"

"Well enough. I have been experimenting."

"And what have you concluded? Have you found anything of practicality? Can you fashion wine from water?"

"I doubt it," Adrienne replied. "I can mediate certain simple changes, but such complex compounds as wine—"

"Hush, Adrienne. You never did know when someone was joking."

Adrienne checked herself and grinned. "My apologies. I spend too much time thinking about this, I suppose."

Crecy nodded. "Still, the 'djinni'—as you insist on calling them— seem concerned that you are reluctant."

"Reluctant? Cautious, rather," Adrienne replied. "The first of my experiments proved to me that even commands which seem simple can have unforeseen consequences. Suppose, for instance, I told them to make lead of copper?"

"Suppose you did?"

"Copper has more philosophic sulfur than lead. Moreover, copper has an extra lux atom per hundred."

Crecy faked a huge yawn.

"What that *means*," Adrienne continued stubbornly, "is that if they simply did as I commanded—made lead of copper by the most expedient means—the lux would suddenly be liberated, with a quantity of philosophic sulfur. The result would be an inferno, even if so much as a coin's worth were changed, charring anyone near to the bone."

"Oh!" Crecy said. "As I said, you should use caution in these experiments of yours—or perhaps work at greater distance from the rest of us."

Adrienne smiled lavishly. "I'll bore you no more. Come!" She put heel to her horse. "Hercule and Duke Francis are just ahead. Let's see what they have to say."

Crecy clucked her tongue and followed. They passed their own carriage, knocking along passengerless; a half dozen artillery wagons; then a crooked caterpillar of infantry a hundred yards long. A black wave of doffing hats followed them up the marching column, which Nicolas took great delight in, pointing stubby fingers and cooing. In fact, he seemed almost to be singing a song.

Beyond the infantry marched the duke's van of musketeers, twenty smartly dressed men, who also doffed their hats as they arrived.

"Good day, ladies," Duke Francis cheerfully cried as they rode up. "To what do I owe my good fortune?"

"That our carriage has become a torture rack, Your Grace," Adrienne replied.

"Yes, the roads are terrible, aren't they? These are indeed unfortunate times."

Hercule snorted. "The roads have never been good," he said. "I traveled tracks worse than this before you were born. And always the roads are worse when armies march."

"You think other armies have marched here recently?" asked Crecy.

"Certainly in the past year, but recently? Not too, for the villages hereabout are still provisioned, and a real army would have picked them clean." He cocked his head. "It is good to see you back in saddle, Mademoiselle de Crecy. I wonder if you would care to again take up a uniform as well? We've few enough officers."

Crecy smiled. "My identity is already known," she said. "I cannot pose as a man here."

The duke cleared his throat. "You would not be asked to don disguise, Mademoiselle."

"Then what is the use? Men will not follow me if they know I am a woman—or if they do, still they would be distracted by thoughts other than obeying me."

"If I say to obey you, they will," Francis piped.

"Please do not take offense, Your Grace," Crecy said, "but I fear that might only compel resentment."

"Well, then," Hercule returned, "at least ride with me and the light horse. We could reminisce on old times."

"Perhaps, then, I too shall ride with the light horse," the young duke interjected gallantly.

Crecy favored him with her loveliest smile. "Perhaps," she answered. "I am not yet up to anything so exerting."

Adrienne patted Nicolas, watching the exchange and wondering at how quickly she seemed to have been forgotten. After weeks of being pursued by Hercule and Francis both, it was strange to feel suddenly ignored in favor of the redhead. She supposed that if Crecy had been in good health all the while, she would hardly have been noticed at all.

Then again, she had been withdrawn lately, and she did have little Nico with her. Children seemed to make women invisible to men, or at least translucent. As Crecy chatted gaily with the two, Adrienne began to excuse herself to go and find Nicolas' nurse. The distant patter of gunshots stopped her.

"Shit," Hercule muttered. "That's from where our outriders were." He raised his voice to a shout, standing in his stirrups. "Captain! Bring up that cannon. Infantry!" He wheeled his horse. "Another time, Mademoiselles." He grunted. "Crecy, you must look to yourselves."

"We will."

A few more shots rang out, somewhat nearer. The duke peered intently ahead, as his guard drew up around him, checking the prime of their carbines and pistols. "It is perhaps nothing," Francis remarked. "Bandits or drunken soldiers play fighting." He drew his pistol and laid it nervously across his lap.

"It is likely nothing," Crecy agreed, "but perhaps we should draw further back."

"I can't do that!" Francis muttered. "My men should not think me coward."

He continued to scan the landscape. They were traveling through a

small valley with forested hills around, just the sort of place a marching army ought to avoid. Behind her, Hercule barked orders, echoes
of his shouts going down the line.

The mud at their horses' feet began to spit at them, hissing and
flinging up droplets, and at the same moment, a red lotus bloomed
from the ear of a young man at the front of the column. He swayed in
the saddle long enough for the sound of gunshots to finally reach their
ears and for Adrienne to realize that the road had just swallowed a half
hundred shots from less accurate snipers. Then the young musketeer
joined them in the mud, and all became chaos.

She flattened in the saddle as guns thundered all around her. A
thin blue cloud drifted from the trees on the hillside above them, but
they could not see the enemy. Their own cavalry screen charged
toward the source of the shots; and as Adrienne watched, two horses
went down. She wondered where she ought to take Nico. Under Hercule's direction, the train was drawing up into fighting order; but they
were already under attack, and it was impossible to tell where the
main enemy thrust would come.

The answer to that question came all too soon, as horsemen in
green uniforms poured down the hill like a wave, sweeping over the
Lorraine cavalry. Hercule's infantry fired a volley, and though a horse
or two tumbled, the general effect was of tossing stones at the ocean.

"Come," Crecy snapped, wheeling her horse about, but they had
nowhere to go, pressed in by the duke's van. And turning only revealed to Adrienne what she knew she would see: a similar wave,
hurtling down the other side of the valley, blades of cloud-gray steel
churning above like foam.

Nicolas pointed at them and laughed, not understanding what was
happening, and Adrienne gritted her teeth, swallowed down the weak
girl she had once been, and did what she had to do. The moment
stretched, frozen in time, as she opened the eyes of her *manus oculatus* and saw the malakim clustered about, awaiting her commands. It
only took an instant to know what to do. Seeing for the blind
malakim, she looked anew at those ranks of swords, saw them linked
by the affinity of the iron for iron, saw further in the iron the bonds of
mercury and sulfur, the shivering lux and damnatum, the spidery
forces that kept them bound.

"Mediate that," she told Djinn. "Strengthen the affinities between the iron, liberate the sulfur. Now."

The webwork connecting the swords thickened, brightened, and then, like lovers divorcing, the mercury and sulfur which made up the iron flew apart. A geometry of lightning connected each blade with the other, pure and white, while the air purred like a giant cicada.

"Now, once more," she said, turning to the other slope.

When the fire faded, there was no sound at all for a long, long moment. The entire army of Lorraine, struck dumb, gaped at the hillsides, where nothing at all moved, save the swords which—now liquid—trickled from seared, dead hands. Adrienne was aware that she still stood in her saddle, her own hand thrust high, the bright glow from it just dimming, and of eyes and mouths turned to gape at her, as if she were surrounded by fish tossed upon a bank.

But then a sound did begin, starting as low, hoarse cries but finally swelling to fill the valley with joyous shouting.

Cheering. They were cheering for her.

She looked again at the dead men on the hills, and the sluggish breeze brought the roasted smell of them to her. She swayed in her saddle as clamor grew louder, handed Nico to Crecy.

"Take him," she pleaded, though she could not hear her voice. "Take him before I faint." And then the saddle fell from under her, and a dark cloud filled her head. And still she heard the shouts, and mixed with them, her name.

1o.

Golem

"Far be it fr' me t' question y'r judgment, Herr Lehrling," Robert muttered, his face a floating yellow mask in the lamplight, "but this hardly seems sanctuary."

"Afraid for your Christian blood?" Ben asked mildly.

Robert's hands appeared, as disembodied as his face, gesturing inconclusively at the low-pressing brick ceiling, the ossuary table and arcane contraptions crowded upon it. "Blood, my eyes. Y'r certain that *it* is gone?"

"No. But the old man said it was, and we've proof enough that the demon haunts the castle now."

"Ah, yes, the wonderful proofs of science. How do you know it cannot haunt *both* places? Or that it has no brother, mother, or uncle left behind?"

"If you knew of a better place to hide, you should have said so," Ben grumbled sourly, picking at the dank floor of the vault with thumb and forefinger, wondering if the larger grit he felt might not be bone.

"Well, let me ponder that," Robert answered, with an exaggerated air of the philosophical. "The emperor tried to assassinate you; soldiers search Prague f'r us and likely will till doomsday—doomsday bein' pretty near—and the only hole you deem hidey-worthy is the cellar of a Jew who commands demons—who, oh, *yes*—you just *robbed*."

Ben chewed his lip, unable to explain what had led him back to ben Yeshua's door. Intuition had told him that the rabbi would not turn even his worst enemy over to the soldiers, and intuition had been right. Besides, who would look for them here?

"Now, I'll grant you I'm no scientific," Robert went on, "but it seems to me that Prague is not where we belong just now. There are other places we might seek our fortune."

"And just where might we go, in your opinion?"

"The Muscovados seem keen enough for your company."

"Well, I'm not for theirs. I'll hear none of that, Robin. You throw in with them, if you wish, but I shan't."

"I've nothing they want, save you," Robert pointed out.

"Aye, and you don't *have* me," Ben snapped. "That's the mistake everyone makes, thinking Ben Franklin is someone's *thing* to be bought, traded, or killed at whim. Don't you make that mistake, Robert—or you either, Frisk. If you think to sell me to anyone, best count on selling a carcass, because I am mightily sick of the uses I've been put to."

"Listen, Ben," Robert said, low. "I'm y'r friend. If I wasn't, I'd have cheerfully left you at the Moldau—or better yet, clobbered you across the back of the skull and left you fer the emperor's bullyboys, for I know they'd not pursue me without you. But from the first day in this kingdom, you've let your pride rule you, and with that tyrant in y'r head, y'r a blind man. Now, think what y' will of kings and nobles—Lord knows I think little enough of 'em—but f'r them there is no treachery, no sin, but only politics an' necessity. If y' don't see that, clear and cold, nothing will keep y'r body and soul together. A leviathan has wakened, and you best keep far from its maw."

Ben glanced up. "Done with your soliloquy, Robin?"

"Done enough. At least until we reach the point of eating one another down here, in which case I might ask y' for the salt."

Ben forced a little chuckle. "Experience is a hard school," he admitted, "but a fool will learn in no other. The thing is, Robert . . ." He suddenly felt very near to tears, and took an instant to force them back. "The thing is, there are things I'm accountable for. There are wrongs of my own doing I have to right. I've spent two years playing at the dandy, trying to forget that; but it always comes back to me. I may not be able to save this city, but who else will even try?"

"Now, listen closely," Robert said, as if explaining to a child. "This here's what I mean by *pride*. Just because you want to do something doesn't mean you can. See?"

"I understand you."

"No, you don't. Y' don't, don't, do *not*! Y' could never have saved London, and if ever there was a thing you could do for Prague, you've missed the chance."

"Robert, you don't understand. I—"

"Listen."

The single word came like the crack of a musket from the almost forgotten Frisk. He was leaning against the wall, arms folded, lips tight, lamplight playing in the craters of his pockmarked face, reminding Ben inappropriately of the moon, and Lenka, and the hope of the night before.

"Listen, you two nurslings. One or the both of you is going to explain to me what goes on here, or I will break your necks. When— if—the Jew returns, I will bow to him and leave him your corpses."

Ben sighed. "Captain Frisk, I'm sorry you've been drawn into these matters."

"No. Don't apologize and don't dissemble. It's my own concern that my lot is cast with yours, but by *God* I will know what game I am playing."

Ben had never heard Frisk's voice like that. He had never heard *anyone's* voice like that. Frisk's tone carried a conviction that Ben *would* explain himself because he *should*, because Frisk expected and deserved it.

Ben lowered his head. "It began when I was a boy in Boston . . ." he whispered.

It took an hour or two, for he and Robert together told Frisk all, the Swede nodding now and then, eyes unwavering and undoubting. When the story was done, Frisk stretched his arms back behind his head, worked his shoulders and neck thoughtfully against them, and smiled.

"Well," he said, "I got more than I expected. How long before this comet rubs away the city?"

"I don't know. Newton seemed in no hurry."

"Well, naturally not. Sir Isaac has the means to leave at his leisure, doesn't he?"

Ben hesitated, and then lifted his hands. "Probably, though I should think that he is watched closely."

"Not closely enough."

Robert frowned. "You know something, Cap'n Frisk?"

"Aye, as would the both of you, if you were more careful about what questions you asked, and of whom."

"And why would you, a simple soldier of fortune, ask such questions?"

Frisk rubbed the stubble on his chin. "Mr. Franklin, in light of your earlier outburst, I think you will not like what I'm about to tell you. I came to Prague in search of Sir Isaac and you."

"I won't say I'm surprised. I was always suspicious."

"You should have been. Though I didn't come to kidnap you, but to win you over—and failing that, to kill you."

Ben noticed Robert tense; his hand had been inches from his sword for some time, and now it slid a bit closer.

"Never fear," Frisk said, pointing languidly at Robert's hilt. "I've changed my plan."

"That were wise," Robert replied softly.

Frisk smiled. "You're a brave man, Robert, and loyal, and those are both rare and valuable things. Certainly more than this boy here seems to appreciate."

"He's young," Robert said.

"I was younger than he when first I took up arms, and far more foolish," Frisk admitted. "I have come to value young Mr. Franklin, despite his flaws. It seems to me that he is a better prize than his master."

"I thank you for your endorsement," Ben said. "But if you want me to fear you, best devise another stratagem. As I've said, I've been bullied enough, and if you think I know horror from your threats, you're as big a fool as I."

"I never did threaten you," Frisk said mildly. "You've explained to me why we sit in this dungeon. I'm explaining why I'm here with you, if you care to hear it."

"I would dearly love to hear," Ben acknowledged.

"I am of the Swedish army," Frisk said. "That far, I told you the truth. But I did not desert my country; I came here for the crown of Sweden, and for no one else."

"King Charles sent you?" Robert queried.

"He did. To persuade you to join us. You see how Russia rumbles down from the north. In all Europe, no army can challenge the tsar's. Already he camps in Holland, in the Rhineland, on the Black Sea. Who will stop him?"

"Not Sweden, I'd think," said Robert. "Fer twenty-two years King Charles has been in the field against the tsar, each year been driven farther from Russia and Sweden both."

"There were mistakes and bad fortune," Frisk confessed. "And yet at times we were so near. So *near* . . ." His cobalt eyes suddenly seemed mirrors for ghosts. "It was the winter that stopped us, not the tsar. Our men died in their blankets, stiff as icicles. Others lived, but their noses and feet rotted off. I still hear their wailing." His mouth tightened. "And still they fought, because their king asked them to! Because *he* never wavered from the front line, never left to rest in warm springs and dine on goose. Because soldiers will follow a soldier in a just war!"

"I doubt that none," Robert replied. "But it matters not how y' were beaten, only that y' were."

Frisk shook his head. "No. We have recovered, and the men of Sweden are ready to fight again—especially now, when all hangs in the balance. And the Turks will join us, if they can be shown we will win."

"But you admit that the tsar is beyond you."

"Moscow may be beyond us, but the king no longer dreams of that. His desire now is to draw a border, to say to the tsar, 'This shall never be Russian.' "

"And this has what to do with us?" Ben inquired.

Frisk nodded. "The king has heard of you. Everyone knows of magical Prague, holding out with scarcely an army, beating back all attacks—not by force of arms but by wizardry. That is what we lack. Men we have in plenty, and swords and guns and cannon. But the Russian drakes and mortars spit lightning and flame, intelligent things that always find their targets. Demons march with them. These are too much for simple bravery and military stratagems. We must have science of our own, gentlemen. I have come to convince you of that."

"Or to kill us, you say," Ben remarked.

"The tsar mustn't have you," Frisk said. "He mustn't."

Ben was quiet for a moment, and then looked frankly at Frisk. "What I see are wars between kings that I give not the slightest damn about. Do you know what concerns me, Captain Frisk? That the butter-headed tyrants of this world think nothing of tossing planets at one another in hopes—in hopes of what? Of calling themselves the lords of a blasted hell? That is what the world is becoming, sir, under their tender ministrations. I want nothing to do with any of it."

"Oh? You were all willing to let the emperor feed you pheasant and clothe you in silk—to make him toys and weapons and whatnot, weren't you?"

"For a purpose!" Ben snapped. "To give me opportunity to devise proofs against the worst of this, to counter sword with shield, not with other swords!"

"Very good. But your opportunity for that is lost here, as our good Mr. Robert Nairne here has made clear. Sweden will offer you that opportunity again, I promise you. We have swords aplenty; it is shields we desperately need."

Ben frowned, hoping for some brilliant response, but his head felt like a cauldron bubbling. There was too much in the pot already, without *this*.

"A moment, Captain Frisk—" he began, but the secret door banged open, and a shaft of light fell down the stairwell.

Frisk sprang upright and armed in a heartbeat, Robert right with him. Ben scrambled to his own feet, clumsy beside the two.

"Come up, thief and friends of thief," a quavery voice called down. "Come up."

Isaac ben Yeshua daubed at his head with a kerchief, both of which were stained bright red.

"What happened?" Ben asked him.

"Well, thief," the rabbi said, "the emperor, it seems, wants you very much. Yes, very much indeed."

"The soldiers did that to you?"

"Yes, thief, for they know that you were here before, don't they?" He indicated a bench next to the wall. "Sit, thief and friends of a thief."

Ben wished that the old man would stop referring to him as "thief," but it was, after all, true; and it would just be another stupid exercise of his pride to try and claim otherwise. He sat down.

"I'm sorry," he said. "Sorry that they hurt you."

"Yes, yes, I'm sure you are. And you are sorry by now that you stole my book." His eyes sparkled with anger, but also a sort of terrible satisfaction.

"Sir," he began.

"Two more have died, if that is what you mean to ask."

"Two more . . . ?"

"In the castle. The Golem has slain two more servants. The deaths are blamed on you, in case that interests you."

"They are innocents, sir. They should not be punished for my misdeed. You must call this—Golem?—back."

"Oh, *must* I, thief?"

"Please. If you wish vengeance on me, I will await it here. I beg you, recall your creature from the castle."

"First of all, *thief,* it is not 'my creature.' It was made long ago, to protect my people. When it became more dangerous than useful, its body of clay was dissolved, but its spirit remained, in case it should be needed again. What *I* did, you see, *thief,* was to keep that spirit here, quiet, harmless. That was all the power I had over it. I am not Solomon or Rabbi Low, to command or unmake such things. I leave it to you, Herr thief-lehrling, to set right the trouble you have caused."

"You could have warned me," Ben said. "I had no choice. My master told me to obtain the book."

"Don't speak such nonsense—you 'had no choice.' How can you talk with so much shit in your mouth? Don't you hate the taste?"

Blood rushed into his face. "What must I do?" he asked.

"Bring the book back here, of course."

Ben nodded. "I will."

Robert grunted as if struck. "Are you mad? You'll never get into the castle."

"Yes, Robin, I will. For more than one reason. I must know what Sir Isaac knows. And if I cannot save Prague, we must at least set about warning her people. And I must retrieve the book. If this Golem were killing the likes of the emperor or the courtiers, that were one thing. But poor Stefan . . ." He had a horrible thought. "I wonder—oh, God, I wonder who else is dead?"

"Two girls: Mila and Anna."

"Anna." Ben grunted, remembering the beautiful curve of her face, the enviable lines beneath her dress. *But not Lenka, thank God. Not yet.* But she was Newton's maid. How long could she survive?

He frowned at a sudden thought. "Rabbi, how is it you know who died in the castle tonight, and the like?"

The old man smiled, fissuring his face with lines. "I have many friends among the servants of the castle," he said. "It is good for us in Judenstadt if we know what winds blow in Hradčany."

"Then you might get a letter into the castle?"

"I know how such a thing could be done."

"Good. Very good. Then may I borrow pen and ink?"

"Why not steal it, thief?"

"Please, Rabbi."

"Yes, yes. Come this way. Steal a writing desk, too."

Ben nodded briskly and turned to where Frisk watched with a careful expression. "Captain Frisk," he said, "you have a deal, but you must wait. The rabbi calls me a thief, and thief I am. You must allow me to steal a thing or two more before we leave. If you do, it will greatly increase my worth to His Majesty of Sweden."

Frisk nodded almost imperceptibly. "And Newton?"

"I will try to fit him into my pocket, too."

11.

Two Storms

Two days later, they sighted sails. This was at first cause for some celebration, but when the count of unknown ships rose above twenty, the American flotilla fled as fast as it could. At least ten of the ships gave chase; it took them three days to lose the last, using every pirate trick Blackbeard had at his disposal. One of the ships came close enough to fire at them, though it was an intimidation tactic only; the nearest balls raised waterspouts more than a hundred yards short. Still, it did not settle the mood of the crew or raise their hopes. The device on the nearest ship looked French, but pirates often flew false flags, raising the blood flat only when victory was imminent. Not even Bienville was willing to risk it.

On the second day of the chase a storm swept upon them. Teach had often remarked on their luck in crossing the Atlantic without bad weather. Now, it seemed, their luck had changed. It was as if the western sky had been gashed with some giant knife, as if the black night that lay beyond the edges of the world were bleeding through, boiling toward them. That dark wind threw up remorseless mountains of liquid iron to stoop upon them, tossing them like corks. They drew down the sails, but even so the mainmast cracked, and five men from the *Queen Anne's Revenge* were swallowed into the white jaws of the waves and never seen again. When the storm finally cleared, it was to a desolate seascape, empty of any ship save their own.

"We should wait here for them," Nairne said, meeting Blackbeard's hard gaze.

"If there is anyone left to wait for," the pirate retorted. "An' that we do not know."

"We can't be the only ship that survived," Nairne persisted. "Besides, the compass attuned to the *Dauphin* still points."

"Aye, an' it would point whether the *Dauphin* were on the sea or below it."

"We can sail to them and discover it," Nairne replied "floating or drowned, they can't be so far from us."

"We need a port," Blackbeard growled. "We need food, rum, and sweet water; and most of all, we need to *repair* this hulk. As it is, we'll run the pumps day and night to keep her afloat. We're in shape to sail only one direction—landward. Now, Mr. Nairne, you will point me landward, or I shall crack your skull, I promise you."

Nairne glared, but raised his finger to indicate the horizon. "It's there," he said, "but my calculations show we've been blown almost to the Pillars of Hercules."

"Uh." Teach grunted. "The Barbary coast."

"Yes, Captain, you see? What port here do you trust well enough to try alone?"

"What port do I trust *anywhere*?" Blackbeard snarled. "And yet we must have one."

"Can we not sail for the space of a day as the needle points toward the *Dauphin*?"

Blackbeard glared at Nairne, arm twitching strangely, and for an instant, Red Shoes was certain he would draw his pistol and shoot Nairne in the head. But after a moment of chewing his beard, he nodded brusquely. "Very well. One day. But if another storm catches us, we're done for."

Up above, the sailor in the crow's nest hollered something. They all looked up as he repeated, "Sail."

"There!" Nairne remarked. "Our discussion is moot."

Blackbeard frowned. "Which direction does your scientific needle put the *Dauphin*?"

"Sou'west."

"Then why is my man pointing east?"

"It's probably one of the others, one of the ones we have no compass for—the *Scepter*, the *Lyon*, perhaps."

"We'll hope so, then," Blackbeard snapped. Then he bellowed, "Ready her for a fight, men."

An hour later, they grimly watched the nearing ships.

"Take her to full sail," Blackbeard shouted.

"Damn," Nairne remarked.

"Not our ships?" Red Shoes asked.

Blackbeard shook his massive head. "No. See there? Those three are *galliots*, I'll wager. See how they jump in the water? Those are oars doin' that. Small ships, fast ships in a flourish. Back behind them are two caravels. No, these are some of those chasing us before the storm."

"Might they be peaceful?"

Blackbeard shook his head. "Corsairs, I'm damned sure. Merchants go under sail, real war galleys are bigger. No, these are our pursuit. Now they see us cut away from the flotilla and move in for murder."

"I'll trust you in that matter," Nairne said.

"And so y' should. It's what *I* would do, were I them."

"We can't out run 'em, as we did before?"

"Not with this gut full of brine. No, they'll catch us sooner or later. But I want to make 'em work for it, especially the caravels, on account of *they* have the real fire. So if we can engage the galliots *first*, we'll have the better chance."

"You really think we can best five ships?" Nairne asked doubtfully.

"If we best only four, then still we die," Blackbeard said. "Edward Teach has no desire to die this day."

He stalked off, shouting orders.

"Can we win?" Red Shoes asked Nairne.

"Stranger things have happened, I suppose. Can you use those hands yet?"

Red Shoes curled his hand's children. They would not fist, but he could move them.

"Enough to fire a musket, I think."

"Have you any magical tricks to help us?"

"I will think on it," he replied.

He did think on it, furiously, as the ships grew nearer, until he could see what Blackbeard meant. The galliots resembled long, wide canoes with sixteen oars on a side, each oar pulled by several men, and were terribly fast. The caravels—three-masted vessels—were slower but much larger. Not so large as the *Revenge*, but nearly so.

Blackbeard seemed more worried about the caravels. Was there anything he could do to them?

He still had his wire-melting shadowchild. He supposed he could send it over, but he doubted that the ships were held together by wire, and something more massive—a cannon, say—was too large for his servant, even if it were made of the same metal, which was unlikely. If the storm were still overhead he might call Thunder, but the clouds had fled the sky. He tried sending his shadowchild for a taste of sail, but like wood—or anything which had once been living—it proved too rich for the spirit.

He might boil some small portion of the sea, but did not think that would help very much, since he could boil very little of it.

Blackbeard was forward, shouting orders again, and in response the *Revenge*, creaking and complaining, finally turned to face her opponents.

Most of the crew were Blackbeard's own, of course, and now they showed it, climbing into the rigging, shrieking curses to tell the corsairs that they had attacked no weak-willed merchant vessel, but the three galliots came on. Red Shoes could see them clearly now, the rippling muscles on the backs of the rowers, the bunched warriors with muskets or naked blades. He propped his own gun on the edge of the ship, checked the prime, and fumbled his clumsy hands to the trigger. He knew tricks for fast healing, for healing things that should not heal, but nothing he knew of could put what he had done to himself right in short order.

"Fire!" He heard Blackbeard bellow, but he held, knowing he would hit nothing at this range, and then realized he had misunderstood anyway as the *Revenge* roared and rocked back as twenty cannon unleashed nearly in unison. Smoke and spray hid the approaching ships for a moment, but when it cleared, they had the satisfaction of seeing one of the small craft spun about in the water and the bloody swath a charge of grapeshot had cut through its gang of rowers. Blackbeard's pirates redoubled their cries, and a volley of musket shots erupted.

Their attackers, however, suddenly changed tactics. One came on, but the other two swung broadside, each in a different direction, one toward their bow and the other aft. Soon they would be fighting in three different directions. Both flanking ships unloaded their guns, and the deck quivered from the dull crunch of impact. Nearby, Tug waved his cutlass and whooped. "Six pounders if even that!" he howled. "Darlin' baby guns! They'll have to do better 'n that!"

But Tug was an exception; a lot of the men seemed worried. And beyond the immediate fray, the sails of the caravels were growing by the moment.

Red Shoes sighted carefully at the oncoming ship. After a second's consideration, he chose the drummer, the fellow whose booming strokes timed the pull of the oars. If any one of these was a sorcerer, it would be that one. He had to move his whole hand to squeeze the trigger; but when the weapon kicked him in the shoulder, it was worth it, for the drummer thrashed to the deck, his rhythm broken forever.

Wood chipped near him, and the air sang with returning fire, but Red Shoes ignored it, methodically reloading his weapon. It was a clumsy business.

"Sweet Jesus," said the fellow next to him, a straw-haired man named Roberts. One of his ears was now missing. He sounded surprisingly calm, considering.

For a hundred heartbeats after that, there was no sound audible save the peal of cannon, as all four attacking ships fired at will. Ten paces from Red Shoes, the rail blew apart, and wooden shrapnel stung his cheek. He winced and continued trying to load his musket, but using the ramrod was almost impossible.

The air slapped him, hard, and the eye of the world blinked. He came back to awareness with Tug shaking him.

". . . boarding," the big man was saying. "You stick next to old Tug, y' hear?" It sounded as if Tug were a very long way away.

Men were fighting on the deck. Some looked like Fernando, with his almost black skin, but most were the color of cypress, clad in colorful pantaloons and head wraps not unlike his own. They swarmed over the gap in the rail, pushing Blackbeard's men back, the fighting spreading to the center of the ship.

The caravels were very near, now.

Red Shoes noticed Nairne, not far away, hanger in hand, hacking at the boarders; and he stumbled in that direction, fumbling for his *kraftpistole*. If he could get a clear shot, he could kill many at once, and then perhaps they could stop the rest from boarding. Unfortunately, Nairne and the rest were in the way.

One of the corsairs hurled himself at them, but Tug hammered him into the deck with a blow from his cutlass, swinging twice more to sever an arm; but after that at least ten corsairs came over the rail. Nairne was still in the way, and Red Shoes found himself having to dodge back from a man in a red-and-black-checked turban. He hated to waste a *kraftpistole* shot on a single man, but it seemed he had no choice, as his attacker drew his own sidearm.

And then his opponent faltered, his face become a mask of terror. Red Shoes did not waste the opportunity; as the man stood transfixed, he clubbed the heavy iron point of the *kraftpistole* across his face, wondering what the man had seen to shake him so.

Then Blackbeard swept by him, a pistol in each hand, and he knew. Teach had plaited his beard and hair, tying each braid with black ribbons. His head was wreathed in smoke from perhaps twenty match fuses stuck under his hat brim, and from that cloud stared eyes bereft of sanity, mercy, and humanity. Blackbeard was death, and any who saw him knew it.

He walked into the crowd of men as if they were not armed at all, firing his pistols point-blank, and two heads exploded like melons. One of the corsairs shot back, but his hand must have been shaking, for the ball merely snapped one of the matches from Teach's hair. The pirate didn't even blink, but drew two more pistols from the braces crossing his chest, fired, drew the last two, fired again, and then pulled out his cutlass. The nearest corsair raised his hand in defense and had his forearm splintered into his face. They fell away from Blackbeard, and still he came on.

Red Shoes followed.

At the rail it finally seemed to occur to the men that they were ten, facing a single man, but by then it was too late. Aiming around the pirate captain, Red Shoes finally had a clear shot. Holding his weapon with both hands to keep it steady, he pulled the trigger, and white fire jagged through the corsairs, pitching all but three of them, burning, into the sea.

The surviving three jumped.

Blackbeard swept his lethal gaze about the ship, and his own men, probably from experience, scrambled out of the way. All their attackers had been driven from the ship. For an instant, there was silence, as if the world were drawing a breath, and then a single cannon shot whizzed over the bow.

Both caravels were drawn up close, broadside, thirty guns between them trained on the *Revenge*.

Panting like a wounded bear, Blackbeard moved up to the rail. A hundred paces away, on the corsair ship, a man in a bright yellow turban held up a cutlass. He must have had a fine voice, for despite the ringing in his ears, Red Shoes could make out his words.

"Surrender. Surrender and accept our escort, and not another man among you shall die."

Red Shoes thought that Teach's eyes would bug from his head.

"Escort to where?" Nairne called.

Blackbeard moved like lightning, whipping his remaining pistol up to Nairne's temple.

"Shut up," he hissed.

Nairne stared into the muzzle without the slightest indication of fear.

"For the sake of intelligence," Nairne whispered back. "Not for the sake of surrendering."

"Shut up," Blackbeard repeated, and then, deliberately, faced the other captain.

"I will make you a better offer," he roared. "Give me one of your ships, and I won't sink the other."

Even at that distance, Red Shoes saw the other captain's eyes widen. A sprinkling of laughter traveled around the corsair ship.

"You misunderstand," the Barbary captain called back. "I may make such offers and demands. You may not."

Blackbeard nodded, and turned to his master gunner, Josiah Warn.

"Blow them out of the Goddamned water," he said.

12.

Jealousy and the Moon

Duke Francis Stephen of Lorraine raised his wineglass. "A toast," he said, beaming. "To Mademoiselle de Mornay de Montchevreuil, our savior and beloved guest."

Adrienne humbly inclined her head as the duke, Hercule, and Crecy drank the toast.

"I would rather drink to the recovery of Mademoiselle Crecy," Adrienne said, lifting her glass.

"Hear, hear," the duke seconded, finishing what remained of his wine. His valet quickly filled his glass again, and he sipped before addressing the company.

"I have been among the men today, and they send their regards. To tell you the truth, I believe that many had begun to fear for the success of our quest, but you have restored their hearts, lady. What man does not take hope when the new Joan of Arc rides with him?"

"Sir!" cried Crecy. "Do not curse my friend so by bringing that name upon her! I, for one, would prefer not to see her martyred."

"Of course," the duke replied, "but Saint Joan was martyred because she was surrounded by fools, and I hope that the present company is not comparable!"

"There are fools in any company," Crecy remarked.

"I suppose you speak of the chaplain," Hercule said.

"He did refuse to join us," Adrienne murmured.

"You must understand that he is not so much a fool as a jealous man. That he, a man of God, is not so favored by God as our dear Adrienne."

"Jealousy is foolish in and of itself," Crecy avowed, with perhaps a hint of irony in her voice. "And in this case, leads to foolish comments. He has been heard to swear that our Adrienne is in league with the devil."

"An unheeded remark," Francis asserted, "for every man among us knows that were she diabolic, she would not have delivered us from the Russians. No, pay no attention to that one, I beg you. He serves his purpose as confessor to the men, but no one will listen to him in this."

"I do not take him to heart," Adrienne added, trickling a little more of the dry wine upon her tongue—watching amusedly as the duke tried to keep his composure, despite the fact that Crecy was stroking his leg with her bare foot. Privately, she believed that the men in general simply did not care whether she served good or evil, so long as she was on *their* side. When she rode along the train, she caught a distrustful glance now and then—but always it melted into a simulacrum of adulation when it found itself discovered. No, she would not be named a witch until either her powers failed or the company reached a secure place and festered there a while. In peace they would turn on her, not before.

The next round was brandy, not wine, and Adrienne took only a bit, having proven in the past unable to withstand the effects of strong liquor. Crecy, however, did not hesitate, matching the men glass for glass, until all three were rather unsteady.

After dinner, they left the duke's tent, Crecy swaying and linking arms with her as the two men smoked what little tobacco remained.

"You are feeling well, Veronique?" Adrienne asked. "Is the brandy well in your belly?"

"Ah, very well, my dear," she answered, her words scented with apricot. "It is good to be drunk again, to be impaired from choice rather than from wounds. And how is it with you, O Sorceress? I note you drank little."

"I have a lot to think on tonight."

"Tha's Adrienne," Crecy slurred. "Always much to think about. I wonder—I wonder . . ."

"What do you wonder, my dear?"

"I wonder what you think of *me* these days?"

"How do you mean?"

"You used to be so helpless. Such a little girl. You needed Veronique then, to wield her sword, to teach you what a woman can do even without a sword. I wonder if you need Veronique anymore."

"Of course I still need you. You are my friend."

"Yes, yes, your friend. Of course I am! And yet, I notice, Adrienne, that you came by less to see me when I could not walk than you might. And that you have seemed less than eager to see me put my sword back on. . . ."

"I only fear for your health, Veronique. What is this? You've never spoken like this before."

"I've never—" Crecy suddenly pushed away from her, so violently that it bruised her arm, reminding her how terribly strong the other woman really was. "I've never been the *weak* one before," she snapped.

"Weak? You aren't weak."

"No? Who is the stronger now? And you surrounded by all these able men, ready to lay down their lives? What need have you of me?"

Adrienne folded her arms. "I am no longer a helpless child who needs your constant protection. Is that so terrible?"

"Or perhaps we became friends merely because you had no choice, no one else to guard you, and now that that condition is removed you disdain my company."

"Veronique, when have I ever disdained your company?"

Crecy pulled her arm away. "Now you treat *me* like a child."

"Veronique! Stop this. I have given you no cause for this."

"No? And yet you avoid me, preferring d'Argenson or the duke or even that little tart Nicole. How am I expected to feel?"

"Crecy . . ."

Crecy's eyes flashed silver in the moonlight. "You will never understand what I gave up for you, Adrienne. But if you don't understand, I at least hold you to remembering."

"Veronique, that is unfair. For more than two years I have been your friend, though you have lied to me time and again. For all that I know, you are lying yet."

"Yes, for all you know, I am. What does Crecy know of truth? Or of love?"

"Hush, Veronique. You have gone too deep into your cups tonight."

But the redhead gathered herself and straightened. "Not too

much," she murmured, "not too. I am sorry, Adrienne. Come and walk with me. Tell me of the stars while still they shine."

Adrienne hesitated. The duke of Lorraine had taken leave back to his tent, and she noticed that Hercule was wandering slowly away.

"You should rest, Veronique. You are in a mood tonight, and I have no patience with it."

"You must have patience with me," Crecy whispered. "I am unused to this, Adrienne. I am not used to being the feeble one."

Adrienne peered into her friend's slightly stupefied eyes and kissed her lightly. "You are not feeble Veronique—merely drunk. Now, hush and good night."

Crecy drew back, her face working through three or four expressions, and then she finally said stiffly, "Good night, in that case." And then, with a touch of her old sarcasm, "And flights of angels sing thee to thy sleep. For they no longer sing for me." She winked and leered slightly. "I think I shall see what sort of man this young duke is—or would like to be."

"Crecy, you warned *me*—"

"Teach your grandmother to suck eggs," Crecy replied, and with that walked toward the duke's tent carefully, as if on a tightrope. Adrienne watched her go, wondering if she should try to stop her—but how could one stop Crecy, once her mind was set?

Instead, she turned her attention to the stars. The Milky Way was just visible, obscured not by clouds but by the burnished brilliance of the rising moon. Saturn was an unflickering light halfway up the horizon. She was wondering if she could use the djinni to bring her reports of such heavenly bodies, when a quiet cough interrupted her. She turned to find Hercule d'Argenson.

"Am I intruding, Mademoiselle?" he asked.

"Not at all. I was admiring the stars, that is all."

"As they admire you, no doubt."

She smiled. "You are in a fine humor tonight."

"And why shouldn't I be?"

"You do not worry, like the chaplain, that I might be some sort of witch?"

"I know for a fact that you are a witch." He stepped toward her. "For you have long since bewitched me."

She closed the yard separating them, feeling suddenly very bold, challenging him with her uptilted chin. "Your talk is very fine, sir," she said. "Your mouth has a very pleasing way with words. I wonder — can you put those lips to some other use, or are they good only for drenching the ear with honey?"

His eyes widened. "Mademoiselle, I—"

"No, Monsieur, you cannot address my question with more words. I demand empirical proof or none at all."

He shut his mouth, then, and reached the back of his knuckles over to touch her cheek. A small, triumphant smile on his face, he gently parted her lips with his finger.

He tasted of brandy and smoke, and the warmth of his mouth was shocking. She knotted her fingers in his steinkirk and pulled him closer, and he crushed against her, hands stroking goose bumps down her back. He painted breath across her cheek, to the hollow of her neck, buried there and planted fire, so that finally she gasped, the heat dribbling into her belly and along the face of her thighs.

"Your tent," she said. "It is empty?"

"Save of air, milady."

"Take me there, then," she whispered.

"Are you certain?"

"Take me there."

Amongst his sheets, she nearly laughed, for he was, it seemed, a man with much experience, finesse, and technique — certainly he was more proficient than any lover she had ever had — and yet he had nearly broken his leg trying to undo his breeches. At last she understood Crecy's joy in lovemaking, in seeing a strong man become endearingly weak. Lying with Louis had been a chore, a repugnant, dirty thing. With Nicolas, it had been a meeting of hearts through the medium of flesh, an act of love. She did not love Hercule, but he gave her something she had never had: simple pleasure, true enjoyment. When they were done, and he fell into languid sleep, she patted his brow, dressed, and went back out to regard the stars, grinning foolishly. She walked in circles around the camp, happy and alone.

In time, she grew tired and made her way back to her own tent, and to her surprise, found Nicolas there, as if awaiting her. "Did you slip from your nurse, Nico?" she asked, stroking his head. He laughed, a funny little laugh, and for a moment she thought he said something— a silvery trickle of nonsense that yet sounded like—*something*. She was just gathering him into her arms when suspicion swept through her like a chill wind. With a little snarl, she opened the eyes of her fingers and swept its gaze through the aether, not knowing for sure what she was searching for. Crecy's story came back to her, of the childhood voices that raised her up, of the changeling process by which she was formed. Was this happening to Nico? For the love of God, if so, for how long?

But the aether was quiet—as quiet as it could be, filled with its strange choruses and plainsong. Nevertheless, she called one of the djinn to her.

"Mistress?" it hummed.

"Watch him," she said. "Watch my son, and let no power touch him. Do you understand? Alert me should any sympathy develop between him and any of your kind."

"Yes, mistress," the creature intoned.

"Good," she said. "Good."

Feeling a bit better, she stroked her son's head. Children, after all, were strange without the aid of unseen intervention. Nico giggled again at her touch, and then pointed at the moon, now risen higher, and she said. "Yes, my sweet. You have not seen her much, *la lune.*"

"Lalooon," Nico repeated, crooning the vowel.

"Nico!" she said. "You've said a word!"

"Laloooon!" he crowed again.

"What a smart boy!" she said. "Your first word!" She felt suddenly very proud, very much in love with this little creature of hers, and she gathered him up, sang him a lullaby about the moon, over and over, until he fell asleep, and then she took him into the tent, crawled into her blankets, and joined him in untroubled slumber.

13.

The Black Tower

Ben tensed at the approaching footsteps, laying his hand on the cold, brass grip of his sword. When he realized what he had done he sighed and withdrew his fingers from the hilt. After all, if it was someone he really needed the sword against, he was done for anyway. In fact, he wished now that he had left the weapon behind. The mere fact that he was armed might scare some would-be attackers, but cannier ones would only take it as a sign that they had best creep up behind him or shoot him from a distance.

He could see the person below him now, a woman as he had hoped, cloaked against the night. He waited a moment longer, trying to perceive whether she was alone, whether she had been followed. After a few moments, with no sign of anyone else, he called softly down.

"Lenka."

The hood turned up to him and revealed Lenka's face, as he had seen it last, pale in the moonglow.

"Benjamin?" she hissed.

"Yes. Thank you for coming."

"I shouldn't have. If I am ever found out—"

"You won't be, I swear. Even if they catch and torture me." He paused, then slithered forward on the tile roof until his head and shoulders hung above her. "Did you bring it?"

"Yes. I only pray that 'tis the right one."

"Toss it up."

"You didn't keep our appointment," she said.

"I am indeed sorry, lady, but I was indisposed."

"They say you tried to assassinate the emperor."

"Oh, indeed," Ben replied sarcastically. "Wait a moment."

He swung around on the roof until his legs dangled over and then inched back, teasing gravity before giving himself to it and rushing to the inflexible stone below.

"Such strange rats scurry about these parts of Old Town," Lenka remarked, as he winced, stood, and brushed at his suit.

"Yes. That's all I've been doing, scurrying." The crescent moon stood straight above, making shadow of her face, but he thought he saw a puckish smile on it. "Do you believe them?"

She shrugged. "No, but neither do I care. Are you hurt?"

"Not as I've noticed. I was lucky." He looked slowly around once more, as much to avoid her gaze as to search for possible threats, and added, "I've heard others were not so lucky."

She nodded and spoke more seriously. "Anna, near Newton's rooms, and Mila, near the Black Tower."

Ben started. "The *Black* Tower? Not the Mathematical?"

"You know what it is, don't you? The thing."

"I tried to tell you the other night," Ben replied, "but you were too stubborn. And I warned the others."

"I know. Anna—she was angry. She and Stefan were sometimes lovers. She thought to see it and—well, I know not what, and neither did she, and so now she is dead."

"Oh. But Mila—"

"Does not even work in the palace but elsewhere within the castle walls. She was passing the Black Tower. Were we in danger the other night?"

Ben had been only half listening. "Us? No. The book was in his rooms, then, and in any event we were in the wrong tower, it seems. The *Black* Tower, eh? Not the Mathematical?"

"Book?"

"Yes. There is a book, written in Hebrew. This thing that kills is searching for the book. Lenka, I must get into the tower, which means I must get into Sir Isaac's rooms and borrow his key. You are certain that he is not in them?"

"He dines with the emperor tonight."

"Good. I'll put a stop to these killings, if all goes well. But if I don't, if something happens to me— Lenka, I want you to leave the castle. Leave Prague."

She snorted. "Such an easy thing to say, so impossible to do. I've no horse nor carriage nor money, and as a woman I'll not be able to get those things save perhaps at the cost of my back—and still I'll be hung if they catch me. Better that you just don't get caught."

"I'll do my best, believe me. Here, let me see that." He took the bundle she carried and unfolded it, and to his relief saw that it *was* his aegis. "Now if only it works," he remarked, shucking off the cloak the rabbi had given him.

"Always getting undressed around me. You'd think you would learn a lesson."

"Not me. I'm too scientific to learn anything practical." He pulled his arms through the tight sleeves.

"Now, watch closely," he whispered and slipped the key into his pocket.

Her gasp told him that it worked, as did the sudden variegated tint he could see out of the corners of his eyes. Satisfied, he removed the key.

"I'd heard about that," she said, "but seeing it is another thing. I guessed that's what I was bringing you."

"And, again, I much thank you for it. I'm afraid I've no way to repay you at the moment."

"Repay me by not getting me hanged," she said. "And now what do you intend to do?"

"I intend to watch you walk safely away from here."

"And then?" she pursued.

"And then I shall march through the front gate."

"I could see—something—even while you were invisible."

"At night, on higher calibration, there will be little to see. Besides, the guards are lax."

Her head wagged from side to side. "Not now, they aren't. Here is what I suggest; you follow me back to the castle, and there I will make some sort of distraction for the guards."

Ben shook his head. "That's too dangerous for you."

"What is more dangerous is that you will be caught, and despite what you think, when tortured, you will tell all."

Ben remembered Prince Eugène's remarks about the Russian prisoner and torture, and reluctantly nodded.

"Besides," she said, flashing a nervous smile, "there is still our bargain. I will accompany you into Sir Isaac's secret laboratory."

"No."

"Oh, yes. It was our bargain."

"Things are very different now."

"Not so different," she replied sweetly. "It is still I who have the key."

He considered that and sighed. "How will you distract them?" he asked.

"Clever," he whispered to the prismatic blur that was Lenka, as they left the guards at the front gate behind them. "Is it safe for me to weaken the aegis?"

"Yes. There is no one in the second courtyard."

His vision cleared enough for him to see that Lenka wore a triumphant smile.

"Clever, you say? I would rather avow that men are such buffoons that the simplest artifice works on them."

"Most men don't expect a glimpse of thigh from a woman strolling up to the castle," Ben replied. Lenka had torn her skirts and feigned distress, claiming that some boys had set upon her and then let her go when she'd screamed. Though unable to see well enough to read the expressions of the guards, Ben had heard clearly enough in their voices that—despite their expressions of concern—they had been more grateful that the "boys" had made off with a fair section of Lenka's skirts than that she was otherwise unscathed. Indeed with the aegis turned down, he found *himself* distracted by the bit of stocking and bare skin flashing beneath the borrowed cloak.

"It also diverted them from asking what business I had outside the castle this time of night. It seems that all men do not share your ill opinion of my appearance."

"Pfah. As you said, men are imbeciles. Show them a little flesh, and all their standards drop."

"I *see*. Well, thank you for making that clear, Mr. Franklin. I and my key shall now take our leave of you, and a good night to you, sir."

"What did I say?" Ben asked. "You must have misunderstood me. I meant to say that even the smallest glimpse of Venus robs men of their wits."

"That sounds more convincing," Lenka decided. "Now, quiet. Some people ahead."

Robbed of banter, Lenka's nervousness became a little more apparent—as did his own—but the courtiers making their way through the yard did not even notice Lenka, much less himself. He reflected that servants had scant need of an aegis to be invisible.

Save to other servants, such as the guards, he reminded himself, for as they approached those flanking the entrance to the palace, they greeted her—though they did not challenge. Doubtless straining for a glimpse of thigh, they too saw him not at all.

In the hall, Ben never let his gaze rest, sweeping here and there, searching for the smallest sign of the Golem, but noticed nothing out of the ordinary. In fact, the wavering of the air near Newton's door was gone as well. More evidence that the book had been removed, likely to the Black Tower, along with everything else.

No one was near when Lenka opened the door and they both stepped through.

Heaving a sigh of relief, Ben detached the aegis key and strode hurriedly across the anteroom to the study.

"You know where he keeps it?" Lenka asked.

"Of course. It's been a long while that I've had my eye on this." He found the little wooden coffer and flipped back the lid, and there it lay, a Pythagorean key, a sliver of metal-bound crystal.

"There, now." He sighed. He turned to Lenka and bowed. "Excellently done, and my highest regards. And now, see if you can find the book, a slim little thing, just so in size." He showed her with his hands.

A thorough search of the study turned up no sign of *The Sepher*, which did not surprise Ben in the least. Nor did he find any notebooks; all, it seemed, had been removed.

"Well." He sighed. "Again, thank you. I'm now off to the Black Tower."

"As am I," Lenka informed him.

"No. Your shapely leg will not get us past the tower guard."

"There is no guard at the Black Tower," she replied smartly.

"No, but there will be guards about—at the Lobkovic Palace, for instance, which if I remember correctly is just next to the tower. Besides, now you have no key to hold ransom."

"Doesn't Sir Isaac have such a garment as yours?"

Ben narrowed his eyes. "A jade after my own heart," he muttered. "But remember that you asked me to keep you from the hangman's noose. Letting you walk into the tower with me might do harm to that cause."

Her lips tightened a bit. "I want to go with you. There is something in the tower that I wish to see as well."

"We haven't time to argue about this," Ben hissed.

"Good. Then stop arguing."

"Rot you, Lenka . . ."

She started suddenly across the room, headed for Newton's wardrobe. "Never mind. I'll find it myself."

Ben threw up his hands. "Cease," he grunted. "I'll show you."

And a quarter of an hour later they opened their second lock, this one on the heavy iron portal of the Black Tower.

The Black Tower was smaller, tighter, and altogether more square than the Mathematical Tower, where Newton's primary laboratory was. What did he work with here, that he should want to keep it separate from the rest, and secret from Ben?

A strong sense of déjà vu gripped Ben as he stepped through the doorway. Almost, he could have been in London, more than two years ago, entering Sir Isaac's study. Three heavy tables were every inch covered with philosophic equipment, notebooks, powders, colored liquids, and tools. In the center of the chamber mounted a pyramidal platform, like the one in London—as before, crowned with a scintillating sphere. Now he regarded all with more learned eyes, however, and knew the reddish luminescence within the globe for what it was—a captive malakus.

But as he moved amongst the tables, he saw that Sir Isaac had not merely re-created his old haunt; there were new things here. The dissected bodies of animals, ambient in glass jars of yellowish liquor. Human parts—arms, legs, a head—treated in the same manner, muscle laid open to the bone. Near each of these receptacles were sketches of the offended flesh, diagrammed in Newton's cryptic hand. Only vaguely did he notice that Lenka, seemingly unawed by it all, had found a crammed bookshelf and was pushing her way through the books.

He knew he should hurry, but like a boy in an old tale stumbling upon the ogre's treasure, he was transfixed. Where to begin?

Along with the dissections and their drawings were strange models: armatures of steel, articulated like bones, muscled with some azure claylike substance, tough and springy to the touch. Some aped the limbs of the once-living specimens, but others bore more resemblance to the legs of insects. In one place sat an aetherschreiber, but without the customary clockwork to drive the arm, having instead more of the bluish integument.

Most strange of all was the *corpus*.

Not a corpse—for it was neither a human being nor anything that had ever lived—but a corpus, a body. Like the smaller devices on the tables, this thing was made of steel, brass, and the muscle-mimicking substance. Its head was a heavy glass globe, more or less featureless save for a faint spectral sheen. Hesitantly, he tapped it, and was rewarded with what seemed to be a sluggish fluid motion inside, and the imprint of his finger left behind on the sphere as silvery stain, fading slowly.

"Philosophic mercury," he muttered. The "head" was a chime, a conduit between matter and aether. He glanced back at the similar sphere, hovering above the pyramid, and a profound shiver ran through him.

"God, Sir Isaac, what have you done?"

The thing reclined in a chair. In its lap rested *The Sepher Ha-Razim*. On the table nearby, an open notebook.

Ben turned to the latter frantically, suddenly aware again that he and Lenka could be discovered at any moment. The half-finished page before him was mostly calculation and alchemical formulae. He excitedly thumbed back through it, searching for some sort of summary.

What it contained was a series of "quaestiones," in Sir Isaac's writing. It was the style he used, and which he had begun to teach Ben before he closed and locked the door between master and apprentice: ask a question and then amass relevant information, observation, and experiments regarding it. Ben found himself staring at "Quaestione Sixty-one."

Quaestione Sixty-one: What is the nature of the animal spirit?

Ye animal spirit must be of a mix'd nature, for some substance must mediate between ye aethereal impulse and ye expansion and contractions of grosser matter. It has been observ'd that ye Malakim are of such mix'd nature, and as such represent an imperfect fit betwixt the two, as they can only alter fix'd substances in most cases; as in ye case of the Seraphim, the Cherubim, who respectively can only thicken or lighten the substance of aer and lux. And yet I might postulate other orders which have a mediating effect on magnetism or gravity and ye other affinities etc. And have devised proofs for detecting such. And further, I have seen by my experiments that there exist those who are universal mediators but lack the power to expand or thicken a particular sort of atom. But likewise there must exist those of a pure animal spirit. And yet to test the basic notion does not require this animal spirit, but merely an atomic one. Take the materia integumenta *as can be made . . .*

(here followed a long alchemical formula that Ben skipped over)

Contrive, by the philosopher's mercury, to give entrance to a spirit of the sort which impinges upon damnatum, and command that it expand and contract in simple manner.

The margins were filled with diagrams of the devices littering the tables. Ben began skimming. Newton had experimented, it seemed endlessly, using his captive malakus to simulate muscular movement in the devices.

Several pages later, there was an annotated design of the thing in the chair. It was labeled *Talos.*

Fascinated and sickened, Ben leafed farther back through the "quaestiones." Each had to do with some aspect of the malakim; many being the dissertations hinted at in the last quaestione. Quaestion twelve was, "For what purpose has God contrived to create the malakim," and there followed some eighteen pages of notes from various books—some in English, most in Latin, a fair number in Hebrew.

He could find not a single quaestion that had anything to do with comets.

"God damn him to hell," Ben snarled—a request, not an idle curse. "Oh!"

He looked up, startled at the exclamation, having entirely forgotten Lenka. She was near the window, was uncovering something draped in a cloth. At first he thought it their old lifeboat—the one that they had flown to Prague in, but realized that it was somewhat larger, painted black with gilt trim. It also had what appeared to be sails collapsed into it.

"Oh!" she cried. "Oh, no."

Ben joined her, looking at the thing. "This is not Newton's," he muttered. "This is an old thing."

"More than a century old, though the sails are newer," Lenka breathed. She seemed very upset, searching about it. Ben noted, behind the thing, a much larger sail of silk.

"Why—'tis a balloon," Ben muttered.

"No," Lenka choked. Ben suddenly understood that she was holding back tears. "No, it is a moon ship."

"A moon ship? What are you talking about?"

"It is," she said again, "a moon ship. Built by Johannes Kepler."

"Lenka, what are you going on about?"

"I can't . . ." She paused in an attempt to control herself.

"What do you know of Kepler?"

She put her face in her hands, but he could still hear her strangled murmur. "He was my father's great-grandfather."

"That's no reason to be so upset."

"No, no. My *father*—"

"Wait," Ben hissed. "Hush."

For he heard footsteps on the stairs.

"Damn, damn," he snarled. "It must be midnight. Who would come at midnight?" But he knew: Newton, who never slept nor ate when he wrestled with some "quaestione."

"Lie behind the boat," he grunted. When she had done so, he

joined her, pulling the cover back over them. Lenka was still weeping, making no sound; but in the tight space he could feel her tremble against him, her head tucked beneath his chin, breath coming in irregular gasps.

The door swung open again, and too late Ben realized that he had not relocked it. Feet shuffled across the floor, and there was silence for a long space. Lenka's exertions lessened, and she lay more quietly against him, a supple warmth that might have been pleasant if he wasn't imagining both their faces purpling above the golden hemp rings of a noose. And yet . . .

Sir Isaac—if it *was* Sir Isaac—might be so absorbed that he noticed nothing. It would be like him.

Ben had no way of knowing, but it seemed an hour passed, and then another, with only the occasional faint click or scratch to assure them that someone remained in the room. They both had to shift now and then, as their limbs numbed from lack of blood, but on their cushion of silk, Ben was sure they made no sound.

He could feel Lenka's heartbeat, a little pattering against his chest. In one place he could feel her thigh, in others her head, her arm. In time, those points seemed to grow warmer, stronger, as if bonds were linking them. It was most disturbing, and worse, though he tried to suppress it, his manhood reacted. He knew she must notice, for that was where her thigh was pressed. It was amazing, he thought, how idiotic the body was, following such whims when mortal danger threatened.

About that time there came a low cough, a clearing of the throat, and then the familiar voice of Sir Isaac Newton breaking the silence.

"Benjamin? Benjamin, is it you in here?"

14.

They watched the *Queen Anne's Revenge* sink by the pearl light of morning. More than one of the sailors, sotted on rum, cried when she went down. Red Shoes felt, not sorrow, but a sort of joy, the joy of seeing someone die well and bravely, leaving the world with a war shriek on the lips.

The *Revenge* had served them well, given better than she got. The two caravels they now occupied testified to that, as did the pile of bound captives, the mound of loot, and the dead corsairs they had been heaving overboard all night. Of course, one of the captured ships was sinking, too, but Blackbeard claimed that with the pumps going full they might reach a port with her. If not, they could all crowd onto the more sound of the two.

"If we can find a port not full of these Barbary pirates," Blackbeard grumbled, "an' that will be a trick."

"What matter, Cap'n?" Tug grinned. "With you a lead'n' us, no doubt we could take a whole townful of these lads."

"Actually," Nairne said, "as to the matter of a port, I've a fellow you might want to speak to."

"And who would that be?"

"One Domenico Riva, a merchant of Venice. He claims that this was *his* ship six days ago, as it is ours now. And he says he can get us to a safe port."

"Does he? When he could not keep *himself* safe? Well, let us have a talk with this Venetian."

Domenico Riva clasped thick fingers together beneath his gray-stubbled chin. "I swear that what I say is so," he said in good English, his coppery brown eyes wide with sincerity. "Sirs, you must believe me, for it will be to the betterment of us all."

"You understand our reluctance," Nairne reasoned.

"Aye," Blackbeard added. "We're naturally wary of the word of a Turk."

"Sir!" Riva exploded, his almost square, fiftyish face blazing the weird scarlet that white men acquired when angry or embarrassed. "Sir, I am not Turk but a Venetian of old family. I will not be referred to as—"

"Is Veneto not a Turkish province?" Blackbeard interrupted.

Riva's mouth hung open for an instant, closed stubbornly. "That is true, sir," he admitted.

"And you sailed under Turkish banner?"

The merchant nodded reluctantly, bright color fading.

"Then despite y'r Latinish name, I will call you Turk as it pleases me."

Riva stared at Blackbeard for a moment or two, and then a little grin crept across his face. "As you wish, sir. I am a merchant, not a politician. If it please you to call me a Turk, I've been called worse things and still bargained with a smile. My point to you is this: You need a port and supplies and most of all, repairs. I tell you clearly that you will not find them on this side of the Gibraltar Straits unless you sail back to America."

"Not in Lisbon? Nor anywhere in Spain?"

"No. Those coasts have been sacked so often by corsairs, the natives will bombard you without asking. If you survive that, they will burn their towns and poison the wells. If, I say, you don't choose a port already corsair."

"And yet you would have us sail into Algiers, the heart of all piracy on the Barbary coast."

Riva rubbed his hands now, all anger and fear evaporated as if it had never been there. Red Shoes began to wonder, indeed, if it *had* been there or if it had merely been a tactic. Whatever the case, Nairne and Blackbeard both were now riveted by this fellow.

"Allow me a moment, gentlemen, to tell something of recent history, if I may. In fact—may I?"

"May you what?"

"Recover something that the corsairs failed to discover?"

The four of them spoke in a rather spacious cabin, lit by the light riddling through ornate latticework windows. Riva claimed it had once been his. He now gestured at a small shelf of books on the bulkhead. Blackbeard shrugged. Riva went to the bookshelf, ran his finger down the edge of it, and clicked something. The shelf opened to reveal a small chamber, containing something bundled in cloth.

"Ah, indeed," he said, unwrapping a crystal decanter, "they would have found it, given time. The bookcase hidey-hole is not the most original one can choose. But it is our fortune that my captors were uningenious."

"What is it?"

"A certain brandy from Venice. Wonderful stuff. Here, let me drink of it first so as to reassure you." From the same cabinet he produced small glass cups and poured a little of the amber fluid in each. He drained his own and smacked his lips. Red Shoes sniffed his; it smelled like rotten fruit. Blackbeard and Nairne seemed more than passing pleased, however.

"On then, with your story, Mr. Riva."

"Indeed. Well, you know of the Rain of Stars—"

"No, we do not," Nairne told him.

"No? Well, there came a night when flaming stones fell from the sky everywhere. I was on Crete, and the sea was a thousand plumes of steam in the moonlight, and the sky was wondrous full of flame. At the time I thought it some charming show of fireworks sent by God. Why, for an entire week thereafter, I attended Mass every day! But then the news began coming in—or in some cases, not coming in. Of how in France, before the rain—there fell a single fire from the heavens, a sort of comet, and that it struck the horizon and made a light like the rising sun but brighter." He shrugged. "I know something of astronomy, as I must navigate my ships, but I had never seen nor read of a like thing. But whatever it was, it left behind ruin in the west, as if the hand of God had smitten England, France, Spain, the Netherlands. From England we have not heard at all; of France we now have reports, but they are all of confusion, barbarism, atrocities beyond belief. France and Spain, I think, are at war, though it is a chaotic kind of war. The navies have turned privateer, and many have simply become corsair. Almost two years ago, the sultan of Morocco invaded Gibraltar, and he gives the corsairs—of any nation—protection in his port if they serve him in invading Spain and defending him from the Sublime Porte in Constantinople. These pirates, you see, are not the old *Corsair Reis* of Algeria and of which you are familiar. They are a new breed compounded of Spanish, French, and Berber."

"And yet you want us to sail through Gibraltar."

"Ah, but I'm not finished. The erstwhile corsairs in *Algeria* have turned more honest. With Spain, France, Portugal, the English, and the Dutch no longer carrying out legitimate trade, the Ottoman Empire has taken up their part. Thus Algeria and Tunisia—still part of that empire—see their profits in keeping the straits open, you see? When you control trade, there is better profit in trade than in piracy. And so a Turkish fleet, some months past, wrested the Rock from Morocco, and any ship under Turkish protection may pass safe into the Mediterranean."

"Such as your own."

"Ah, well, there, sir, was my mistake. I sailed *beyond* the straits, in hope of finding trade along the coasts of Europe. It was a gamble—one I'm sad to say did not pay me—but there you are and here *we* are. But if you allow me to negotiate for you, I can find you a haven in Algiers, and I dare say come to some arrangement of commerce with the Americas, now that we know the strait is clear and there is someone across the Atlantic to receive our goods."

Blackbeard chewed his lip in silence for a moment, regarding the Venetian. In the pause there came a light rap on the door. Teach signed for Nairne to open it. It was Coleman, the boatswain.

"Sir," the young man said, "some news."

"Aye?"

"We've sighted sail."

"More of the same?"

"No, sir. It's the *Dauphin* and the *Scepter*."

Blackbeard grinned fiercely. "Good. Now we have some strength, and our own escort. But I'll consider your words, Mr. Riva."

"That's all I can ask, Mr. Teach."

"Mr. Riva," Blackbeard said, rising, "if you are lying to me, you will find you had been better off with the corsairs."

Riva smiled, nodded understanding, and poured himself more brandy.

On first seeing Algiers, Red Shoes could make no sense of it. Against the olive roughness of the hills stood an alabaster mountain, shining so brightly in the noon sun that no details could be discerned. He wondered where on that strange mountain the city was.

As they drew nearer, his perspective changed. The "mountain" was a mound of ivory cubes, in numbers he had no words for—as if an entire field of white corn had been husked, shelled, and piled to dry. A little nearer, he saw the windows and doors piercing the "corn kernels" and understood that each cube was a house, and that his idea of *big* had changed forever.

The sky was big. The Earth was big, the sea, big. But those were all created in the beginning times, by the Ancients of animals, by Hashtali, whose eye is the sun, and so of course they were big.

But a town of human beings? It was unbelievable. Nothing in his experience—not Charles Town, not Philadelphia, certainly not Chickasaway—the largest Choctaw village—had prepared him to understand this place. It was walled and gated, guarded by a fortress bristling with cannon. The harbor teemed with ships, rendering their own flotilla inconsequential.

Here is what he had thought to see in England, the discovery he would make on this voyage. The kind of place that the white people were intent on building in his country. It was frightening, repugnant. It was beautiful, awesome. He had no words for it in Choctaw or in English. And so he stared, as details came more clear, antlike people appearing to his eyes.

"This must be the largest city in the world," he breathed.

Tug, beside him, chuckled. "Naw, not by a long distance." But then he sobered and said, "Well, London was a lot bigger. But I guess now—maybe now this *is* the biggest. But that Venetian fellow says 'Stamboul is still there, and I've heard tell that it would make this place look a country village."

"Oh."

"Anyhow, you let old Tug show you around 'Jiers."

"You've been here?"

"Once, years ago."

"Do you have any kin here?"

"Kin? I don't think so."

"Then who will feed you?"

Tug just laughed at that, and Red Shoes reminded himself how very different the Europeans were from his own folk, and how far away from home he was.

Nairne wandered up to them a few moments later, clad in his best red military coat and dark brown waistcoat. "What are you two talking about?" he asked.

"Tug was offering to show me Algiers."

Nairne frowned. "Take no offense, my friends, but that may not be so sound an idea."

"You doubt I can keep 'im safe?" Tug grunted. "Me an' the boys'll look out for him."

"I don't doubt that, but I have my worries about this place. Pirates do not turn honest so easily."

Tug frowned. "Who say's that pirates hain't honest? How is it we are less honest than some filly-gree lord on his manor? At least we work t' eat our bread. And I'll say this about pirates and pirate ports, 'specially this one. They don't give a good damn what family y' come from, or whether you pray to Mary, Mahomet, Jesus, or Beelzebub. I can't say as much for yer fine European cities."

Nairne regarded Tug coolly. "I'm not going to argue with you, for I'll wager you know the truth deep down in you. What I am saying is that we were nearly lost ourselves in England, and this place seems even riskier."

"You can't be sayin' we won't go ashore?"

Nairne sighed. "If it was up to me, yes."

"Then you would have mutiny. How long do y' think good men—
or bad—can go without wine, song, a good thrum? Everyone knows
the tales of 'Jiers, and many enough have sampled the wares. Try and
stop 'em, Mr. Nairne. Try and stop *me*."

"I said if it was up to me. It isn't. Teach and Bienville both agree
with you."

" 'Cause they know sailing men better 'n you."

"Perhaps. What I really meant was, I don't think our Choctaw
friend here should go ashore."

Red Shoes frowned and rubbed his hands. They felt as if they
itched, deep in the bone, a sign of healing but annoying nonetheless.
"Why?" he asked.

"Remember what you told us at the start of this. If we should lose
you, your people may declare war on us."

"That's your risk," Red Shoes replied. "I told you I came here to see
this place. I will see it."

"There is more reason. You councilmen are to attend a meeting of
the Divan with Riva. To talk about trade."

"That doesn't interest me," Red Shoes remarked. "Not now. You go
in my place. I give you my vote."

"The rest won't like that."

"I'll tell them if you wish. But I've decided."

Nairne seemed to struggle with himself for a moment, and then
nodded grimly. "Keep him well, then, Tug. And stay away from strong
drink."

"By the prophet, I shall!" Tug promised, winking at Red Shoes.

Algerian streets seemed made for drunkenness; they were so narrow
that the walls were always there to support you should you sway.

Red Shoes normally avoided the bitter water in quantity; it made
men crazy, turned warriors into madmen and then into wretches. And
yet in this place it seemed fitting somehow, and, besides, Tug and Fernando were powerful persuaders. As well, the drink helped to dull the
horrible smell of the streets—worse even than New Paris—and blunt
the sharp, rude regard of the natives.

As a consequence, he had long since lost track of where they might be going, though he suspected it involved women. This far from upset him; he had done his best to put women from his mind on the voyage, but here they were everywhere, in every hue. Few, by his standards, were beautiful, but all were exotic, all spoke to the male parts of him. What he could see of them, anyway—most wore a cloth covering their faces, so that only their bright eyes could be seen. The mania the Europeans had for covering every inch of a person in cloth, despite the weather, seemed even more pronounced here, but that was, in its own sick way, more intriguing than what he was used to. Especially with bitter waters coursing in his blood.

Algiers was a dirty place, once you were there, and much of the population seemed to be wretched, clad in rags, their eyes mean or empty. It reminded him of the Indian settlements near Charles Town, people without pride or hope, who drank rum like water, dogs waiting for scraps to fall from the English tables. When he had seen that as a boy, it had been a powerful lesson. He had promised himself that the Choctaw would never be like that. But here was the home of that sickness, multiplied beyond belief, and he himself was sick. He suddenly felt very stupid and sad. He should not have taken the disease into himself.

He frowned and shook that off. He would not be defeated; sometimes you had to take something into you to understand it, and he desperately wanted to understand this world across the ocean. Bitter waters were a part of it.

The four of them—Tug, Fernando, a gunner named Embry, and him—entered a building, a close, dark, reeking cave, paradoxical when he remembered how white, shining, *clean* the city had been from a distance. He sat with Tug and the rest on a carpet, a low table in front of them. A girl—probably no older than twelve—came by and Tug gave her a coin and said something to her in a language Red Shoes did not know. She nodded and walked off.

"What do you think of it?" Tug asked loudly, waving his bottle of wine around and then upending it.

"It's big."

"It's big," Tug repeated, and then laughed coarsely. "Aye, it's big."

"I thought we were goin' to find us a doxy or two," Fernando said.

"I've just done that," Tug promised. "We'll just have t' wait here a tick." He passed the bottle to Red Shoes. "We'll find y' a fine oyster basket," he promised.

He took the bottle, wondering what an "oyster basket" was, only to discover his hands would not grasp the glass strongly enough. It slipped from his fingers, falling to the carpet and spilling the red fluid out like blood.

"Damn you, Indian!" Embry snapped. He was a block-jawed man from the *Jack*, one of the ships of the original flotilla, whom he had never met before. "You spilled our damn wine. Damn stupid savage!"

Red Shoes reached for the bottle again, mumbling an apology, when suddenly Tug's massive form bolted up from the floor. In two strides he had knotted his fists in Embry's shirt and lifted the fellow into the air, slamming his head into the low ceiling. "Wha' d'jou say?" he roared. "What did you just say?"

Embry's mouth worked, and Tug threw him back contemptuously, so that he crashed into another table full of dark men in turbans. Tug walked over and kicked him, hard, ignoring the shouts of the indignant Algerines.

"This here's the bravest damn man I've ever seen, you slug," Tug went on. "Fernando saw it, didn't you?"

"I saw it," Fernando agreed. "I will never forget."

Something bright appeared in Tug's hand. "You know why he dropped the bottle? Look at his hands!"

Embry began fumbling at his own belt.

"You pull your knife an' I'll skin you! I swear, God rot you!" Tug bellowed, tears running down his face. Around the room, revealed steel gleamed.

"Tug!" he said. "Tug! Be calm. He meant nothing."

"Damn if he didn't. Didn't you, Embry?"

"I didn't mean nothin'," Embry agreed, and then, to Red Shoes, "I'm sorry."

"You see, Tug? This is nothing to fight about."

"Look at your hands," Tug said, his voice faltering a little. "Why did you do that? How did you do that?"

"It was the only thing to do."

"Embry here couldn't have done it."

"It's not important." But he felt something inside him swell. Tug's admiration felt good; it made him proud.

Fernando clapped Tug on the shoulder. "If Embry says another word," the black man promised, "I'll cut out his tongue myself, good? But for now, I think we best quiet. Look, isn't that your girl, calling us over?"

"Why quiet? Are we afraid of these?" Tug brandished his knife at the crowd of Algerine faces. "You think I'm afraid of them?"

Red Shoes came to his feet. "No, my friend. I don't think you are afraid of anything. I have never seen a braver man."

"No?"

"No. But I want to see these women."

"Women. Aye, women. M' pipe is fit to explode." He looked around the room once more. "So long as they don't think I'm a coward."

"They don't," Red Shoes assured him.

The girl led them into a narrow alley, and then down another. Overhead, the light was fading, and Red Shoes wondered how deep night would be. Finally, after another moment or so, they were led into a room lit only near the doorway. Inside were three women. One was little older than the girl who led them there—she might have been fourteen. The other two were older, one perhaps thirty, the other perhaps ten years older than that. Tug gave a loud whoop.

"Here we are! An' without Embry, no need to share." He lurched into the room, grabbed the closest woman, the oldest, and began kissing her. She made no protest, but Red Shoes didn't notice any enthusiasm, either.

Fernando patted Red Shoes on the back. "Take y'r choice," he said.

A sudden dizziness overcame him, and he realized that he had drunk even more than he thought, first rum and then wine. He was not used to it, that was certain, and again he felt a hint of sadness.

The youngest girl was very pretty. He chose her.

Young she might have been, but not to the business of love. He lay back on the rug as she undid his breeches, kissed him, and then, slipping from her loose dress, slid her slim form against him. He shuddered, darkly delighted, reaching to caress her face. She pressed her cheek into his hand, and the ash light from the door filmed her eyes. They looked as dead as the eyes of a corpse.

He was making love to a dead girl.

He pushed her off him, trying not to be rough. At first she misunderstood, thought that he wanted a different kind of pleasure, but he kept fending her off with his hands, insisting, "No, no," softly.

And then, it seemed, the world fell away. He was suddenly in the Bone House, surrounded by the dead, the girl a child's skeleton. He stifled a cry of anguish, suddenly realizing how unnatural this sudden feeling of grief was. Unnatural and familiar at the same time.

His shadowchild—the one he had made in England—was gone, ripped from him so subtly in the fog of alcohol he hadn't noticed. But now he knew, and knew as well that he was under attack. His tormentor pulled away from him even as he knew it, and though he stabbed at it with the weapons of his soul, it fled, laughing, into the night. He thought he recognized the hoarse voice of Kwanakasha, the *oka nahollo*, the dreaded *na lusa falaya*. He tried to reach after the thing, to take vengeance on it for what it had done, but it was gone, only its evil scent remaining.

Sobbing, he backed into a corner, shaking, and his hand found his knife. For a terrible instant he wanted to plunge it into his own throat, end his suffering, flee from this house of death, this funeral city, life. He gripped the hilt of the blade for a long moment before his hand's children, throbbing painfully, finally uncurled. The world spun and he vomited, grinding his head against the stone, wishing for oblivion, and finally finding it.

Only vaguely was he aware, much later, of being carried, of Tug's grunting laughter, of the salt scent of the sea, and he hoped that he, too, was not dead.

Red Shoes rubbed his aching head, caught Mather's disgusted look from the corner of his eye.

"We've got a little time to decide," Blackbeard said, "but it were best done now, so we can provision."

"We've got something of what we came for," Bienville ventured. "I've found Frenchmen who have given me some report of France. My feeling is that we should return to the colonies."

Mather shook his head. "I don't agree."

Riva, across the cabin, spoke up. "Sirs, whatever trade agreement you may conclude here, I can get you more and better in Venice. From there you can deal directly with the Ottoman sultan."

"Not to mention your own family. Could it be that you will receive the dispensation to carry on trade with the colonies?"

Riva cracked a bare grin. "I've never claimed a lack of self-interest. But as I say, this will benefit us all."

"That's well," Blackbeard said, "for I've never trusted a man who had no interest in a matter."

"Sir," Bienville said, facing the Venetian but clearly addressing them all, "I have agreed that it is improprietous to ask this expedition to press my interests in France. And yet, it seems that some vestige of France remains, and I must contact it, decide what faction to support. I fear that it is time for our ships to part company. I regret this, but we all knew it might happen."

"We agreed to stay together and abide by our covenant," Mather reminded him. "I hope you will not break it."

"You put me to a difficult decision," Bienville said. "To choose between covenant and country."

"But you made clear what your decision would be at the outset," the preacher insisted.

"No. I promised that I would not join my countrymen against you, would even defend you against them, if it came to it. Neither situation exists here. What we have found is far different from what any of us had imagined."

"Sir, listen to me, I beg you," Riva said. "Take your ships and sail back to France, and the corsairs will swallow you whole—there is nothing I can do to protect you. But if you agree to help me back to Venice, I can outfit you with three more ships and the protection of the sultan as well. If there is trade yet to be had in France, I will find it, and your aims will benefit from that. I will benefit from your help, since you are a French gentleman and an officer of the court. All I ask of you is a bit of patience." He lowered his voice. "The time will come, gentlemen, when Venice casts off the Turkish yoke. An alliance needs to be made in Christendom, else we will find all of our children

Mussulmen. Whatever you may think of Venice, her heart is still Christian, and we have secret ways that the Porte knows nothing of. Think, all of you, whether you would rather trade with Mohammedans or Christians."

"You know what my answer is," Mather said.

"Oh?" Blackbeard growled. "Will the Puritan throw in with the pope, now? I myself care not who Charles Town gets her goods from so long as they are the cheapest possible."

"Popish or not, they are Christians," Mather answered, diplomatically, though Red Shoes was certain he had heard the preacher say otherwise in times past. "I will take my chances with them."

Bienville sighed heavily. "I must admit, you make sense, Monsieur Riva. But my heart chafes to find my countrymen."

"You will find some of them in Venice," Riva promised.

"Very well," Bienville said. "I will agree to this—I will accompany you to Venice, but I can promise no more until I have word from France."

Blackbeard made a disgusted noise. "The Mediterranean is the sultan's bear trap," he snapped. "This is foolhardy."

"Once again," Mather said, "it appears as if our Choctaw friend might break the stalemate."

Red Shoes looked wearily at all of them. "I want to go home," he said quietly. "I have had more than enough of your Old World."

"And our wine, I should say," Mather said acidly.

"And your wine. Yes, I want to go home."

"Well, then—" Blackbeard began.

"But," Red Shoes interrupted, "that would be cowardly. That would not be doing what I said I would do. My uncle and many men I loved died on the journey to Philadelphia, and only I remain. I am the eyes of the dead—and the eyes of my people still living—and despite what I wish for myself, I must act for them. I say that we go on to this Venice." *And I want to know who or what has attacked me,* he thought grimly. *Why only after I cross the ocean to the world of the white men I meet this grief.* The warning of the *oka nahollo*—that the Europeans would be the death of both spiritkind and the Choctaw— He had to know if it was truth or lie. And if it was a lie, what truth was it painting over?

He noticed all but Nairne looked at him in blank surprise for a moment. Finally Mather crooked his eyebrow.

"I should say," he remarked, "that it is decided."

"So it is," Blackbeard grumbled. "Nine coffins, bound for Venice. 'Twill be a pretty good sight."

In his heart, Red Shoes could only agree.

15.

Saint

Crecy came beside her about midday, mounted on a handsome roan. "I'm sorry," she said, without any preamble.

Adrienne smiled generously. "Given the tempests you've endured from me," she replied, "that was only a zephyr."

"Still. Wine can wake hurtful words."

"You seemed the one in pain, Veronique. I suppose I thought you incapable of pain, or I would have tried to be more thoughtful."

"Please!" Crecy sighed. "Any more thoughts in your head will surely make it explode." She glanced off, as if surveying the horizon, and then added, "Well—if we are mended, let's spend no more time on this. I feel like a silly girl, and I don't believe it suits me."

"Very well," Adrienne replied, a little relieved. "And how is his grace, the duke, this morning? Does he grin?"

"If so, only at his imaginings. Morpheus defeated Eros a moment or two inside the tent." Her eyes glinted a bit evilly. "But I notice Hercule has some unusual swagger in his step today."

To her vast surprise, Adrienne felt a blush creep up her neck. "I thought we were against schoolgirl talk."

"Oh, yes, indeed we were. How do you find the sky today, my dear?"

"With happy eyes!" Adrienne returned, and was rewarded by Crecy's genuine chuckle.

———

An hour later, there was nothing happy about the sky at all, for it began to bleed flame. Adrienne saw the first of it, a stream of incandescent gobbets poured into the heart of the artillery. There was no sound save a sort of crackling hiss, like grease striking a hot griddle. For a space of two breaths, there was not even human noise, for the sight was so weird—beautiful, even—that no one understood what it meant.

Flesh was not as easily fooled as the eye, however, and the blackening figures that writhed from the sudden blaze, liquid fire clinging to them like impossibly hot honey, shrieked until their lungs charred. As molten columns splattered all around them, more took up the chorus.

Adrienne remembered little after that; she was too busy, her sight caught between the aethereal world and that of matter. She thickened the air, chilled it, struck waves of repulsions about her, but the screams of pain and terror only mounted, as the air choked with heat and black ash. She did not know what to do, even how to begin, as those who trusted her died.

She thought she heard her name, as a desperate prayer. They thought she could save them.

It was all chopped into brief portraits in a stream of nonsense. Crecy leading her horse, Nicolas howling—not with fear, but in imitation of those around him. Her glowing hand, a flaming horse thrashing in its harness. Nicole, beating at the fire on a soldier's back, face grimly determined. Shattered wood stinging her face. Muskets and artillery clattering like a troop of drummers.

And all the while she strove, but her thoughts were slow, so terribly slow. Her djinni finally learned of bullets and began to turn them aside. Lead she knew.

Heat touched them, fierce, and they rode through a tunnel, amber-walled. They kept going.

Adrienne snapped back to herself, finding her nightmare of falling all too real; she only barely managed to catch her horse's mane in time to save her a plunge to rocky ground. Shaking herself, she surveyed her surroundings. Crecy, tight-lipped, rode a few paces to the left with Nico in her lap, Hercule on her right, a bandage made from the hem of her own dress binding his head, nearly saturated with blood. Encircling them some eight of Hercule's light calvary listed in their saddles, while behind a line of some thirty horsemen straggled wearily beneath the leaden twilight. In the distance—it was hard to say where in this hilly, echo-filled country—guns yipped and cannon barked.

So she had slept only a moment or two. A moment in—was it two days or three?

Weakly, she tried to use the djinni to find the rest of the army and found a glimpse of a few hundred men, marching in good order but under near-constant harassment by horsemen, with no cavalry of their own to counter. The horse were all here, who knows how many miles away, and each hour taking them farther.

Hercule shot her a narrow, feverish glance. "How do you fare, milady?" he asked.

"Weary," she said. Then, "I have failed you."

Hercule shook his head. "It is I who failed. I should have persuaded the duke to another course, but failed. I should have forced him southward after the first attack, but failed there, too. He was so confident—"

"Yes, because of me."

"If so," Hercule said, "that wasn't your fault."

She lay her head forward on her horse's neck.

"What shall we do now? How can we rejoin the duke?"

Crecy, at her other side, laughed sharply. "We cannot, and soon there will be nothing to rejoin. We must watch for ourselves now." She smoothed Nico's hair, her gaze going down to him and back to Adrienne significantly.

"The duke needs the horse. . . ." Hercule managed.

"Dead cavalry will do him no good. If we turn any direction but north, the Russian infantry catches us in its teeth," Crecy said.

"Yes, yes," Hercule muttered. "They herd us like sheep. But to where?"

"Away from the army of Lorraine, of course."

Hercule sighed heavily, bowing his own head. "Of course," he acknowledged. "In any case, I do not think the men would return, even if we led them."

Adrienne had no answer; she felt her heart growing chill, for she knew what came next, as their little band lost all purpose save survival.

She got her proof two days later, when they happened upon a small village. Scouts reported that it lacked troops, and Hercule gave the sign to ride down, though a small screen was left to patrol. Unlike many of the earlier villages, this one was not abandoned but had perhaps some forty people in it.

A cluster of them—some five or so—were gathered to confront them in the square when they arrived, led by a priest, an elderly man who nevertheless carried himself proudly, steadfast as the ragged horsemen approached.

"*Guten Tag, meine Damen, meine Herren,*" the priest said, as they drew up to him.

"Do you speak any French?" Hercule asked, trying to keep his shoulders back.

"Aye. A little French. How is it with you, Monsieur?"

Lacking his customary tact, Hercule merely said, "We need food and drink for ourselves and for our horses."

The priest nodded, but his tone was anything but welcoming. "Sir, we some hospitality for you can give, but if feed your horses, we survive not the coming winter. I pray you, however, take what little we have to offer."

Adrienne glanced around the village. It did not look to be starving—its inhabitants appeared well fed.

"We rode through half a day of pasture," Hercule noticed, "the hay all cut and the grain harvested. I saw fat swine in pens as we rode in. You cannot offer us a single day's feed for our mounts?"

"Sir," the priest said, "we already feed one army."

"I see. The Muscovite one."

The priest hesitated. "What choice we have?"

"Little, perhaps, for they are stronger. Do I notice a musket in that house over there?"

"We protect ourselves, mein Herr, from outlaws."

"We are not outlaws. Of late we marched with the duke of Lorraine to the aid of your emperor in Prague—until the Muscovite army you so kindly provided for cut us apart. At least show your friends the same decency you show your enemies."

The priest's face contorted in anger. "You not our friends! Muscovys not our friends! The emperor not our friend. All of you take, and nothing you give us back! Nothing you will take. Nothing!" And with that he dropped to his knees and began to pray, crucifix held before him.

He dropped the cross when it suddenly turned red-hot, and leapt back to his feet, gaping at Adrienne, whose raised fist still flickered with eldritch light.

"Give us what we need," she said. "Please." Then, lower, "You don't think we can control these men, do you?"

But the priest was still staring at her hand. "*Eine Hexe,*" he muttered, and then, shouting in a voice that suddenly filled the square, "*eine Hexe!*"

An angry hornet stung her cheek, as her horse screamed and bolted forward. Distantly, she heard a second shot, saw beads of blood appear on her mount's neck. Before she could comprehend that, the priest jerked like a puppet in the hands and twisted to the ground, vomiting life from four or five wounds as the air swarmed with lead insects.

The villagers didn't have a chance, of course. A handful of muskets, blunderbuss loaded with nails and rocks, and a dozen swords forged almost a hundred years before, during the Thirty Years War, were no match for even the most bedraggled group of trained soldiers. Some villagers ran and some tried to fight; most of the latter fell in seconds.

In instants, guns were empty and sword work had begun. The men—earlier so disciplined—were suddenly raging madmen, unleashing all their anger and frustration on the hapless townspeople. Adrienne, stunned by her wound and the sudden eruption of chaos, was dragged by Hercule to an empty cottage. Crecy came with them, Nicolas in one arm, broadsword in the other, eyes darting about like a bird of prey's.

"Stop them," Adrienne managed weakly. "Stop them. I'm not

hurt." Blood rolled down her face and pooled at her collar, but the cut on her cheek, while deep, was far from mortal.

Hercule nodded wearily and patted her shoulder. A moment later she heard him barking orders. The shrill screams continued, however.

She could not stand it. "Pox on this," she hissed. "I won't live with brigands again." She followed Hercule back outside, despite Crecy's protests. Her legs felt like pillows, but within she felt strong, energized by a paradoxically composed rage, her anger simplifying everything, bringing order to the confusion around her.

Houses were already in flames, and as she watched, two of the Lorraine soldiers dragged a girl—she was at most thirteen—into another building.

"No," she snapped. "No! Crecy, we escaped this life."

"Illusion," Crecy murmured. "We were on holiday."

"No. No! Watch Nicolas."

She strode purposefully across the square, calling her djinni to her, telling them what to do. In the house, she found one of the men sprawled atop the girl while the other stood guard. The latter's eyes widened when she swept in.

"Lady . . ." he began, but never finished, for she struck him in the mouth with the butt of her pistol. It was not a hard blow, but it was a sufficient surprise that his head snapped up and he took two jarring steps backward before tripping over a stool and falling.

She cocked the pistol and placed the muzzle against the rapist's temple.

"Get up."

He did so, murmuring protestations, while the girl, eyes mad, kicked her way across the floor and into a corner.

"The three of us are going back into the square," she said, "or I shall strike you both very dead."

"But, lady," one said, gesturing at her cheek, "they did *shoot* you."

"Did *she*?" Adrienne asked, stabbing her finger at the cowering girl. "Will you tell me that *she* shot me? And that poking your prick into her will heal my wound? Goddamn you, answer me that!"

His face transfigured in horror then, and she realized that her hand was flaring due to her continued orders to the djinni, now assembling overhead. She sneered at his fear and motioned him toward the square. Both men followed without further protest.

When she reached the middle of the square, her djinni did two things at her command. First, they created a vacuum above them and suddenly filled it again, so air clapped like a bell shattering. Second, they lit the sky with a fine mist of flame, harmless but effective in attracting attention. In under a minute, she had a mute audience gathered in the square.

"Listen to me," Adrienne shouted, her body shuddering with anger, "Listen to me, you *brave* soldiers, you men of Lorraine. You may take food for yourselves and your horses. But the people of this village, save those who try to harm you, you will not touch. If they lift ax or gun or sword against you, kill them. But otherwise, if you touch them—for pleasure, for perversity—I shall smite you dead, I swear it by God almighty. You are men, not *dogs*! If you behave like dogs, I will treat you as such, and bring you to heel."

They ate, fed their horses, slept in short shifts and were under way again before dawn. There were no more incidents, the townsfolk supplying everything they asked. As the east rouged herself with sunrise, Adrienne counted their number at six less than it had been the previous evening, and was not greatly surprised—two of the missing were those she had stopped from raping the girl.

"I expected it," Hercule commented quietly.

"They misliked my command," Adrienne replied. It seemed almost that she should apologize, but could not quite bring herself to do it. "It is just that I have seen men at their worst, and I cannot ride with such again," she explained instead.

"Nor will you," he vowed. "They may *have* resented you, but that is between them and the devil. You did what was right, what *I* should have done." He reached over and squeezed her hand.

"Thank you," she said. "You are a better man than you pretend, Hercule d'Argenson."

"And you a better woman than I have ever known."

That struck deeply, somehow. It was the sort of easy compliment he always gave, but this time he used no bantering tone, affixed no suggestive addendum. It troubled her to hear him so serious, but then, their situation was serious. When they came on better times, he would reform.

At noon they reached a small river—no one knew which—and paused for half an hour to water their horses. Adrienne sat with Nico beneath a tree, surveying the brambled, abandoned fields that stretched to the horizons, broken only by the dense hedges which now forced their flight into a labyrinthine course—a league north, a league east, a league north again. The djinni could no longer show her the duke and his forces, whether because they were dead or simply lost she could not say.

She turned when someone approached, and to her surprise saw that it was one of the men, a young fellow everyone called Mercure, for his fleetness of foot.

He bowed to her as if she were an empress, swallowed, swallowed again.

"Sir?" she prompted.

"Milady. The men have elected me to speak to you."

"Concerning what?"

"They wish to apologize. You did remind us that we are soldiers and not mere cutthroats, and we are grateful for that. I, that is, we—" He stuttered off as he reached into his haversack and withdrew a wad of cloth—several steinkirks such as the men wore around their throats.

"What is this?" she asked.

"The men, the ones who—ah, went too far yestereve—"

"The ones who deserted."

"Oh. No, milady, they did not desert. We—well, we punished them for you. We executed them. We kept these as token."

"What?"

"Without you, we have no hope, lady. These men displeased you, and to the rest of us, that is a great sin. We wanted to make it clear that your word commands us."

A peculiar feeling tickled in her belly, a sort of horror, and yet it also felt . . . something else. Pleasing, almost.

"Hercule was involved in this?" she asked, fighting for composure.

"No, Mademoiselle. We did not bother either of you with it. The lady de Crecy told us that we should not."

"Crecy? Crecy came to you with this plan?"

A frightened look crossed Mercure's face at her rise in tone, and he quickly shook his head. "No, milady. We went to her, once we made up our mind. To make certain we were doing right." He looked down at his feet and added, "She told us that we were."

Adrienne gazed at him for a long moment, remembering the girl, remembering her days with Le Loup and all the things she had witnessed. She smiled what she hoped was an encouraging smile. "You did the right thing," she told him. "Tell the men that I thank them. But do not do this again without asking me or Hercule, please."

"Yes, milady."

"You may leave the cravats. I will keep them."

His flush and furtive smile were so young, so endearing, that she could scarcely believe he had been a party to the calculated murder of six men. She watched him go, and, when he was out of sight, covered her mouth, fighting a sudden wave of nausea, but it passed. Nicolas hummed softly, paying no attention to any of it, beating a little rhythm on his leg with hands half closed.

16.

Matter and Soul

"**S**tay hidden," Ben hissed to Lenka, "no matter what."

He could not see her, but she shifted, and he felt the sudden tickle of breath on his cheek. "Be safe," she said.

"My word on it," he replied, and then quickly—before Newton himself came to investigate—slid from beneath the tarpaulin and stood, straightening his waistcoat, seeking as much dignity as one crawling from hiding could manage.

Sir Isaac sat at one of the tables, red waistcoat unbuttoned, steinkirk hanging undone, shaking his head. "It *is* you." He rose, a very peculiar expression on his face. "Where have you been?"

"Where have I been?" he asked, incredulously. "You ask where I've *been*? I've been hiding from the army of the Holy Roman Empire, or don't you remember a certain hunting trip? I do hope you weren't inconvenienced, sir. I hope you did not need me to find you another book."

"Don't be so dramatic, Benjamin. Of course I remember. I only meant to say that—well, I'm happy to see you alive, though I wonder that you came back to the castle."

"Well, sir, I do not intend to stay long," he said, but it did not come out quite as forcefully as he'd intended. Newton sounded *concerned*—from him that was almost shocking.

"Not long, eh? And yet you have some sneak-thief business in my private laboratory."

"Yes, sir, I do," Ben retorted. "I have been neglected by you, nearly murdered by the emperor, chased through wood, river, and alley—

and oh, yes, attacked by a demon—and I'm damn well past the point of needing the by-your-leave of anyone to do what I think needs doing."

"And what is that, Benjamin?"

"I don't have enough fingers to count."

"Try."

Ben pursed his lips. There was something odd about this confrontation. Newton remained calm, even reasonable seeming, while he found himself nearly shouting in rage. Not that he didn't have the right, no. But an angry man was a stupid man, as his father used to say. This was no time to be a stupid man.

"Well, then," he said in a quieter voice, "here is what it comes to. The first thing is to stop your murdering innocents."

"My murdering?"

"The monster that guards *The Sepher Ha-Razim* has killed at least three servants in the palace on account of you. I intend to end its threat."

"Very well. Please go on."

"I have also taken it as my duty to discover whether your claims of a 'new system' have any substance, whether it can avert a comet, and if so whether you have any intention of *trying* to. If not, I shall raise the alarm."

Newton nodded, his brow puckered but otherwise calm. "Despite how shamefully the emperor has treated us?"

Ben snorted. "When I see *you* chased through the woods by hounds and falsely accused of assassination, I'll allow that you have been treated shamefully, Sir Isaac. Do you know the reason for that theatrical?"

"Of course. The emperor is trying to frighten me into explaining my new system and giving details on what happened to London."

"If only he knew how little regard you had for me, he could have saved substantial effort."

"Indeed," Sir Isaac said mildly. "He could have merely contracted you to steal my secrets for him."

Ben suddenly found himself nearly shaking with fury. "God strike you for saying that. He offered me my life to betray you, Sir Isaac, and I did not. It isn't the emperor I came here for. Most people in this city have nothing to do with these petty intrigues, and they do not deserve to die—not for the emperor and not for your damned secrets."

"I see." Newton calmly reached for a decanter of red wine, poured himself a glass, and beckoned Ben closer. "Would you care to sit while I answer your charges, Mr. Franklin?"

Ben shook his head. "The subject stands while his majesty reclines. I shall continue standing."

Newton sighed. "Very well, Benjamin, if you insist on childishness." He sipped his wine. "Let me first congratulate you on entering the tower. It must not have been an easy thing, and I would never have known that you were here were it not for my servants."

Ben bit his tongue; he was sure he knew what "servants" Sir Isaac meant, but there was no point in saying so. He hoped Newton did not also know about Lenka.

"Next, let me ease your mind as to that first matter. The malakus that guarded the book has been contained."

"Contained?"

"Yes. It took me some small time to contrive it, but it is no longer a threat."

"Meantime three people died."

"What would you have me do? I did not intend that they should die. May I go on?"

Ben set his mouth stubbornly. "Contained how? Where?"

Newton smiled, and waved in the direction of the strange automaton. "It is there, in my talos, and entirely under my control. Now, the rest requires a longer answer. Perhaps I was mistaken and should have taken you into my new system earlier, though I don't see that it would have helped anything. In fact, if I had not made it clear to the emperor that you had no knowledge of it, you may well have been tortured. The emperor must *not* have my knowledge. As to this supposed comet of which the Muscovite kidnapper babbled—I assure you, Benjamin, there is no comet."

"No comet? But—"

"A tactic to frighten and confuse, nothing more. I have secure methods of discovering such things, and I assure you that there are no heavenly bodies threatening Prague. Really, Benjamin, did you think, after London, that I would leave myself no means of warning?"

"Begging your pardon, but how am I to believe that? You are the one who taught me only to believe the evidence of observations. You've as much as said that you would abandon Prague to its fate. How can I be sure that this isn't merely a device on your part to convince me to leave? You do intend to leave, don't you?"

"Yes, presently. If I do not, the emperor will lose all patience. At the moment he is mollified, for I gave him part of what he wanted, but that will not last long."

"What did you give him?"

"Youth. In the end, he will not thank me, I think."

"I . . ." Ben was stunned. "I thought you said you could not replicate that feat."

"Replicate it, yes. Comprehend it, no."

"I don't understand."

"You will. I am forced to it, now, Benjamin. If you will sit, and be civil with me, I'll give you what you came here to steal. I will explain my new system to you. And I will also explain that your fear of Prague becoming another London is the least thing that mankind has to worry about."

Newton said, after a moment, "I must tell you of events that occurred some years ago. Exceeding strange events which changed the direction of my thoughts. My *Principia* had just been revised, and some fresh questions came to my mind. I began reflecting upon the prophecies and chronologies of the ancient kingdoms, and I saw that the ancients had knowledge of the laws of gravity, of the inverse-square law, and the like. I came to realize that they knew everything I had 'discovered,' and much more besides, and that this knowledge had been lost. Or, rather, not lost, but stolen—stolen from mankind by the malakim."

"Stolen? How do you mean?"

"More patience. It was about this time, you see, that I had my first contact with the malakim. They wrote to me upon my aether-schreiber. Naturally, I was at first skeptical of what they claimed to be, but I made certain tests—asking them to observe experiments that I conducted near at hand—and in the end I was convinced that there were, indeed, mysterious intelligences in the aether. I continued to correspond with them, and at first they seemed a great help to me."

"Do you know what they are?"

"Surely you have guessed. You tell me."

"They seem— Well, if atoms are bound by ferments into particular forms, we can also guess that ferments exist without there being matter in them."

"Yes, as Boyle proved. Go on."

"I surmise that these malakim are ferments without matter, but ferments of a very special nature, such as those, perhaps, which contain our own souls."

Newton nodded indulgently. "Very fine reasoning, and insofar as my experiments show, correct. They exist as configurations of harmonies and affinities, but with little or no matter in them. I have postulated that there may be a fifth sort of atom, a particle which makes up souls, but none of my investigations have borne it out conclusively. I now believe souls propagate more in the fashion of a wave, like the affinity linking aetherschreibers, an instantaneous wave unfettered by distance, as gravity and magnetism are."

"You have proven the existence of the human soul?"

"Certainly—we have two of them. I have the proofs."

"And the malakim are bodiless souls?"

"Not exactly. They are more and less than that. I would be disingenuous if I claimed I understood them entirely—as I said, many of my experiments have not borne fruit. The Bible and cabalistic texts speak of a separate creation of the malakim and human souls, and I am inclined to that view." He leaned back, brow furrowed in thought.

"In any event," Sir Isaac began again, "they are creatures of the aether. They 'see' and 'hear' not light or sound, but the higher harmonics— mostly those which are absolute, or mathematically instead of exponentially proportional to distance."

"That's why they contacted you through the aetherschreiber!" Ben exclaimed. "It's an absolute affinity!"

"Precisely. Gravity, magnetism, aural harmonics—these things they are nearly as blind to as they are to matter. But the other affinities— those closer to God—"

"Closer to God?"

Newton blinked. "Surely you see that. God is all-being, all-knowing, everywhere the same. Light is matter, and travels at a fixed speed.

Magnetism and gravity weaken with distance exponentially. If He were composed of anything with such finite, limited properties, He could not be all-knowing. If He had to wait for light from the far reaches of the universe to perceive— You see?"

"I do see," Ben said, warming to the notion, so fitting to his own speculations. "But can you prove it?"

"Of course."

"But I have drawn you from your original point, sir. How have these malakim robbed us of the knowledge of the ancients?"

"I have faith that you will see that soon enough, too. The malakim, in their natural state, thus have little power to manipulate matter, or even the grosser attractions and repulsions. And yet, by our ingenuity, we can construct devices that allow it, enhance their abilities."

"I see you have been at that," Ben replied, gesturing at the talos. "But what is the benefit?"

"The benefits are great. They are blind in our realm, we in theirs. And yet, through science, we can see into theirs. That is what we have done, in constructing our laws. We are like blind men, feeling this and that part of something, trying to imagine the whole. As you know, it is a taxing process. The mathematics upon which even so simple a thing as an alchemical lanthorn is based are prodigious. But the malakim, once directed— once provided with a way of 'seeing' gross matter— can alter ferments instinctively, with no need to understand what they do, just as you or I can boil water with fire or lift a stone without knowing how fire excites atoms or understanding the manifold properties of gravity. It is enough, once the bridge has been provided, to merely explain to them what result you want." He smiled slyly, reached into a drawer, and withdrew something. "For instance," he said, passing a heavy metal ball to Ben.

"This is gold," Ben noticed, turning it in his fingers.

"Indeed. It once was copper."

"Then you have solved the equations for the vegetation of metal? You have mapped its ferments?"

"No. Aren't you listening to me? I merely commanded it and it was done."

"Oh. Like that fellow in the Arabian tales."

"Yes, you see? Useless."

"I would hardly call gold useless."

Newton snorted. "The gold is not useless, but the process by which it was made is. Likewise my returned youth—and now the emperor's—the levitating globe that transported us here from the English Channel, and so on. I do not understand how these things were done, though I can command that they be done again."

"But still . . ."

"Benjamin, I could see light before I understood its nature. Which is more important, seeing it or understanding its laws?"

"Well, in a general sense I would say seeing it—"

"Nonsense. Perfect nonsense, if you speak as a philosopher."

But Ben already understood. After all, hadn't he just been arguing this to Robert? "It is not science, this use of the malakim."

"No, of course it isn't."

"But then why do you continue with all this?" He waved at the laboratory and its weird apparatus.

"Because they can be used, Ben, used to *understand* what they do. By making them do it and then observing, in a thousand experiments, *how* they do it—something that even they themselves do not know, any more than an unlearned peasant knows how he breathes. And I have been, in part, successful. But it requires holding them captive. While they are willing enough to do certain things—like create that gold—they will not hold still to be examined. It is not their *wish* that we understand them. So I must force them—and, naturally enough, protect myself against them, for since I began my experiments, as long ago as London, they have tried in many and cunning ways to murder me. Indeed, it was my first thought, on our hunt, that the panther and its familiar sought to kill me, not you." He rubbed his hands together. "In any event, there is much more for us to do, and I am ready to teach you again."

Ben arched his eyebrows, but gave no other indication of his deep distrust of that remark. "There is the little matter of the hangman's noose," he pointed out instead. "I am no good to you hanged."

"But of course we must leave Prague. You see now why I cannot satisfy the emperor's whims. If I gave him the malakim to command, think of the results."

"Oh, Lord, yes," Ben said, as the implications sank in.

"Best we leave soon," Newton went on.

Now would be the time to tell him about Frisk and the offer of the Swedish king. But, still, he hesitated. "Sir, you must swear to me that there is no comet, that Prague is not in danger."

"There is no comet," Newton repeated. "As I have already told you. The malakim could easily detect it, and they have not."

"Mightn't they lie to you? You suggest that they have sinister designs on mankind. Why should you trust them?"

"It is true, they have no love of mankind, and I believe that they have contrived the downfall of our race countless times in the past and now do so again. But 'my' malakim obey me not from love of me, but because they *must*."

"You are certain?"

"Yes—and you will question me no more on that. I grow weary of your incredulity. It is insulting. The greatest philosophers in the world have huddled at my knees, and yet my seventeen-year-old apprentice remonstrates with me as if I were a naughty child in grammar school."

Ben clenched his jaw, but kept his peace. As things were going, he might soon know enough about this system of malakim to see how it really worked. If he went too far with Newton now, the older man might simply reveal him to the emperor's men, and that would not do.

"Very well, sir," he said. "What is your plan?"

"Since you are here, help me gather the things we shall take with us."

"When do we leave?"

"Tomorrow night. Meantime, perhaps you should continue to hide here. It may well be the safest place for you. Besides, someone needs to prepare an airship. Do you remember how to do it?"

Ben glanced at the glowing, enthroned orb and repressed a shudder. "I can do it," he said.

When the door had been closed for perhaps twenty seconds, Ben rushed back to where Lenka lay. To his surprise and amusement, he found her asleep, and tugged gently on her arm to waken her.

"What's happening?" she asked.

"Newton is gone," he told her. "How could you sleep?"

She grinned a little sheepishly. "It was boring. I could not understand your English, and when it became clear that the emperor's soldiers weren't going to rush in and take us captive or anything, I grew sleepy. And so what has happened? Your master came and went. Are you reconciled?"

"That's difficult to say," Ben temporized, "but things seem better than they were. Sir Isaac has done away with the Golem, so there will be no more deaths among the servants. He also started explaining all *this*." He motioned to indicate the room.

"Is your mind set at ease about the danger to Prague?"

Ben smiled his brightest smile at her. "No," he said, and then froze, unbelieving. He had meant to lie to her, he really had. What had happened?

"Damn it all," he muttered, not sure to whom.

"No? Then this doom you spoke of is coming?"

"Er—" It was done, now. "He told me that no such disaster was coming, but—"

"Enough. Tell me the nature of this doom, Benjamin Franklin. I deserve that much, for my troubles."

"Now look here—" Ben began, but her expression stopped his tongue. He took a deep breath and began again. "You've no doubt heard of the destruction of London?"

"Of course, though none knows the cause."

"Sir Isaac and I know. That is one of the secrets the emperor meant to force from Sir Isaac by killing me."

"The stories are of fire from heaven . . ."

"Do you know what a comet is, Lenka?"

"A comet? It is like a planet, is it not?"

"Yes," Ben said, relieved that he could start at that point, and not by dispelling some superstition. "They are very like planets, save that they are smaller and have more eccentric orbits—they go very far from the sun and then approach very near. The wind of light blowing from the sun pushes the atmosphere that surrounds them into a tail and makes it to glow, and that is what we see in the sky."

"Very well. That sounds sensible."

"Good. Now, there are also comets of a sort that have no atmospheres, and so though they pass by us, we do not see them. One of these was made to fall on London."

"*Made* to fall?"

"Made to fall by philosophers, enemies of England. Imagine a stone a mile across, traveling at greater speed than a musket ball, striking a city."

Lenka paled, and for the first time since Ben had known her, crossed herself. "*Matka Bozhye,*" she whispered. "This will happen to Prague?"

"Newton says no. I don't know whether I believe him, especially since he prepares to flee the city."

"He is leaving?"

"Aye, as am I."

"You promised to raise the alarm."

"And so I shall. But, Lenka, I made that promise before it was death for me to be seen here. I will write a letter, with diagrams and all, and send it to the emperor—I will send another to Prince Eugène. It is as much as I can do."

She lifted her chin. "That is true. No one could ask more of you." She turned and clasped her hands behind her back, then—when she remembered that her skirt was still torn—dropped her hands and pinched the cloth together.

"Wait a trice," Ben told her. It took him only a few moments to find an iron pin. "There."

"Thank you. And so will I have to arrange a new distraction to manage you and Sir Isaac through the gate?"

"Oh," Ben said, trying to both look and not look as she pulled the cloth together, hitching the skirt and then pinning it. "No. Sir Isaac and I will be leaving as we came." He gestured out the window and thumped the wooden boat. "We shall fly."

"Using this craft? Johannes Kepler's boat? You can make it fly?" A strange light seemed to film her eyes.

"We can make *any* boat fly. But I suppose as this one is a *moon ship*, it should fly spectacularly well."

"That is no joking matter!" Lenka snapped. "It *is* a moon ship, or was meant to be. Some say Kepler did *go* to the moon in it, so as to write a treatise upon it."

Ben arched his brows skeptically. "I doubt that very much," he said.

"Why? If *you* can make a boat fly, why couldn't he?"

"He hadn't the means. Look, Lenka," he said, pulling at the cloth. "This was a balloon. It may have flown, yes, filled with hot air—"

"Dew," she corrected angrily.

"Dew? As in that Frenchman's silly story? Lenka, it would most certainly have not flown anywhere on dew. Hot air, yes. If a fire were built under it, and the envelope filled—yes, it might rise until the air began to cool, and then 'twould sink again, no great distance away."

"Is there no way to cause the air to remain hot?"

"If you could keep a fire going beneath it, or build some sort of alchemical device to produce heat. Just so long as the air is kept in a rarefied state. As a boy, I used to put candles in paper lanterns and fly them aloft."

"But couldn't this boat have a magical heating device?"

Ben looked at her in mild surprise. "I don't know. Do you have some reason to think it does?"

She looked away. "Yes. I have seen it flown. There was no flame."

Ben frowned at the boat, and then began to push back the silk. "Even if it did have such a device," he explained, "the distance to the moon is staggering, and in regions between here and there no atmosphere exists for a man to breathe. He would smother on the journey."

"Smother?" Her face was a sort of stony mask as she nodded and said, "I see."

"Lenka, how does this concern you? What is this obsession you have with the moon and means of reaching it?"

She did not answer right away, and an instant later he had almost forgotten that he asked the question. For there, in the bottom of the boat, was bolted a device about the size of a man's head. A nearly globular bowl, polished and smooth on the inside, its aperture was partially closed by eight overlapping plates, like flower petals but curved inward so as to resemble a whirlpool. A lever on one side dilated or closed the opening. At its widest, he could just fit his fist into it.

Ben whistled. "Lenka, I've found the device."

"Really? Can you reckon how it works?"

"It is some sort of catalyst. Some substance is placed in the receptacle and generates warm air."

"Dew," she said. "Dew. Morning dew. They say it comes from the moon, but in the morning is attracted back."

Ben shook his head. "No, that can't be. Dew is merely water, condensed from the air by cooling—chemically no different from any other water. But—it might have *been* simply water." He crouched down, staring at the thing, and then leapt back up. "Yes, find me some water."

The two of them hunted for several moments before Lenka found a bottle labeled *aqua*. His estimation of her rose again; the glass was colored, and so she had clearly read and understood the Latin label. He hoped that the label was accurate—just plain *aqua*, and not *aqua fortis*, *aqua regis*, or some other alchemical stuff. Eagerly, he went back to the device and sprinkled some in.

It hissed, sputtered, and vanished, without steam or smell.

"It's not hot," Lenka observed.

"No. No, it need not be, for I jumped to conclusions. Here . . ." He searched for a few more moments until he found a piece of parchment. He then folded it deftly into a sort of box enclosed on five sides, open on the bottom.

"This is what I was telling you about a moment ago," Ben told her. "If you make something so, and put a small candle in it, 'twill rise under the power of the hot air. Now, I hold it over this little cauldron, and you pour in more water."

She nodded and did so, and almost immediately, Ben felt a tug on the edge of the little balloon. When he let it go, it drifted up to the ceiling, while behind him, Lenka vented a wordless exclamation that gratified Ben somehow.

"Amazing," he said. "All those years ago, they had built such a thing." He remembered his ruminations over the astrological clock in the Old Town Square, and then Newton's claims about lost knowledge. How could knowledge be lost, with such inventiveness in the world? How was it that this device had languished here in obscurity for a hundred years?

On sudden impulse, he decided to try another experiment. He

jogged across the room and picked up a funnel-shaped device he had noticed earlier.

"What's that?" Lenka asked.

"An aquafier. It condenses water from the air."

"Ah." She watched as he unbolted the other device from the boat, and then affixed the aquafier over its mouth.

"Get one of those silks and help me draw its mouth over this," Ben told her. "I want to see how quickly this generator works."

She nodded enthusiastically and dragged one of the envelopes over. They arranged the opening over the device—which was now dripping and hissing with a will—and weighted the edges down with books.

"There," Ben said, pleased. "We shall see."

"If it works," Lenka asked, "we can use it to leave?"

"I suppose, but we won't. The means we have is more practical. It would be impossible to launch such a balloon ship from this tower, for one thing; we would have to move all down to the square and—" He broke off and stared at her. "We?" he asked.

"Yes. I want to leave Prague with you, in the airship—however you go about making it fly."

"Lenka, the danger is too great."

"No greater, I think, than remaining here. Once you two have fled, if the slightest suspicion falls on me—and remember that the guard saw you and me go together into the Mathematical Tower—then I may suffer a great deal and perhaps even be killed. You promised to prevent that."

"Well, yes I did," Ben admitted, "and yet fleeing with us hardly seems safer."

"A chance I'll take," Lenka said, "to fly in an airship."

Ben pursed his lips, trying to find a valid objection, but the only one he could think of was that Newton would never stand for it. "Very well," he said, "but Sir Isaac must not know—you must remain in hiding until the last moment, when his objection will come too late. Be careful while I am gone."

"Where are you going?"

"I must get word to Robert and Frisk."

"That's stupid; you will never slip out of the castle and back in with only one aegis."

"Robert has two. I'll find them in his room." He paused, and then glanced over to her. "You got word from the Jew of where to meet me. Who was the go-between?"

She hesitated for a moment, and then said, "Klaus. One of the dwarfs of the archduchess."

"The archduchess Maria Theresa?"

"Yes."

A slow smile spread on Ben's face. "Then, indeed, I have a plan."

17.

An Archduchess, a Sorcerer, and a Rain of Fire

"Rehaset Ramai."

"*Hmmf?*" The eyes of the little archduchess flew open at his whisper, and she turned her head on her pillow.

"Rehaset Ramai," Ben repeated.

"Apprentice? Where are you?" she inquired crossly, rubbing her eyes and sitting up.

"I am by your side, invisible, your Royal Highness. I have passed many dangers to come to you, and beg your pardon for waking you at this hour."

"My father is very angry at you! And *so am I!*"

Ben wished he could see better, but all the girl's servants—dwarf and tall folk alike—seemed either absent or asleep, including the diminutive, loudly snoring nurse who shared her room. Ben had the aegis on low calibration and that, along with the near darkness in the room, was his only protection. He had come in through the bedroom window, which Lenka knew to be almost always open—but only a great deal of stealth had gotten him past the guard outside. He was pleased; it seemed that he was becoming well versed in stealth.

"Answer me or I shall scream!" Maria Theresa promised, her voice already too shrill and too loud for Ben's comfort.

"Soft, Archduchess. The music of your voice might awaken your servants, and none but you must know that I am here. I have come to you because you are the only one who can save the Holy Roman Empire from the evil Turk, from the black sorcerer *Wazam*—eh, *Ha Razim*. Please, Archduchess, the fate of the empire is in your hands."

"Why? Wazam who?" she asked, and Ben congratulated himself on her softer, curious tone. He had her, at least for the moment.

"Much has happened," Ben whispered. "Among the Turks is a most foul and cruel sorcerer named Wazam Ha Razim. It was he, through evil magics, who brought about the fall of Vienna."

"I *so* loved Vienna," the girl said dreamily, though Ben guessed she was repeating what she had heard others say. She had been scarcely three when the great city fell.

"I have never had the pleasure of seeing it, but I yet hope to. But first we must defeat this devil, this Wazam. He is black of heart—and that heart he keeps in a secret jar, across seven seas, thirteen deserts, and five mountains in a place called Khitai. He keeps it there so that no cannon shot or sharp sword can slay him. But most monstrous of all, Wazam Ha Razim can take any form he likes. He can appear a dragon, a griffin, a beautiful woman—most recently, he has taken *my* form."

"*Your* form?"

"Yes, Your Highness. So that the guards at the gate would let him into Prague—into the very castle."

"We must tell my father!"

"Soon, Archduchess, but—if it please you—hear the rest of my story."

"*I'm* listening."

"I know you are, because you are wise and sensible, a true Habsburg princess. Now, once in the city, he came upon me asleep, and by his spells bound me up in a casket, and threw the casket into the Moldau so that I would float away. The last thing I heard was his evil laugh, and his bragging how he would murder your father and take you for his bride."

"He's stupid. I would never marry such a bad man."

"You wouldn't *know* he was bad, not at first. You would think him handsome, chivalrous, and wise—for he can seem all of those things."

"I guess so."

"Anyway, in my shape, he tried to murder your father, but he failed because Sir Isaac is as good a magician as Wazam, as white as Wazam is black, and made some spells to protect your father. In the meantime, I managed to free myself from my watery prison—"

"How? How did you do that?"

"I had, in my possession, a small philter," Ben replied, delighted at how smoothly the fabrication came to his lips. The archduchess, after all, was female, which seemed to inspire his best in such matters—with the unlikely exception of Lenka. "I meant to make a present of it to you, Your Majesty—but I was forced to drink it. It shrank me to the size of a gnat, so I was able to squeeze through a crack in the casket. Then, with my magic shoes, I walked back up the river—only to find that every guard and soldier in the country was searching for me, thinking me an assassin. But I had to come here to warn you, for I am the only one who knows that Wazam is still in the city—probably still in the castle, plotting his next evil deed."

"Who does he look like now?"

"I cannot say. He could be anyone. One of the Gentlemen of the Golden Key, one of the servants, one of the guards. That is why we must be so very careful, so *very* careful who we speak to." He sighed heavily. "And so now I have told you the story, Archduchess, and you are the only one who can save us. Will you help?"

The archduchess rolled her eyes and folded her arms in front of her. "Yes, of *course*! I am a Habsburg!"

"Good. Then I must ask you to do some things, and these may seem odd to you."

"Well?"

"First, there is a certain fellow in your staff, one Klaus, whom I know to be trustworthy. When I have gone, you must impart to him a package I will give you, and he must run right away to deliver it."

"Make yourself visible, so that I can see you."

"Very well, Your Highness. But no one else may know that I was here." He reached to his pocket and removed the key, Maria Theresa giggling and clapping as he became visible. On the other side of the bed, the nurse grunted in her sleep, but did not waken.

"If you had not given me our secret sign," the archduchess confided, "I should think *you* were Wazam."

"But he cannot know our password," Ben said, "and there is where he made his mistake. Now, the other thing you must do is this." He drew forth a small bottle, tightly corked.

"Is that my potion for shrinking to the size of a gnat?"

"No, Archduchess—I was forced to use that myself, though in time I can make you another. No, this is a very special potion. You see, I believe that Wazam hides near the gate of the castle—either invisible, as I am, or in the shape of a guard. I believe that he will be there near noon, awaiting the time when your father will pass to go shooting. What you must do is lead your courtiers once around the castle, from the end of Saint George Street back to the front gate, chanting some words I will teach you. Sprinkle a bit of this as you go along, but save most until you reach the gate. There, you must pour what remains upon the ground. It will make all things invisible visible and give all false seemings their true appearance. And you must do this precisely at three o'clock. Can you do this?"

"Just pour it on the ground?"

"Yes. Meanwhile, I will be waiting, and when he appears I shall catch him with a special noose. Is this plan to your liking?"

"Very well," she answered gleefully. "Very well to my liking. Papa will be very pleased."

"Yes, he will, but you must take care not to tell him—or anyone else—of our plan. For all you know, even your father may not be who he seems. Anyone could be the black-hearted Wazam. Even your own servants, except for Klaus, so you must not explain to them why or what you are doing."

"I know. You don't have to tell me *that*."

"Of course not, Archduchess. And now, I must go to prepare my sciences. I hope that I will see you again. Wish me luck!"

"Of course we will meet again. And then you shall join my court. And maybe one day we shall be married."

"Ah, Your Highness, I am but a commoner—though a great magician, I reluctantly admit. I would never be allowed to marry you—I can only hope to serve."

"When I am empress," the girl said a trifle petulantly, "I can marry any man I want."

"Quite true. Now, do not forget—as soon as I have gone, you must send Klaus on his mission. If word does not reach my friends, all shall be lost."

"I won't forget," she said.

Morning crept up the sky as Ben did back to the tower, and as the light drizzled through his eyes, so did a few doubts into his head. What had he just done? Gambled all of their fortunes on the whimsy of a little girl. If she should tell anyone of his visit, if the letter and aegis came into the wrong hands, their doom was secured.

But there was no gain without risk, was there? And his clever story was surely convincing to a child.

The guard was changing in the street near the tower, but the two men distracted one another well enough with their talk that he passed them easily. Lenka came from hiding when he softly called her.

"All went well?" she asked.

He shrugged. "I can only hope. The archduchess seemed enthralled."

"She is easily enthralled, but also capricious. I don't like your plan."

"You should have spoken more forcefully when I proposed it, then."

Lenka vaulted her eyebrows. "I seem to remember I did raise an objection. Your ears, I think, are stuffed with your own self-importance."

"Likely so," Ben admitted, "but it is too late for that now. Help me prepare the airship."

Ben hated touching the orb. The malakus within seemed to radiate malevolence, and he felt a cold tickling in his brain, a disorder that he was sure did not come from himself. He did his best to ignore it. Since he was not certain what part the pyramid played in controlling the willful malakus, he left the globe there, dragging the boat nearer and then affixing the cables. He and Lenka then spent the next few hours testing the ancient vessel for rotten places, packing up books and notebooks, along with whatever food and drinking water they could find—which was not much. Ben hoped Newton would think to bring some back with him.

He included the instruments that seemed most needed: a compass, an astrolabe, a small telescope. Amongst the various instruments he found several sympathetic compasses as well, whose needles were tuned to like needles or objects elsewhere, allowing for a fixed reading of some place other than north. One of these pointed in a westerly direction, leaving Ben to wonder if its twin needle was in London, having somehow survived the comet. He included that among the articles on the boat, thinking it might help them navigate. Another pointed southeast, but when he moved it, the needle swung sharply. Confused, he wondered if it was broken; with each step he took the needle changed direction.

The real solution was so simple that he felt stupid for not seeing it immediately; the matching needle was somewhere in the laboratory. Once he had that thought in mind, it was easy enough to locate using the compass. The "needle"—a bar of metal about three inches long— was in a desk drawer. After a bit of thought, he hid the bar in a crack in the stone of the tower, scratched "Prague" onto the brass casing of the compass, and placed it in the boat.

His gaze then crossed to the talos, and he shuddered. Was the spirit of the Golem really captured in it? It had not moved or otherwise given any outward sign, but somehow he did not doubt what Newton had said. What he did doubt was that the murderous thing was really tame. He made a point of staying as far from it as possible.

As three o'clock neared, he went to the window facing into the castle.

"What are you watching for?" Lenka asked.

"The archduchess and her dwarves. I'm going to join them. If she fails to do what she should with the potion, I will empty my own."

"That is, I think, a very bad idea," Lenka opined. "Why lay such an elaborate plan and then not trust it?"

"You've answered your own question," Ben said. "Elaborate plans are most prone to failure. In the best of worlds, all will go as I hope, and the archduchess will empty her potion bottle onto the ground. However, as a Frenchman I once knew was prone to argue, this is *not* the best of all possible worlds. I owe both Robert and Frisk my life. Besides, we need Frisk, if we plan to find the army of Sweden. I don't know where it is." He smiled and winked at her. "But I'm pleased you are concerned for me."

She frowned. "If you are captured, Sir Isaac will discover me, and without your persuasion, will leave me here. That is the nature of my concern."

"Oh, I see," he said, with an exaggerated air of disappointment. "Well, let me show you something." He beckoned her over to the craft. "Did you notice this?" he asked, rapping a board on the small deck.

"What?"

"It's very cunning. You see?" He depressed one of the ornamental crenelations on the side of the boat, and with a small click, a section of the deck popped up a bit. With his fingernails, he lifted a hidden hatch. Beneath was a space; cramped, but easily large enough for a person Lenka's size.

"I found this when you were hunting for food," he explained. "I put a few things in here I didn't want Sir Isaac to know about."

"What sort of things?"

"A *kraftpistole* from my quarters—"

"You went to your rooms?"

"Yes. Also my water-walking shoes, a musket, powder, and shot. But I left most of the space empty—for you."

"Me? In there?" She regarded the tiny space dubiously.

"He won't let you on the boat, Lenka. I've thought about it, but he won't, not with Frisk and Robert, too. Best wait until we are aloft to reveal you. If anything happens to me—or if Newton should return early—you hide there."

"For how long?"

"Not long. Newton will not throw you out: I know him that well, at least."

"I hope so."

From the window drifted the sounds of drums, cymbals, and hautbois.

"There they are. A kiss for good luck?"

"You don't need luck; you need some sense."

"Well, a kiss for good sense then."

"I've never noticed nor even heard it rumored that a kiss gave a man sense. Quite the contrary."

"Hmm. You need less theory and more experimentation," he observed.

She folded her arms and smiled her daunting little smile, at which he shrugged his shoulders and started down the stairs, activating the aegis as he went.

The archduchess' entourage was just coming around the corner from Golden Lane, and as Ben had anticipated, in full regalia. The guard was nowhere to be seen, and so it was an easy matter to slip in behind that last dwarf, one of five in the parade wearing luminescent golden lanthorn armor. Ahead, the sedan chair of the archduchess was surmounted by gently bobbing metal birds, the chair itself bedecked with glowing jewels. In such a procession, his own ghostly form was likely to be unnoticed or ignored as more magical frippery.

And in their train, a light mist arose, at which Ben smiled hopefully.

The procession marched on until it came to the gates, where the guards hastened to perform the Spanish genuflection to Her Royal Highness. Ben, meantime, searched across the great square and its border of ornate palaces, looking for ghosts like himself.

Up ahead, he heard Maria Theresa shout, "Show yourself, villain!" In a short time, the soldiers began shouting as well, as a thick cloud appeared and rapidly expanded to fill the yard. At the same moment, across the square, the geometrical black-and-white façade of the Toscana Palace seemed to waver, and Ben clenched his fists in jubilation.

A few moments later, he thought he heard his friends run by, and turned to race into the less misty precincts of the third courtyard, and then, for certain, he made out two optical distortions moving down Saint George Street toward the Black Tower. The strident shouts of the archduchess and bellows of the guards faded behind.

Even in his triumph, he began having second thoughts. The guards at the gate would not dare to question the archduchess about her strange behavior, but they would report it, and then someone would question her. How long before—advertently or inadvertently—she gave an answer that led them to the Black Tower?

He hoped a few hours, at least.

In the distance, a titan stuttered and then moaned, a long, drawn-out shuddering of the air almost below the level of hearing. Stone quaked beneath his feet. Puzzled, Ben looked up, but the sky was still blue, nowhere grayed or blackened by storm clouds. He stared, frowning, and suddenly was surrounded by blinding light.

He screamed and shut his eyes, but it filled his head, pulsing, and his belly seemed to open. On that dazzling backdrop his panicked brain painted an image: a black-tailed comet, its nucleus the mocking red eye of a malakus. Newton had been wrong, or lied, and in an instant or two now it would all be over, when the thing struck them with hideous speed, scattering the very atoms of the castle.

And yet, a moment passed and he was still alive, though his eyes burned, and some rational part of him fumbled for the aegis key and removed it.

He was a few steps from the basilica, spots before his eyes still blackening the largest part of his vision. A group of black-clad nuns began pointing at him, shouting. That cured his paralysis, and he started to run again. Not far ahead, Robert and Frisk staggered like drunks.

"This way," he shouted.

"Ben?" Robert gasped.

"Hurry!" The explosions in the distance were as steady as heart-beats, and as his vision was restored, he saw with dull understanding that the sky still carried a rainbow patina. Not because the colors of the aegis had been burned into his corneas, but because the city shield was on.

Prague was under attack.

"What in hell happened?" Robert snarled as the three of them ran up Saint George Street. Crowds were darting into the narrow lane, but none were paying attention to the three men, pointing instead to the sky and shouting.

"The city shield is on. It is a sort of aegis built large, and so when it went on while we wore ours—" He didn't have the breath to explain: two lens, separate, were magnifying glasses. Placed in line they were exponentially more powerful. Something like that had happened with their "garments of Adam."

"Never mind," Robert shouted. "Wait till we reach safety."

A throng coursed out of the Lobkovic Palace, just next to the tower, and in the press, the guard nearly missed them. At the last moment, when they began shouldering past him, the guardsman shouted and raised his halberd. Frisk broke his nose with the hilt of his saber, and the soldier fell groaning to the flagstones.

Ben led the way up the winding stairs, at the end of his wind, car-ried along by sheer purpose. It was as if the world had suddenly begun tearing apart around him, like the time he had come back to the print shop to find James murdered, the shop in flames, and a devil after him. He had a sudden, clear understanding that this was how life really was: insanely chaotic and unplanned. Men constructed fantasies, explanations to try to make reality seem coherent, but it wasn't, any more than a crazy dream was because you spent an hour discussing it.

That hung in him, a crystal caught in his throat, as he reached the door and battered into it, found it locked.

"Lenka!" he howled, pounding on the heavy door. "Lenka, open the door!"

Only then did he realize that he had the key.

He gaped for an instant at what he saw when he opened the door. Or rather, what he didn't see. The glowing globe, the wooden boat, all the things he had packed up—all were gone. Of Lenka there was no sign.

One section of the roof stood open to the shimmering sky. Outlined against that was the moon ship, red light winking above, and standing in the prow the unmistakable figure of Newton, vermilion coat as clear as a distant cardinal on a winter landscape.

And farther away, across the expanse of golden Prague, a fleet of black ships sailed the winds, suspended from points of sanguine light, raining fire.

Part Three

THE DARK AER

At our service are very wise spirits who
detest the bright light of the other lands
and their noisy people. They long for our
shadows, and they talk to us intimately.
Fiolxhilde to her son, Duracotus.
—Johannes Kepler,
    Somnium, 1634

1.

Vasilisa

Adrienne rested her cheek against Hercule's chest, imagining it a universe: the hard muscle and skin its outer boundaries; the dark hollow within swirling with jeweled, mysterious planets; the thumping of his heart the tempo to which they danced, the single, simple rhythm behind the music of the spheres. In the universe of Hercule, his heart was God; without it all of his orbs would become still, the stars of his eyes dim, the warmth of his lips cool forever.

"Thinking again?" Hercule whispered, stroking her head.

"Yes."

"May I ask of what?"

"Why, of you, my dear."

He grunted in satisfaction, and afterward seemed content, gently dropping off to sleep, the meter of his solar system diminishing.

The real universe must have such a heart, she insisted to herself. Must have. And yet, though she could see the tracery of a thousand forces, watch the djinni burrow through the aether like worms through rotten meat, she could not perceive the beating heart behind it all. She could not, in short, see God.

Could it be that the Korai were right after all? That their superstition of a world damned to exist without God was true? And if that were so, how could one achieve grace, forgiveness, salvation?

For certainly she needed all three.

And yet, she almost had to smile at this thought, for it was not one she would have had, traveling with Le Loup, not one she could have tolerated. Then she could not feel, or think, or speculate. Now she could, though once again she rode with orphans of civilization. Now she could, because though she sat a wild horse, she had at least one hand on the reins.

Hercule was warm, and in her drowsy mind her own body became a planet, lazily spinning about the axis of her brain, even more sedately falling along an elliptical orbit, so that, year after year, she moved through the same places: now near the sun and its bright warmth; now, at aphelion, farther from the life-giving rays. In that moment of near dream, she experienced a hard kind of comfort: that her life was not an ascending or descending arc, but like this, a repeated path. And yet, even the orbit of a planet was not fixed. The gentle tug of other bodies created subtle harmonies, never the same; and so, as her life repeated itself, it did so always with variations, like a fugue. In time, the sum of these would ruin her orbit and send her to dwell forever with the sun or in the dark regions beyond.

Thus, for a moment, though harried and pursued through an unfriendly land, Adrienne de Mornay de Montchevreuil knew a moment of peace, knowing also that it was transitory but that it would come again. In that pax between sleep and dream, a voice spoke to her. It was the voice of one of her djinni—and thus her own voice—and yet the cadence of the words was not at all like anything she had heard before from her aethereal servants.

"Mademoiselle, how fortunate that I have found you," the voice said.

"Who has found me?" she asked.

"One who has long searched for you."

Adrienne felt a faint tingle of worry. This was something new. Cautiously, she called her djinni to stand near her. Was this one of the *malfaiteurs*, the murderous faction of which Crecy had warned her?

"Reveal yourself, then. Are you human or djinn?"

A suggestion of a chuckle. "I am no malakus, if that is what you ask. I am human, Mademoiselle, as human as you. I am your sister."

"Sister? What nonsense."

"Not nonsense at all. *Chairete, Korai, Athenes therapainai.*"

A shock ran through Adrienne, as almost reflexively, she answered *"Chairete."*

"Enthade euthetoumen temeron," the voice chanted.

"*He glaux, ho drakon, he parthenos,*" Adrienne finished, and then— forcefully, "Enough of this. Who are you?"

"One of the Korai."

"You only tell me what is obvious. Tell me your *name.*"

"That is hardly fair," the voice said. "For I do not know yours. Still, it is my wish for you to trust me. My name is Vasilisa Karevna."

"A Muscovite name," Adrienne guessed.

"Yes, Mademoiselle, a Russian name."

"You are among my enemies, then."

"Were I your enemy, I would have given you a false name, with no hint of Muscovy in it. Were I your enemy, I would command the troops surrounding your company to slay you all—"

"There are no troops," Adrienne said. "My djinni would tell me of them."

"You are not the only sorceress, my dear," Karevna replied, "nor have you been at it the longest. There are tricks of which you are doubtless unaware. The djinni, as you call them, are not bright creatures—at least not those you and I deal with. They are limited and easily deceived."

Adrienne could hardly argue with that. Were they really surrounded? She hoped that did not mean the sentries were dead. "What do you want?"

"I want my sister Korai at my side, of course. In this world of men, we need each other, you and I."

It sounded almost like something Crecy would say.

"That is no answer. You want me for what? To do what?"

"Why, to join me, of course. To join me where we might talk in the flesh, where we might—"

"Whom do you serve?"

"I serve the Korai." And then, it seemed, reluctantly, "I serve the tsar of all the Russias. He values our kind, Mademoiselle, as other kings do not."

"Values the Korai?"

"Ha. Of course, he knows nothing of the Korai. No, I mean to say that he values philosophers, scientifics. He gives us refuge, solace— the things we need to continue with our studies. Do you have that now, Mademoiselle?"

"Until your tsar's troops slaughtered my friends, yes."

"That was unfortunate, but not my doing. The duke was bound for Bohemia, and Russia is at war with Bohemia."

"I remember no chance to surrender."

"These are hard times, and, as I say, that was not my doing. Still, I find it difficult to believe that you had library and laboratory in your camps along the way. If you believe the so-called Holy Roman emperor would have supplied you—a woman—with such things—then you are mistaken."

"But the tsar is different," Adrienne said skeptically.

"The tsar is a realist. He is not bound by the nonsensical conventions and delusions of the European courts. He chooses people by their merit, rewards them by their merit. Under his rule, the lowliest peasant can become like a lord if he—or she—has sufficient talent and ingenuity. His own empress was a Lithuanian slave, his closest advisers of common birth. And I—also of humble origin—occupy a regarded position in his court."

"How did you find me?"

"Need you ask? You have used the power of the malakim freely, without guile. Naturally you have been noticed; the reports came to me by aetherschreiber, and I hastened here to find you. Now I have found you, and I am glad. And you should be glad that it was I who discovered you first."

"I'm sure I am."

"Mademoiselle, you must understand me. I can save your life; more, I can save the lives of your companions. But I will not mislead you: to his friends, the tsar is magnanimous. To his enemies he is remorseless. You eluded him for a short time, but that time is over."

Adrienne smiled without humor, her head still pressed against Hercule's gently moving chest. "Then it is a matter of joining you or dying?"

"I suppose."

"Well, what an unusual offer. I think I should discuss this with the others."

"Please do so."

"And I think you should come here, in the flesh, to present your terms."

"I agree completely. Shall we say tomorrow afternoon, around six? I shall bring repast."

"I fear I have forgotten my clock," Adrienne retorted.

"I shall send a—what did you call them?—djinn to remind you. On the morrow then?"

"Tomorrow," Adrienne agreed.

"How can we trust her?" Hercule asked.

"Oh, that answer's simple," Crecy replied. "We can't."

"What have the scouts seen, Hercule?" Adrienne asked.

Hercule grimaced and brushed mud from his riding boots. They sat together in a copse of ancient oaks, gazing out over a plain, speckled purple with thistle. Behind them spread a dense forest whose un-friendly inhabitants had been sniping at them for three days.

"They are there," he said, thrusting his arm toward the western horizon, "and there," pointing north. "There," east. "Of the forest I don't know, but if I were at a gambling table, I would not wager against it."

"Then in that sense we can trust her," Adrienne said.

"In another as well," Crecy said, tilting her nose east, where Adri-enne suddenly made out eight horses approaching.

Hercule nodded. "Just eight of them. They have stones on them, these Russians."

Adrienne chuckled. "At least one of them does not."

Hercule leaned and kissed her ear. "The women of my acquain-tance these days carry bigger stones than most men."

"Can we escape them? Fight our way through?"

"That all depends upon you. Can you best this sorceress of theirs?"

"I would guess not," Adrienne admitted.

"Do not be deceived by her, Adrienne," Crecy warned. "She may present herself as accomplished, but it may well be a façade. This could all be a trick by your lesser, a peasant conniving to rid a knight of her sword."

"That could be true. But that many men . . ."

"Let us hear their terms," Hercule said reasonably.

"Agreed," Adrienne replied.

Crecy only shrugged, and decapitated a thistle with the point of her sword.

Vasilisa Karevna was a tiny woman with night-black hair and slanting, almost Oriental eyes. She wore a riding habit of bloodred velvet, a cape of heavy black fur, and a cylindrical hat of sable. The men with her wore the typical green Russian coat and black tricorns, but their faces had the same foreign caste to them that Karevna's did. Their saddles bore twin *kraftpistole* holsters, and exceedingly heavy, curved sabers flapped at their sides.

"Good day," the Muscovite said as she approached. "I hope you are in the mood for a picnic."

One of her men dismounted, carefully keeping his hand far from his weapons, and began to unload baskets.

"I would prefer to talk," Adrienne said quietly.

"Surely we can do both. You are . . ."

"Adrienne de Mornay de Montchevreuil. These are my companions Monsieur d'Argenson and Mademoiselle de Crecy."

Karevna made to slide down from her saddle and, pausing, glanced at Adrienne. "If I may?"

"Please."

The sorceress finished her descent and then curtsied. "So happy to meet you all. Mademoiselle Crecy, your reputation precedes you."

Crecy smiled faintly. "How unfortunate," she said.

Despite Adrienne's admonition, the horseman had begun unpacking the baskets. Adrienne suddenly found her resolve to refuse the meal weaken as plump quail, black bread, wine, and roast boar appeared. It was a violent assault on senses weakened by hunger and rough meals.

Trying to ignore her salivating mouth, Adrienne gestured at the ground. "I'm afraid we left our *chassetes* and armchairs back with the duke."

Karevna shrugged, and, carefully arranging her skirt, folded gracefully down.

"You're certain you won't eat first?"

"Very certain," Adrienne replied.

"Ah, well—then shall we cover the business at hand, so that we might then enjoy our meal?"

"I very much doubt that we will enjoy it, Madame," Hercule interjected, "after we hear what you have to say."

She looked at him in surprise. "Is monsieur a reader of thoughts and futures? If so, he should know that I am a mademoiselle, not a *madame*."

Hercule frowned, but did not answer. Karevna took this as a sign to continue. "This is what the tsar offers you," she said briskly. "For you and your close companions, Mademoiselle de Montchevreuil, rooms in the palace in Saint Petersburg."

"Rooms? Prison cells?"

Karevna shook her head. "Not at all. You shall have freedom of movement not only within the palace but also within the city, on certain provisions. You must swear to serve the tsar, and you must not leave the city itself without permission from the tsar—or perhaps from the director of the scientific academy."

Adrienne tilted her head at that, and Karevna smiled. "Yes, I thought that would interest you. You, Mademoiselle, may join the academy as a full member."

Adrienne blinked. "How can such a thing be possible?"

"Because it is so, Mademoiselle. I will not pretend to you that all masculine philosophers are particularly happy about this state of affairs, but it is nevertheless true. The tsar places men—and women— as he sees fit."

"And Mademoiselle de Crecy, Monsieur d'Argenson?"

"Why, they may do what they wish, though the tsar is most pleased by those who show some industry. Crecy, I know, has manifold qualities, as, no doubt, does monsieur."

"And the men?" Hercule asked, waving at the nearby clusters of faded and bloodied uniforms.

"The men shall be well cared for, or they may remain here, whatever you please. They must be disarmed, of course, but aside from that . . ."

Hercule frowned deeply. "If you leave them here, disarmed, it is as good as killing them."

"They may come with us, I said, if they swear allegiance to the tsar. Some useful work can be found for them, too—in the shipyards, casting cannon—"

"They are soldiers," Adrienne interrupted. "They keep their weapons and remain as my personal guard."

Karevna's smile took on a slightly frozen quality. "That is quite impossible," she replied.

"Well, then, pack your picnic back up and return to your tsar. We will all die together."

"Mademoiselle, do not be extreme. Be prudent."

"This is prudent. I can only be certain these men are treated well if they are near me. I personally guarantee that they will never lift arms against your tsar, so long as he keeps his word. But they remain with me, under the command of Monsieur d'Argenson, or we fight."

Karevna looked steadily at her for a few moments. "This is not within my power to grant you, Mademoiselle."

"Who has the power, then?"

"Only the tsar himself."

"Well, then, tell your tsar."

Karevna lifted her delicate shoulders. "Very well," she agreed. "What do you say we go see him together?"

"In Saint Petersburg?"

"Ah, no, he is much nearer than that. We will march together. In the meantime, your men can keep their arms and remain under your command. Agreed?"

Adrienne searched the other woman's face for some signal of deception, but nothing palpable presented itself. If she refused this offer, in all probability they would not live until morning. Lie or not, this journey the Muscovite proposed gave her more time to gauge the strengths and weaknesses of their foes. She looked to Hercule, who lifted one brow slightly, his sign that it was her decision. Crecy pursed her lips, the same signal.

"Very well," she said. "We agree."

"Good. And now can I convince you to join me in a meal?"

Crecy coughed quietly. "I, for one, would be delighted. But I hope you do not take it ill if I ask that you have yourself served first."

Karevna grinned broadly at that, and said something in Russian.

The men with her chuckled, too, and one replied to Karevna in the same tongue.

"They say you have the heart of a Cossack," Karevna told Crecy. "I quite agree."

"I would be much obliged," Adrienne said, "if you would provide our men with food. I shall not eat until they have at least bread."

Karevna smiled even more broadly. "And you, my dear, have the heart of the tsar."

2

Charles

"I'll assume that was our way out a' here," Robert remarked from behind him.

"Damn, damn," Ben answered, pounding the windowsill with his fist. "Why couldn't he wait another two—" He broke off and looked around wildly. "Lenka!" he called.

But he already knew that there would be no answer.

"What are those?" Frisk asked, surprisingly calm, gesturing at the flying ships.

"Death from the sky," Ben muttered. "And all I could think of was comets. It could have been anything."

"Ships. Ships in the air. Tsar Peter must be *so* pleased," Frisk remarked.

Ben leaned against the wall, vaguely aware of the disjointed nature of the conversation. But one did not see an armada aloft every day.

"Well, then, what now?" Robert asked, voice suddenly briskly practical.

"Flee another way," Frisk said. "In the confusion of the battle, that should be simple enough."

"Not so simple," Robert answered. "Someone is coming up the stairs. A lot of someones, by the sound."

"Lock the door," Ben snapped. "Give me a moment to think."

Robert was already at the door, but instead of closing it right away, he drew a pistol and leaned around the frame. An instant later, the room reverberated hollowly with a sharp explosion, and gray smoke billowed in. A chorus of shouts went up from below, and then Robert had slammed the heavy portal shut and drawn the bolt.

"Not a long moment, please," he said.

"No, it's clear what we must do," Ben said. He went to the crack where he had hidden the compass bar, pocketed it, and then turned back to the others. "We'll have to jump."

Robert glanced dubiously at the steep hillside some fifty feet below. "I assume that in scientifical language 'jump' has some other meanin' than in common speech."

Ben, grinning mordantly, shook his head no. "Have you heard the story about the governor who was defenestrated?"

"Who what?"

"In times past, Prague was Protestant, but the governor was Catholic. One day a mob threw him and his secretary out an upper-floor window of the palace. They survived because their cloaks billowed out, resisting the air and slowing their fall." He nodded his head toward the corner of the room, where the envelope he had placed the gas generator beneath had developed a pronounced hump.

"Oh, no," Robert said. "No.

"We could tear it t' strips and braid a rope," Robert protested, nervously knotting his fingers into the silk.

"We've no time. They'll break through soon."

As if to emphasize his words, the door's iron hinges squealed a metallic complaint, and the pounding outside redoubled.

"We have to jump all together," Ben cautioned.

"Aye, so's we die simultaneous," Robert countered.

"If you've a better solution, out with it now."

The three of them stood in the now-open wall of the tower, each holding a corner of the envelope. It was considerably less than half full, shaped like a mushroom well past its prime. The gas in it was not sufficient to lift the envelope itself into the air, much less the three men clutching its corners.

"As long as we keep the mouth open and pointed down, it should fill with air and slow us," Ben explained.

"The ground will slow us considerably more," Robert grumbled.

The door whined again, and this time bulged into the room. Then the sound stopped.

"Not a good sign," Frisk said. "They must have something more effective."

At that moment, a jet of flame licked the door from the mouth of its frame. Outside, someone shrieked in pain, presumably from the backlash of whatever they had just used.

"Go!" Ben shouted, and jumped.

Frisk was with him, but Robert an instant too slow, so that they swung like a pendulum. Ben suppressed a shriek as there was suddenly only space beneath his feet, and he was sure that the giant bag would simply fold and fall with them. It might have, when it swung back, but the tower wall was there, and instead the three men smacked into it. Robert hit hardest—Frisk and Ben being in some part cushioned by Robert—but that stopped the balloon's swinging. It yanked fiercely at Ben's hands as it filled with air. Gritting his teeth, Ben held tight, watching the ground approach with surreal rapidity. Then they crunched into the underbrush at the tower's foot, and below that the unyielding earth rammed straight through Ben's feet into his head, never minding the organs between.

When they untangled themselves from the now-tattered silk, musket balls were whizzing down at them from above, and, ducking their heads, the three men half fell down the slope, accompanied by Robert's steady, imaginative cursing.

A few moments later, out of line of sight from the tower, they came together for a moment. The Moldau curved below them, placidly unconcerned with the explosions and sheets of flame that illuminated the skies around Prague. Some of the eruptions splattered against the sky like great starfish, indicating that the shield protecting the city still held; others spewed columns of soot and fire from the earth, proving it had begun to weaken. Across the river, in Old Town, Ben could make out people swarming in the street like ants from a hill, kicked by some titan. Many clustered near the river, which was thickening with boats.

"Are we all living?" Ben asked.

"In pain, but alive. I think my ankle is broken," Robert complained.

Frisk snorted. "If it were broken, sir, you would not be running so well on it."

"Perhaps. Men an' their ankles are capable of great things in times of emergency."

"Come on," Ben said, starting off again.

"Where to?"

"To where our boat awaits. On Venedig Island."

"Hell," Robert muttered, "more swimming."

A perimeter of nervous soldiers stood guard at the island, but they weren't firing, merely shooing back terrified swimmers with their smallswords and sabres. As the three crawled from the water, two of the fellows approached, grim faced, though their expressions mellowed when they saw that the three were dressed like gentlemen.

"Your pardon, sirs," one of them said, "but as we are under attack, we must guard His Majesty's boats all the more. I understand that you are frightened, but—" He broke off, staring hard at Ben. *"Der Lehrling!"* He exclaimed. "To arms! Murderer!"

Ben had a second to regret how highly visible he had made himself in the last two years. Was there not a single person in Prague who would not immediately recognize him?

Then Frisk, cold eyed, had drawn his saber, and, with no sound, launched himself at the guard. The fellow's eyes widened in terror as the heavy blade swept down, and he lifted his own weapon—a narrow little thing, more for show than for anything else. Steel rang, and he stumbled back, but Frisk gave no respite. Robert drew his Spanish rapier and attacked the other guard, just as a third was arriving.

Ben uttered an oath and clumsily pulled out his own smallsword. He had chosen it for its look, not knowing much about swordplay; it had an inventive brass griffin on its pommel that appealed to him. Gripping the hilt uncertainly, he brought it up to guard, as Robert had shown him.

His opponent grinned wickedly—whether from the way he stood, from the look in his eyes, or from the way he held the weapon, Ben had no idea—but suddenly the fellow was there, the sword darting toward Ben. With a strangled cry he beat at the blade, trying to keep it away from him, scuttling backward at the same time. The other, sure of his footwork, advanced.

Ben parried two more strokes, and then suddenly the steel was at his chest, in it, and Ben felt the strangest pain he had ever felt in his life—a numb cold that shot through his entire body at once. Stopped from screaming only by his throat closing in terror, he dropped his sword.

At about the same instant, the flat of Frisk's blade smashed into the guardsman's face, crushing his nose. The fellow pitched over backward, sobbing in pain.

In the next instant, Robert was by his side. "Ben? Come on, Ben."

He wanted to tell them he couldn't, that he was dying, but he couldn't get the words out. He could only watch, stunned, as blood welled between the fingers clasped over the wound.

The guards had never drawn their pistols, so Robert and Frisk took them. Then, bearing Ben up between them, they hurried toward the boathouse, which itself looked like a small castle. It wasn't defended as one, however. The guardsmen patrolling the island seemed to be all that remained, the rest doubtless gone to their units, since, after all, a more important battle was raging. A single young fellow met them, but he quickly surrendered his weapons, which consisted of musket and a heavy short sword.

"Which one?" Robert wondered. Moored at the king's quay were mostly pleasure craft: a barge, several small yachts designed to resemble full-size sailing ships, one with a prow shaped as an eagle.

"Any of them," Frisk said, "and hope that the Muscovites are not guarding the river."

Robert looked up at the older man. "Why should they care if someone *escapes* the city, s' long as they don't stay t' defend it?"

"They'll want to keep the emperor from escape. Hurry, now. We took a short route here; soon floods of nobility will pour down from the castle, to make good *their* flight."

Ben found his tongue. He could at least save his friends before he died. "That with the sea-horse prow," he murmured. "That one."

"Why that one?"

"It's magical. Like my shoes, if 'tis finished."

"Ah. In that case . . ."

The ship indeed had a sea-horse prow and crenelated gunnels, as if it were a warship. It was, however, only some fifteen feet in length.

"Too big to row," Frisk objected.

"Steam engine," Ben muttered. "Robert used to drive a locomotive in London. You won't need me. Fare thee well, my friends. Find Newton. Make sure Lenka is well. Tell my father—"

"Will y' please shut yer maw?" Robert snapped. "Y' a'n't dyin'."

Ben looked down at his shirt and nearly fainted. It was wet and red, as if someone had thrown an entire bucket of paint on it. "I think I am."

"I'll tend him," Frisk said. "I've unmoored us. If you know aught about starting the engine, do so quickly."

"Aye, aye," Robert said.

Ben, for his part, lay back on the deck. Above, rainbow skies shuddered a final time and then flashed white.

"That's it," he murmured. "The end of Prague. Me and Prague together."

Frisk was fooling with Ben's shirt, doing something he instinctively knew he didn't want to watch. "It isn't the end of Prague," Frisk said. "The Bohemians have had German rulers, now they will have Russian ones. Prague will remain. And so will you. Now, take a deep breath."

Puzzled, Ben did so, as the deck beneath him began to throb with the awakening of steam. Then something hurt very, very much in his chest, and a fist of darkness closed on his brain.

He awoke to the same gentle throbbing and starlight. A thick sickle moon hung in the sky, and for a long moment he couldn't remember where he was. He lay there, watching mists glide by the moon, trying to recall, straining at the familiar sounds of Robert and Frisk talking quietly. When he moved, and a serpent seemed to bite into his breast, it came to him.

"Robert!" he managed weakly.

"Ah! He comes alive!" Robert said from somewhere. A moment later his face appeared as he crouched beside Ben.

"How are ya, boy?"

"Am I going to die?"

"Am I a priest?" Robert grunted. Then, more gently, he said, "Not at the moment, I'd say, though I'm no surgeon. All looks well. The blade went into muscle and bone, but Frisk thinks it stopped short o' lung. An' it's on the wrong side f'r the heart. Frisk cauterized it for you with gunpowder."

"Are we away from Prague?"

"Maybe. One of them air boats is followin' us. They can't catch us. This is a fast boat, Ben, terrific fast."

"It's the one I was having made for the emperor."

"The problem," Frisk said, "is that we must meander with the river, while the air boat travels in straight lines. They almost caught us twice, while you slept. If they get far enough ahead, they will land and block our route. Our speed may have confused them, but mark me, if they persist, they will catch us."

"If they persist," Robert said. "But why should they?"

"This boat is clearly scientific—not the sort of thing a peasant would have. They may be convinced that the emperor or someone else important is aboard."

"Are we sailing upstream or down?"

"Up. Down is in the wrong direction, if we are going to join my army."

Ben nodded. "Ah. But you also claim that the Russians are bound to catch us, sooner or later."

"True, if we stay on the river."

"Where else to go?"

Frisk frowned impatiently. "Even if we stay on water, we shall soon run out. The headwaters are not far south, and it will become unnavigable even before we reach them."

"Y' have a suggestion," Robert observed.

"Yes. Abandon the boat, and then go to join my men."

"You mean for us t' walk all the way to Vienna?"

"No. I mean my men who are camped near the city—and, as it happens, in the south of it, not far from here."

"You've said nothing about men, Captain Frisk."

"It didn't seem the sort of thing to bring up."

"How is Ben to travel with that wound?" Robert asked.

"I've seen men travel with much worse than that."

"An' I'm sure that some of 'em died," Robert retorted.

"No, Robin, I can make it, if one of you gives me a shoulder to lean against. Sir, how shall we find your men?"

Frisk pulled something that resembled a watch from his pocket. "I have an aethercompass," he said. "It tells me where they are."

Ben sat up, wincing as he did so. "We have to find Newton. That was part of your mission, wasn't it, Captain Frisk? To win over Sir Isaac or kill him?"

"Yes."

"Then you must help me find him."

A faint, enigmatic smile crossed Frisk's Teutonic features. "I've an idea where he might be headed."

"Oh? And how might you know that?"

"I made him the same offer as I made you. He never accepted, but if he wants to avoid the Muscovites, he has no other place to go."

Ben blinked. "When did you do this?"

"It wasn't me, exactly, but one of my men, some time ago. I came because there was no response."

"And you never told us this?"

"It didn't seem—"

"The sort of thing to bring up. Yes, you say that quite a lot, Captain Frisk. And still you expect us to trust you?"

"I expect you to trust that I'm the only man who can help you right now."

Ben considered that, remembering Frisk's secondary task was to kill him. Could Robert outmatch Frisk? Somehow, Ben didn't think so.

"Let's find your men, then, while we still can."

For the most part, they carried him, though Ben tried to keep his feet going. He groggily reflected that losing blood felt like being drunk. Certainly the fields and farmsteads they passed were blurred images, ghosts of real places to his brain.

At one point, Frisk and Robert bought some mounts from a fat man who spoke loudly in very poor German. For perhaps the third time in his entire life, Ben then found himself on a horse, clutching Robert from behind, wincing becoming a part of his breath.

Despite the pain, on the horse he nodded in and out of sleep, until he was roused by a chorus of cheers. He forced his eyes open and saw some thirty or more men, uniformed much like Frisk, waving their arms and exulting, all clearly excited to see Frisk.

Ben was taken to a surgeon's tent, where he drank a wine that seeped into his fevered brain and doused it with midnight.

Slowly, what he had taken to be the droning of insects began to become sensible, resolving itself into German. He opened his eyes to cheerful firelight and the smell of mulled wine.

"Must have struck a deal with the sultan. Damn this Turkish treachery."

"Yes, Majesty," said a young man with coppery hair. "It is thought you had best seek refuge."

"Seek refuge? For nine years or more I have had refuge with Turks. I have fought battles for them, lent them the blood and bravery of my men, and now this betrayal? No. We ride for Venice this very night. I will face the cowards before they withdraw, and with God, reverse this situation."

"But, sir—"

"Lieutenant, over a thousand Swedes await in Venice, and I will not abandon them. You should know that."

The man grinned, a little ruefully. "Yes, Majesty, we all know that. But we had to try."

"Majesty?" Ben managed, raising up on one elbow.

"Ah, Mr. Franklin," Frisk said, nodding.

"One more thing he didn't believe worth mentioning," Robert muttered, from behind him. "Let me introduce to you Charles XII, the king of Sweden."

Ben didn't have the energy to gape. He just nodded—not because it wasn't a shock, but because no other action presented itself.

Frisk—or, rather, Charles—grinned slightly. "One day soon, Mr. Franklin, you and I will resume our earlier conversation about the worth of the institution of monarchy, but I'm afraid now that will have to wait."

"Sir? I mean, Majesty?"

"Sir will do," Charles said. "We have very pressing business in Venice, all of us." He turned to the lieutenant. "Send word ahead by the aetherschreibers. Have men we trust provide us with fresh mounts." He motioned toward Ben. "He cannot ride, so someone will have to carry him. I want to break camp within the hour. In five days I want to be in Venice."

"Five days?" Robert exploded. "Venice is five hundred miles from here if it's a league."

"Well, that's only a hundred miles a day, isn't it?" Charles replied.

"Why?" Ben asked. "Why such a hurry?"

Charles leaned forward, his voice low and hard. "Because if we do not hurry, we shall find Tsar Peter there, waiting for us."

3

The Sinking City

"The streets *are* water," Red Shoes noticed, squinting to see into the distance.

"Aye," Tug agreed, "I tol' ja. Han't it a wonder?"

Red Shoes searched for wonder and found it, but it was the wonder of a rattlesnake, a spider, an eel. Algiers had seemed impossible; Venice was far worse. Staring at it, he recalled his dream conversation with the pale chief of the *oka nahollo*—or whatever the apparition had truly been. He remembered that sunken city of stone and rotten wood, how its citizens made their captives into things human in form but more kin to the crawfish and the leech at heart.

Here was a city of stone and rotting wood that might have been raised from the deeps yesterday: a city where none ought to be, an abomination. With a sinking heart, he remembered also that his foe had suggested a close kinship between himself and the Europeans. Venice, after all, was the first real *nahollo* city he had ever seen—the people of Algiers were darker even than he. But he remembered other tales, now—of the Dutch, for instance, who also lived in cities with streets of water, below the level of the sea. He had met Dutchmen, and they were white indeed, as close to the *oka nahollo* of legend as any people imaginable.

The Choctaw were said to have emerged from that watery world beneath in *chanshpo*, the Beginning Time, to have split out of skins like crawfish to become human beings. But that had happened long ago, and the Choctaw had been ages in the sun. Perhaps the Europeans had emerged more recently, were closer to the underworld. That would explain their love of narrowness, of closed spaces, their mania for covering their skin, their unpredictable ways. They were creatures caught between, either rising out of the muck or sinking into it.

He stared down at his European clothes, trying to remember how long it was supposed to take the *oka nahollo* to turn a Choctaw into one of them, and repressed a shudder. He liked some of these people, but he did not want to *be* one. He wanted to go home, marry, plant a garden, hunt deer, kill a Chickasaw now and then. He wanted to stay Choctaw.

Everyone else on the ship seemed happy enough though, even people like Fernando who were far from white. They jabbered of the pleasures they would discover, of the qualities of Venetian women. Tug had already promised him another "good time," but Red Shoes wondered if he could survive another such night, especially in a city where the streets might literally swallow the drunken.

No. If he went into the waters of Venice, the waters of Venice would not go into him. It would be all his unknown enemy needed to destroy him, as he almost had in Algiers. And that enemy was still there: Three times on the voyage to Venice he had caught the gaze of covert eyes upon him, three times his foe had vanished without a trace.

Nairne paced up nervously beside him. "You look worried," he said.

"Do I have cause to worry?"

Nairne frowned. "So far, everything has gone as Riva said. No one bothered us on the Roman Sea, and here our welcome was pretty courteous, I have to admit. But did you notice the Turkish ships putting out?"

Red Shoes smiled ruefully. "I still have trouble telling one floating house from another."

"Well, in the few hours since we arrived, I've watched seven Turkish ships leave. And look around you—it seems to me that everyone else is readying to go, as well."

"You think Venice is in danger?"

"I think something very strange is going on."

Perhaps the underworld is preparing to swallow Venice once more, Red Shoes thought, *and take her home.* "What does the Venetian say about it?"

"I don't know, as he went ashore. I hope he returns."

It was five hours later before Domenico Riva returned, and his face had a rather grim cast to it.

"You said y'd return in an hour," Blackbeard grumbled dangerously.

Riva shook his head and raised his hands helplessly. "I'm sorry. Things are . . . You'd best summon your council."

Blackbeard turned his head slowly, eyes narrowing.

"I am reckonin'," he said, his words clipped casually, "that you had best tell me what goes on, and you had best do it now. In an hour, our ships'll be the only ones in this harbor. I want to know what *they* know that I do *not* know."

"I beg your pardon," Riva said. "I did not mean to be mysterious. It seems that Venice will soon be invaded."

"Invaded?"

"Yes. A Muscovite fleet is on its way even now."

"What? From where, the Bosporus? The Turk would cut them to pieces."

"Not so, and for two reasons, Captain."

"Being?"

"The one, because the tsar and the sultan have concluded a pact. The Turkish ships withdraw, not out of fear, but from arrangement. The second—" He paused, looking distraught.

"Out with it."

"The second is that, this is no ordinary fleet."

"What do you mean?"

"An ordinary fleet would need water to sail upon," Riva said. "The Muscovite armada does not."

The council, for once, all seemed in agreement.

"There's nothing in this for us," Blackbeard said. "It isn't our fight."

"Even if it were, what could we do?" Mather wondered.

"We cannot risk our ships," Bienville added.

"I see your concern," Riva murmured. "And, truly, I do not know how things will run. It looks bad, but in its own way, this is an opportunity, and I would like a chance to convince you that it is *your* opportunity."

"How so?" Mather asked.

Riva clasped his hands. "For almost twice ten years the Turk has lorded over us. You see the minarets of their mosques, do you not? If you come into the city, you shall see more. But now—now, at long last—they withdraw."

"Only so the tsar may move in."

"Yes, but you see, it is all a ploy. The sultan long ago tired of King Charles of Sweden—perhaps even fears him, as the Janissaries respect him so much."

"What matter?" Bienville asked. "The Janissaries are merely soldiers, are they not?"

Riva shook his head. "No. The Janissaries are powerful indeed, and willful. They have removed sultans from the throne. Once, they may have been pliant to the wishes of the Porte, but that was long ago. Especially in the provinces, like Venice, their power is great. The long and short of it is that a command to simply arrest the Swedish king and his men would be ignored, for such has happened in the past. But the sultan, you see, wants peace with Russia, and that peace can never be concluded with Charles still a guest in the Ottoman Empire."

"Aye." Blackbeard shrugged. "So the Turks withdraw, with no invitation to Charles to go with them. The Moscovados take the city and Charles in the process."

"Aye. But then the Russians withdraw again, and the Turk comes back. They stage a sham battle perhaps, so everything looks well, but in the end that is the plan."

"I still don't see what this has to do with us."

Riva stared at them intently. "I told you that there were those of us who would shake the Turkish yoke. This is the time. If we could defeat the Muscovite—"

A belly laugh erupted from Blackbeard. "Defeat flying ships?"

Riva blushed, but plunged on. "They expect no resistance."

Blackbeard laughed some more.

"Let's say you do defeat them," Bienville said. "What prevents the Turk from crushing you next year?"

"Several things," Riva said. "The first is that the Turk has no flying ships, and Venice has always been a tight oyster to shuck. Our loss to the Turks those years ago was as much luck on their part as design. *Secundo* — if we beat the Muscovites, it will be because the Janissaries have come to our side."

"Why should they do that?"

"They have lived here for many years. Their children are, for all purposes, Venetian. It would be possible, I think, to establish a council that was both Janissary and Christian — in short, to become a regency instead of a colony. We could claim that we defended the city for the greater glory of the Porte. With the Janissaries on our side, the sultan could hardly disagree."

"So you would keep the snake in the garden," Mather muttered. "You would live on with the Mohammedan."

"We live together as it is. The Porte allows all religions to exist, but Christians have no say. That, at least, would change." He paused. "There are those of us who think as you, that all of the Mussulmen must be cast out, that Venice must be ruled only by those descended from the old families. They are somewhat fanatical; we call them the Masques."

"So your junto is split, then," Blackbeard noted. "I suppose these 'masks' care little for the Janissaries."

Riva shrugged. "They know who has the power. Our plan is not theirs, but they will cooperate until the Muscovite is driven away and the Porte held at a distance."

"But you are not one of these," Mather said.

"No. If we alienate the Porte, the Janissaries, *and* their children, how shall we survive? In a sea controlled by the Turk, whom shall we trade with? How will we beat off invasion year after year?"

"Come to the point," Bienville said. "What is it you want from us?"

"Only this, for now. A council of the Janissaries is meeting in a few hours. I ask only that you attend. If the Janissaries do not swing to Charles, then all hope is lost, and I happily bid you sail home. But if they do —"

"If they do, you want us to fight," Blackbeard said grimly. "Fight against magical ships an' demons."

Riva held up his hands. "Please. I ask only that you come and listen, delay sail for another day. The Muscovites will have no reason to pursue you."

"We've only your word for that," Bienville pointed out.

"True. But what difference will a few hours make?"

"And what will we get out of this?" Blackbeard asked mildly, "besides a missionary glow?"

"A partner in commerce on what I can promise you will be very, very good terms. And a friend should the Turk ever turn his eyes toward America."

Nairne quirked his lip. "I see. And by attending this meeting, we become a part of your argument, yes?"

"What do you mean?" Riva asked innocently.

"You can parade us as proof that there is trade to be had beyond the Mediterranean—an incentive for the Janissaries to stay here and become merchants."

"Well—" Riva said, staring down at the boards.

"This is a dangerous game you play," Nairne went on, wiggling his finger. "How many factions are attending this council only because they have been promised that some other faction may be there?"

Riva chuckled throatily. "All of them."

"So none are firm."

"Oh, no," Riva said. "The Masques will fight; there is no doubt of that. They even think they may have obtained some advantage, a scientific one."

"How so?"

"A few days ago, a man came into the Veneto—in a flying boat—and ensconced himself on one of the near islands. At first we thought it an advance Muscovite, but new rumors have arisen. It is said that it is some mighty wizard, perhaps Sir Isaac Newton himself!"

"Newton?" Mather said, his voice rising.

"Yes. It is well known that Newton has been at the court of the Holy Roman emperor in Prague. Prague has recently been overrun by the tsar. It is said that Charles offered him refuge here."

"Here is an odd twist," Mather said. "And these Masques think to gain Newton's aid?"

"We all do, of course. It is well known that it was only he that enabled Prague to stand as long as it did. At the moment, he staves off all intruders with a magical force. If anyone can help Venice stand alone, it is Newton."

"And yet," Nairne said, "you don't know for certain this man is Newton, nor has he offered his help to anyone."

Riva shrugged. "The wizard—Newton or not—has been invited to the council. Perhaps he will come."

"Well," Mather said dryly, "if nothing else, this council should prove more than interesting. Besides—if this really is Newton and not some godless warlock, it could be worthwhile for us all."

Blackbeard smiled his evil smile. "Aye. I would not want to miss this kind of squabble."

Bienville, surprisingly, seemed to have lost his reluctance. "I will go, if we are allowed to speak."

"All may speak at the Divan," Riva assured him.

"Red Shoes?" Mather asked.

Red Shoes shook his head. "This time I have no opinion. The situation is too complicated."

"No," Blackbeard muttered. "No, your instinct was good in England."

"Perhaps not so good in convincing you to come here."

"That remains to be seen, Choctaw. What do you say?"

"It never hurts to hear a talk," Red Shoes replied.

"Well enough," said Blackbeard. "A talk we will hear."

4

Tsar

Amidnight quiet settled on the company, though it was only an hour past noon. But high midnight is the time of dreams, of phantasms. Climbing the last hill, Adrienne and her companions entered that realm.

Besides, what was there to say of a monstrous ship of war—complete with cannon, pennants, and men standing at the rails—hanging so impudently in the air? One could not rant that it was impossible, for there it was.

As they drew nearer, Adrienne understood *how* it was possible: the ship was supported by a number of iridescent gloves, eggshells of twisted forces enveloping djinni yolks. She tried to sit straight in her saddle, to show no sign of fear for her men to seize upon and thus kindle their own fears. The green-clad soldiers marching in front, behind, and to their sides were a reminder of what would happen should panic erupt. And so she smiled—that same smile whose constancy Louis XIV had so admired, that her true love Nicolas had so disliked for its falseness—and she rode on until the ship blotted the sun. In its shadow, Vasilisa trotted ahead to meet a group of soldiers, dismounting gracefully near a tall, forward-hunched, fierce-looking man. He asked her a question, presumably in Russian, and a brisk conversation followed as Adrienne veiled her apprehension behind a placid face. The man—dressed in a nondescript military coat with no obvious sign of rank, tricorn tucked under his arm—raked his gaze over them. Adrienne was momentarily taken aback by the animal intensity of his black eyes, the exotic barbarity of his swarthy face, thick lips, ferocious mustache. Shoulders bunched, head lowered, he came forward.

"You would dictate terms to the tsar of Russia?" he asked mildly in comprehensible French.

"Sir—" Hercule began, but the Russian cut him off with a sharp glance and an admonishing finger.

"I spoke to the lady, sir. Milady?"

"In fact, I would," Adrienne remarked coolly. "Mademoiselle Karevna assured me that I could present my case."

"And so you shall. So you shall. I am informed that you accept the terms but wish your men to remain armed, as a sort of personal guard."

"Yes, Monsieur . . ."

"Captain Alexevitch," he supplied.

"Thank you, Captain. Yes, that is my wish."

He nodded, and his face suddenly twitched spastically, followed by a brief, disconcerting smile. He nodded.

"Very well." He gestured up at the ship. "Will you come aboard to speak further of this?"

"Will we meet the tsar?" Hercule asked, and then frowned as a little flutter of laughter traveled through the group of soldiers. Vasilisa smiled also.

"I think," Adrienne said, "that we already have."

The tall man tilted his head. "At your service," he remarked. "And, again, if you would be so kind as to join me above, I will consider your request. I love my men, and respect those of similar inclination."

"Then you will understand if I question the safety of these men in our absence, Your Majesty."

"I give you my word that they will be safe, Mademoiselle. You may speak to them if you like."

Experience had taught Adrienne to mistrust the words of kings, but as she had walked them all into the tiger's lair, the only choice was to speak to the tiger.

"That is very gracious, Your Majesty," she told him.

"Shipboard," he said gently, "I prefer 'captain.' "

"Thank you then, Captain."

As he turned, she noticed them. They were trying to stay hidden, his entourage of djinni, but they could not hide from her. At least three attended him, one of an unfamiliar sort. Silently, she called out to her own servants and doubled her aethereal guard.

Once they had completed their vertiginous ascent—drawn up in a large wicker basket—the tsar put on a different demeanor—like a schoolboy showing playmates his new toys, bounding about enthusiastically, explaining this or that. Notwithstanding her concerns, Adrienne found herself quickly infected by his ebullience.

"And what of these?" she asked in the wheelhouse, an airy, pavilion-like structure. Around the chart table were several raised banks of brass dials, labeled in a script that looked a little like Greek.

"Ah," the tsar exclaimed, another curiously ferocious smile plucking his lips. "Perhaps you can guess?"

Adrienne examined them again. They seemed divided into discrete groups, each with a clock and three dials of varying calibration. The Russian numerals, at least, were those the rest of the world used.

"The clocks, I presume, are *horologium aetherium*, for determining the longitude."

"Bravo, Mademoiselle."

Crecy coughed meaningfully, so that the tsar lifted an eyebrow. "Mademoiselle?"

"Captain, I fear that I am no scientific," she explained in her most endearing tones. "I wonder if you could explain further?"

"Yes, yes, of course," the tsar said. It was peculiar, Adrienne thought, that such a large man would fold his shoulders inward, the way he did, as if trying to escape notice, as if some natural reluctance had shaped his very body. Fierce and shy, bold and retiring. A strange man, this king who would rather be called captain.

"For reasons I won't go into," the tsar said, "it is impossible to determine longitude without an accurate clock. And no clock, you see, has ever been invented that keeps good time on a ship, because of the constant odd motion. But here we have a clock whose works are back in my house in Saint Petersburg, you see?"

"Ah! Like an aetherschreiber, but instead of translating writing across the airy spaces, it sends out the proper time."

"Yes, precisely."

Adrienne gestured at the indicators. "And the other dials—wind speed and force, perhaps? And barometric pressure?"

"Yes!" the tsar almost shouted. "Yes! At a glance I can know something of the weather in any direction! Mademoiselle, my dear Vasilisa has estimated you well, I think. You do not disappoint. I cannot wait to see your face when we return to Saint Petersburg and I show you the facilities which await you."

"I look forward to it, Captain, though we first must settle the matter of our men."

"It is settled," the tsar replied. "They will swear, each one, loyalty to me as well as to you, and I will want the same promise from you three." His eyes hardened somewhat. "Do not betray me. I do not care for betrayal."

She glanced at Hercule, who nodded imperceptibly. "This is most generous of you, Captain," she said. "And I promise you that you will not regret it."

"And you sir?" the tsar asked, addressing Hercule. "I hope I have not mistaken the chain of command."

Hercule grinned a little sheepishly. "I am, I suppose, the captain of the guard. But Mademoiselle Karevna has given you the right notion: Mademoiselle de Montchevreuil owns their hearts."

"Does she? What of the duke of Lorraine?"

Hercule shrugged. "I doubt not that the men retain some affection for him—if he still lives—but I believe their devotion to Mademoiselle is greater."

"I should tell you that the duke does still live," the tsar said. "The desire of my officers was only to keep him from reinforcing Prague. That point is now moot, though I'm afraid the division which you had the ill fortune to try and march through had not yet been informed of this, for fear of spies learning my plans."

"What do you mean?" Hercule asked.

"The invasion of Prague began two days ago. Today, the city is ours. There would have been nothing for the duke to reinforce. I regret the loss of life, I truly do."

"I see." Hercule said, his face carefully blank. Adrienne was remembering the flame falling from the sky. "And the duke?"

"The duke is a guest on another ship such as this one."

"Ah. He is well, then, and perhaps near at hand. That presents me with something of a dilemma, Captain."

"You have sworn loyalty to him, I presume?"

"Yes, Captain."

"That need not be a dilemma—I shall explain why at dinner. It's good that your loyalty is not lightly given."

"No, sir, it is not," Hercule replied. To Adrienne, he sounded relieved.

"In the meantime," Adrienne interjected, "I hope you will show us the rest of your fabulous ship."

"And so I shall." The tsar grinned.

The food was good, not at all outlandish. The tsar cut his meat with knife and fork, more civilized in that respect than Louis XIV had been.

"What is this wine?" Crecy asked.

"It is rather excellent, is it not?" the tsar replied. "It is my favorite—*Tokaji*, from a region in Hungary. They make it, they say, from raisins."

"Very good," Crecy agreed.

"None has been produced in almost three years. The strange weather has destroyed much, and grape harvests—all harvests—have been poor. Fortunately, *Tokaji* can keep well for more than a hundred years."

The tsar's cabin reinforced the opinion Adrienne was forming of the tsar. It was quite simple, rather Dutch in decoration—the cabin of a captain and not a king. Louis XIV would have had every surface encrusted with gold and ornament, but Louis—for all the immense power he had wielded—had never truly been secure, had always needed to emphasize that he was king. This tsar did not seem to need to underscore his authority. The single extravagance was one she approved of: a glass portal in the floor that allowed one to watch the terrain pass beneath.

Hercule coughed softly. "Would it be rude, Captain, if I were to bring up the matter of the duke again?"

"Not at all. I said we would discuss this matter at dinner, and this is dinner, isn't it?" He took a long draft of his wine and then settled back, steepling his fingers beneath his rounded chin. "You must understand that I have no desire to make Bohemia a Russian colony. Add her to our empire, yes, as a buffer against the Turk, and perhaps, eventually, to stage the restoration of Vienna to Christendom, but I have no intention of placing a governor there. And yet I do not—cannot—recognize the claim of Karl VI to the so-called Holy Roman Empire. His pretension to the Bohemian throne, in particular, is baseless. Nevertheless, *someone* must rule Bohemia, preferably someone legitimate and mindful of the greater scheme of things."

Someone easily controlled, Adrienne thought. Now, at last, she saw the king in him.

"Francis Stephen?" Hercule asked, in a puzzled tone.

"Not precisely. Karl VI has a daughter whose claim to Bohemia—though of course not the 'empire'—is secure. She is very young, and I think could benefit from marriage to a more experienced ruler who could act as regent."

"Ah," Hercule said, suddenly grinning from ear to ear, as Adrienne remembered that such had been the young duke's aim all along.

"He seems amenable," the tsar added. "If all goes well, you may rejoin him if you wish."

Hercule hesitated. "I will think on it, Captain."

"Good. I would be pleased, of course, to have you in my service, along with Mademoiselle." He turned significantly to Adrienne.

She felt a moment of her old fear, the fear of making irrevocable choices, but it quickly passed. She knew her decision; she had made it the instant she saw the airship, or perhaps even earlier, when Karevna mentioned membership in the scientific academy. But there was no reason to appear too eager. "I have never sworn an oath of loyalty to Lorraine, nor do any oaths bind me to any nation, as matters stand. The thought of at last being able to pursue my study of science is most compelling." She lowered her eyes. "I wonder if I can give you my answer in the morning."

"I'm afraid not," the tsar said. "We must cast off very soon—in an hour, in fact. I can give you until then, and let you alone to talk among yourselves."

"Though your company is most enjoyable, Captain, that would be a great kindness. Thank you."

"It is nothing," the tsar said. "I must attend to the preparations in any event. I will see you in an hour."

He stood, bowed briefly, and then left the cabin.

"Well?" Hercule said, when he had gone.

"A moment," Adrienne replied, circumambulating the room with her servants, making certain that no hidden ear—human or djinn—would eavesdrop upon them. "There."

"It seems an overgenerous offer," Crecy noticed.

"Yes, but sincere enough."

Hercule looked skeptical. "This is the man who went and invaded the Dutch republic on the pretense of helping them rebuild their dikes. Sounding trustworthy is not the same as being so."

"Did he help the Dutch rebuild?" Adrienne asked.

"So I hear."

"Well, then, I think we should consider him at least half honest. In any event, what choice have we? Should I refuse his offer, he could easily compel me. Why not maintain at least the illusion that we freely chose?"

"Illusions are dangerous," Crecy pointed out.

"Which you should know well," Adrienne returned. "Listen to me, Hercule; you are the one who said it. Rome has fallen, and now the barbarians struggle over who will be the new Charlemagne. And yet here is a most unusual barbarian, one who seems to care little for the trivialities of the old regimes, recognizes where real power lies, and values science. As you said, we could rise far serving such a one."

Hercule smiled sardonically. "I am sure that I have said the like. But I am surprised to hear you speak so."

Adrienne sweetened her smile. "It only shows what a good influence you have been on me, dear Hercule." She glanced at Crecy. "What do you say?"

Crecy shrugged. "I care not. Where you go, there go I. Life on the terms promised us is certainly better than brigandry—or nursemaiding a poppet in Prague."

Hercule nodded at that, too.

"So are we agreed, then?" Adrienne asked.

"How nice of you to ask," Hercule replied, a trace of bitterness in his tone.

"Hercule—"

"No, my apologies. Of course, I agree. How can I not, with you quoting my own philosophy to me? But I say we sleep lightly. Our future may not be as rosy as we wish."

"It was never rosier, though," Adrienne replied. "Though at times it has been pleasant." She reached for his hand, and he returned her small squeeze.

"I believe," Crecy said, "that our 'captain' is not a man to do things in half measures, ordinarily. So seeing that he left this bottle of wine only half empty, I propose we save him any possible remorse or embarrassment by making certain that when he returns it is completely so." She raised the bottle and refilled their glasses. "To the three of us," she said, "and to our future in Saint Petersburg."

And they drank.

The tsar returned when he said he would, and they made their agreement. The men from Lorraine boarded—not without trepidation, but comforted by their weapons. Adrienne and Hercule outlined their situation to them, and though it was offered, none returned to the ground.

When all was settled, the ship began to fly, climbing forward and up at the same time. Adrienne held Nico near the rail as the landscape below became plains of lichens and forests of club moss, but he seemed unimpressed.

Hercule was not so phlegmatic. "By God," he breathed. "Who could have dreamed?"

"It is wonderful, is it not?" the tsar—who had just come up—said. "That is the marvelous thing about this age of wonders, Monsieur. What we dream can be made real." He leaned over the rail, farther than Adrienne thought wise.

"I have always loved boats, you see. As a child, I had my own sailboat, but where could I sail it? On the river, on the pond? Yes, but I dreamed that Russia would have saltwater ports, that I would sail the seas. I went to Holland and learned to make ships with my own hands. I helped make this one!" He laughed. "It is ironic, don't you think, that I fought so hard and so long to secure saltwater ports, and now I have no need of ports at all!"

"Captain, might I ask where we sail?" Crecy asked. "To Prague, the scene of your victory? To Saint Petersburg?"

"Alas, no," the tsar replied. "I have a debt to settle in Venice first—it will not take long."

"Are we going to battle?" Adrienne asked, tightening her grip on Nico a bit.

"Never fear for your son, Mademoiselle," he assured her. "I do not think it will come to battle, and if it does, it shall not be much of one."

Adrienne nodded, but she had been made such promises before, and did not find herself particularly reassured. She continued to watch the tiny landscape, wondering now what it would be like to fall from such a height.

5

Veneto

Ben thought wonder had been bled out of him. His feet oozed like tar in his boots, blood glued his stockings and breeches to the saddle, fever chattered his teeth. Five days and nights on horseback had spread the ache in his chest from head to toe. He felt close to death and did not care.

And yet when the sea came in sight—a dawn plain of coral, quixotic spires like rosy mists ascending from it—it stunned him how much better it was to live than to die, to see such sights; and he shuddered with what felt like laughter but which his weary eyes mistook for tears.

So rapt was he that it took him long moments to note that they had stopped, not so he could contemplate splendor, but because their way was blocked by what seemed soldiers from his fevers, a company of colorful, whimsical, almost laughable men. Most of them wore floppy red caps embroidered with gold, baggy white shirts, and even baggier pantaloons tucked into yellow boots. They were unmounted. He had seen clowns dressed thus, in the court of Bohemia.

But these were not clowns. There were perhaps fifty of them, with fifty sorts of faces, comprising in complexion a spectrum from pale and freckled through almost black, in form from round to jagged, noses from mountainous to flat. But in demeanor they were all alike, each visage a grim promise of violence. It was a look he had come to know, and he knew it in this rainbow of men bristling with weapons.

Turks. The ravagers of Vienna, the conquerors of Venice, the implacable enemy of all Christendom. Turks.

He knew he ought to be afraid.

Charles XII, always at the fore, rode yet a few steps farther toward the strange troops. Hand raised, proud and straight in his saddle, only the dark hollows of his eyes hinted at his fatigue.

"Greetings to the *ochak*, and to you, *Corbasi*."

The man who seemed to be the leader of the Turks—an olive-complected fellow with curly hair, a scar below one eye, and four feathers in his cap—bowed. "*Inshallah*, Iron Head," he replied.

Charles nodded acknowledgment. "How courteous of you to bring your *boluk* to escort me to the city."

The Turk bit his lower lip and continued in thickly accented German. "I regret," he said softly, "that such is not our purpose."

"No? Then might I ask you, one soldier to another, to briefly address your purpose? My men have ridden hard and long, and some of us are wounded."

"I have come to warn you, O King. A friendly gesture from men who respect you."

"I value the respect of the Janissaries, though I am unworthy of it. Speak your warning, my friend."

"It is just this. The Sublime Porte is withdrawing its protection from the infidel city."

"So I have heard. But as an infidel, how should this trouble me?"

"Iron Head, you have long been friend to the sultan, the enemy of his enemy, the Russian tsar. He therefore wishes you to understand that, with his protection withdrawn from Venice, he cannot speak for what will happen to you without his sword and shield above you."

"The sultan sent me this word himself?"

The Turk shifted uncomfortably in his saddle. "We in the *ochak* know the sultan's mind well enough."

Charles smiled sardonically. "Well enough to give a warning that the sultan might have neglected?"

"As you say," the Turk responded, his face like stone. "The sultan is very busy."

Charles nodded knowingly. "I deeply appreciate your words, my friend, but I also have many matters weighing on my heart. Indebted as I am to you for this warning, I fear I cannot heed it. My soldiers are quartered in Venice—"

"At a word from you, Iron Head, they can be escorted safely from there, if haste is made."

Charles paused for a bare instant before continuing. "My soldiers are there," he repeated, "and I will see them. And I will speak to my brother the beylerbey, a final time."

A brief look of what might well have been contempt flitted across the Turk's face. "He leaves by morning."

"Then it's fortunate that I arrive now. But more important than the beylerbey, I wish to speak to my brothers the Janissaries. Do you think that possible?"

"In Allah, all things are possible," the Turk replied. "But you have a full *boluk* before you. We are the eyes and ears of our brothers. What would you say to us?"

"I would say it in the city," Charles said. "Would you hinder me?"

A long tense silence followed, before finally the Turk shook his head. "We would not hinder you, Iron Head. We will escort you to the city. And we would be honored to have you in our kitchen."

"The honor is all mine," Charles replied.

"A city wi' streets of water," Robert murmured, as the procession of Janissary longboats bore them up a broad canal. His gaze moved from side to side, where liquid alleys wound back into the city, crowded with elegant gondolas jostling one another as might pedestrians and sedan chairs in a more mundane city.

"It is a place of wonder," Ben agreed, "though I could hope for a better smell." The scent was that of Roxbury flats on a bad day, a sour, briny odor with a considerable bouquet of sewage added.

"It is a bit on the nois'm side," Robert allowed.

The seduction of the city had not diminished with contact, though it had lost something of its ethereal quality. Ben mused that it was like seeing a new lover unclothed for the first time. The view from a distance was like the fancy clothes, the paint and powder, hiding imperfections, accentuating assets. Closer, one saw the pores, the warts, the irregularities. And yet for Ben that had never made a woman less enticing, but rather more so. So too, with Venice, now that he could see the crumbling pilings, the dark forms of rats scampering along narrow ledges, offal and human waste floating by. Venice gained strength over him as she gained reality to his eye.

But in all of this discovery, there was yet discord. To gain the city, they had passed the massive forms of Turkish galleys, ornate and Oriental, their myriad oars awaiting the hands of slaves to row them, swarming with colorful figures preparing to lift the hand of the sultan from the Veneto. Under ordinary circumstances, that would be a cause for celebration, for the Turk had ruled in Venice for near twenty years. But when they were gone, more terrible ships would stoop from the skies. How long did they have?

"Do you know what passed earlier?" Ben asked Robert wearily, trying to raise his hand to wave back at a group of girls leaning from an upper window.

"Something, I think, from speaking with the Swedes. These fellows—" He gestured at the Turks in the other boats. "—are Janissaries."

"So I gather, though I know not what that may be."

"Soldiers, but of an especial sort. Many began life as Christians, but were captured by the Turks in childhood, enslaved, and raised to be perfect warriors. They're called fanatical, without mercy 'r pity."

"And yet they seemed well disposed toward King Charles."

"King Charles has earned their respect, at least as his own men tell it. From what I gather, some think better of him than their own sultan, who is, after all, no warrior. They see a kindred spirit, a fellow madman-soldier. What I think happened back there is that the Janissaries disobeyed their orders."

"How so?"

"We know that the sultan and the tsar have struck a bargain; the Turks will withdraw from Venice, leaving King Charles without their protection. He will either have to flee back toward Sweden—which is now mostly in Moscovado and Danish hands, and so no haven—or further away yet."

"But the Muscovites and the Ottomans are enemies."

"Perhaps both see fit to settle their differences and divide the world between them," Robert said. "If so, that leaves only the problem of Charles, for the tsar will not conclude peace with him here, and

Charles will never stop trying to incite the sultan 'gainst the tsar. Add to that the Janissaries—the real power and backbone of the empire—are disposed to listen to our friend 'Iron Head.' "

"So Venice is a trap. The Turks withdraw, the Muscovite hosts move in—"

"And the rumor is that once Charles is captured or fled, the tsar withdraws as well."

"Leaving Venice to whom?"

"The Venetians, perhaps. More likely the Turk will then return. Who knows?"

"Shell games!" Ben muttered. "The shell games of tyrants."

"Don't forget our friend Frisk is such a tyrant."

"But a very unusual one, Robin, one that labors earnest for his respect."

"Aye, and see where he is. A valiant insect about t' be trod beneath the feet of giants."

Ben shrugged. "More's the pity, for despite his deception, I like our King Frisk very much. But you and I cannot be bothered with that, now. It's for us to find Newton and Lenka."

"Oh? And how will you find Newton? Assuming Frisk was even correct to say that Newton came here?"

Ben mustered the energy to grin as he pulled something from his pocket; a metal bar, dangling upon a thread. It swung aimlessly for a moment and then pointed with unusual certainty into the deeps of the city. "I know not precisely where Newton may be," Ben said, "but his boat lies yonder."

"Near?"

"Watch how the needle moves, as we do. Were he far away, we would not discern any motion."

Robert nodded, staring at the lines of the buildings against the sky. "It's a strange course we've steered, Benjamin," he grunted.

"I doubt not 'twill steer stranger before all is done."

Robert nodded, turning his head farther, and gasped.

"Holy Jesus! Look there, Ben!"

Ben turned his head, and for a moment did not understand. The canal before them opened into what could only be described as a vast aqueous plaza, bustling with gondolas, small sail craft, barges, long-boats. But beyond them—through a gap that led to open sea—lay deep-going ships, at which Robert seemed to be vaguely aiming with his finger. But then Ben saw. Among the Byzantine galleys, brigantines, tartanes, pinks, galliots—amidst a chaos of banners and sail—stood the straight, tall mast of a New York sloop, the same as he had watched coming into Boston harbor a hundred times. At its highest point, proud in the Mediterranean breeze, fluttered the king's jack.

Tears starting in his eyes, Ben reached over to clasp Robert's hand for an instant. "I believe," he said, "that we can add one more thing to be done."

He awoke in a narrow but comfortable bed, puzzled. The last thing he remembered clearly was watching that improbable king's jack and the sudden, deep conviction that things would be well.

He rubbed his eyes and looked around, and the hair on his scalp pricked up.

Turks. He was in a room full of Turks, and no European to be seen anywhere.

"You feel better, English?"

Ben looked up, startled, to find a young man in a striped gown behind him. He looked perhaps eighteen, had large, black eyes in a long, almost feminine face.

"You speak English," Ben said, stupidly. In close to three years he had heard his mother language only from Robert and Sir Isaac, and it was a shock to hear it on the lips of this foreign man.

"Yes, some. It has been a long time since I use it. Can you eat something?"

"Can I?" His belly felt like a cavern. "Indeed!"

"Good. I return anon."

He turned and strode down the room, a narrow gallery with high, bright windows. There were a number of other beds, some occupied. He counted five Turks in the chamber—all men—who gazed at him for a moment and then returned to chattering in their own language.

Ben noticed that he was clean, and wondered who had bathed him and why he hadn't wakened. He also noted that his chest was freshly bandaged, and that the throbbing there seemed considerably tamer. He wondered where Robert, Charles, and the rest were.

A few moments later, the young man returned, carrying a dish of bread, crumbly looking cheese, and small, black, oblong fruits. Ben started into the bread and cheese like a starved animal.

"What are these?" he asked, through a mouthful, gesturing at the fruit.

"Olives. Careful of pits."

"Olives. Huh." He knew olives from the Bible, of course, but had never paused to wonder exactly what one might taste like. He tried one tentatively. It wasn't bad, exactly: a little bitter and quite salty. By the time he finished the last, the taste had begun to grow on him.

"Thank you," he told the fellow, and then, sticking out his hand said, "My name is Benjamin Franklin."

"Hassim," the boy replied, taking his hand.

"Thank you, Hassim. May I inquire where I am?"

"Yes, of course. You in my father's house."

"Your father is one of the men who brought me here—one of the Janissaries?"

"Yes," Hassim said, proudly. "He is *Corbasi.*"

Charles had used that term, Ben remembered, in speaking to the leader of the Janissaries. "I'm afraid I don't know what that means."

"It is like—eh—general? Colonel? He commands the *orta. Orta* is like—like regiment."

Ben nodded. "And you? You are a Janissary, too?"

Hassim cast his face down a bit. "Allah does not will it. Son of Janissary may not be Janissary."

"Oh." Ben shifted uncomfortably. The room smelled sweet, as did Hassim. Like perfume or incense.

"Hassim, where are my friends?"

"King Charles is waiting to meet with the *ochak*—"

"*Ochak?*"

"Janissary. It means—a place where cooking is done for many. Because we say the Janissaries always eat together, you see? Like family. So they are called *ochak.*"

"Like family." Those diamond-eyed men, like family? He tried to picture them eating, talking, joking together.

"What of my other friend?"

"Another room, sleeping. You want to see him?"

"No—no, wait until he wakes, thank you. I—" He stopped for a moment, wondering whether it was wise to bring the matter up, but then plunged on.

"Have you heard of a man arriving—um—arriving in a boat flying through the air?"

Hassim's eyes widened. "You mean *sihirbaz?*"

"*Sihirbaz?*"

"Come flying in boat, four days ago. Small boat."

"You saw this?"

"Others saw. Think him *sihirbaz* sent by tsar."

"*Sihirbaz?* What is that?"

"Ah—warlock? One who puts spells."

"And is he still there? Still at that place?"

"As I hear, yes. Some went to talk to him, but could not. *Sihirbaz* in old fortress there, sealed it up with spells. Janissaries can't get in."

"No one has spoken to him?"

"He says he will speak only to Iron Head."

"Ah. Was there— Do they say there was a woman with him? In the boat?"

Hassim shrugged. "Do not know of that."

Ben pursed his lips. No matter how mad he was, Newton wouldn't have hurt Lenka. Surely not.

Hassim bowed slightly. "I have duties," he said, sounding apologetic.

Ben fought down an impatient snarl. He wanted to ask more, but honestly couldn't think of how to pursue the matter. Clearly, it was Charles he needed to speak to.

"Can you tell me where Iron Head is?"

"No," Hassim finished, and grinned briefly. "He moves much. Always moving." With two fingers he pantomimed a man walking, and Ben nodded agreement.

"Where does he sleep?" Ben asked.

"Remains to be seen. Has not slept yet," Hassim said, and then, nodding politely, went on, "I will ask—about woman, about Swedish king, yes? But now I must go."

"Thank you," Ben said, "and tell your father I thank him for his hospitality."

Hassim grinned and nodded.

If it is hospitality, Ben thought. *If I am not merely a prisoner in a pretty prison.*

Once Hassim was gone, he tried standing, and found that his feet— and to a lesser extent, his legs—were a mass of running sores, blisters that had burst, formed again, burst again. Still, it was not as bad as he had envisioned, and the more general pain in his muscles was fading to almost the pleasant soreness of regeneration. The only wound that still worried him was the sword cut, which pulsed feverishly now and then. Or was that, he wondered, in part perhaps something else, not on his chest but *in* it?

Standing, he could gaze out the windows, at the broad stretch of water he had seen while coming up the canal. He picked through the masts of the ships again until he found the English flag, and sighed in relief, afraid it had been some illusion. In fact, now he could see at least three and maybe a fourth—the sloop, a caravel, and a big frigate obscuring possibly another. He found himself growing excited again. Who were they? Were they from London? Was there, after all, a chance that the city had survived?

But English ships had sailed every sea in the world. There was no reason to become hopeful about the impossible, not when he had so many tasks remaining him. Contacting the English ships was important, and it seemed the easiest of what lay before him—if in fact he had freedom of movement, and if the Muscovite ships did not arrive too quickly.

Reaching Newton and Lenka was another matter. His needle might point to the boat, but even if they were near, how would he find the place, in a city where he spoke none of the languages? What did they speak here, anyway? Some Italian dialect, he supposed, and Turkish, of course. One of the Turks had spoken German, but he doubted that German—or English—would get him far in the streets of Venice.

Streets? There might not be any streets. He would need a boat, or money to pay a boatman. He had a few Bohemian crowns left, but they might not pass as currency.

It suddenly occurred to him that he had no idea where his clothes were, which meant that he didn't know if he had any money or not— or even his compass needle! He frantically cast about in search of them, heart sinking. To his vast relief he found them in a striped cotton bag laid neatly under his bed. Money and needle were both there.

To that extent, at least, these Turks were honest, not at all what he had expected given the tales he had heard.

Well, then, he knew roughly where Newton—and, he hoped, Lenka—were. If they were still alive.

The thought of Lenka being dead did nothing to improve his spirits. In fact, it made him somewhat sick—and now that he thought upon it, he was much more concerned about finding Lenka than Newton. He supposed that made sense, since he was responsible for whatever mess she was in, whereas Newton could damn well take care of himself. Then, too, was the elementary fact that Lenka was a lovely girl, and so naturally he—

He blinked. When had he begun thinking of Lenka as beautiful? Hadn't he first thought her rather plain?

He frowned. He did not like this, this thing his mind had done without his permission.

"Well, my young Turk," a voice called from behind. "Shall we raid the *harim* together?"

He turned, shaking his finger at Robert's familiar voice. "Best watch your tongue, infidel, around the faithful." Indeed, he noticed that a few of the men were glaring at both of them. Robert, who wore a sort of dressing gown and looked a good deal cleaner than last Ben had seen him, noticed too.

"Wup," he said. "Maybe both of us should. Y' never know what will set this sort off."

"Have you just wakened?"

"A few moments ago, but I held off on sleeping longer than you. If they'd desired to drown *me* in the tub, they'd have had something of a fight. You, on th' other hand—"

"I slept through bathing?" Ben marveled.

"It did give them all great amusement," Robert said, "I'll not hide that from you. But look at us, here, alive, clad in fine robes in some pasha's palace—"

"We've done well enough," Ben agreed. "Shall we discuss our plans?"

"I think it best we get the lay of the land, first."

"What do you mean?"

"I just spoke with one of the Swedes. He said that the king's discussion w' the *bey-yay*-what didn't go well. Apparently his Swedish majesty burst in on this Turkish potentate, complete with grime and blood and horse sweat."

"No!"

"Yes! He demanded that the Turkish withdrawal cease, that they stay here and fight the tsar. The bey did refuse, an' scurried from the city this morning, as the Janissaries said he would."

"But the Janissaries are still here."

"Aye. Waitin' t' hear what Charles'll say to 'em."

"Hassim mentioned something about that. When does he speak, and where?"

"Why, in this very house, come another hour. That's what I mean by the lay of the land. And there is another thing; there's been intelligence about the Moscovado ships."

"That being?"

"It may be that they will reach Venice in three days."

Ben stared back out at the water. "And then what?" he wondered.

"Well, that depends a great deal on what happens in the next hour, I would say," Robert replied.

"Have you heard aught of Newton?"

"I've heard the tales of the flying ship. The Janissaries have laid siege to some place—on a different island, I think—where he landed, but it seems Sir Isaac brought some sort of aegis with him, an' they cannot get through it. I've heard no more than that."

"Nothing of Lenka?"

"Not a thing."

"I've got to see King Charles."

"I don't think that's awful likely afore the meetin'," Robert guessed.

"Then it's certain," Ben grunted, "that at the meeting, he will hear me, for we shall be there."

6

Geography

Peter stared through the window in the bottom of his cabin, fascinated by the changes in the land. Each moment was a subtle surprise, as this or that feature of the jumble of images below was suddenly understood, as the greater patterns became recognizable. Rivers in particular were enthralling. For every living river, two or three dead ones crowded near, ghosts, abandoned channels that now and then still contained stagnant water in isolated oxbows, but more often had been drained and cultivated. Human settlements and their fields followed rivers, too, strung out along them like another kind of channel, another sort of ghost.

Of course, he knew that rivers changed course now and then, after a large flood, after a dam broke. But to see the whole made him understand that it was not an occasional incident but had happened continually since creation. He wondered briefly what had become of the towns along those old rivers, those abandoned channels. Had they moved? He squinted, wondering what form evidence of this might take.

There was a science, here, he thought, an entire new realm of study made possible by his airships. On a pragmatic level, better maps could be made, and better maps meant a better ability to wage war, maintain borders, conclude treaties. But at another level, the level of wonder, it was amazing to think what might be learned. He would, he decided, create a select body of philosophers to study the Earth from the air, and grinned as he pictured the exploratory ship he would build, the places it would sail—to the ends of the Earth, and perhaps beyond. History would remember Tsar Peter not merely as an emperor, but as the father of a new science.

A knock at the door brought him back to the moment.

"Enter," he called.

The door swung open, and a man of about thirty years stepped in, gray-eyed, his slightly weak jaw partially hidden by perhaps two weeks' growth of reddish beard.

"Come in, Captain Androkov," Peter said, quietly.

"Sir."

Peter settled into his armchair, indicated a similar seat facing him. "Sit, please."

Captain Androkov complied, his face betraying none of the worry he must be feeling.

"Captain, you have served me and Russia well in the past. I particularly recall your bravery at Pruth."

"Thank you, sir."

"I gather that you love your country."

"I hope you do not doubt that, sir."

Peter felt a surge of anger, and his facial muscles spasmed, which made him only the angrier. How he hated that affliction! As he spoke, he found it impossible to keep his voice entirely steady. "Why, then, Ilya Mikhailovich Androkov, have you chosen to grow a *beard*?"

Androkov's face registered dismay, perhaps at Peter's question, more likely at his obvious anger.

"Well?" Peter asked, a bit louder.

"Sir, the priests say—"

"Priests? Priests? Who is tsar of all of the Russias, Ilya Mikhailovich?"

"You are, Captain."

"And to whom do the priests—and the patriarch for that matter—owe their allegiance?"

"To you, Captain."

"Yes, to *me*. Of course, to *me*." He slapped his chest for emphasis.

"But, sir—begging your pardon, sir—also to God."

"God? God? Do you think that God the Almighty cares whether you wear a beard or not? Hmm? Do you? Does that make any sense at all to you, Captain Androkov, that *God* should care if you have a beard?"

The captain squirmed just a bit. "Sir, it is the old way. The priests say we will be lost without our old ways."

"The patriarch regrets that he is not a tsar, Captain, and the priests that they are not governors; and acting as you have, you have allowed yourself to become a pawn in their game. That was stupid of you. These 'old ways'—these were the 'ways' that kept us in darkness for a thousand years, beggars at the doors of the kingdoms of Europe, even our tsars peasants next to a Dutch merchant of common birth. The priests would see us back to that, I'm sure, for then they had more power and influence."

His face betrayed him again, and he took a deep breath. "Listen, you fool," he began again. "You think this is nothing, a simple act of piety. It is not. It makes you my enemy. God does not care whether you wear a beard or not, but I assure you, the tsar of Russia *does*. In my eyes, this is a badge of alliance with the Old Believers and what remains of Strelitzi sympathizers. You remember the Strelitzi, I presume? The royal guard that thought they knew better than their tsar how Russia should be governed? Were you too young to see their heads rolling in the snow?"

Androkov's nerve finally broke, and he looked down at his feet, unable to meet Peter's gaze. "I remember, Sire," he mumbled. "My father took me there, to see."

"Yes. And so, listen to me, Captain Ilya Mikhailovich, for I have a most important question for you."

"Captain?"

"It is simply this," he said, picking up a leather case on the table next to him, opening it to produce the gleaming blade within. "Do you wish to live, and serve me—and thus Russia—or do you wish to join the Strelitzi in hell?"

The captain squared his shoulders and looked at Peter again. "I am not a coward, sir."

"I did not say that you were, Captain. In fact, I believe I opened our conversation by saying something quite different. It does not change the question or the consequences of the answer."

The captain paused, then nodded his head. "I am sorry, sir, to have grown a beard."

"Hold still, Captain," Peter said, grimly, unfolding himself from the chair. Androkov watched him approach, his eyes fastened on the polished, almost liquid metal.

Peter was not gentle, and before he was done, blood slicked the razor, but when he stood back to admire his handiwork, it was with a certain satisfaction. Androkov had uttered no sound throughout, which was also pleasing.

"Very good, Captain," he said, as he wiped the sanguine razor. "If you grow it again—if you let just two days' growth accumulate—I will see your beard *and* your head struck clean from your shoulders. Do you understand?"

"Yes, sir."

"You may go now."

Androkov rose, his face bleeding profusely from where the keen edge had sliced into flesh. But he had no beard now, and Peter felt better. He watched the door close behind Androkov, then went to a cabinet for a half-empty bottle of brandy. He poured himself a healthy draft and swallowed it, felt its potent warmth fall into the pit of his belly and glow there.

The Old Believers were growing in power again; he could no longer deny it. For years he had intended to abolish the obsolete position of the patriarch, had been moving to do so when the time of disasters began. Since then, more immediate battles had commanded his attention, but now he saw his mistake. When his own trusted officers began growing beards, it was time to act.

"I have been at war too long," he muttered, "too long."

"You do what you must, Great Tsar," a voice whispered.

Peter poured more brandy, staring hard at the amber liquid. He rarely saw the ifrit when awake, in daylight, though it spoke to him often enough. He made no effort to look for it now; its appearance made him uncomfortable.

"What I must do," he said, "is to return to my people. Whenever I turn my back on them, the Old Believers crawl back out of their holes and breed vipers to strike me."

"But the winters grow colder, great king. Already the north is almost uninhabitable."

"We have the new alchemical furnaces my philosophers developed, to warm those in the coldest places. I, myself, shall never abandon Saint Petersburg, and my people will take heart from that. Science will help us survive the winters, science and Russian fortitude, not more war."

"But they must eat. Frozen earth grows no wheat."

"I know that," Peter snapped. "But now we have Poland, Bohemia—even as we speak, we are consolidating France. Those nations may be colder, too, but a good Russian farmer can get a crop from those lands. I will stop for a while. After Venice, I shall take my airships to France and finish up that business. I have my ports and a fresh alliance with the sultan. Best, I shall finally have the cursed king of Sweden out of my affairs."

"But the winters shall grow colder, Great Tsar, and colder yet."

"Have you turned oracle, now?" Peter snapped.

"No, Great Tsar. But my kind knows sciences that yours does not."

He shook his head. "My people must heal before they fight again. We will rest for a time. I *cannot* keep my back turned forever on the Old Believers. You know much, you people of the aether, but you do not know what it is to be tsar."

"More than you might suspect. I can help you with the Old Believers."

"What?" Peter asked, astonished.

"You know how I appear. You have expressed your discomfort."

"Yes. You look like a saint." Or rather, the gilded image of a saint, like a living, glowing icon. The ifrit had styled itself an angel when it first came to him, but Peter had never really believed that. Once he had learned their true, scientific nature, he had taken to calling them ifrits. He knew, however, that part of the reason he had done this was to push away that image of the angel, the beatific saint; for his worst, most spidery fear was that the damned Old Believers were right, that everything he had ever done was wrong, a lie.

"Go on," he muttered.

"When I first came to you, I named myself an angel," the ifrit said. "I did so not to deceive you, but because it is a word used to describe me in the past."

"I understand that."

"The fact that I look like an angel or a saint to you is no coincidence, but not from the cause you fear. It is rather simple, actually. At times in the past, your people saw my kind and mistook us for the saints of your God. We do not look like these 'icons.' They look like *us*."

"I begin to see," Peter breathed. He felt something in him relax. Of course the Old Believers, those gullible fools, were not *right*. "And how does this help me?"

"Suppose that the saints were to begin appearing again? Suppose that they perform a miracle or two?"

"I have already heard of such happenings," Peter said, a bit suspiciously. Indeed, he had quietly begun an investigation into such occurrences, confident that the "miracles" were the products of scientific devices.

"Those rumors are not of our making," the ifrit assured him, "but if they were, we could make certain that the saints said the sort of things a tsar might *want* said."

Peter frowned. "It is a good suggestion," he admitted. "But I mislike using superstition so. It will make my people more gullible, not less."

"People change very slowly, Great Tsar. If you desire to triumph over the Old Believers, you must beat them at their own game."

Peter felt his face twitch again, and finally nodded. "Begin discreetly," he said, "very discreetly. The Old Believers already suggest that I am attended by demons. If it became known that the 'saints' were merely my 'demons' in disguise—"

"No one who sees a saint will consider that they might have seen a devil," the ifrit said. "No one wants to believe that they have been fooled. If our own philosophers have learned aught of Man, it is that."

"It is just as important," Peter said softly, "to understand what they will do when they realize that they *have* been tricked."

"Worry not, Great Tsar. We will proceed at the pace you instruct, doing as you instruct. I do not presume to know as much about Man as you."

Peter sighed, finished his brandy, and stood. He had things to do. "Thank you for your advice, ifrit. As usual, it has merit. I think perhaps you see Man more clearly because you are *not* one."

"You flatter me, Great Tsar."

"I think not. Now, if you will excuse me."

"I will return later, O Tsar."

But as he left his cabin, Peter suspected—as he had before—that ifrit never really left him, ever. He did not know whether to feel comforted or angry.

"You did not mention that we would be impressed directly into battle," Adrienne reproached, eyeing Vasilisa Karevna through the plume of steam rising from her coffee.

"It should not be much of a battle," Vasilisa replied. "What weapon can reach us?"

"Yes?" Crecy asked, propping her elbows on the small table and resting her chin upon a bridge of interlocked fingers. "Then how will you take the city? I understand that in Prague, land forces marched below you, so that your aerial attack merely softened the city for invasion. The pace we set now, however, makes that impossible—not to mention the fact that the land forces would still have to cross the lagoon to Venice. That suggests to me that you must land some of these craft to disgorge soldiers."

Karevna smiled wanly. "At Prague, we were unnecessarily cautious. After all, Sir Isaac Newton and his apprentice were there, and might have had unpleasant surprises prepared for us. As it turned out, they did not. But you are very astute, Mademoiselle. Once Venice has surrendered—or been bombarded into submission—then ships will land with troops. This ship, however, will remain at a safe height, I assure you. Prague was well defended and we lost not a single ship. Venice is not defended at all. Does that reassure you both?"

Crecy allowed a thin grin. "I have discovered that the essence of war is the unexpected."

Karevna laughed. "That is the essence of *life*, Mademoiselle."

"My child has experienced very little of life," Adrienne noted sardonically. "I would like him to experience a little more."

"You think you were safer on the ground, with your ragged little band of soldiers, in unknown territory?"

"No."

"Good. Then I urge you to stop thinking of our small expedition to Venice as a hazard and treat it as an opportunity."

"What do you mean?"

"The tsar favors you, Mademoiselle, but the tsar is *most* favorable to actions. If, in the coming battle, you demonstrate a willingness and ability to aid our cause—"

"I thought we would be out of the action." Crecy frowned.

"Above it, yes. Safe, most probably. But we will play a role in our own unique way. For my own part, I will direct those malakim I am in communication with to the best effect I can imagine. You . . ." She paused for an instant, and Adrienne tried to gauge the look that crossed her face. Was it admiration or jealousy? "They still talk," Karevna continued, "of how you destroyed that first attack on you. Even I have not ascertained exactly what you did. But if you can perform similar feats *for* us, you will have begun an early ascent in the tsar's estimation."

"I see," Adrienne said carefully, sipping her coffee. It had been a long time, it seemed, since she had tasted coffee. "I thank you for the advice, Mademoiselle Karevna. I will consider it most carefully."

"I suggest you do. I would be overjoyed to have you by my side when we reach Venice."

A few hours later, Karevna was gone, and there came a knock at the door.

"Who's there?" Adrienne called.

"It's me, Hercule," came the muffled response.

"Oh!" Adrienne said, chagrined. She hadn't even wondered where he had been. "Crecy—"

The redhead nodded. "I'm sure I have some business somewhere, for an hour or two," she muttered.

"Thank you," Adrienne said, taking her arm.

Crecy blinked at her, unable to hide a slight bitterness in her eyes. She leaned over and kissed Adrienne on the head. "Of nothing," she said, voice tight.

She opened the door and went by Hercule without a word.

Hercule watched her pass with a raised eyebrow, then shrugged. He glanced around the cabin. "Your accommodations seem comfortable enough," he noticed.

"Yes," Adrienne replied. She walked over to him, very deliberately took his chin in her fingers, and brought her lips up to his. He responded rather ferociously, and for an instant she was taken aback until her own underestimated desire erupted to match his. Not so much a desire for sex as such, but for the comfort of flesh against flesh, the mindlessness of motion.

She was undoing the buttons of his waistcoat when he gently pushed her away.

"What? What's the matter?" she asked, studying his suddenly serious eyes.

"I've volunteered to lead one of the ground assaults."

"You've *what?*"

"I dislike asking this, but I think you should give the men your approval."

"Why, Hercule? What nonsense is this?"

He sighed heavily and brushed past her to gaze out the small porthole. "I must do something quickly to prove my new commitment to the tsar. Otherwise—"

"Karevna has been talking to you."

"Adrienne, you have powers I don't begin to understand, usefulness which is undeniable. I, on the other hand, am a simple soldier, one among many."

"Your place is secure if mine is," Adrienne said.

He snorted. "Yes, as your lapdog, the popinjay captain of your guard. My aim is at a higher target, my dear. If I am to seek my fortune with the tsar, I must be bold."

"You will be of no use to anyone dead, Hercule."

He turned and leveled a dark gaze upon her. "I have considered that, of course, but it is of no matter."

"And what of us? Is that also of no matter?"

"Yes, what of us, Adrienne? What does your heart say of me? Do you love me?"

"That is unfair, Hercule. Love has never been a part of our discussions before. Was it love you were pursuing in me? I think not."

"No," he admitted, "perhaps not. But it is what I have found. What have *you* found?"

Her chest tightened, and her next words felt labored. "Companionship. Happiness. A dear, dear friend."

He nodded and turned back to the clouds outside. "But not love?" he asked.

"How am I to know what love is?" she demanded. "And why do you present me with this just before committing suicide?"

"I see you have little faith in me."

"Hercule, I have every faith in you. But everyone who has loved me— and most particularly everyone I have loved—seems to desert me."

"Nicolas did not desert you. He died that you might live." He hesitated. "And there is Crecy."

"You cannot be jealous of Crecy."

"She is jealous of me, always a good sign that one should return the sentiment."

"Enough, Hercule d'Argenson. You presume far too much."

He laughed bitterly. "Yes, I suppose that I do. And believe me, I feel foolish. I have always considered myself the cavalier, a rogue lover, a rake, and to find myself thus entrapped—"

"Entrapped?" Adrienne snapped, almost too angry to speak. She took several deep breaths to calm herself and continued. "I assure you, sir, you are in no way entrapped. Nor, I suspect, are you in love. You and I have been walking through graveyards together, surrounded by the dead. We sought life in each other's arms and found it. Now you mistake that for love. When we have found a place of peace, a place where you have the opportunity and leisure to pursue other demoiselles, I'll see your attitude change."

"I thought you had faith in me."

"By God, d'Argenson, do not twist my words!" she shouted.

He lowered his head for a long moment. "I apologize, Mademoiselle. I misspoke."

She bit back an agreement, approached him, and hesitantly touched his arm. "Do not do this, Hercule. I love you enough not to see you dead."

He turned back to her. "I must think of myself," he said. "I don't have your heart, and so I must think of my advancement."

"You rogue. You would think of your advancement whether you had my heart or not."

Finally, almost painfully it seemed, he grinned. "You know me well. Do you wonder that I love you?"

"Do not speak of that again," she said. "Do not."

"Very well," he said, tightening his lips a bit, "I shan't. If you don't try to dissuade me from the assault."

"I have said all I can, I suppose."

"In that case, Mademoiselle, I must bid you good day."

"Is this all you came here for? It did not seem so when you kissed me."

"Such are your charms, Mademoiselle, that all reason deserts me when I see you."

"Perhaps you should discard reason, then."

He grinned ruefully. "It's said by some that only reason divides us from the animals. Would you have me discard that?"

"For the next hour or so, yes."

"I thought you were angry with me."

"I was. I remain so."

"Then—"

"Your punishment," she said simply. "When you find your foolish death, I want to give you one more regret to carry with you to hell."

"Mademoiselle—" he began, as she pushed up his waistcoat and shirt, pressed her lips against his chest.

"Mademoiselle!" he repeated, in quite a different tone. She began working on the buttons of his breeches.

"By God," he groaned, after a moment. "Your wrath is terrible!"

She stopped what she was doing and looked up at his glazed eyes. "You have barely begun to taste it," she murmured, and pushed him over onto the bed. She shucked the loose gown Ka-revna had given her over her head and pressed herself atop him, almost shocked by the pleasure of her breasts against his bare stomach, the adherence of one damp skin to another. She began placing judicious kisses as he struggled the half-buttoned waistcoat over his head.

"Adrienne—" he moaned.

She paused. "No talk of love!" she cautioned. "Unless it is to deny you love me."

"I—I—" He stuttered. She nipped at him, then crawled up his length until her lips were on his ear.

"Say you do not love me," she whispered. "Say it."

"Madame," he managed, through choppy gasps, "if you would have it so, I despise you."

"Say it again," she said, pushing his breeches down his legs with her feet.

"I hate you."

"Good."

And for a time, she found her forgetfulness, her moment of motion and passion. But afterward, when Hercule kissed her and went on his way, she found that she was perhaps not as happy about getting her way as she should have been. She did something she had not done in a long time; fumbling to her knees, she knotted her hands beneath her chin and begged God to preserve Hercule in the coming battle. She found that she had enough faith left to believe God heard her, but no confidence at all that he would grant her wish. Troubled, she watched from her little window as the sun bloodied clouds and died a slow, gray death.

7

The Divan

Ben regarded himself critically in the mirror, wondering if the outlandish clothes fit as they ought. The azure robe with its gold floral brocade was pleasing in pattern and color, but it hung straight and unpleated, like a stiff dressing gown. The pantaloons felt ridiculous. He determined to keep his hat tucked under his arm, both because it looked silly with the Turkish costume and because he didn't know enough about Turkish rank to know who he should remain bareheaded around.

After shifting the coat this way and that on his shoulders, he finally shrugged, wondering what his father would think to see him preening so in front of a mirror—what his father would think of *him*. Was there a single thing the old man had taught him that he had not managed to unlearn? In three years he had replaced honesty, thrift, and humility with deception, vanity, and pride. What was left of Josiah Franklin's boy? Did anything remain that his sire—if he was still alive—would find to respect?

He looked back in the mirror, and for a moment beheld a stranger, a doppelgänger mocking him, and felt a sensation almost of falling, of rushing away. Boston, which had seemed for so long like another life, a distant dream, suddenly came back to surround him, painting over his Oriental surroundings as if *they* were the shadows.

He set his jaw and pushed it away. He loved his father, and once he had respected him. But his father's way was a naïve one, a philosophy that an older, kinder age might tolerate but that had no place today— not for those who would prosper. The meek were not inheriting the

Earth, that was certain enough, and God—if there was a God at all—did not watch over Ben Franklin, eager to reward him for virtue or punish him for vice. In the days when he had striven for virtue, he had caused more harm than good. Now he understood that there was more honesty in healthy selfishness than in some pretended notion of doing good, and it was certainly less dangerous to those around you.

He had thought to save London and failed; so be it. He had thought to save Prague and failed; so be it. He had begun to think of saving Venice, too, but that thought now seemed absurd. What did he want? Really want?

And then he knew. He wanted Newton's notebooks, and he wanted Lenka, and he wanted to be on board one of those English ships sailing far away from here. He gave not one damn what happened to Newton, or to Venice, or Charles XII. No he didn't. He and Robert and Lenka safe and sound, and with Newton's notes and his own ingenuity, he would soon make a place for himself. Let other idealists dig graves for the living from now on. He grinned as the stranger in the mirror became himself again, and was both astonished and pleased at how much wiser he looked, how much more the man.

He was just stepping away when Charles entered the room. The king looked haggard, though clad in a fresh blue-and-yellow uniform.

"And how do you fare, my friend?" the king asked.

"Not too poorly—ah, Your Majesty," Ben answered.

"Good. You will attend the Divan. I had a better sort of suit sent to you, that you might make a good impression."

"Yes, Majesty, and thank you. But I wondered if I might discuss a certain matter with you."

"Be brief. We must go, and quickly."

"I'm sure you've heard the rumors that Sir Isaac has planted himself on a nearby island, awaiting your word."

"Yes. The man is quite troublesome. I commanded that he be conveyed to me, but he refuses to leave his haven, insisting instead that I attend him. Obviously I have no time to do so."

"May I suggest that I speak to him? I know him best."

Charles frowned. "If all goes well, I have a battle to plan and if not, to flee in ignominious haste. Either way, Benjamin, I shall need you near me, for you are the only person I trust who can advise me of what

I face in these Russian contrivances. There is no time, I tell you, to send you to cajole your old master. I am at the end of my temper with Sir Isaac. If he does not come to his senses, I shall order the island bombarded so that he can be of no use to the Muscovites should they triumph."

"Sir, I can talk sense to him."

"For which I have no time. As I say, if the Divan decides to fight, I shall need you with me."

"Majesty—"

"No, enough. Don't forget yourself, Mr. Franklin. As Peter Frisk, I stood silent before your impertinence, but now I have no inclination to do so. If all goes well, and we defeat the Muscovite here, then I promise you I will see to your desires. If not, there will be no point, for Newton will be dead and we will be flown." A shallow smile touched his lips for a second. "I assure you, my young friend, that the age of kings is not yet over, no matter what you might wish. Now, we have a council to attend."

What could he do? Ben nodded and bowed.

The chamber of the Divan was sheer hubbub, a hundred babbling men packed beneath its vaulted roof. As the guards at the door checked them for weapons, Ben could only goggle in astonishment. For him, the words "council meeting" evoked something more stately than a roomful of brightly clad thugs jostling one another and shouting.

When Charles entered and began pushing his way through the crowd, the commotion redoubled. Ben, Robert, and Hassim followed close, lest they be swallowed by the throng.

"I translate for you," Hassim told Ben and Robert. "Heed; you may not use fist or hand here. You may kick."

"Kick? What do you mean?"

But just then fierce clamor erupted as another group entered, led by a rather small fellow in flamboyant silks who raised his arms as some faction of the mob howled "Riva." Though "Riva"—Ben knew not whether that might be a name, a title, or an insulting epithet—was clearly the one drawing the crowd's attention, he did not hold

Ben's; for behind him, looking dazed at the spectacle, entered two men Ben knew on sight. The recognition was like two short, quick blows to the head as Cotton Mather—a preacher from his home town—and Blackbeard the pirate stepped into the hall. *Together.*

His knees weakened suddenly, and he worried that he had fallen back into a fever dream or simply gone mad. He put his hand on Robert's shoulder, both to steady himself and point, when suddenly Robert shouted, in a voice that carried above the din, "Uncle!" And began plowing though the mass toward Mather and Blackbeard. Ben, scalp tingling, followed. They all converged at the base of the dais where Charles and the leader of the Turkish soldiers from the day before—Hassim's father?—stood together. The Riva fellow joined them, and the tumult rose toward fever pitch.

"Uncle!" Robert repeated, and this time a fellow in a red English coat spun and gaped in astonishment. In the next instant the two were grappling in a hug. Ben hung back, trying to rebuild his understanding of what was going on. Blackbeard was frowning at the two embracing men, and then his gaze moved to Ben. For an instant, his fierce eyes held puzzlement, and then they passed on, dismissing him.

Ben released his breath. Teach hadn't recognized him. That was good, as the last time they had met—three years ago—he had tricked the pirate into putting to sea in a sabotaged rowboat. Of course, that had been only fair, as Blackbeard had twice tried to kill him, but Ben somehow doubted that such would matter to Ned Teach.

Well, he was a head taller now, his features much more grown up, his dress entirely different. With any luck, Blackbeard would not make the connection. Of course, when the time for introductions came—as seemed imminent, the way that Robert and the red-coated fellow were hollering in each other's ears—that would be a whole other pipe of brandy.

That discovery, fortunately, was delayed, for suddenly Charles' voice roared above the din. "My brothers!" he shouted in German, and nearby a fellow with an equally powerful throat began spitting and hissing in Turkish. "Janissaries! The finest warriors that God's earth has ever seen—well, save the Swedish, of course!"

As he said this, a huge shout erupted from some thirty men clad in

Swedish yellow and blue, and a garden of fists sprouted all around Ben, waving. The din was awesome.

Somehow Charles fought above it. "We all know why we are met here. It is to decide your future, the future of your city, Venice. It is to decide what will become of your children, your wives, your businesses—"

A man screamed something from the audience, shrilly interrupting the Swedish king. Behind him, a group of what seemed to be supporters shouted some phrase in unison, over and over again.

Hassim leaned close as the fellow shrieked. "He say that this not about Venice at all, but about King Charles. He say only one at risk here is Charles. Charles want the Janissaries to defy sultan for his own reasons, not for Venice. His fellows chant, 'Back to Sweden, Iron Head.' "

The general roar was suddenly supplemented by howls of pain, and Ben suddenly understood what Hassim had meant by kicking. The group that presently had the floor was engaged in a kicking match with the Swedes and presumably pro-Charles Janissaries, viciously stamping at feet and shins. One fellow had fallen, and two men were booting him in the ribs and head.

The speakers ignored all this, as a second Turk leapt up and began shouting as well. "Him say that Charles want us to fight a battle we can't win, against jinn and peri, against flying ships—all to protect his own pride," Hassim translated. "He say, who will pay us for this? The beylerbey and the sultan pay our salaries. Will Charles pay? Will he pay for all we lose if we fight the Russian devils?"

Charles held up his fists, and somehow, as if damped by the sheer force of his will, the pandemonium subsided. Perhaps it was the look of haughty fury on his face, the soldier set of his shoulders. "You weak-kneed women!" he shouted. "Where are the Janissaries that brought down matchless Constantinople, who swam up rivers of their own blood to the walls of Vienna? Where are you now? Counting your coins for the day of your retirement? Waiting to watch your grandchildren grow old? But what will you tell those grandchildren, those Venetians, when they ask what happened on that day, on that day when you could have been warriors, but instead you chose to be old women, to let the Russians who murdered you at Pruth walk into your city without the slightest resistance, take your wives and your daughters to lie with them in *your* beds? What will your grand-children hear of you, you *brave* Janissaries?" In two brief strides he was suddenly in the crowd, aiming a powerful kick at his last oppo-nent. The man yelped and went down, and though his followers surged up to Charles, they did not strike him.

Behind Charles, the Turk took up the oration.

"That my father," Hassim said proudly. "He say, the sultan tell us to leave our homes. Sultan tell us to leave our children, our wives, our business, our honor. Sultan should be ashamed, sultan has no honor. Maybe Janissaries no longer have honor either."

Another man bolted up, pointing out that they would have no busi-nesses if they rebelled against the Porte, no one to trade with. At that point, Riva joined the fray, speaking of Blackbeard and the others, ex-plaining that not only did they have ships to throw into the battle, but that here stood men with whom they could negotiate a fruitful and ex-clusive trade with the Americas.

It was surreal, the way the shouting match became a mercantile meeting, with terms of trade suddenly added to the hot words about courage and cowardice. It seemed, for a time, that the discussion of *whether* to fight had been replaced by one of what to do after the battle.

But after perhaps half an hour, the argument suddenly swung sharply back to the central issue.

"We cannot fight them! Where are our sorcerers, to pit against these demons? What weapon have we that can fight against ships of the air?" someone shouted.

"Go, then," Charles returned. "Scurry off to your holes! I will fight them alone! I will defend your city for you, keep safe your children and your women whilst you cower in whatever wilderness the sultan grants you. Go!"

"That is big talk! But explain to us—how will you fight them? How, Swedish King, how?"

That hung pregnant for an instant, and Ben suddenly felt the bal-ance around him. The debate hung in equilibrium between pride and common sense. Common sense told the Janissaries not to fight. Pride told them they should. Under normal circumstances, Ben would have advised them to keep council with their sense, but on the other hand, if Charles was forced to flee—or fight desperately and alone—Ben would never see Lenka or Newton's notebooks again. They had to be convinced to stay and fight, and what's more, that Newton was the key to winning.

And so, as the din dropped slightly, Ben spoke up, shouting as loudly as he could manage. "I know how to fight them! I know how they may be beaten!" The translator shouted his words more loudly, and suddenly the hubbub subsided to nearly nothing. All eyes were suddenly on him.

"Who is this boy?" someone shouted.

"He is the apprentice of the great sorcerer of Prague," Charles shouted. "You ask who will fight the djinni, the sorcerers—he is the one!"

"Show us!" someone yelled. "Show us your wizardry!"

Deliberately, Ben reached beneath his robes. There, dirty, smelling of horse and human sweat, he wore his aegis. He slipped in the key and vanished.

Pandemonium.

After a moment he reappeared.

"A trick!" someone shouted. "What use such tricks?"

"I have many tricks!" Ben shouted. "Many ways to destroy the flying ships! I cannot tell them all here!"

"Now!" Charles shouted. "Now, you see? Now only cowardice can hold you from the glory of battle!"

It suddenly seemed as if everyone in the room went from merely mad to completely rabid. The meeting dissolved into a hundred eddying kicking fights.

A looming presence in the corner of Ben's eye warned him to turn, and his vision was filled by a nastily grinning Blackbeard. At the same instant, a heavy boot smacked painfully into his shins. His legs buckled in shock, and the pirate kicked him again viciously. Too late, Ben angrily lashed back, but he had hardly recovered from his wound and frantic ride, and his attack was weak. The next kick from Teach sent him heavily to the floor, and then fierce blows rained on him from every direction.

Red Shoes was entirely baffled by the Divan. Riva had provided an English translator, but the man had a weak voice and could rarely be heard over the din. And, of course, he was situated nearer Mather than Red Shoes.

He didn't really care; instead he watched the ebb and flow of the arguments. The blue-coated man that he'd been told was a king and one of the Turks stood together with Riva; other factions were evident by their spokesmen and by the chants of their constituents. It was unlike the councils he was used to, which were usually a little more deliberate, the participants speaking in order of rank and prestige.

He wondered who was the auburn-haired man Nairne was talking to, and the young *isht ahollo* that Blackbeard kept edging toward, the one who had somehow slipped himself into and out of *hoshonti*, a cloud of concealment such as certain legends spoke of. After that, his attention was riveted, the more so because he could make out no shadowchild nor spirit accompanying the young man, which made him powerful indeed.

What he did not anticipate—nor, apparently, did anyone else—was Blackbeard's violent attack on the fellow, under cover of the general bedlam of the Divan. Nairne's friend was the first to react, leaping forward and driving his fist straight to Blackbeard's chin. He remembered that the use of fists was forbidden in the Divan as he watched Blackbeard stagger back. Nairne seemed to have kept the rule in mind, however, and was warding off blows from the nearby Turks kicking the disappearing man. Red Shoes, still uncertain of the situation, stepped in to help the dazed fellow to his feet.

In the meantime, bellowing, Blackbeard recovered and lurched toward the auburn-haired man, who held his ground before the huge pirate until the last instant, then nimbly danced aside, snapping a vicious kick at the pirate's shin that sent him tumbling into the crowd. The surrounding Turks, fickle, began kicking Blackbeard as well. Blowing like a whale, Blackbeard thrashed among them, finally coming up with both fists knotted around a Turk's neck.

That was when the armed men appeared, seemingly from nowhere. With halberds leveled at him from every direction, Blackbeard, growling, released the Turk. Glaring, Teach allowed himself to be led from the room. Riva whispered a few words to their translator, and the rest of them—Nairne, Mather, the sorcerer boy, the fellow who had punched Blackbeard, Bienville, and himself—were ushered through the throng and out of the room. Red Shoes helped Nairne's friend to support the sorcerer boy, who, though conscious, did not seem able to walk.

As they departed Red Shoes felt something like a knife at his back and jerked his head about, ready to do battle. For a bare instant, he thought he saw wings, scales, glowing eyes—but then there was nothing, just Nairne and Mather and a hundred strange men.

Ben winced at the bright sunshine and pulled a painful breath. Robert supported him on one side, and a man who looked for all the world like an Indian on the other.

"Thanks," he managed weakly, to both of them.

"I wonder what made Captain Teach treat you so," said the man in the red coat.

"Blackbeard and I have met before," Ben explained. "I was hoping he'd not recognize me, Mr. . . . ."

"Nairne," the fellow said. "Thomas Nairne."

"Nairne?" Ben echoed.

"My uncle," Robert clarified. "Are you well?"

Ben blinked through his astonishment. "I think so. Sore."

"Uncle Thomas," Robert said, "let me discover to you Benjamin Franklin of Boston."

"Franklin?" Mather said. "Not a relative of Josiah, or the murdered James Franklin?"

"The son of the first and brother of the second." Ben coughed. "You may not remember me, Reverend Mather, but it pleases me mightily to see you." He paused trepidatiously, heart near his throat. "Do you know aught of my father?"

"Well enough. Mourning three sons, now. Son, it would please me terribly to hear your story."

"And well would I love to exchange it for yours," Ben replied, "which we will do if only Blackbeard doesn't kill me. Where did they take him, anyhow?"

"For holding," Hassim supplied. "He attack Janissaries with hands in Divan. Not a good thing. You can speak for later, if you wish."

"Frankly," Mather said, "I would be pleased to be rid of him, but we need him to control his men, I imagine. But more important, I wonder when the Divan will reach a decision?"

"Already decide," Hassim said. "Janissaries fight."

Ben grinned in triumph, but Mather's next words sobered him.

"God help us all," the reverend said, not a blasphemy, but an earnest prayer.

8.

Stratagems

Two hours later, as he and the others were led to an audience with Charles, Ben still felt light-headed. Not from the pummeling or earlier injuries, but from the revelations that the Americans had provided—most especially their description of what had once been London. He had known, of course, what the comet must have wrought, but to have it described in detail . . . Even the wonderful news that his parents were alive did not balance that.

But it was settling out, bit by bit, and in his mind a plan was starting to form. It seemed, altogether, that the colonies—English or French— were safer than Europe, a smaller pond to swim in with fewer sharks and barracudas. A man with his talents might become someone of importance there, and not owe his livelihood and very life to the whims of thin-blooded monarchs.

Charles and the Janissary leaders had installed themselves in the beylerbey's palace, which before him had belonged to the doge. It was imposing and beautiful, a baroque European lady in Turkish costume. As Ben and the Americans were ushered in, Charles stood up from behind a large table, at which were seated a dozen or so men. Ben recognized a few—Hassim's father and Riva among them.

"Gentlemen," Charles called in German. Translators began speaking to the English and Frenchmen. "We have weighty matters to discuss, and battle plans to draw."

The Frenchman named Bienville cleared his throat. "Your pardon, Majesty, but we have not yet agreed to aid you."

Charles nodded. "I realize that, Monsieur. But it is true, yes, that should Venice become a sovereign regency, Louisiana would welcome our trade on good terms?"

"Of course. But I, for one, remain unconvinced that you can triumph in this battle. If what we hear is true—"

"It is true, sir, but I assure you, I would not consider fighting unless we had a good chance of victory."

Bienville laughed. "Your pardon, sir, but such is not your reputation. It is said that you would stand alone against an entire army with naught but a paring knife, were it the only way to confront the tsar."

Charles pursed his lips. "Men have been given to exaggerate my deeds," he said. "But be that as it may, if you would join us for the moment, I would be pleased."

"I will join you," Bienville said, "but if I remain unconvinced in two hours, I will raise sail."

"We need you," Charles said.

"We know that," Bienville said. "What you must convince us of is that *we* need *you*."

A man across the table rose. "Monsieur de Bienville," he said, "*peut-être que je peux vous aider, dans cette affaire.*"

"*Pardon?*" Bienville replied. "*Qui parle à moi?*"

"My pardon," Charles interrupted. "Sieur de Bienville, I introduce to you Louis de Rouvroy, the duke of Saint-Simon, governor of Naples and representative of His Majesty, the king of France."

Bienville blinked, and then a slow smile crept across his face. "France does exist then? And has a monarch?"

"Sir," Saint-Simon replied, "France is smothered by Muscovite hordes, but the Crown survives. It is imperative that our Italian and American possessions—and our Venetian friends—remain free of Russian rule. Thus my presence here, and my own appeal to you as a Frenchman."

Bienville bowed. "I know you, sir, and we have even met once, you may remember, at Versailles. I would very much like to hear more of the state of our country."

"And so you shall, Monsieur, and it will make your blood boil, I assure you."

Charles smiled broadly, clearly pleased by Bienville's reaction. "Captain Teach shall join us in a moment," he said. "In the meantime—"

"Sir?" Ben interjected impatiently. "Your Majesty, may I have a brief word with you in private?"

"Of course," Charles replied, frowning. "Pardon us, gentlemen." He rose and guided Ben into an antechamber.

"I have you to thank for the decision," Charles told him. "You swung opinion our way."

"Thank you, Your Majesty, 'twas my intention."

"But now you must explain in detail," Charles went on. "The leaders of the factions are all met. We convinced them with shouting; now we must convince them with more reasonable words. Especially, we must keep your friends in the ships here, for we will have need of them." He frowned slightly. "You *do* know how to defeat these flying ships?"

"Of course I do," Ben lied. "But I will see Newton before I publish it to you."

Charles' eyes grew colder. "What?" he said slowly.

"Majesty, I believe I was clear."

"Are you blackmailing me? We must speak to these men *now*, explain your magical solution *now*. You can go see Newton immediately after."

Ben pursed his lips and decided to modify himself a bit. "Sir, I must needs obtain something from Newton to be convincing. Feed them dinner, give them wine. Persuade them in other ways, and I will return as quickly as possible."

"Mr. Franklin, do not try me."

"Do not try *me*, Your Majesty. I am willing to help you, as you helped me in Prague. But you must let me go about it my own way."

Charles' frown deepened, and then he nodded. He beckoned one of his men over. "Lieutenant, take this fellow to the madman on the island. Bring him back in an hour. If he will not come, bind and gag him and return him here. Do not let him stray from your sight."

"Yes, sir."

Charles turned away from Ben. "Go," he said.

Ben spent the gondola ride knotting and unknotting his fingers, acutely aware of time slipping away, of the depth and possible repercussions of his lie. He knew of no certain way to defeat the Muscovite airships. Oh, he had an inkling, but it all depended upon Sir Isaac.

The men on the island looked suspiciously at him when he came ashore, but Hassim—sent along as a translator—reassured them some, and the note hastily scrawled by Hassim's father even more so.

The sun was half past meridian, the harbor gold-flecked lapis, antique, Egyptian. The building—a church? a castle?—wavering witch-light. Newton had brought one of the large aegises with him, perhaps built into the very boat.

"Where has he been heard?" he asked one of the men, through Hassim. The fifteen or so Janissaries regarded the ensorcelled structure balefully, and one of them pointed.

Alone, Ben strode to that point, and when he felt the slick-cool surface of the aegis, stopped. "Sir Isaac!" he bellowed, and then again, "Sir Isaac!"

A long pause followed, and then, thinly, "Benjamin?"

"Yes! Let me in. I have to talk with you."

Another considerable pause. "Is King Charles with you?"

"No, sir. He has pressing business, and you are angering him with your demands. Sir, if you would live, I suggest you speak to me. There is no other chance!" Try as he might, he could not keep the desperation from his voice.

"Move to your right fifteen paces." The reply floated down. "I will unbar the door and unhook the aegis for a few seconds. Only you may enter. Do you understand?"

"Aye!"

Teeth grinding, he did as directed. After perhaps ten minutes he heard a bolt slide, and an instant later a weather-pitted stone wall appeared. He quickly opened the heavy wooden door and stepped in, and was staring at a distorted image of his own face, framed by a sphere of sea and sky. He cried out softly as he understood he was facing the automaton that he had seen, dormant, in the Black Tower.

No longer dormant, it reached for him, and he threw himself violently aside, feeling just slightly foolish when it continued past him, and closed and barred the door.

Silently, it turned, crossed a dusty floor of red marble, and began to ascend a stair of verdigris stone. Ben followed the thing up, fascinated despite himself at the way its artificial muscles flexed and bunched.

Newton looked worse than Ben had ever seen him. His stained waistcoat was open, the shirt beneath a dirty ivory rag. His hair hung in greasy strands about his face, and his eyes stood like carbuncles in black abscesses. That febrile regard darted to Benjamin, lit on him for an instant, and then flitted randomly about the room.

"I'm glad to see that you survived and escaped the fall of Prague," Newton muttered, his voice somehow uncertain.

"Are you? Well, no thanks to you, you will admit."

Newton shrugged. "I did what I thought was best. Who is more valuable to the world, you or me?"

"Oh, that's a pretty robe to put on coward's ways," Ben returned, surprised at how calm he felt. "But to the devil with you, sir, in any case. I came for Lenka."

"Lenka?" Newton asked.

Ben gasped in abrupt horror. "God! She was in the hidden place in the boat!" He had a sudden image of her, locked there for six days with no food or water, Newton oblivious to her pounding and cries.

"Oh!" Newton said. "The girl. Really, Benjamin, I think it was rather extreme of you to pack one of your little bunters for the journey—"

"God rot you!" Ben snapped. "She was no doxy, you stupid old man. Is that all you see when you look at a woman—any woman? A whore? No, don't answer me. I don't even care. Just tell me where she is."

Newton's eyes suddenly snapped into focus, as if seeing Ben for the first time. "Benjamin," he said, "I am really most remorseful about abandoning you. I regretted it instantly, I assure you. I just—" He faltered, and Ben gathered that Newton was weeping. "I've never learned, you see. People are so difficult. Much more difficult than calculus and optics. Much more."

Ben paused, feeling his throat catch, and for an instant he was three years younger, on that terrible and wonderful day when Newton had asked him to be his apprentice. "Sir, I—" No. He could not let himself be distracted. "Where is she?" he demanded.

"I don't know. She was here, then she wasn't."

"What?"

"She was here, ranting, annoying me. I told her to go and find King Charles. I suppose she went to do that. I haven't seen her in several days."

"You—" He broke off, thinking furiously, trying to ignore that Newton now had his face down in his hands.

Hassim had said that no one had seen Lenka. What had happened to her? Had she been snatched up by the Turk for some harim? Had she drowned, trying to swim to Venice?

"Lenka!" he cried, running around the room, searching for other doors. He descended the stairs, shouting her name, spinning dust into clouds, sending rats chittering into darker corners until his body—still much the worse for wear—began to fail. Panting, leaning against a smooth, cool wall, he slid down to the floor.

She was alive, he was certain of it. She was alive, in Venice or— He squeezed his eyes shut. Not on the beylerbey's ship, already a day gone! Would she have been taken slave so quickly? Was there a trial or something, before a free woman was made slave?

He didn't know. He didn't know *anything* about Turks.

He did know that he would find her, somehow. This was his fault. This was his fault, and he—

Nothing. He nothing. He would find her because she deserved to be found.

And then he saw, with a blinding clarity, what that actually meant. It meant staying in Venice or sailing to Constantinople or wherever the bey's ship had gone. He had to admit that he might need more than three days for that.

In three days, the Muscovites would be here.

All in all, it was a very simple equation. He would have to save Venice, as he had promised.

Taking a deep breath he rose, steadied himself, and went back up the stairs.

He found Newton as he had left him.

"Well," Ben said, "it seems you are correct."

"This girl meant something to you, I take it?"

"She was a person, so she meant more to me than to you." He winced at his tone and held his hands up. "Let it pass," he whispered. "I will find her. I have something else to speak to you about."

"Oh? And will you remonstrate with me further?"

"I don't know. That depends upon you, sir."

"Meaning?"

"Meaning, what are your plans now?"

Newton looked steadily at him. "I promise you, Benjamin, I will not leave you again. This time, we shall go together. Somewhere safe, where I can carry on my work." He brightened a bit. "Look! See you my talos?" He waved at the man-thing.

"Oh, indeed, I did see it, and have seen it before," Ben replied dryly. "A useful servant, I should think—perhaps a replacement apprentice?"

"No, no. Benjamin, it is more than it looks. It is the key to the wisdom of the ancients. To describing the malakim!"

"I see."

"No, you do not. But I can teach you, Ben. Many secrets are in our grasp now, many new systems. It is more than ever I dreamed."

Ben felt a bit of hope stirring, but he had heard Newton speak so before. "Listen to me, sir," he said. "Know you that the Muscovite fleet comes here now?"

"Here? Why here?"

"It is too long in the telling. They come to conquer Venice; that is enough."

"Well then, we must flee immediately."

"No!" Ben snapped, amazed that he could be so angry at Newton for planning nothing more or less than what he himself had been contemplating an hour before: find Lenka, convince Cotton Mather to sail, and leave Venice to her fate. He couldn't do that now, because Lenka was here somewhere, and suddenly he felt a tower of righteousness. It was astonishing what was lying there below his pragmatism, and he marveled to hear it come out.

"I have fled Boston, I have fled London, I have fled Prague. By God, sir, here, for once, I stand and fight."

"With what? You saw the ships at Prague."

"I did see—and I know, sir, that you must have noted that they are propelled by caged malakim."

"Yes. Mrs. Karevna must have thieved away my design."

"Be that as it may. You made these things, sir. Can you not *unmake* them? Loose the affinities that bind the malakim to their service and let them fly free, so the proud Muscovite ships plummet earthward?"

Newton's eyes widened as if he had never thought of that, and for a long space Ben watched the problem churn behind the master's eyes. At last the philosopher looked up at him. "Perhaps," he replied. "But it is too dangerous. I will not risk myself so for a city I owe nothing to."

"Tell me," Ben snarled. "I shall do it. I care not what the danger might be."

"But *I* do, Benjamin, and I will not expose you to it."

"But you would expose me, unprotected, to the bombs and shot of the Muscovites? For I swear to you, I am standing with King Charles in this."

"I would expose you to nothing. I would have you travel on with me."

"I have friends who will not abandon me at their slightest fear," Ben mocked. "I have friends who love me and whom I trust. You are not one of those, Sir Isaac. You are *not* one of those, and I would rather take my chances with musket fire in defense of my friends than escape with a man I do not trust and do not like!"

"Benjamin—" Newton began, and then again, "Ben—our work is more important than this. You must believe me."

Ben let out a measured breath. "Oddly, sir, I do believe you. But I must do what I must do."

"Then I cannot help you."

"Is there nothing I can do to stop the ships?"

Newton shrugged. "Perhaps. You have always been the handy one with contrivances, Benjamin. Perhaps you will invent something. Now, if you please, my talos will show you back down. I must ready for another flight, it seems."

Ben paused as he approached the stairwell, but did not turn as he said, "You best fly quickly. Charles was talking of having you bombarded, so as to keep you from Muscovite hands. Farewell, sir. I do not think we shall meet again."

His only reply was the faint bell of the talos' feet on stone.

Red Shoes shook his head to clear it, glad to be back in the open air, even the fetid air of Venice. His initial impression of the city had only been confirmed. The paths of water between the houses, the sinking, decaying buildings, the smell! He found himself always looking for enemies. Whatever had attacked him in Algiers was here: he knew it, could feel it. Below the waters of Venice, something dread waited to claim him.

He had meant to try and sort out what the "quiet" council had agreed, but he found he could not force himself to care. No matter what was said or done, a battle would be fought here, and he, Red Shoes, was going to be a part of it. Ostensibly, it remained to hear from Benjamin Franklin what plans he had for attacking the flying warships. In truth, it was decided.

Europeans could not bear to be alone, among aliens. It was a sentiment he could understand. Away from his people, what was true and right began to lose its meaning; and he was fast becoming a chip of wood, tossed about on the water, weighed down by it, closer to sinking each day. Nairne, Mather, Bienville—even Blackbeard—might be from different nations, but it was clear that they thought themselves a sort of tribe apart from the Muscovites and the Turks. Venice might be ruled by the Turks, but in their hearts they thought of it as the last remaining part of a world that had once held England, France, Spain. Venice was all that endured of the Europe they knew, and they would fight to save her, he was sure. The Americans would not let Riva and King Charles die. Even Bienville now saw a chance to save his doomed colonists, and he would take it. But for the final decision they waited for the sorcerer Benjamin Franklin. Red Shoes had decided to wait outside.

It was perhaps because he strained so for warning of a sorcerous attack that he did not sense the physical one until the last instant. A cudgel slapped him across the shins, and he collapsed in agony, grasping for his pistol or ax and realizing that he had never retrieved them after the Divan. Fighting the pain, he lashed wildly with his legs and had the satisfaction of striking someone, hearing them gasp. Then three sharp points dug into his flesh at neck, ribs, and kidney.

"Be still," someone hissed in heavily accented English. "Make no sound or you die."

His hands were yanked roughly behind his back and bound there, and a blindfold tied over his eyes—though as they rolled him he caught a glimpse of four men in black hats and bizarre masks.

"Avant'! Prest'!" a man with a voice like a jay squawked. They hauled him to his feet.

"Walk," the English speaker said. Red Shoes tried to comply, but found himself mostly dragged along. Not much later, they put him in a boat. He could feel its motion—hesitating between pole strokes, winnowing slightly upon the thin skin of the underworld. In the shadows behind his eyes lurked movement, and he stabbed out with his ghost vision just in time to see it vanish, a figment in the corner of his vision. *Coward!* he shouted in the silent language of shadow. *Coward, come try me!* But no answer came.

Frustrated, he settled into the forest of sound around him: the chattering of a hundred nearby mouths; the plaintive whine of a cat; the cooing of pigeons; harsh grating of metal; and, farther still, the windy strains of a song played on an instrument unknown to him.

Finally, the boat came to a rest.

"Now," his captor said, "I want you to listen very carefully. I'm going to tie a rope around you, and after that I'll drop you in the water. Hold your breath, and don't struggle. If you follow my directions, you will most probably live. If you do not, you will die. Do you understand?"

His mouth went dry as the man's words sunk in. "I can't swim," he said.

"That's what the rope is for," the fellow grunted. "Like I said, listen to me or die."

Red Shoes nodded, stood, and kicked hard at the sound of the voice. His foot grazed someone and he was rewarded, first by the sounds of chuckles, then by a powerful slap across his face. He reeled back—and someone caught him by his shirt—and he realized that light was seeping in through the rags over his eyes. The slap had moved the blindfold just enough for him to see the face of his captor, a darkening, canalside alley, and a hanging yellow sign with the picture of a bee on it. Then rough hands were all over him, and the blindfold tightened painfully.

"You've got spirit," the voice said, disembodied no longer. Red Shoes now had an image of a narrow, tapering face, an aquiline nose, mussed brown hair. "You could almost be a Venetian. But don't try that again. Now, take a few deep breaths."

Red Shoes fought back his panic as they tied a rope beneath his arms. "Now a *very* deep breath."

He sucked in air until he could find no more room in his lungs, and they threw him into the water. It was cold, amazingly cold, and terror roared through his body in a wave, an explosion that was almost sensual in its intensity. He tried to summon the detachment that had allowed him to grasp the burning iron; but this was different, a thing he had never even considered inuring himself against. He summoned images of dry earth—of hunting deer in the small, bright prairies of his homeland, of the bald ridge of a hill he knew—but all these came in disjointed flashes, drowned before they could afford him any comfort. His panicked lungs heaved futilely. Then, finally, he caught an image that brought some solace, that calmed him, afforded a measure of dispassion as the rope tugged him through the black water. It was no pastoral scene, no sunlit landscape; it was the face of his captor, the look of surprise as an ax split it in two.

He came up gasping, and someone gripped him below the armpits and hauled him from the water and marched him along. The rotten stink of the canals clung to him, but by the stillness of the air and sandy smell of wet stone, he knew he was in an enclosed space. He counted paces, but there were only fifteen before he was forced roughly to sit. His bonds were cut, but an instant later cold manacles replaced them. His blindfold remained.

Someone said something authoritative to him that he did not understand, and then he heard footsteps recede. He could not decide if there were enough leaving to account for all his captors, but he suspected that at least one had remained as guard. He tested the chains and manacles anyway; they were solid. He might escape them with the aid of a shadowchild, but that would wait until he had thought for a few moments.

Who had kidnapped him, and why? He remembered Riva and his talk of the Masques, the extreme Venetian faction. His captors had been masked—it seemed reasonable to assume that was who they were. But why?

"*Wer sind Sie?*" He started at the sound of the woman's voice. He did not understand her words, though they were clearly a question.

"I don't understand," he replied. "Do you speak English?"

"*Nein. Parlez français?*" she asked.

"Yes," he replied in French. "I speak French."

"Very little, I. You are captive also?"

"Yes. And you?"

His answer was a rattle of chains.

"Do you know what they want?" he asked.

"No. No. But they make me write letter."

"A letter?"

"Yes—to—friend of mine, Benjamin. You know him?"

"Benjamin Franklin?" he asked. "We just met today."

"That Benjamin, yes. My name is Lenka."

Ben paced over what seemed to be one of the few solid streets in Venice, thinking furiously. How could one combat ships of the air? They could fly well out of range of the most powerful cannon, wreak havoc by dropping stones, mortar shells, and arcane weaponry. He had pinned his hopes on dissolving the bonds of the malakim and thus depriving the ships of support, but he couldn't formulate a method for that on his own, not in three days' time.

So deep in thought was he, that he didn't notice the street urchin running toward him until the guard Charles had sent with him suddenly interposed himself between Ben and the young fellow. The guard barked something in Italian.

"*Per Benjamino,*" the boy said, waving what looked like a letter. "*Benjamino Franco!*"

"What?" Ben grunted. "Let me see that." He took the sheet, made somewhat grubby by the boy's dirty fingers.

He broke the seal—nothing more than a spot of wax—and quickly read two short notes. The first was in English.

For the honorable Mr. Franklin.
We have taken into our protection a foreigner in our city, a Mrs. Lenka. She publishes that you are a dear friend of hers. We will keep

her safe for you until such time as the Moscovados are defeated. Before your reunion, we would very much like to discuss with you matters Turkish and Venetian.
Humbly yours,
The Masques

The second was in German, and bit longer.

Dear Benjamin,
I am captive of some men who say they will deliver this letter to you. It was imprudent of me to reveal our acquaintance, and I fear they may have misunderstood the depth of our friendship.

I never finished the story I was telling you, the one about the man whose great-grandfather was Johannes Kepler. He believed, you see, that Kepler had flown to the Moon in his fabled airship, and was determined to do so himself. He flew off, the court bidding him bon voyage, and his little daughter, a girl scarcely five, waving her handkerchief, calling out for him to bring her back a bit of green cheese. He never returned, and the little girl never saw him again, but she always imagined that he was on the Moon, there, looking down at her. That is, until one day, she found the airship, high in a tower, empty, and learned that men who fly too high suffocate from lack of air. She understood then that the ship must have gone no great distance at all, had been quietly found, returned to the castle, locked away.

I have finished this story, and I trust it explains many of the inconveniences you have suffered on account of me. I am sorry for these. Do not let my present circumstance also be an inconvenience, I beg you. Thank you for showing me the mountains of the Moon and for the opportunity to sail the air. Do not worry for me, for I am now content.
Yours very truly,
Lenka

Ben carefully folded the note and put it in his pocket, and the last of his doubts dissolved. In his mind's eye, he saw again the moon he and Lenka had shared, and felt a dark grin creep across his face. He looked toward the north. "I have nothing in particular against you, Tsar Peter," he said, "but God help you, now." *And God help the Masques.*

Ignoring the puzzled looks of his companions, he continued toward the palace, his stride firm and resolute. "Bring the boy," he commanded over his shoulder. "He may know something useful."

Benjamin Franklin cleared his throat and looked frankly at the council. "I apologize for the delay, gentlemen, and thank you all for waiting. I wanted to consult with Sir Isaac Newton before proposing my countermeasures, which I am confident will prove adequate to end the Muscovite threat."

"I thought you were certain before," the now-present Blackbeard grunted, a dark fire burning in his eyes.

"I was," Ben replied. "But Sir Isaac, after all, is the master and I the apprentice. 'Twas best I first consult."

"Why isn't Sir Isaac here?" Cotton Mather asked. "Why can't he consult with us directly?"

"He is too busy with matters of his own."

"Preparing his own measures?" Riva asked.

Ben hesitated for an instant, but by the look that flashed across Charles' otherwise impassive face he knew that for one person, at least, it was an instant too long. "Yes," he said anyway.

Everyone at the table seemed to relax a degree.

"Now then," Charles said quietly, "what are your plans?"

"Should I wait for the Indian fellow?"

Thomas Nairne shook his head. "He's a strange one, given to wander. I will inform him later."

Ben nodded, wondering how convincing he could make his half-formed ideas sound, but determined that he would, indeed, convince. "This will require much work in a short time," he said. "But I think Venice is equal to the task. There are things I must know first, however, of the city's present defense."

"That being?" The speaker was Hassim's father.

For an instant, Ben felt dissected by the man's gaze, revealed to the Turk as a charlatan. But that had never stopped him before, and it did not now. "Do you have a fervefactum?"

"We have fervefactum," the Janissary confirmed.

"Of what use will that be?" Charles asked impatiently. "We have two, as a matter of fact, positioned to guard the entrances to the city. They were effective enough when enemies had to approach by sea, but they can scarcely boil a bowl of water if the distance is greater than twenty yards. The tsar need only stay above that range and land his troops in the interior of the city—once he had bombarded away resistance."

"I know the limitations of the fervefactum, gentlemen," Ben replied. "We will not be using them in the usual way. Can they be removed from their placement?"

"They are quite massive," the Janissary chief replied.

"But can they be removed to a ship?" Ben persisted. "To one of the American ships?"

Now everyone in the room looked puzzled.

"Come, gentlemen. The fervefactum is used in siege to boil the blood of those approaching key points in a defense. The effect is most intense—indeed, almost unbelievably intense—near the device."

"What does that have to do with my ships?" Blackbeard grunted.

Ben smiled. "Drop the device in the sea, and what do you suppose will happen?"

"*Pardieu*," Bienville muttered.

"An eruption," Mather breathed. "Steam."

"Indeed," Ben replied. "A column of steam that will rise high and continue to rise—a miniature storm, if you will, that can be used to disrupt the movements of the airships and perhaps overturn some. If we carry one suspended on a ship, we can position it to its best advantage."

"I like this thinking," Charles murmured.

"It's nothing," Blackbeard snarled. "A minor trick. But then my ships are vulnerable to every sort of attack. And what can I do in response? How will my guns reach these flying ships? What will repel the mines they drop upon me?"

Ben rubbed his hands together. "I have answers to all those questions, Captain Teach, gentlemen. The fervefactum is the most minor part of my plan."

"What other things do you need to know?"

"Venice is famed for her stores of silk, true?"

"Only China has more silk," Riva said.

Ben's grin broadened even more. "In that case," he said, "we shall have a good defense indeed."

9.

Three Magi

Adrienne first saw Venice as a fey glimmering beneath the roots of black cloud mountains. As they drifted, the numinous range shattered, and the sky opened to receive the faint iodine breath of waters far below. The city was glowworms nested on a sea of ink.

Between her and that suggestion of sea and city, she saw sailing a squadron of what resembled red fireflies marking the rest of the Muscovite fleet, lowering themselves for nocturnal invasion. It was such a wonder, all of it, that Adrienne could scarcely believe it a prelude to violence.

"How low are the lowest ships?" she wondered aloud, her eyes still fastened on the marvels below. Her voice broke the momentary silence that had transfixed them all when Venice first came into view. Even the tsar, conferring with his officers a few yards away, had fallen silent. Now he cleared his throat.

"You worry about d'Argenson, Mademoiselle?"

"And the men with him," she said. "I thought this was to be an assault from on high."

"Look there," the tsar said, indicating the glowing islands of the Venetian lagoon. "Have you ever been to Venice?"

"I have not."

"Nor have I, and I would despise to see her only in ruins. I would take her without raining flame."

"Even at the cost of your soldiers' lives?"

"If I expected a high cost in lives, I would not pursue this particular course," he explained. "When morning comes, they will see our troops already occupying key points of the city, our ships poised to strike decisive blows. They will see how little they stand to gain by resistance. Our design is to take the city with no bloodshed at all."

"Do you truly believe it will happen?"

The tsar sighed. "Charles is an intractable foe, Mademoiselle, and perhaps mad. I do not expect him to go quietly. But I dislike the idea of pulverizing a city like Venice merely to dispense with a troublesome Swede. The Venetians deserve their chance."

"How can I help?" Adrienne asked quietly.

The tsar beamed at her. "Help Mademoiselle Karevna locate scientifical defenses. Fervefactum, firedrakes, airy shields such as protected Prague. We will then know where to station our ships."

"Anything that looks strange in the aether," Karevna put in. "All which the malakim recognize as unusual."

"Very well." She flexed her *manus oculatus*, beckoned her minions, and told them what to do. As they dispersed, their eyes became hers, and she sorted through their perceptions as she might a book of diagrams.

In djinn eyes, the water was a vast canvas; land, smudges of paint. The lights of Venice were smoldering embers, the drifting smoke of shattered ferments—alchemical lanthorns. She found the faint, slow-throbbing energies of a fervefactum and several cannon with unusual properties she could not identify. One of the tsar's engineers worked quickly with surveying tools to map their locations as Adrienne pointed them out.

More worrisome was a general and almost undetectable wavering in the aether, a sort of glimmering here and there, mostly on the water.

"I didn't notice that," Vasilisa admitted, when Adrienne mentioned it.

"Might it be some natural effect?" the tsar wondered.

"So far as I can tell, Captain, my djinni do not note processes we consider natural—evaporation, heating, cooling, the slow vegetation of metals. They help me see and understand these things if I direct them, but natural processes do not catch their attention. Only direct manipulation of the aether does that."

"You think it a danger?"

"I will study it more, Captain."

"Do so." He sighed. "This disconcerts me. Surely they cannot be considering an actual defense of the city, given what they face."

Adrienne gave little of her attention to the conversation, for as she had promised, she was concentrating on the strangeness below. It was subtle, merely a hastening of natural sublimation. It was no wonder that Vasilisa had missed it. "I think," she said softly, "that they are raising a mist—a forced sublimation, perhaps by some powdered catalyst. To the eye it looks natural." Indeed, the lights of Venice were beginning to blur.

"Ah. One wonders what they hope to accomplish," Vasilisa murmured.

"We cannot bombard what we cannot see," the tsar growled.

"Yes, Captain," Vasilisa went on, "but Adrienne and I can peer through that mist. If they prepare an alchemical weapon, we will know of it."

"But *they* do not know this," the tsar said. "They could not, and so foolishly prepare to fight."

"That is their mistake," Vasilisa said grimly.

"Unless—" Crecy muttered, a faraway look in her eyes.

But she was interrupted by a flash of light, a billowing globe that limned one of the ships below—the *Bogatyr*—in a shroud of flame. An instant later, the sound and the shock wave hit them, buckling the deck beneath their feet. Panicked shrieks and commands suddenly filled the air.

"Unless the weapons aren't philosophical," Crecy shouted over the noise. "Where is Nico?"

"He is with a nurse, below deck." She hesitated an instant. "Crecy, go get him."

"Is he not safer there?"

"Not if *that* happens to us!" Adrienne shouted, pointing. The *Bogatyr*, flaming, wrenched in half, each side still supported by its ifrit. In the light of the flames, she saw men spilling from the ship as if from the belly of an eviscerated whale.

Farther away, a second new star lit the night.

A thunder of cheers erupted on deck of the *Carolina Prophet*— Blackbeard's new flagship—when the first explosion broke the night stillness, a firework visible even through the creeping fog. Despite his exhaustion—he had spent the last three days working nonstop, pausing only for the briefest naps—Ben shouted as loudly as any of them, and at least ten Janissaries slapped him on the back in congratulation. He nearly wept with fierce pride. His plan was working! He had claimed it would, convinced it would—and yet, deep down, perhaps never believed it himself.

Now if it would only continue to work.

He knew that they needed the fog—made by the same agent as that he had given the little archduchess Maria Theresa—but he wished it weren't there. Likewise he wished it were not nighttime, though it was absolutely to their advantage. But he longed to see what he saw only in his mind's eye: the sky filled with the myriad forms of hastily sewn silk balloons, filled with hot air from a thousand fires, bearing their deadly, explosive burdens to the Muscovite ships.

Another explosion, and another, though it was difficult to see what effect the bombs were having. The effect should be good; the Venetian magazine contained helios, one of the newest and most powerful alchemical explosives, and it was with this that the balloons were armed.

"Congratulations, Mr. Franklin," Charles said, shaking his hand. "You have given us a good start. Striking the first blow is always important. I hope your other ideas work as well."

"Believe me, sir, so do I. Perhaps the Muscovites will even retreat."

Charles shook his head skeptically. "That I doubt, I'm afraid. We've shaken them, but for every one of those balloons that does some damage, thirty float away."

Robert grunted, pushing his hat back on his head and folding his arms. "I should say someone downwind'll receive an unpleasant surprise."

"Oh, God," Ben said. "I hadn't thought of that."

Charles shrugged. "Most will land in the sea."

"Most," Ben replied, thinking that it seemed to him that the wind was blowing toward the mainland. But the balloons would drop quickly as the air in them cooled.

Charles rested his hand nervously on the pommel of his sword. "When will the *Madman* be ready?"

"Another thirty minutes, I should think," Ben replied.

"Why so slowly?"

"It's a larger envelope and takes longer to fill. And rifts were found in it when they began the inflation."

"It must be ready while mist and night still hold. I don't trust your airy shield."

Privately, Ben didn't either. He had cobbled the aegis together awfully fast, and was far from certain how effective it would prove.

The sky blazed twice more, and then suddenly the sea and shore erupted as the Russians counterattacked. The string of concussions slapped across the water, somehow out of keeping with the unbelievable size of the explosions; and Ben's triumph turned to a sudden, suffocating fear. When those ships stood over Venice, they were doomed. Of course, that's why the command had been placed on the *Prophet*, but in some ways that made them all the more vulnerable.

"We need to get more balloons under them," he muttered. By necessity, the balloons had been strung out in a perimeter around the city—on the other American ships in the deep channels, on flatboats and skiffs in the shallows, as well as on the islands that dotted the lagoon. When word came from the watchers on land, the ships rushed to release the balloons where they could be most effective. Ben had seen at least one of those ships—he could not be sure which—struck by the Muscovite counterattack. The others were rushing to interpose themselves between the attackers and Venice itself. The *Prophet*, on the other hand, was hiding, motionless, some four hundred yards from the city, directing the defense and readying its own slender hope of attack. But if even a single Russian ship came on, Venice would be rubble.

Lenka was in Venice, so he could not let that happen.

A runner shouted something in Charles' ear.

"The kites have gone up," Charles said.

"I hope there is enough wind."

He turned to stare at the map, where Charles and his tacticians were scribbling furiously as reports came in. The Russian ships were approaching in an arc from land—though it seemed certain that some had been sent to surprise them from the sea. *This is insane,* Ben thought. *What did I ever think I was doing?*

But another explosion, high in the air, reminded him; and at the same moment, a weird sensation shuddered through his body, one he well recognized. It was the touch of a malakus upon his soul. He closed his eyes, swaying with sudden nausea, his mind screaming, *Go away.* But it would not stop. In the babble and confusion, no one saw him slowly drop to his knees.

"What is this?" Tsar Peter roared hoarsely. "What attacks us?"

"I do not know, Your Majesty," Vasilisa replied coolly. "We are trying to discern that now."

Adrienne stepped grimly to the rail and set the air alight in a sheet that rolled, waving and down, stairs worn smooth by the feet of the gods. In it, they saw the rising forms of what might be jellyfish, if the air were ocean.

"Balloons," she said. "That's why we didn't see them. They are not scientific weapons at all."

"Balloons? Not scientific?"

"They make no unnatural mark on the aether for the djinni to scent," she explained.

"Stop them."

"I've already begun," Adrienne replied quietly.

"It would seem that the Venetians had more fight in them than I thought," the tsar admitted.

"Yes," Crecy agreed. "It would seem so."

"Your Majesty, we must fly higher," Adrienne said.

"Why?"

"My science will work better from a height." It was a lie, of course, but she was thinking of her son. What other nasty surprises did the Venetians have awaiting them?

Meanwhile, her djinni, obedient as ever, followed her commands. Now that she knew what to look for, the balloons were clear enough: air ferments more agitated than the rest. Hot. It needed only to cool them a bit, and they would sink instead of rise.

Red Shoes felt rather than heard the dull *crump* of distant explosions, but by then he already knew the attack had begun. The air was shrill with the noise of spirits—one-eyes, *Lowaks, Shimoha*—and somewhere, lurking, the thing that stalked him. For two days in darkness he had labored to make himself invisible, to stop the creatures from underneath from finding him. Now with so many shouting voices in the spirit world, it was easier.

"Did you hear that?" Lenka asked.

"I heard."

"What was it, you think?"

"A bomb—maybe a cannon."

"Then attack is beginning."

"Yes."

"I saw them attack Prague—or part of it, after Sir Isaac let me out of the boat's compartment. They to drop bombs from air, big bombs. I don't think we safe."

"No, I don't think so," he agreed. It was time to do something. In the first day, he had tried to melt his chains where they joined the wall, but the metal proved too conductive of heat. He might be able to stand the pain of red-hot irons on his hands and feet, but he would be in no shape to escape afterward—or even to free Lenka. He had been working at weakening the stone, but that had borne little fruit, especially as he had to be wary, recall his shadowchild each time he felt his enemy near.

He had gradually—and reluctantly—formed a plan, but now it was probably too late to put into effect. He supposed he must try, however, or be here, helpless, when the sky began to rain thunder and fire and that horde of spirits he sensed no longer had anything to do save search for him. Further, he had taken a liking to Lenka, and wished her to live. He could not delay his own confrontation forever.

And so he cut another shred of his shadow from himself and hesitated a moment, wondering who to make it for. Nairne? Tug? But they might be at sea, or otherwise unable to help. No, he knew who he would make it for, though he barely knew the man.

But Lenka knew him well. And so he took the little taste of breath he had captured, the breath of Benjamin Franklin, wrapped it about a dream, and sent it away to find him. Gritting his teeth against the vacuum within, he tried to staunch the wound, bleed as little shadow as possible; and he waited for his enemy to come to the scent.

Ben shuddered as the images poured through him, sickened, knowing they made no sense. He was pulled through a tunnel beneath the water, had a glimpse of a man's face, of a canal and an alleyway, pain, remorse— *Lenka's voice*. Speaking a language he did not know, but her voice. And somehow, in all that, the Indian who had vanished three days ago.

He thought his head would split—worse than the worst hangover he had ever had—but he staggered to his feet to find Hassim. Mercifully, he found him quickly, gawking at the flames across the water.

"Hassim," he yelled. "Quickly! An alley, with a yellow sign. A yellow sign with a bee on it. Do you know where this is?"

"Yes. Hassim believe he knows."

"Good. Take me there."

Where was Robert? He cast about for his friend, but he was no longer near. And Ben didn't have time to find him.

A number of craft—small boats and gondolas—were moored about the ship. Ben gestured for Hassim to start down, and made to follow himself. A small sound warned him to turn.

Blackbeard stood less that a yard away, pistol aimed between Ben's eyes. "I missed y' once." He grinned. "But at this range I think there's no question."

"Then shoot and be done with it," Ben gritted. "For I've business to be about."

"Still the same stupid-tongued boy. And your smart trick with the longboat—that was nearly the end of me."

"You tried to kill me, remember? Did you think I would just let you row away?"

Blackbeard chuckled. "I suppose I did. But I was a pirate then, and I'm a right legitimate captain now. So you tell me, why are you desertin' my ship? So I'll know what I'm killin' you for."

Ben stared at the barrel an instant longer, and then very deliberately started for the rope ladder. "A friend of mine—and the Indian fellow that came with you—they're being held hostage."

"I know. We got a letter about him."

"I know where they are."

"And y'r going to the rescue, all of your lonesome?"

"Aye." He was now four rungs down the ladder, and Blackbeard hadn't fired. He looked up. "Captain Teach, if you don't think you and I are even by now, that's fine with me. But be man enough to let it go until I've done this."

Blackbeard made no other comment, but when Ben reached the boat and looked back up, Teach no longer stood at the rail.

As Ben began to row, another ball of flame appeared in the sky, north. It looked as if the Russian ships had slowed, if not stopped. That was both good and bad; they had learned respect, but with it, caution. He only hoped this new caution would give him enough time to reach Venice, rescue Lenka, and return.

A white ribbon of light as straight as a geometry lesson cracked against the black sky, wreathed a sky ship in an argent umbra. For an instant all Ben could think of was the old tale about Jack who went up a beanstalk.

The Russians had discovered his kites.

Adrienne saw the flash of light for what it was.

"That was a *kraftpistole*," she said. "I've seen them fired before; this is the same."

"Impossible," Peter snarled. "No *kraftpistole* has that range."

"That one did, Captain," Adrienne said quietly. "And that," as another flash erupted. She wished she could see the actual stream of the bolt—something seemed strange about it. Another lit, and another.

"Damn!" the tsar stormed. "It's like a wall." His face worked furiously. "I've been too hasty," he muttered. "Give the order to fall back!" he shouted over his shoulder. "We've let them guide us into their traps— No more. Night is doing them more a service than us. We'll rise high and finish this in the dawn. The hell with Venice. I've given them their chance."

His face wrenched itself grotesquely as lightning struck again, again, again.

1o.

Canals

The gondola rippled through the still water as if through some stygian pool, some dark and narrow place beneath the earth. The sphere of lanthorn light was bounded by walls and darkness, the glittering red eyes of rats, larger movements that might be merely shadows and might be something more sinister. Ben reminded himself of Lenka—kidnapped, hidden away, possibly tortured or already dead. He needed that thought, that frustration and anger, to inspire his body when exhaustion, the leaking wound in his chest, the battering he had taken at the Divan, and three days without sleep all conspired to drag him to defeat.

"How the lightning?" Hassim asked.

"What?"

"I know about balloons—float up, explode like mines on the ocean. But lightning?"

"Oh." Ben grunted. "Kites. Kites can fly very high, and the people of Venice make good kites."

"Yes. You should see festival—many kites, and very beautiful. I saw the men go with kites in their gondolas."

Ben nodded, remembering the sight. Hundreds of the slender craft, dispersing across the dusky lagoon, kites rising in the sea breeze.

"The string we treated with a kind of iron," Ben continued. "Tie the point of a *kraftpistole* to the string and fire it, and then—um, lightning— runs up the string to the ships. You see?" The problem had been getting enough *kraftpistoles*. Only seventy had been found—or rather, relinquished. These had been given to the fastest gondoliers, that they might take them where needed.

A fragile plan—all of it improvised, contingent on the cooperation of too many people. And yet, it had borne fruit, the more so because the Russians had attacked at night. It had been Charles who had guessed that would happen. He understood the tactical mind of the tsar and his generals better than any man alive—any enemy, that is.

Ben realized that it had been some time since he heard the crack or boom of combat, and wondered what that meant. Retreat? Victory? How soon before Venice began to shatter around him?

He hoped the Russians meant to spare the city. What use a city in ruins? But the tsar was undoubtedly angry by now, and his anger was legendary.

"Here," Hassim murmured, as they came around a corner.

Even by lanthorn light, he recognized the yellow sign of the bee, and that renewed his conviction.

Now what? He closed his eyes, remembering. Water, suffocating him, a rope. Ben's eyes flew wide as it came back with sudden force. He felt his lungs squeezing smaller and smaller, panic rising. . . .

"No!" he muttered angrily. He was not afraid of swimming, below the water or upon it. Even as a boy, he had been the strongest swimmer he knew; and in Prague, he had taught lessons in swimming. Why these feelings?

But he knew the answer. They were not his feelings at all, but those of whatever malakus had assaulted him. Of course, that meant that he might be walking—or, it seemed, swimming—into a trap.

It didn't matter. Too many people had suffered or died in his wake: his brother, parents, John Collins, Sarah Chant, the archduchess. At seventeen, the list was already too long. At that rate even the high worth he placed on his own skin would require outside moneys to justify.

He stripped off his coat, waistcoat, shirt; unbuckled his shoes and lay them in the bottom of the boat; and then shucked his stockings. "If I do not return soon, Hassim, go tell the others where I went."

"Where *did* you went?" Hassim asked, clearly puzzled.

Ben pointed at the water.

"Ah. Hassim go with you."

It came to him that he had not been thinking of Hassim as a person, but as a sort of thing—a Turk he could talk to. Hassim's limited fluency in English helped that impression, filtering out many of the nuances that made a person unique. Now Ben suddenly saw the great hope, fear, need of the boy; and it came as a shock.

An epiphany he did not need right now.

"Do you know the way underwater?"

"No," Hassim admitted.

"Then I would rather you stayed here, to bring word should I be killed or captured."

"Hassim cannot be Janissary like his father," the boy said, trying to sound fierce, "but he can help!"

"You *have* helped me, and will help more if you wait."

Hassim looked uncertain, but Ben had no more time. He had done what he could. If the boy followed him now and got himself killed, it was no longer Ben's fault. He eased himself into the canal. The water was cold and dirty, repellent; but he took the lanthorn, a deep breath, and kicked downward, letting the "memory" guide him.

The first two dives he found nothing, but on the third, he located a cracked and crumbled place in the building, well below the waterline. The lanthorn light did not carry very far into the breech, but it appeared to be a low-roofed room, full of water. Perhaps it had once been a cellar. Had the sea risen or the building sunk? He went back up, gasped deeply for air, and then dove again, kicking in through the hole, hoping he chose the right direction—that there *was* a right direction.

Adrienne rocked Nico, awaiting the dawn, trying not to wonder which of the ships Hercule had been on. He had taken most of the men from Lorraine, leaving her a guard of five. She remembered giving them her blessing, remembered the ridiculous trust they placed in her; and her heart felt cold.

In the hours since falling back, they had discovered that six ships had either been destroyed or damaged so badly by fire and blast as to be useless. Losses had been great, especially on the packed infantry carriers. That left sixteen ships in the windborne fleet; and so, despite everything, the tsar was still confident of victory. Victory would mean little to Hercule if he were on one of the lost ships.

It would mean even less if something happened to Nico, but in the small hours of the morning, she had turned her thoughts to providing for that. "Here, little darling," she whispered to her son. "I want you to do something for me."

He looked guilelessly up at her, seeming attentive. She took him over to a large wicker hamper—one of the smaller ones used to pull food and supplies up from the ground. She had modified it a bit: four iron wires wove through it like lines of longitude on a globe, forming a sort of dome above. "I need you to stay in this basket, Nico. Can you do that? I will be near, and Crecy, and your nurse. But you *must* stay in the basket."

He blinked at her and smiled, which she decided would do for a yes, but resolved to have Crecy keep an eye on him.

"Some protection for Nico?" Crecy asked, emerging from the shadows aft.

"Yes. I've set four djinn about it—I've shown them the iron and they can see that. They will deflect bullet and flame, lightning— anything else I could think of. Should the ship fall, they will bear him down gently to the earth." She pursed her lips. "It is not good, but it's the best I can think of."

Crecy mussed the boy's hair. "You've your own airship, now, Nico! What do you think?"

"La loon," the boy replied, quite seriously.

"I should hope it won't fly that high," Crecy answered fondly. "Now, be a good fellow, and soon enough we'll be living as dukes and duchesses in the Muscovy land."

"Yes indeed," Adrienne answered. "You shall have a room of your own, and toys, and when you're old enough, a pony. . . ." He looked so fragile, sitting there in that basket, and for an instant she felt a surge of panic. Trying to push it down, she turned to Crecy. "I've solved the mystery of the lightning bolts," she said.

"Oh?"

"The conducting strands are borne aloft by kites. Like the balloons, they write no unusual sign in the aether for me or Karevna to read."

"You have to admire them," Crecy said. "Who would have thought of such things?"

Adrienne crooked a little smile. "I like to think I would have. What I wonder is why Vasilisa and the other philosophers gave no thought to such countermeasures?"

"They have not encountered them before. As I say, who would think a balloon or a kite might be a weapon?"

"Anyone thinking clearly, knowing an attack was coming from the sky."

Crecy shook her head. "No. Men have been thinking on how to wage war by land and sea for many thousands of years, and that many years of contemplation wears deep ruts. Look, even, at this amazing fleet. With ships that can move at will through the very air, why would the tsar sweep in from the most obvious direction? Why in a single front? The maneuvers are still naval maneuvers, though there are a thousand better uses for a fleet like this. Why attack at night, when balloons and kites could go unseen?" She shook her head. "No, the sort of ingenuity we see below us is rare."

Adrienne shrugged. "I prefer to think you exaggerate. At any rate, I'm sure the tsar will shift tactics now."

"It's still misty below?"

"Yes. I believe that small boats are constantly renewing the mist."

Nico pointed at something in the darkness and laughed.

"I hope I'm doing the right thing," Adrienne said softly, studying her son's face.

"I can think of no better plan," Crecy said.

"Nor I. But thus far I have failed."

"Ah, but you have done more than Karevna. The balloons and kites, at least, are no longer a threat—thanks to you, not to her. The tsar will remember."

Adrienne shrugged. "My concern now is with the survival of my son and friends, not with the tsar's grace."

The east was graying, and the highest clouds powdering themselves pink. The battle would begin again, soon, and because of her, men would die. Listening to Nico's soft cooing, she found that she could accept that, so long as the right people lived.

Ben tunneled through the murk, feeling more like a mole than a fish, the lanthorn grasped in his teeth. Finding his way was easier than he thought; the rope in his vision was not there, but the marks where it had laid in the muck were clear. At the end of that wormy trail he would find Lenka, he was certain.

By the time he reached the end of the marks, he still had breath to spare, if not much. The problem was that the track led to what looked like a cellar door.

A closed cellar door.

For just an instant he hesitated; he might just barely be able to make it back to the canal. What if the door were locked from the other side?

He pushed on it, gently, but it stayed firm. He shoved harder. Now his lungs were starting to hurt, and he knew he had forfeited his chance to go back. Fighting panic—both his own and that which he had been poisoned with—he let drop the lanthorn, braced his back beneath the slanted doorway, steadied his feet on the step below him, and pushed with all his might. Black spots appeared in his eyes, and now his panic became all his, running out from his aching lungs, strengthening him as he strained once more.

More than a little rotten, the wood tore, and he burst up through it and another foot of water and was breathing again. The air was sweet, but not so sweet that he did not notice a man, some thirty feet away, pop-eyed and gaping in the flickering light, raising a pistol.

Snarling, Ben drew his sword and threw it, following it as fast as he could, water sucking at his legs. The man—seated on a small stool—cursed and scrambled away from flying steel, lost his balance and fell to one knee. The smallsword spanged against the wall behind him, and though he kept his pistol, he did not manage to get it back around in time to meet Ben's charge. Ben crashed into him, and the two of them smacked into the wall, the guard getting the worst of it. Ben got a brief impression of a roundish face and the stink of wine, felt the stranger's hard muscles writhe beneath him before the gun clubbed against the side of his head. Yowling, he jerked back, and a hand fastened onto the front of his face, clawing at his eyes. He punched weakly at his opponent's gut, and then, as nails dug around his eye sockets, drove a right fist into the fellow's throat. The claw on his face slackened, and Ben hit him again so hard that it felt as if his hand were broken. The man let go completely then, and Ben scrambled up. Seeing his opponent still trying to rise, Ben kicked him hard, once in the side of the head and once in the ribs.

The guard stopped moving, though he continued to breathe, and Ben spun wildly around, feeling a hundred other pistols aimed at him. But there were no other guards, and no place for them to hide either, and so he relaxed and finally let himself glance at the two figures chained to the far wall, a man and a woman.

"Lenka?" he said. "Lenka?" She was manacled with hands behind her back, blindfolded. The Indian was next to her, contorting, trying to get his feet up and through his arms so that his hands would be in front of him.

"Benjamin? Benjamin, is that you?"

He rushed over and nearly collapsed next to her, tugging the cloth from her eyes, stroking her hair. "Are you hurt? Lenka, did they hurt you?"

Her eyes were bloodshot, her hair bedraggled, her face smudged with dirt. He thought her the most beautiful woman he had ever seen. "No," she said. "No, Benjamin, I'm well. We have to hurry. There are more of these men."

"Lenka, I—I'm very glad to see you."

"And I you. But quickly!"

Ben nodded, a little chagrined, wondering where that perfect thing to say had gone. He returned to the guard and searched him, discovering a ring of keys in his coat pocket. He hurried back and tried them in Lenka's manacles until one fit and reluctantly turned. She shook her hands free, groaning.

"Thank you," she managed.

"Lenka—"

"Red Shoes," she muttered, crawling toward the Indian. She removed his blindfold, revealing haggard, dark eyes.

"*Merci,*" he mumbled, and then to Ben, "Many thanks. You are a brave man."

"I told you we would be freed," Lenka said, squeezing the Indian's hand.

Ben snapped out of his paralysis and unshackled Red Shoes.

"I am sorry for any discomfort I may have caused you," the Indian said, stretching his arms and trying to rise.

Ben stared at him without comprehension for a second, and then gaped. "You! You sent me the vision."

"Yes. I hoped you would understand."

"But *how*—"

"Please," Lenka said. "Please, talk later."

"Aye," Ben said. "Lenka, can you swim?"

"She is weak," Red Shoes said. "You must help her."

"And you?" But the vision surged through Ben again, and he knew that the Indian could not swim.

"I will follow you."

"But you can't—"

"I will follow you," Red Shoes insisted, his black eyes sparkling. "The rope is still there?"

"Yes."

"Take her, then."

Ben nodded. "I can come back and help you, too."

"No need."

Ben nodded and hurried to retrieve his sword. He eyed the gun, but saw no point in carrying it with him through the water. Besides, he had a pistol in the boat.

"Come on, then," he said to Lenka. "Hold around my neck."

She nodded, and they entered the water again. His fight with the guard had given him a febrile new strength, but it was now flagging, and he found even Lenka's slight form a burden, though one he bore gladly.

They came up, gasping, in the dark of the canal.

"Hassim!" he hissed.

"Here," came the answer, and a slender hand closed on his own. Treading water, he helped Hassim draw Lenka into the boat and then painfully dragged himself in, too, nearly upsetting the gondola. For a long moment, he could only lie back and draw labored breath.

"We go now?" Hassim asked.

"No," Ben managed, "one more coming."

"Yes, and someone there, too," Hassim said, gesturing. Down where another canal connected with the one they were in, the corner of a building was visible, illumined by an approaching light.

"Shh," Ben hissed, feeling around for his pistol. He found it, wishing he had enough light to check the prime, and cocked back the lock. A moment later, two gondolas came around the corner, lanthorns dangling from their jutting, ornamental prows. For an instant, his heart seized as it had when the Golem touched it, for beneath their black tricorns, the faces of the passengers were bone white with almost no features.

"That's them," Lenka gasped, even as the masked men began shouting. Ben did not know Italian, but he knew a curse when he heard one, and now he heard a string of them. He also noted them reaching into their dark cloaks.

"Hold!" Ben shouted, standing in the rocking craft, pistol pointed at the closest man, a fellow with a red plume in his hat that Ben guessed to be some mark of distinction. "Hassim, translate!"

"No translation is necessary," one of the masked men said.

"Well enough. Let me tell you who I am. I am Benjamin Franklin from Boston, the apprentice of Sir Isaac Newton, and I am the one with gun already drawn. You, sir—" he said, waving at a fellow in the back, shadowed, who seemed to be moving stealthily, "if you please, do not move, or I shall be forced to kill you."

"You can only shoot once," the English speaker said reasonably.

"Not so. This gun can shoot many times. Do you think that the man who invented the firedrake and the fervefactum cannot make a pistol that will fire more than once?"

He could not tell what effect this had, but he noted that the men in the boats seemed to have become quite statuelike.

"Now," Ben went on, "I've told you who I am. Let me tell you who you are. You are the men who wronged my friends."

"We do what we do for Venice," the fellow replied.

"Well, and here I would be saving your precious Venice were it not that I had to come and fetch my friends from the likes of you. Now, understand this: I don't really give a good God-rot-you who owns Venice in a few days, or whether she sinks into the sea—far less what happens to you clown-faced fellows. But at the moment, I do care; for I am her guest, and I do not want my accommodations moved to Muscovy. And so I will go back to defend your city, whilst you brave patriots skulk here in the dark after fierce young women to kidnap. You have my leave to go, my fellows."

"That won't do," the man said, reaching into his cloak.

"Well and good," Ben replied, and shot him clean in the face, smashing the mask below the nose and all his teeth besides. "Away," he snapped to Hassim, reaching for his other pistol, marveling at the luck of his shot. He was amazed at how cold and calm he felt.

A second gun—one of the enemy's—blazed in the narrow way, and Ben heard the bullet whine from one wall to the next. Hassim had begun working the oar when Ben pointed carefully, slowly, the way Robert had taught him, and fired again, producing a harsh gurgle from someone.

Then Ben turned on his aegis and tried to stand so as to shield Lenka and Hassim.

"Red Shoes—" Lenka shouted from behind.

"Later!" Ben grunted. "It'll have to be later!"

Then the real thunder began, and Ben had barely time to hope that the aegis would withstand a fusillade better than it had a single bullet back in Prague. Weirdly enough, it seemed that the shots somehow resounded, not just in the alleyway, but in the sky itself.

11

The Long Black Being

Red Shoes stretched his stiff muscles and glanced around the chamber, knowing that he didn't have long to prepare himself. The scent of his soul drifted thickly in the deeps surrounding him, and he had no place left to hide.

A pragmatic part of him noted the guard's fallen pistol, and he picked that up, taking his smallsword and dagger as well before manacling the unconscious man where he himself had been imprisoned a few moments before. That done, he righted the stool, sat on it, and began a chant.

> "Red Panther of the East
> Loan me your eyes,
> Loan me your strength,
> I stand amongst graves in the Darkening Land.
> I have need of you.
>
> "Red Peregrine of the East
> Loan me your sharp breast,
> Loan me your flint talons,
> The Imprecator names me in the Ghostland.
> I have need of you.
>
> "Red Thunder of the East
> Loan me your copper war club,
> Loan me your rattlesnake armbands,
> The Black Spider watches me from the Sundeath Country.
> I have need of you."

As he chanted, his ghost sight awoke. In his weakened state, it was hard not to be pulled entirely in, to forget about his mortal eyes—as had ancient Panther Dreaming in the village of Abika, who never remembered how to see the living world again, who mumbled constantly of things unseen and did not notice the drool on his own chin. Thus did *isht ahollo* die, when they died. Not the harsh, bright victory of a battlefield death, but the terrible unraveling of soul bereft of shadow.

Courage, he thought, and chanted a little more of the war song, the quickening song, the song for remembering the path. And now the spirit water engulfed him. He took it into his lungs and began to drown.

A ball of molten shot spattered red an inch from Ben's eyes, but the other projectiles twisted around him, struck sparks from the walls; and despite himself he laughed. Hassim had his stroke, now, and the gondola was gliding fast. As they turned the corner, their attackers remained stationary, frantically reloading their weapons or trying to doctor their companions. In the distance, titans still pounded on their drums. The attack on Venice was renewed.

"We have to go back for Red Shoes," Lenka insisted.

"We can't," Ben said. "I'm sorry. I'm grateful to him, for he helped me find you; and I swear that afterward, if I can, I will find him. But listen! The tsar is firing his cannon, and we do not want to *be* in Venice when he reaches her, I assure you. Never mind that I am sworn to be elsewhere at the very moment, that many more people are depending upon me. The Indian made his choice."

"He might not be able to swim. Did you think of that?"

"I thought of it," Ben snapped, angry at his own guilt—for he *knew* the Indian couldn't swim. "But if we go back, those men will kill us, do you see, and this will have all been for naught, for I'm *not* going to let you die."

A shaft of light glanced down from a high window, and her face appeared for a moment, determined, tear wet, astonished. "Listen," he said, "Red Shoes was ransomed, too. They won't do anything to him."

"You *shot* some of them," she said. "That might make them a bit unreasonable."

"What was I supposed to do?" Ben asked, exasperated. "Leave you to have bombs dropped on you? Hand you back to those nice fellows? Come, Lenka, with your sharp tongue, tell me what, in hindsight, I *should* have done!" He caught his breath for a sullen second. "And to think that I thought—" Then he checked himself, glad for the darkness, and took another deep breath, and another, relieved to have stopped short of making an even greater ass of himself.

"Thought what?" she asked.

"Nothing. Keep quiet—they might be following."

She did keep quiet, too, long enough for him to begin to regret himself. He was so tired, so worn—yet Lenka must have endured much more, chained in the dark for days.

"Listen," Hassim hissed, but Ben had already heard— Among the duel of giants, from back the way they had come, a sudden flurry of small gunfire echoed. Lenka gasped, but said nothing, and they traveled for a while in silence.

Drowning, he gazed into the stillness of a swamp, its water like iron in the last minutes of the sun's rays. Between the sinewed columns of cypress rose the inconstant green glow of fireflies, and the air creaked with frog songs and the disconsolate imprecation of a whippoorwill. He knew where he was: near the beginning of things. The obscure shadowed hill behind him was Nanih Waiyah, from whose caves the Choctaw had first emerged. It was a thin place on the skin of the Earth, saturated in the swamp his people called Lunsa, the Darkening.

Something across from the Darkening, grinning a faintly phosphorescent grin. It was as long and lean as a snake, nearly as sinuous, but as it emerged it unfolded narrow limbs—like a praying mantis or a walkingstick, with fingers as thin and sharp as porcupine quills. Its skin was not uniformly black, but mottled like a frog's, or even more like the tail of a peacock, darker and somehow more iridescent. As it towered over him, eyes blinked open in its palms, fingers, wrists, elbows, scattered across its torso, green as the fireflies with the vertical black pupils of a copperhead.

"I have been awaiting you, Long Black Being," Red Shoes said.

"Indeed?" The thing even sounded drawn thin, as if its voice were still under the earth and water, traveling up through a long pipe. "I thought you were hiding from me."

"Waiting. To meet you when *I* wished."

"What a pity. You seem to have failed."

"You are welcome to believe so," Red Shoes said. "Do you have anything to say before I kill you, Long Black Being?"

The spirit giggled, a remarkably childish and entirely chilling sound. "Only that you were warned. Only that you have betrayed us."

"I never betrayed you. You tried to claim me; I claimed you instead."

"You were chosen. It was not your place to refuse or twist our intent. You should have listened to the guide we sent you as a child. You should not have provoked *me* into coming. Now we can leave you nothing. We must empty you out and fill you up, that through you we may hunt others of your traitorous kind."

Red Shoes smiled wanly. "I do not think it will come to that, Long Black Being. Can you see into the living world, the world above?"

"This is the living world. Yours is naught but clay."

"Yes, yes. Can you see into my world? No, I think you cannot—or not well, not without human eyes."

"Make your point."

Red Shoes could feel the strength of the thing; it was beyond belief. And he was so weak. If it should strike, catch him with those claws, it would do as it said: wear his skin back to the land of the Choctaw and slay his kin. It would never come to that.

"Kwanakasha," he said, calling up the diminutive spirit from its prison. "Go kill that thing."

Kwanakasha seemed to sprout up from the ground between him and the Long Black Being. It still looked like a little man, but its face held both terror and anger. "I cannot kill a great one. You cannot set me upon him."

"I can and do," Red Shoes said. "You were the one who summoned him, yes? Who complained to him of your treatment? Well, I do not think that I will die alone, Kwanakasha. It is always sweeter to die with an enemy."

"Do not waste my time," the Long Black Being crooned. "It will only make me angrier."

"Yes," Kwanakasha pleaded. "Do not waste his time."

"I taught you some tricks," Red Shoes said. "Use them now, and perhaps both of us will live."

The Kwanakasha seemed to swallow its dismay. It clenched its eyes shut for a moment; and when it opened them, they were flame. It turned to face the monster.

"This is not of my choosing, master," the dwarf said.

"Then do not do it," the Long Black Being said.

"He is yet strong. But when you kill me, he will be without strength."

"Then I shall kill you," the creature said, whipping outward like a chain made of knives.

Kwanakasha darted forward with the speed of a musket ball. For Red Shoes, the scene became confused, for the appearance his mind made of them was not what they were, and the battle they fought was not of flesh and blood. Like hearing a slightly known language spoken too quickly, he could not sort it all out. They were whirlwinds, sparking wheels, joined and separate, braiding and unbraiding, knotting and, finally, tearing. In the end what he saw was Kwanakasha swallowed, moving down the throat of the Long Black Being like an egg down the length of a snake.

But in the meantime, Red Shoes had a moment to do what he now knew he must. He raised the pistol with both hands and placed the muzzle between his eyes.

"Another," Crecy said, peering through the spyglass, "the largest I've seen."

Adrienne turned to see what Crecy meant. The fleet proceeded with more caution now, and following her suggestions, used more prosaic means of detection. The biggest surprise that morning had brought had been the ships. While it was clear that most of the balloon bombs had been deployed from small craft, the real bases of operation were a number of large ships—ships of the line, sloops, caravels. More strange yet, they flew not Venetian or even Turkish standards but British and French ones.

It was one of these ships at which Crecy was now pointing. Straining to peer through the artificial fog, Adrienne saw two balloons of truly immense proportions inflating on the deck. They were attached to something she couldn't make out.

"What is it?" the tsar pressed.

"Captain, I do not know. Two more large balloons, that much is clear. But what they are attached to—"

"Can you render them quiescent, as you did the rest?"

"Yes, Captain."

"Do so then." He paused for an instant, his chin pressed hard into one fist. "Board that one," he grunted to one of his officers. "Send down the word. I want that ship boarded. I have a feeling . . ." He seemed vague for a moment, as if listening to distant music, and Adrienne suddenly noticed a malakus, almost imperceptible, drifting—no, rather, merged—with the tsar.

"Charles!" the tsar muttered.

Below, one of the ships dropped lower still. And then, quite suddenly, the balloons and their mysterious cargo vanished.

Charles XII stood fuming at the rail of the *Carolina Prophet* as Ben, Hassim, and Lenka arrived.

"I should kill you," he shouted down.

"Who will fly the *Madman* if you do that, Captain Frisk?" Ben retorted, catching the lines thrown to him.

"The only reason I don't shoot you!" Charles hurled back. "Even now, I doubt me that there is time!" He gestured at two of the hulking airships, moving toward them.

"Yes," Ben said, "but the balloons—" A flight of balloons lifting toward the underbellies of the airships paused just fifty feet from the surface and started to fall again. Men scrambled into the water as the first touched gently down, and then a fountain of flame obliterated the view.

"Sweet Jesus," he gasped. "They've some way of cooling the air!"

He was on deck by now. "Your Majesty, is the *Madman* loaded?" He could see the billowing, inflated envelope. So, certainly, could the Muscovites.

"Yes," Charles said impatiently.

"Then activate the aegis, now, and best tell Captain Teach to set sail!"

"It's only you we've been awaiting." But he shouted the order over his shoulder.

The ships were close, one high, one very low. Even as Charles spoke, so did the Russian cannon. The water around them was suddenly alive with spray, and the main sheet—halfway up, in preparation for sailing—suddenly burst into flame. A ball of fire appeared fifty feet away almost on the bow, flinging men from it like scraps of meat.

"Jesus," Ben swore again. "Lenka, with me! Hassim!" He reached down and hugged Lenka beneath her arms, lifting her onto the deck.

"Not on the *Madman*," Charles snapped. "We've no room."

"You'll make room unless you want to fly it yourself," Ben returned, leading Lenka across the rocking deck. "The *Prophet* is no safe place!"

Blackbeard met them halfway to the *Madman*.

Charles bowed to the pirate. "I thank you again, sir, for the use of your ship. You have done us all a great service."

Charles spoke in German, of course, and so Ben had to quickly translate. Blackbeard nodded grimly and gestured at the approaching Russian ships, looming lower each moment. "I don't know this new-fashioned aerial fightin', but I'll be damned if they don't look as if they want to board us. Get this Swedish king off my ship, Benjamin Franklin. I'll show these Moscovados the proper way to hell."

"I don't doubt you know it, Captain." Ben grinned.

"I'll see you there, one day, Franklin, never doubt it. Go, and show them up at their own game."

Ben nodded, and they jogged onto the afterdeck.

The *Madman* was a strange, hybrid thing: a light wooden frame, roughly the shape of a longboat, but covered in and out with taut, tough canvas. Her sails were two enormous silken envelopes. Whereas the smaller balloons had been inflated mostly by open flame, two scientifical furnaces had been found to give the *Madman* her lift. The furnaces changed the state of air passing through them, though more slowly then Ben would have liked; inflating and keeping the great balloons swollen had turned out to be a chore.

Of course, he could see none of this, for his command had gone ahead, and the aegis that he had cobbled together was in operation. He only hoped now that whatever science had been used to cool his balloons could not penetrate the unpredictable force, or the last hope of Venice was done.

As the three of them drew within a yard of the ship, the aegis suddenly twinkled out, revealing Robert and eight tough-looking men— four Swedes and four Janissaries. The ship itself, straining at the tethers, suddenly seemed to sag a bit.

"Hurry!" Ben boosted Lenka into the craft, but Hassim hung back. "Come, Hassim. Things will be very hot on the *Revenge* in a moment or two."

"Yes," he said. "And Hassim stay here to fight."

"No. Come on," he repeated, but when Hassim shook his head, he wasted no more time debating, but just stuck out his hand, gave Hassim's a brisk shake, and then leapt into the ship.

"About goddamn time," Robert snapped.

"Had business." Ben grunted, gesturing at Lenka. "Cut the lines."

The sun suddenly turned prism. The boat shook gently as the mooring cables were cut, then more fiercely as the Muscovite cannon spoke again. The *Prophet*, her cannon upslung in hastily modified carriages, replied, and the world became smoke.

The *Madman* was not lifting.

"They cooled us, somehow," groaned Ben.

"Boarders!" Charles shouted tightly. "They're dropping them down on ropes!"

The distinctive rattle of murder guns cut over Charles' proclamation, small-bore cannon spitting clouds of molten lead, followed an instant later by clashing of steel. Ben did his best to ignore all that, struggling instead with the small firedrake mounted near the prow.

"Help me, damn it!" he shouted. Robert was already there, and now one of the Swedes, who was assisting him in wrenching the alchemical weapon from its mount. Shadows wrestled in the corner of his eye, one of which had to be Blackbeard, by the bellowing it produced. They got the drake—a thing like a cannon some two feet long—positioned and aimed straight up the silken canopy.

"It'll burn it!" Robert snapped.

"Maybe yes, maybe no," Ben replied. "But experimentation is the essence of science." He pulled the trigger, and a jet of blue flame hurled itself up into the envelope. Ben gasped on a mouthful of air so hot it burned his lips and singed his eyelashes. The *Madman* shuddered, her prow lifting and swinging aimlessly. He pulled the trigger again, and at the same instant something struck the *Madman* so hard that she flipped nearly over, a deafening explosion ringing their ears. The firedrake rocked in his grip and the sulfurous jet ran up against the silk envelope.

"G'd rot it," Ben cursed, but then caught himself. Though blackened and smoking, the envelope was not aflame. What's more, with excruciating slowness, the *Madman* finally began to rise.

"Well done," Charles shouted, barely audible over the roaring of guns.

"Aye, and thank you," Ben replied. "And now all we have to do is find a wind to blow us to a Muscovite ship, invade her with our compliment of eleven, and use her to blow the rest of these out of the sky."

"No more than that," Charles replied soberly.

Ben stared at the king, and it occurred to him that Charles of Sweden might be more insane than he was brave.

"Holy God," Robert breathed, staring down. In rising they had just missed bumping into the descending Muscovite ship, and now it nearly eclipsed the *Revenge*. Even through the rainbow distortion of the aegis, they could see soldiers pouring over the rails. Above them and around them, the circle of flying ships closed like a noose around Venice.

Charles stood, despite the swinging of the boat.

"We are invisible to them?" he asked.

"Barely visible, I should say," Ben replied.

Charles held a finger in the air, shook his head, and turned instead to watch the smoke below. "They sail against the wind and we with it," he murmured. "And so we should meet one of them. A most happy circumstance indeed. Keep near the harpoons, men."

Ben settled the drake firmly on the deck and turned to arm himself from the small arsenal on board, wondering what sort of circumstance Charles would not find "happy." He supposed it would be one with no risk of painful death.

Red Shoes tightened his finger on the trigger at the same moment that Long Black Being flashed toward him, and for one instant feared he would not be quick enough. Perhaps he would not have been, save that something—a sort of silvery needle—appeared, impaling the monster, slowing it fractionally while he squeezed the trigger. The prime hissed in the pan and he understood that he had drawn his last breath. Then something slapped him—hard—the gun exploded, and for an instant he heard music before his head thudded against the wall.

At first, he thought his body was shuddering, the way he had seen a deer shudder when shot, but then he realized that someone was shaking him. His ghost vision faded, and he saw Tug's ugly face an inch from his own. Something burned along the side of his head, before the dream drew him back to Nanih Waiyah, to the swamp.

The Lond Black Being was gathering itself up to strike, but not at him. Rather, its target was an old man, all in black and white. He stood straight but noticeably shaking, a thin line of blood trickling down his face. He held something bright in his hand, like a star with long rays.

Cotton Mather. Red Shoes could hear him praying, both with his real ears and with those of his shadow.

"Deceiver!" the reverend shrieked, as the monster laughed at him and attacked; and again the strange turbulence of shadow combat. How had Mather, a white man, learned to do this thing, to impress his substance into the ghost realm? He remembered the preacher's talk of witches and science, of the "invisible world" and its nature. Had Mather been shown the way here by his God or his Science? Or were they the same, after all? However he had gotten here, two things were clear: He had somehow harmed the Long Black Being—and he was losing the battle.

Red Shoes balled up what little strength remained in him, crushed it down, concentrated it with anger until it flamed, emptying more and more of himself, becoming a cave of flesh. All of his shadowchildren, Kwanakasha he had imprisoned so long ago—all gone, save one bright point of life, burning so fiercely now it could last only moments before his soul and shadow shook free. It was the worst and the best thing he had ever known, anguish and rapture bound so tightly he could not tell them apart. In that moment, he saw what he could do. As the Long Black Being fell again upon the faltering Mather, Red Shoes stepped up and swallowed it as it had swallowed Kwanakasha, filled himself with it, and then tightened, tightened, before it could understand what he had done.

When it understood, it was like a wildcat inside him, trying to chew out; but he constricted himself, his shadow swelling with stolen strength. He crushed the places where its awful dark thoughts crawled, until they went out, one by one, like the embers of a fire. Until its soul was dead and its shadow was his.

It seemed like years had passed, but Tug still had hold of him. He was crushed against the big man's chest, and the pirate was weeping. "Tug . . ." he managed. "I can't breathe."

Tug thrust him back, his eyes widening. "Y'r alive!"

"Sorry to disappoint you."

"You shot yerself in the damned head, y' idyot! If I hadn't a' slapped you, the ball would a gone straight into y'r teeny Indian brain 'stead o' scootin' along yer skull like so." He tapped a scorch mark along Red Shoes' scalp.

They were still in the place where he and Lenka had been held. Fernando stood by nervously, cutlass drawn. Two other men—Nairne and a young Janissary—stood over Mather's body.

"How did you come here?"

"I heard that Boston boy talking to the cap'n. Told 'im you was held here. We followed Franklin as best we could, be he lost us in the canals till we heard the gunfire. We came around the corner an' found some fellows in a boat. Killed all but one, but he told us what we wanted to know."

"Thank you, Tug."

The big man shifted, embarrassed. "Han't like I don't owe you a turn or two. Hell, all the boys feel that way."

"Mather?"

"Damned if he didn't insist on comin'. He kept jabbering about Satan an' angels and whatnot."

"Let me over to him."

Mather's eyes were open, but he didn't seem to see much. When Red Shoes took his hand, he understood the touch and squeezed, hard.

"I defeated it?" he managed.

"Yes, Reverend."

"I feel such despair."

"It will pass. I did not know you had such power."

"No one is pure, no one perfectly good." Mather gasped. "Jesus Christ knows my sins. He knows I let myself be deceived. For all of my talk, it was my own desire . . ." His pupils were pinpricks. He turned his eyes upward to the dark ceiling, or perhaps the heaven he envisioned beyond.

"The invisible world has always been my armor against doubt," he whispered. "It is the unseen that gives faith. If there are devils, there must be a God, and if there are evil angels, then good ones as well. So I thought, though my church does not preach it. But I could not believe, you see, that the angels of light had all left the Earth. I fasted, and I prayed, and the good angel came to me."

His breath whistled harshly for several moments.

"Jesus," breathed Tug.

"Yes, Jesus," Mather whispered. "The angel said it had been sent by Jesus, to answer my questions, to defend me against the devils. They killed my child, the demons did—I proved it scientifically, you see, I knew they incited against me. I fasted, and I prayed. . . ."

"It was with you all along, hidden in you, hidden in your skin." Red Shoes understood. As it was now hidden in his, albeit on different terms. The sheer power, to disguise itself in the very shadow of a man.

"It is gone now."

"It told me. . . ." He blinked, slowly, like a tired lizard, his voice very queer, *"Behold, he was a Cedar in Lebanon, with fair branches, and with a shadowing shroud, and his top among the thick bows."*

Red Shoes noticed the device curled in Mather's hand. It was difficult to tell what it was, since black, cracked fingers stuck to it. "And this? In your hand?" he asked softly.

"God showed me the way," Mather answered faintly. "Through science. In my experiments with the girls afflicted, I discovered that the evil spirits could be rendered scientifically sensible, and, moreover, affected through the medium of the philosopher's mercury." He gasped. "I think I will see my lord Jesus soon," he finished, and then, weeping, "but no, for I was deceived. I was taken in by a devil. Ah, God, forgive my pride." He gurgled, and then, almost singing, he said, *"The waters made him great, the Deep set him up on high with rivers running about his plants. His height—his height was—exalted—"* His back suddenly arched high, and spittle flew from his mouth. "Oh, God, I see—I see—" He sounded terrified.

"If I were stronger—" Red Shoes began. In fact, he could feel a deep, hard power in him, but it was nothing he knew how to use. He could not help Mather as the old man's face slackened and his eyes dulled. "Heaven?" he mumbled, and then a slurred mewling.

"What's wrong with 'im?" Tug asked in hushed tones.

"He is dead," Red Shoes answered.

"He still breathes!" Tug grunted.

Red Shoes shrugged. "He is dead, I promise you. The only mercy now is to free him from his body."

Tug looked uneasy. "I don't know . . ."

"Look away," Red Shoes whispered, realizing that he was weeping. "I will do it, and I will make it quick."

And so he did.

12.

The Tears of God

Ben fired the drake back up the envelope, cursing himself for not realizing that the little furnaces did not produce enough hot air for rapid rising. If he had thought of the drake earlier, it might have been mounted, sparing him singed eyebrows and all of them the danger of conflagration. He also wished there had been time enough to test the vehicle and practice in it; it was most difficult to gauge the affect of the drake-warmed air. Whereas he had meant to continue their ascent at a steady rate, his last firing of the flaming weapon had sent them bolting upward, making it clear that they would not pass close enough to their intended target, a rather small airship on their right.

"Never mind, anyway." Charles grunted, waving at the higher sky. "I'll wager that the loftiest is also the command ship. The tsar's ship. Steer us there."

"The problem, sir, is in the *lack* of steering," Ben remarked. "We can climb—and fall as the air cools—but otherwise we suffer the vagaries of the wind."

"We need only come near enough to sink in a harpoon," Charles noted. "Some sixty yards. Can you manage that?"

Ben gauged the distance. If they rose just a tiny bit faster, it might be possible. He fired the drake again, trying not to think of what would happen should he be successful. "I'm sorry, Lenka," he said. "I wasn't thinking clearly. I've taken you from one fire to the next."

She shook her hair back. Her face was drawn and pale in the morning light, but her eyes held an unmistakable excitement. "Never mind, Benjamin, for I'm guessing that there is no safe place right now." She smiled wryly.

"Just you keep your head low, Lenka, for I've no desire to have your being hurt on my conscience."

"My, how my life has changed since meeting you," she murmured.

"For better or for worse?"

She laughed and replied, "For richer and for poorer."

Ben had an even wittier reply, but he lost it as the Russian ships suddenly filled the sky and the *Madman* rocked from the recoil of her three-harpoon-gun broadside.

"I keep losing it," Adrienne complained.

"It distorts the aether," Vasilisa said. "Doesn't it?"

"Aether, light, gravity—all wrap around and vanish. My djinni cannot retain sight of it."

"Sir Isaac had such a device," Vasilisa said, "but I was never able to examine it. Do you even roughly know where it might be?"

"In the air," Adrienne confirmed. "Whatever it is, in the air, I . . . Did you feel that?"

"Yes." Crecy grunted. "Something struck our hull."

The tsar began bellowing orders in Russian, and musketeers came along the rails. Adrienne was a bit taken aback at how few troops seemed actually to be on the flagship, but reflected that it did make a sort of sense. They expected to be safe, far above the action, while the bulk of the men were needed for the ground assault. But nothing seemed to have gone in accordance with the tsar's plans, and she feared that this was no exception.

Something bounced violently from the deck next to her, a musket. She stared at it for an instant before looking up. She saw two ropes standing up from the side of the ship, fastened to thin air.

The soldiers around her made this out at more or less the same moment, and suddenly the muzzles of muskets, pistols, *kraftpistoles*, and murder guns all began to shout heavenward, and the sky cracked open.

———

The harpoons bit and the balloon continued to rise, swinging them over the prow and yanking the *Madman* so that her deck was halfway to vertical. Ben hung on and gaped; fifty feet below him lay the deck of the Russian ship, soldiers lining its rails. Quite near, strangely, were three women: a redhead and two brunettes. One of the brunettes seemed familiar.

Then someone—one of the Swedes—cursed, and a musket dropped for what seemed like a long time to the deck of the ship below.

"Ready?" Charles asked.

He was answered by Muscovite guns. The ship's aegis held a few seconds, and then suddenly flashed white and was gone. Ben had the presence of mind to activate his own, hoping Robert had done the same as the balloon shredded apart above them, and they dropped laconically toward the deck.

He turned to Lenka, saw the blood, and realized that she, of course, had no aegis at all.

As they crashed into the Russian deck, Charles managed to fire the murder gun, and Ben saw perhaps ten of the green-uniformed men collapse in the mist of molten metal. He drew his own *kraftpistole* and began to fire, screaming.

Brick and tile fell like rain, the flesh and bone of Venice, chewed and spit up by Russian bombs. The air shuddered with what seemed a single explosion gone on and on. The airships had reached Venice at last, and they were making her pay for her resistance. Red Shoes hardly cared. Better that such a place never existed; better it return to the deeps.

The Venetians had a different opinion, that was clear. From every wall and rooftop, the Janissaries fired cannon, pistol, musket, murder gun, firedrake, *kraftpistole*, and even crossbow, to no obvious effect. The ships dropping the bombs came in high, though some could now be seen approaching at lower altitudes, presumably so that they could disgorge ground troops in the areas already bombed clear of resistance.

"God almighty," Tug shouted, pointing across the water.

It was the *Prophet*. One of the airships sat practically on her mast, and her deck swarmed with green figures. Red Shoes made out Black-beard, fighting on the forecastle, shrugging men off him right and left.

"Faster," Tug urged. "We have to get there."

Red Shoes wearily felt for the ax at his belt, wondering how long he would last. At least he would die in battle, and not as Mather had.

As they drew nearer, their hearts sank. The surviving crew of the *Prophet* and their Janissary allies—perhaps ten men—had drawn into a clump near Blackbeard. The pirate was streaked and spotted scarlet from head to toe, but there was no telling how much of it was his own blood. While they watched, the giant staggered as a pistol was fired into his chest, point-blank. His bellow was audible, even at that distance. Teach decapitated the offending attacker, and then, as if not content with the place he had chosen to die, suddenly began charging forward. Those with him fell in behind him, cheering, and for an instant they made headway, cutting a steady, bloody lane through the sea of attackers. But where were they going? To the side of the ship, to jump overboard?

Nairne understood first.

"The fervefactum!" he gasped.

"The what?" Red Shoes asked.

"It's hanging beside the poopdeck there, you see? Covered with a cloth."

Red Shoes wanted to ask what a fervefactum was; but at that moment, Nairne stood, aimed, and fired his pistol. Tug and Fernando followed his example.

"Go, Cap'n!" Tug shouted. "Go, ye great, bloody bull!"

The fighting converged on the tarp-covered device, swirled in confusion for a moment, and then stopped, rather suddenly, when every man on the ship suddenly fell to the deck as if their legs had been cut from under them. A hundred inhumanly tortured cries rose up beneath the belly of the Russian ship.

"A siege weapon," Nairne muttered, voice shaking, "It boils blood. We loaded her on board last night."

"For what?" Red Shoes asked, staring at the shipful of dying men. "It kills all alike."

"We had a different plan— *Mother of God.*"

A shuddering figure had arisen from the dead and dying, smoke from the matches in his hair and beard mingling with the steam rising from eyes and mouth. He swung his cutlass once, twice. Two of the cables holding the massive machine slackened, and for an instant it remained, slanting, on the persistent restraints. Then a third cable snapped, a fourth—the rest, and it plunged into the water.

"Oh, God, hold tight," Nairne said.

And then the sea itself seemed to lift from her bed, throwing herself in a boiling column, up through the *Revenge*, up through the Russian ship. Red Shoes had time to see the airship spin and flip completely over before the bottom bloom of shock and steam struck the longboat back toward burning Venice like the fist of a thunder god.

"Tsar!" Charles shouted. "Tsar!" Lightning crackled from his unseen *kraftpistole*, igniting three green uniforms. Ben stood straddling Lenka's body. His own *kraftpistole* had given up the ghost after four shots, its supply of catalyst exhausted. Now he jabbed his sword viciously into the chest of an approaching Russian. The young man looked astonished and horrified, struck as he had been by an unseen ghost. Somehow angered by that pitiful expression, Ben ran him through the heart and watched him fall.

They were doomed. Each of the men on board the *Madman* had been equipped with alchemical weapons and protections—aegis and adamantium—but already three of the hastily built shields had failed. Janissary and Swede alike fought like devils, but there were too many Russians. It had always been a desperate plan, Ben knew, with little likelihood of success, but he had imagined somehow that he would not actually be here. After finding Lenka he should have followed his normal custom and run, rowed for the mainland, hoped for the best. Fortune usually favored Benjamin Franklin when he lived close to his wits and far from his courage. How was it he had not thought to flee?

His brain had tricked him again. Looking down at Lenka's bleeding form, he wondered if she were already dead.

A fierce hail of fire erupted nearby, and two more men became visible as their aegises failed. One of them was Charles, who still wore a breastplate of shimmering adamantium. His broadsword rose and fell like a terrible machine, surrounding him in a cyclone of blood.

Four men attacked Ben then, apparently having noted his faint appearance when he slew their comrades. Heavy swords slashed at his aegis and were deflected, but the sheer force of their attack was communicated to him, and he went back beneath them, managing to stab one in the belly before they all crashed into the deck together. He winced away from a blow that should have cut his face in half at the bridge of his nose, struggling to free his trapped arms.

One, two, three men fell away from him, as another blur intersected them. "Ben?" someone shouted. It was Robert.

"Yes, it's me. Thanks to you, Robin."

"This is a rout, Ben. We've got to get away."

"What? Where to?"

"We might hide."

"But Lenka—"

"They won't kill her if she isn't dead."

"But Charles—"

"A madman."

Charles was still on his feet, back-to-back with one of the Janissaries, fighting ten men. As many Muscovites were closing warily on Ben and Robert.

"I think we will not be able to hide, Robin. I think that we will have to kill them all."

He felt pressure at his back and knew that his friend stood there. "Well enough," Robert said.

"You've been a dear friend, Robin, better than ever I deserved—"

"Shut up y'r overeducat'd mouth, Ben Franklin," Robert said. "Save y'r breath for fighting."

Adrienne found herself swept away from the skirmish in a press of the tsar's personal guard, frustrating her attempts to organize her djinni in any concerted counterassault. Their attackers wore the same sort of aetheric armor, as had their balloon; but since she could make out where they were, they were more vulnerable. If, that is, the damned soldiers would release her.

Suddenly she got her wish, as the outer shock of a murder gun struck them. Three of her protectors dropped, groaning, and she was suddenly free. Through the melee she saw Nico's basket spinning across the deck, and screamed, clawing her way toward him.

She noted the blur coming toward her almost too late, understood in the same flash that he was probably moving past her and toward the tsar. But she was in his way, and the blast of the *kraftpistole*, while it did not touch her skin, seared her lungs. She staggered. Then Crecy was there, of course, her broadsword a liquid arc. As Adrienne put her back to the rail and gulped the cool sea air, her Lorraine guards were suddenly around her, a phalanx, supporting her.

Crecy's unseen foe scored a blow on her cheek, marring the perfection of her face, and Adrienne felt filled up with murder. This man was between her and Nico! He had hurt Crecy! But even before she could react, Crecy beat viciously against the unseen, again, again — and suddenly, in a flash of light, there he was, a stone-jawed Swede twice her size, gray eyes shining with malice. Visible, Crecy's sword took him in less than two seconds.

"Nico!" Adrienne shouted, gesturing. She could just see the basket, a few yards past Crecy, his little head peering curiously out. He was still alive! She opened her hand and called her djinni, for now that she had seen the shield fail, she knew how to make the rest fail as well. At the same time, she began to press toward her son, her guard around her.

But then the aether filled with a most peculiar shrieking, a horrible cacophony of mingled triumph and pain. It took only an instant to understand what was happening. Above her, the globes which held the ifrit were unraveling. In seconds they would begin to fall — she, Crecy, the tsar, Nico. . . .

It was a very long way down.

Grimly, she reached up to the ifrit. "Keep to your task," she commanded.

"Lady, you do not command us," one shot back. "Our restraints are gone, and we fly."

"They are not yet gone," she replied. In an instant they would be, however. What was happening? And then she saw the unraveling harmonic that spoke to the globes above them. It was strong, subtle, perfect, the hand of a maker unmaking.

She threw the weight of her servants around the globes, adjusting, probing, adding her own voices to the disruptive harmony until it no longer had any effect.

She could not do it for long. Despite the strain, she opened her mortal eyes and saw what she had expected.

Hercule, she thought, despairing. *Not you, too.*

Red Shoes clung to the capsized boat, gazing at a sky gone more than weird, even in his ghost vision. Something stronger than he had ever seen before was stretching its grasp over that sky. No, not one something, but two, locked in combat.

He was very, very tired. He barely blinked when the Russian airships began to fall from the heavens, conjuring only enough energy to hope one did not fall upon him.

Ben managed to send three more men down before his aegis failed, and then he set his jaw grimly, for he knew that he could match not even the least swordsman if they could see him. There weren't actually that many Russians left in the fray. Most had withdrawn across the deck, presumably to protect the officers, or the tsar if he really was aboard. Others seemed fascinated by something over the rail. This only angered Ben the more—they should at least be *watching* when he died.

The three men he still faced grinned almost in unison when he appeared, happy to see the devil they had been fighting was really hardly more than a boy with little clear idea how to hold a sword. But almost immediately, their expressions changed, eyes drawn up as if to an angry God, and they scrambled away from him with the same unanimity with which they had smiled. Swaying, Ben watched them go, puzzled. Charles, back against the rail, side to side with a Janissary, also gawked, then redoubled his attack. He caught one blade in the palm of his hand, cut its wielder's neck so viciously that the head flopped over like a marionette at the end of an act. In two more blows he was free, hurling himself toward Ben.

I don't understand, Ben thought.

Then a rope ladder hit him in the face, and he, too, looked up. A small airship stood ten feet over him, Newton's concerned face looking down from the rail.

"Take hold," Newton shouted. "The talos will pull you up. You are safe for the moment." A chorus of muskets barked, balls whining harmlessly away as if to underscore that point.

"Lenka!" he shouted up. "I won't go without her!"

Newton pursed his lips in annoyance, and then nodded curtly. In the next moment, the silvery body of the talos leapt into view, falling gently to the deck. He took up Lenka in his arms.

"Climb," Robert gasped.

He did, struggling up the ladder. When he dragged himself over the rail, Newton clasped him. "I'm sorry, my boy," he said. "I've tried to make it up to you."

"You might have helped sooner—" Ben began, but then he saw the sincere pain in his mentor's eyes, and he stopped and returned the embrace. Behind him, Charles and the Janissary followed Robert onto the ship, even as the talos settled back onto the deck, Lenka limp in his arms. Groaning, Ben rushed to her. There was so much blood that he could not tell what sort of wound it was, or even exactly where—somewhere in her abdomen, it seemed. Blood bubbled from her nostrils, so she was still breathing.

"We must go," Newton said. "And quickly. There is something here I do not understand. The ship below us should have fallen by now."

"What do you mean?"

"The rest have already fallen," Newton explained, as the ship swiftly rose. "I saved this one for last, but something interrupts the process."

"I thought you said it was too dangerous, this process."

Newton didn't answer, but instead said, "You remember how to steer this ship?"

"Yes, sir."

"Do so. I must see to the talos."

The creature now stood in the bow of the ship; Newton stepped up behind it and placed his hands against its back, and suddenly a sort of sheen—not like the aegis, but a silvery film—sprang up around them.

Adrienne gnashed her teeth in frustration; her servants were failing, and there seemed nothing she could do about it. They had managed to reach Nico's basket—and Crecy had tight hold of it—and so, finally, she could stop dividing her efforts. She stared at the ship above them almost curiously, at the strange gray-blue automaton—the source of the lethal harmony. It was a sort of djinn, but more powerful, more focused than any she had ever seen before. And it was something else, too, something familiar. . . .

The entire ship lurched as one of its supporting globes disintegrated and the captive ifrit went howling free. She grasped after the willful spirit, but her control was stretched thin maintaining the others. Crecy seemed to be shaking her, but she ignored her, seeking the answer, the sum. How could the—thing—be familiar?

She could not fail. If she failed, Crecy and Nico would die, and her own hopes would be at an end.

Another globe went, and the deck jolted to a peculiar angle. From the corner of her eye, she saw Crecy slam into the deck, still gripping the wire hoops at the top of the hamper. She and Nico fetched against the rail and hung there, as the boat tilted farther and farther. A terrible thing broke loose in Adrienne then, something so far beyond fury that it had no name. She drew her djinni to heel beneath her feet and around her hips, and compelled a wind from them, wings to bear her up, for in that instant of clear-eyed rage, she saw everything. The automaton was like her hand—a chime, a pathway, a universalizer. It was a tool, the man behind it the real power. And yet, there was also a resistance between them, a reluctance, perhaps even anger. . . .

Then she laughed, an utterly humorless laugh that was as much agony as anything else, and she reached with her hand and twisted a single unguarded constant, changed one small harmonic. Then, her will spent, she fell.

As she hit the still-tilted deck, she had a glimpse of Nico's basket, floating languidly out into space. He was waving at her.

———

"There went a second globe," Robert chortled. "Whatever he's doing, it is virtuous!"

"No other ships remain aloft!" Charles said, his voice strangely humble. "What—"

"Enough of that," Ben snapped. "One of you see to Lenka. Please, I must—" He knew he could leave the complicated tiller for a moment, but he could not bear it if Lenka died in front of him. Besides that, he had no medical knowledge at all.

In the end, it happened incredibly fast. Ben had a glimpse of a woman in a dress as blue as lightning, black hair cascading around her lovely ivory face like a thunderhead, one hand an actinic slice of starlight. He heard her laugh, a perfect, cold laugh of absolute malice. She was floating in the air. Her fingers spread wide, and Newton screeched, and then the talos turned and seized him.

"Ah, God, no!" Newton wailed. "Benjamin, I've lost—" The talos gave Newton's head one sharp twist; Ben heard the bones of the neck crack like lighter knot popping on a fire. Then, quite casually, the talos tossed Sir Isaac Newton into the morning air, and, as if in afterthought, leapt after him. Ben lurched to the rail and watched them fall, a spot of blood, a dot of gray, until they were lost to the distant, yellow sea. He stayed there until Robert dragged him gently back to the tiller, for they were rising fast and aimlessly. The Muscovite ship dropped off steeply shoreward.

I have no tears to weep, Ben thought, watching the pearly clouds gathering above. *I have no tears. They are gone, and no science can bring them back.*

But moments later, a gentle rain began, and Ben thought, bitterly, that though God seemed to have few other virtues, he had tears enough for them all.

13.

A Bundle of Arrows

Ben stood for some time, gathering his courage, listening to the ululating song of a mullah filtering into the long hall and, as if in counterpoint, the tolling church bells above. Did God care whether he was beseeched by way of bell or song? Probably not. And for the moment, to all appearances, neither did Venice, for the balance of her inhabitants—Catholic, Protestant, Mussulman, Jew—were in celebration over the victory against the Muscovites, whatever differences they might have amongst themselves for the moment set aside. For the first time in almost two decades, the city was free, ready to govern herself.

Ben wished her well.

He had gathered all the courage he could, he realized. Sighing, he pushed the door open, bowing to the nun who greeted him.

Lenka was as pale as the lilies surrounding her, and as beautiful. His breath caught unnaturally in his chest as he approached her still form and knelt, hoping his heart would survive.

Gently, fearfully even, he touched her cheek.

She stirred, and her eyes fluttered open, confused for only an instant when she saw his face. "Where is this?" she asked, flicking her gaze from side to side.

"A convent," Ben replied. "You've been rather unwell, and the sisters here have been tending you."

"Unwell?"

"A musket ball pierced your belly."

"Indeed?" She rose up to look, then winced. The nun—only a few feet away, and quite watchful—snapped something rather stern in Italian.

"Am I going to live?"

"It seems so."

"Oh. Well, that is good. How long have I slept?"

"Almost two days." He paused significantly. "We won, of course."

"Of course." She frowned a bit. "That Indian—"

"Red Shoes is safe and sound," Ben replied.

"Good. I remember riding up in the balloon—"

Ben laughed harshly. "Yes, I remember that, too. It becomes very confusing thereafter, but I will try to tell you about it later. They say now you are still weak, and can stand visitors in small doses only."

"Doubtless I could stand visitors other than you in larger quantities," she replied, a devilish spark in her eyes.

"Doubtless. You see, already I tire you."

"Yes. You promise that I am not dying?"

"I promise."

"Good. So Venice is saved. What happens now, Benjamin Franklin?"

"Now?" He shifted uncomfortably. "Now I go home. To America. To Boston."

She blinked at him, and he plunged on. "This is no place for me, this Old World. There is so much that needs to be done, so much that must be understood. How can I accomplish anything here, with this war or that war always interfering? They tell me that America is quieter, at least for the moment. And they need me there."

She nodded. "Very well," she said.

"Very well?"

"Yes." She yawned. "I tire now, Benjamin. But I need to tell you something quietly, if you would lean close."

"Yes?" he said, bending his head.

"Closer, you fool," she muttered.

He bent nearer still, and her lips brushed his cheek. They felt like the warm petals, immeasurably sweeter than a lily. "And what shall I do in America?" she asked very gently.

Ben swallowed hard and found that he did, after all, have the courage he needed. "I suppose," he replied, "that you might consent to be my bride."

"You suppose quite a lot," she said.

He kissed her on the lips, then, carefully. They tasted very sweet indeed, until the nun tugged him up—much less gently—by his hair. Lenka did not notice; she had fallen asleep, her lips still pursed for kissing.

Adrienne lurched against the rail, trying to stay upright, trying to see, to *see*. But there was nothing.

"You must come away," Hercule said. "You must rest."

"He is alive," she managed. "My son is alive."

"You determined that his guardian spirits are not," he reminded her gently.

"I know what I said. They are gone. But he is not. Tell the tsar I will search more."

"He—" Hercule touched her shoulder lightly. "He has already given the command to return to Saint Petersburg. We are under way."

"I will remain, then."

"He will not let you."

"I saved his fleet. Does he think he can stop me?"

Hercule was silent for a long moment. "Crecy said—"

"Crecy!" she managed to snarl.

"You should speak to her."

"I cannot."

"You must." Crecy's voice came, from behind. "If you want to see him again, you must. He is not here, Adrienne."

Adrienne spun too quickly, so that her exhausted body failed her. Only Hercule saved her from joining Nico over the rail. "You let him go! You released him!"

Crecy trembled visibly. "I did not. I *had* him. I would have fallen and died before I let him go. He was *taken* from me, Adrienne. He was . . ." And then tears started in her eyes. She clenched her jaw and then went on, voice quaking. "The *malfaiteurs*. They made use of your basket and took him."

Adrienne broke free of Hercule, staggered toward Crecy. "Why?" she rasped. "Where have they taken him?"

"I don't know. I only felt them at the end."

"You were *one* of them!" She slapped Crecy so hard that a red handprint remained on her pale cheek. "What do they want with my son, Crecy?" She knew her voice had taken on a note of hysteria, but it seemed a somehow distant thing. Crecy, eyes sparkling with pain, shook her head again. Adrienne hit her again, and again, and then with both fists, while Crecy did nothing but absorb the blows, until her broken lips smeared Adrienne's hand sanguine, and Adrienne collapsed, sobbing, into the redhead's arms.

"Crecy . . ." she murmured. And for the first time they cried together, salt of blood and tears mingling, intertwined like their fingers.

Red Shoes stood at the rail of the *Scepter*, watching fragments of the sun sink into the waters, and found he no longer feared Venice, or the underneath.

"It'll be good to go home," Tug said from nearby.

"Indeed it will," Red Shoes replied.

"What'll y' do there?"

"Go back to my people. Tell them all I have seen." He smiled at the big man. "Take you with me, if you want. Show you what a Choctaw woman looks like."

"I would'n mind it," Tug said.

"What *have* you seen?" Nairne asked, from his right.

Red Shoes smiled at the white man. "I really don't know," he said truthfully. "But I know this: Our folk go into the future together, whether we like it or no. Our destinies are bound, I think."

"Are they?"

Red Shoes nodded. "I know what you are thinking—that my people might try to push you back into the sea. A good time for it, too. Would England send troops to fight us? France? Spain? I don't believe so."

Nairne nodded grimly.

"But I will advise against it."

"May I ask why?"

"It's the story of the bundled arrows. A single arrow can be easily snapped. A bundle of arrows held together cannot." He looked out at the distant horizon. "If I am not wrong, we shall need every arrow we can find to face what is coming."

And in his shadow, something dread stirred, as if to confirm his words.

Ben had coffee with Robert and King Charles in a room flooded with sunlight and the scent of honey. The monarch poured, left-handed— his right thickly bandaged from having grasped a living blade.

"Well, my good Captain Frisk," Ben inquired, "what plans have you now?"

Charles shrugged. "I am a soldier," he remarked, "and I have always sworn I would never shrink from a just war."

"So you pursue the tsar back to his cold homeland?"

Charles raised his cup in salute. "I do not shirk, but I do rest. For now, I've made promises to Venice and I will keep them."

"You will reign here as monarch, then?"

Charles laughed sharply but with real humor. "There will be no monarch in Venice," he said. "They will not have one. The Janissaries hold their own council and distrust strong leaders, and the Venetians are no better. For near a thousand years Venice was a republic, and now they will be a republic again."

"Now see, this is what I was talking about earlier, Your Majesty," Ben said. "When I said that the age of kings was over. It's time for men to rule themselves."

"Yes, we said we would return to this conversation again, didn't we?" Charles said. "But I won't debate a philosopher. Perhaps you are indeed correct. But in my own experience, men have little faith in themselves. It takes a strong man to accept both the responsibility and the blame for his own actions, and few are equal to the task. Most would rather have a king—even a foolish one like me—make their decisions for them. It isn't kings that must change, Benjamin, but men."

"And you won't miss being a king?"

"I am still king," he said, with polite formality, and set his cup down. "And you, Benjamin? Would you remain here, as a favorite of the king? There is much to be done."

"I'm sorry, Captain Frisk, but my struggle is elsewhere. Mankind has a worse enemy than the tsar of Russia or the sultan of Turkey. Despite all his flaws, we have lost our best defender against that foe in Sir Isaac. I must take up where he left off."

"Do you *know* where he left off?"

Ben shook his head. "No. I have many of his notebooks now, but it may take me years to understand what he has written." He lowered his head. "I am not his equal, and it grieves me that only his death proves that to me."

"Bah," Robert snorted. "You are not his equal; you are his better, for you have a *heart*, where he had none."

Ben continued staring at the floor. "He came back for me, Robin. He came back for love of me, and it killed him. And he died without a kind word from me."

"He saved us all," Charles said. "You should be proud of him."

"Proud I am," Ben said. "But I fear to wear his shoes."

"Fear teaches us the most," Charles replied.

"Then I suppose you will never learn a damned thing, Captain Frisk," Robert said. And the three of them laughed together genuinely. Sunlight came in through the window, and Ben felt a stab of triumph, of fierce, heady victory, a hope more blinding than the sun.

Nicolas

Nico laughed at the dark air and waved at the stars. Earlier he had been frightened by the noise and the strange lights, by the worried sound of his mother's voice. But then his friend had come, and the gentle motion of the basket had rocked him to sleep, to happy dreams.

Stretching awake, the sky had greeted him with these thousand funny lights. They reminded him of his mother, of her pointing at the lights and saying words—those strange words that buzzed in his ear rather than appearing as words ought to, inside him, where his own words did, or as when his friend spoke to him.

He hoped his mother would return soon; he missed her. Lately she had been away from him often, which had upset him at first. He did not care for strangers. But his friend had always been there, telling him strange and funny things, and that had made it better.

He stood and toddled to the side of the basket, but he could see nothing below, only an empty darkness, and on the horizon, a great orange sphere.

"La looon!" he cried, recognizing it. "La loon."

Naming it the way his mother would, with a sound, reveling in the strange feel of making his word into a noise and the noise back into a word again.

First it made him laugh, and then it made him afraid. *Where was mother?* Where was *everyone?*

"You are safe, little prince," the voice of his friend murmured. "You are safe, and you need have no fear."

"Maman?" He had known the sound-word—like so many words—but had never thought to use it before.

"She is safe," his friend told him. "She has put you in my care. Soon you will have a wonderful new home, as befits a prince."

Nico did not know what a prince was, but the feelings and images that came with the word were ticklish, warm, happy. He looked out at the moon again, reached to try and touch it.

"La loon," he cooed again. Content once more, he watched the night go by.